PRAISE FOR THE BRIDGE KINGDOM SERIES

"Heart-pounding romance and intense action wrapped in a spell-binding world. I was hooked from the first page."

—Elise Kova, *USA Today* bestselling author of
A Deal with the Elf King, on *The Bridge Kingdom*

"Exquisite, phenomenal, and sexy, *The Bridge Kingdom* is the epitome of fantasy romance perfection. I adored Jensen's world and characters. Aren and Lara were magnificent individually and together, a couple you'll root for from beginning to end."

—Olivia Wildenstein, *USA Today* bestselling author of
House of Beating Wings

"An epic, action-packed tale of love, revenge, and betrayal."

—Jennifer Estep, *New York Times* bestselling author of
Kill the Queen, on *The Traitor Queen*

"The next installment in the Bridge Kingdom series is not to be missed. Do not walk to pick up this book. Run."

—Jennifer L. Armentrout, #1 *New York Times* bestselling author of
From Blood and Ash, on *The Inadequate Heir*

By Danielle L. Jensen

The Malediction Trilogy

Stolen Songbird
Hidden Huntress
Warrior Witch
The Broken Ones (Prequel)

The Dark Shores Series

Dark Shores
Dark Skies
Gilded Serpent
Tarnished Empire (Prequel)

The Bridge Kingdom Series

The Bridge Kingdom
The Traitor Queen
The Inadequate Heir
The Endless War

Saga of the Unfated

A Fate Inked in Blood

THE
ENDLESS
WAR

THE
ENDLESS
WAR

DANIELLE L.
JENSEN

NEW YORK

Published in the United States by Del Rey, an imprint of Random House,
a division of Penguin Random House LLC, New York.

DEL REY and the CIRCLE colophon are registered trademarks of
Penguin Random House LLC.

Originally published in slightly different form as an audio original by
Audible in 2023 and subsequently self-published in print and
digital formats by Danielle L. Jensen in 2023.

LIBRARY OF CONGRESS CATALOGING-IN-PUBLICATION DATA
Names: Jensen, Danielle L., author.
Title: The endless war / Danielle L. Jensen.
Description: New York: Del Rey, 2024. | Series: The Bridge Kingdom series ; 4
Identifiers: LCCN 2024043317 (print) | LCCN 2024043318 (ebook) |
ISBN 9780593975275 (trade paperback; acid-free paper) | ISBN 9798986139333 (ebook)
Subjects: LCGFT: Fantasy fiction. | Romance fiction. | Novels.
Classification: LCC PR9199.4.J455 E53 2024 (print) |
LCC PR9199.4.J455 (ebook) | DDC 813/.6—dc23/eng/20240916
LC record available at https://lccn.loc.gov/2024043317
LC ebook record available at https://lccn.loc.gov/2024043318

Printed in the United States of America on acid-free paper

randomhousebooks.com

1 2 3 4 5 6 7 8 9

Book design by Sara Bereta

Map: Damien Mammoliti

For everyone fighting to change their stars . . .

THE
ENDLESS
WAR

1

ZARRAH

THE DECK ROSE AND FELL, THE ROAR OF THE SHIP SLAMMING against waves deafening. Rough water, which Zarrah knew from experience meant violent storms in the Tempest Seas, the elements standing guard over Ithicana while the kingdom recovered its strength. Not that it had much to fear, given that the eyes of Maridrina and Valcotta were firmly fixed on each other.

And Zarrah was the fuel that had turned the embers of the Endless War into an inferno.

In the hours and days since her aunt, Empress Petra Anaphora of Valcotta, had condemned her to imprisonment on Devil's Island, Zarrah had swiftly come to understand why she hadn't been granted a traitor's death.

The empress *wanted* war with Maridrina.

More than that, she wanted to destroy the man she believed had ruined her plans to burn Vencia. The king who'd become her obsession.

Keris.

Zarrah bit down on her gag, her chest hollowing as his face filled her mind's eye. Always the same moment: them standing on the highest reaches of Southwatch Island. The moment she'd realized that Keris had taken the information she'd given him about the plan to save Ithicana and used it to save *her.*

People were always going to die, Zarrah, the phantom of Keris's voice said to her in the darkness of her cell. *There was always going to be a battle. I just changed the grounds it was fought on.*

Eranahl.

Keris had changed the battleground from the bridge to the city Ithicana had been so desperate to defend, knowing it would lure out every soldier in its arsenal. Had ensured it would be a swift and decisive battle so that there'd be no chance Zarrah could reach the city in time to join the fight.

Load your ships and sail home, Zarrah, because no one can accuse you of wrongdoing. The empress's spies will have seen that Vencia remained too strongly defended for you to attack. As for you coming to Southwatch, given my father is about to gain uncontested control of the bridge, the empress is going to look the fool for not doing more to stop him. At least you tried.

She *had* tried. But she'd also been the fool who'd given their strategy to the enemy.

Regain her favor and secure your position as heir. Become empress. Do all the good you dreamed of doing. I'll do the same . . . We could change our world, Zarrah. Create a peace between two nations who've been at war for generations. Save thousands of our people's lives. But that doesn't come without sacrifice, and that sacrifice is Ithicana.

In the end, Ithicana had been victorious. But in that moment, she'd believed Keris had sent Aren and his kingdom to their doom, and her accusations repeated in her mind. *You say you did it for our kingdoms, but that isn't it, is it?* God help her, but she'd remember the pain until she was dust in the grave. *You did it for me. To save me. Admit it!*

Zarrah—

Admit it!

I couldn't . . . I couldn't let you die.

Keris hadn't liked her plan, her strategy, her *choice*, so he'd taken it away. That Ithicana had prevailed and defeated Maridrina didn't matter because that had been luck. That had been the arrival of a storm—and Ithicana's queen—not Keris's design. *I never want to see your face again. Never want to hear your voice. And if we cross paths, I will kill you.*

Zarrah shivered as the last words she'd spoken to him faded. There was no chance of Keris falling to her weapon, because thanks to the Magpie delivering the truth of her relationship with Keris to the empress, she'd never be free again. The ship she was aboard sailed to Devil's Island, and no one in the history of the infamous prison's existence had ever escaped.

Devil's Island.

Every time Zarrah thought of the ship's destination, nausea roiled in her guts. It was the prison for the worst criminals in the Empire. The vilest and most dangerous. Men and women for whom death was too kind a sentence.

Not for people like her.

True to her aunt's word, Zarrah had received no trial. Yet neither had there been public condemnation, no parade of shame through the streets.

Nothing.

It was as though her aunt wished to keep what Zarrah had done a secret from everyone in Valcotta.

Or perhaps to erase her existence entirely.

Footsteps sounded on the deck, pulling Zarrah from her thoughts. A hooded figure appeared before her cell, carrying a lantern, though it wasn't bright enough to reveal the individual's face beneath the shadows of the hood.

Not that it mattered. Zarrah would recognize her aunt's stride anywhere.

She reached through the bars and pulled out Zarrah's gag. "Hello, dear one."

It was a struggle not to flinch at the endearment, especially given that Zarrah's ribs still bore the bruises from her aunt's rage. "Empress."

Her aunt sighed and drew back her hood, revealing her halo of curls, the silver strands gleaming in the light. If recent events had taken a toll, it didn't show, for her brown skin held its usual luster, the only sign of her age a crinkling around her coal-rimmed eyes. Gold jewels glittered on her ears and her throat, and the faint scent of her floral perfume drifted into Zarrah's cell. Placing the lantern down on the deck, the empress then sat with her back against the wall opposite Zarrah's cell with her knees up, the laces of her military boots swaying.

Silence stretched, and Zarrah's heart beat faster with every passing second. Why was her aunt on the ship? What did she intend that demanded her presence during Zarrah's incarceration? What did she plan to say? Why was she here? What did she want?

What her aunt said next was not at all what Zarrah anticipated.

"I hate this," the empress said softly. "Hate him for having come between us. For having damaged our love so badly that I fear it is beyond repair."

Zarrah stared, struggling to comprehend what madness motivated her aunt's words even as some cowardly part of her wanted to latch onto them. Wanted to beg her aunt for mercy.

But she was no coward.

"It *is* beyond repair, Imperial Majesty. But not because of Keris's actions."

Her aunt sucked in a breath as though Zarrah had slapped her.

"Hearing his name from your lips is a knife to the heart, dear one, because I can hear the affection you still hold for him."

Zarrah knew her feelings for Keris were still there. Hated that they were still there. Yet she said, "You are mistaken."

Her aunt regarded her for a long moment, then looked away, face crumbling with grief. "God spare us, but the rat's claws have sunk deep into your heart, and it is my fault." A tear trickled down her aunt's cheek, and she wiped it away angrily. "I prepared you for life in so many ways, but I neglected to teach you of the devilry of men."

Zarrah snorted in disgust. "I'm a woman grown, not some fifteen-year-old maid who has never been kissed. He was hardly my first lover."

"The fumbling of soldiers. Whereas a man like him uses seduction with the adeptness of a courtesan. You never had a chance, and that is my fault, dear one." Her voice dripped with pity. "I should have made arrangements so that you'd have had the experience to resist his charms."

Zarrah's cheeks burned, and she cursed herself for allowing her aunt to get to her. "He had no idea who I was when we met and didn't learn my identity until . . . after."

"After you had *sex* with him?" The empress sighed. "You claim a woman's experience with men but speak of intimacy like a girl."

Zarrah clenched her fists, aware that she was rising to the bait but unable to stop herself. "I can—"

Her aunt held up a hand, silencing her. "The rat knew you were Valcottan. That you were a soldier. Your speech would have told him you were from a certain class, and therefore a certain rank. All of which made you a challenge worthy of his attention. A prize to be claimed, and a prize to be *used* once he learned just how valuable you truly were."

"You pretend knowledge of something you know nothing about." Why was her aunt pursuing this angle? What was her goal? What was the point of delving into Keris's intentions when Zarrah had already forsaken him?

"If you were just a lover and not a prize worth keeping, why did he take you to Vencia? Why not arrange for you to escape?"

"He tried," Zarrah retorted even as she debated whether it was better to fight or remain silent, or if it mattered at all. "You ordered that I be abandoned; Yrina told him so when she was captured."

Silence.

"Have you stopped to consider that the rat is the source of everything you hold against me?" her aunt asked. "He manipulated you, Zarrah. Put his deft fingers between your legs and played you until you forgot who truly loved you. Forgot what really mattered to you."

"That is *not* true." Zarrah wasn't certain whether she was defending Keris or herself, only that her aunt's words twisted the past year of her life into something dark and ugly. "You speak of things that you don't know."

"I know that all the things he did to make you sing made him king of Maridrina and you a traitor to your people," her aunt answered. "I know that he sits in luxury in Vencia while you sail toward Devil's Island. While you defend him, he entertains himself with orgies, showing particular favoritism for a woman named . . ." She drew a scrap of paper from her pocket and glanced at it. "Lestara. A Cardiffian princess, she was the youngest of Silas's wives. Very beautiful, I'm told, and well trained in the arts of the bedroom. He's made her the head of his house, and there is speculation he might make her queen, though I think that is wishful thinking. Maridrina never allows women that much power." Tucking the paper away, she added, "You will starve and suffer while he fucks and feasts."

Zarrah clenched her teeth, Lestara's face rearing in her mind. It was no secret to her that the harem wife had long had her sights set on Keris. It would seem she'd finally gotten her way, for her aunt's spies wouldn't give her unconfirmed gossip. Her stomach hollowed, pain tightening around her chest like a vise, and her aunt shook her head. "I know this grieves you, dear one, for he no doubt made promises of forever. But they weren't promises; they were lies. Surely you see that now?"

Sickness swam in Zarrah's stomach, for though she had no right to expect Keris to maintain any level of fidelity after she'd threatened to kill him, her heart seemed to have believed he would. Her heart was a fool.

"You are Keris Veliant's victim." Her aunt's hands balled into fists, and she moved onto her knees, eyes locked on Zarrah's, the intensity in them matching the fierceness of her voice as she said, "I intend to make him pay for what he has done to you. What he's done to us."

Zarrah's eyes stung, anger and guilt and shame threatening to choke her, but she managed to get out, "If I'm his victim, then why are you sending me to this place? If it's Keris you're so angry with, why am I the one you are punishing?"

"Because it's the only way you'll learn." Her aunt reached through the bars to wipe the tears from Zarrah's face, then cupped her cheek. "If there are no consequences, what is to stop you from making the same mistake again? What is to stop you from being lured back into his bed with sweet words and promises of pleasure?"

Nothing. And everything.

"You're sending me to a prison for murderers and rapists to learn a lesson about the ways of men?" Zarrah spat in her aunt's face. "Fuck you."

Quick as a viper, the empress caught hold of Zarrah's shirt and jerked her against the bars. Her breath seared Zarrah's cheek as she shouted, "You're going to the island because you betrayed Valcotta. Because you allowed yourself to be duped by a Veliant. Because you allowed the blood of the one who slaughtered your mother—my beloved little sister—to fill you with his seed."

Zarrah cringed, trying to pull away, but she couldn't get leverage with her wrists bound together. Wood creaked as though someone approached. She willed them to hurry, but the passageway remained empty.

"But despite all that you have done, I still love you." Her aunt's voice quivered with emotion. "You have been my everything, the daughter I never had, Zarrah, so while others counsel me to put you down, instead I am giving you a chance to earn back your place at my side. To prove yourself worthy of once again being Valcotta's heir. Every hardship you endure, know that it is because of *him* that you suffer. And every moment you survive, know that it is because of *my love* that you live."

The anchor chain rattled, lowering into the depths, and Zarrah's pulse throbbed with renewed fear. "You're mad if you believe I intend to fight for your forgiveness."

"They say love is a form of madness," her aunt murmured. "And despite all the pain in my heart, there is no one I love more than you, dear one. Nothing I look forward to more than being reunited with you again."

There was no denying the faint tug in Zarrah's heart, a longing for a time when her aunt had been a bastion against every hurt, the warrior who had delivered her from the enemy and promised vengeance against those who'd torn their world apart. For all her aunt twisted words to serve her ends, it was the truths within them that held the most power.

Heavy footfalls echoed down the passageway, and then Bermin

appeared. Her cousin inclined his head to his mother. "It's time, Imperial Majesty."

Her aunt rose to her feet. "We part today, Zarrah. I hope you will take this opportunity to contemplate the decisions you have made, but more importantly, the decisions you *will* make when you earn your freedom from this place." Not allowing Zarrah a chance to respond, the empress turned on her heel and walked away, saying to her son, "The arrangements have been made?"

Bermin nodded, pressing his muscled bulk against the wall as though a cobra slithered past rather than a woman.

"Good." The empress glanced back at Zarrah. "Ensure she arrives at the prison alive. This isn't an execution—it's a test."

Her cousin waited until his mother's steps reached the main deck, then pulled a key from his pocket and approached the brig. "What did you do, little Zarrah? I've never seen her in such a rage. Not even Welran could calm her."

It was so rare for her cousin to mention his mother's bodyguard that Zarrah blinked twice before refocusing. "What did she tell you? What reasons has she given for imprisoning me here?"

"Nothing." He unlocked the bars. "And no reason, beyond that you required punishment." Her cousin's large hands closed over the bars, the whole structure groaning as he leaned against it. "There was a whispered rumor among her guards that she'd accused you of betraying Valcotta to the Maridrinians, but that has since been silenced. In truth, as empress, she need not have a reason for sending you here. Her whim is enough."

This was Zarrah's last chance to share the truth. The last chance Valcotta might ever have to learn that the only reason the war would not end was that their empress didn't want it to. "I was trying to end the war, Bermin. There are like-minded Maridrinians who wish for the same. I warned them she intended to raze Vencia, and they were able to thwart the attack."

He cocked his head. "Just as they thwarted the planned attack in Nerastis."

It was the attack Bermin had been intended to lead, and she knew how desperately her cousin had wanted the glory of retaking the contested city back under Valcottan rule. Denying that she'd stolen his opportunity would be an obvious lie, and even if he didn't forgive her, she needed Bermin to believe she was telling the truth. "Yes. Innocents would have died by the thousands, and for what?"

"Honor and vengeance," he answered without hesitation.

"No." Zarrah shook her head wildly, knowing she was running out of time. "Hubris and greed. We keep fighting, not for the good of Valcotta, but to appease the empress's ego. The war doesn't need to continue, Bermin. We could end it."

His brown eyes bored into her own. "These like-minded Maridrinians . . . Is one of them Keris Veliant?"

Truth or lie? Truth or lie? "Yes. He'd agree to peace, if we gave him the chance. But the empress will never lay down arms. She's obsessed with destroying Maridrina, and she doesn't care what it will cost in blood and lives. There's something wrong with her, Bermin. Something missing from her heart and mind that makes her—"

"Monstrous?" Bermin gave a cold chuckle. "That might be a revelation to you, little Zarrah, but I've faced that monster all my life. Suffered her cutting words and derision. Never good enough, no matter what I did. All made worse the day she made you hers, the girl she'd sculpt into the perfect heir, never mind her own flesh-and-blood son. She cast me aside like trash, yet you were blind to her nature until she turned her venom on *you*."

He wasn't wrong. Over and over, Zarrah had seen how her aunt treated him and had said nothing. Done nothing. But the worst part, in hindsight, was that she'd believed her cousin had deserved the contempt his mother bore for him. "I'm sorry."

"I'm sure you are." Abandoning his grip on the bars, Bermin reached through and shoved her gag back into her mouth. "Perhaps if you'd cared about me, I might be helping you now."

Swinging open the bars, he caught hold of her bound wrists and dragged her down the passageway and then up the ladder into the open air.

It was night, the cold wind carrying the scent of pine and ice.

Zarrah squinted against the brightness of the many lanterns illuminating the vessel. The deck was empty, the crew all below while she was delivered to the prison's guards, who waited by the ship's rail.

Except it wasn't the guards that drew her gaze.

Beyond, a cliff reared, its sheer face split by a gap perhaps half the width of the vessel on which she stood. A curved stone pier joined both sides of the cliff opening, fortified guard towers built where it met the rock. At the outermost point of the curved pier, a singular dock illuminated by torches jutted out into the sea like a burning tongue.

Devil's Island.

The prison was infamous, the tales about the island itself as numerous as those whispered about the prisoners condemned to it. For all her elevated rank, Zarrah had never had anything to do with the prison, for any criminal whose capture she'd orchestrated was sent to Pyrinat for conviction. But that didn't mean she hadn't heard rumors about the waterway carved through solid rock that spiraled inward to encircle the prison itself, endlessly sucking the sea into its core but never allowing it to flow out again.

As though the water circled around and then down into hell itself.

"This is the condemned?" one of the guards asked as Bermin dragged her closer.

"Yes," he answered. "It is the will of the empress that she be given to the island as punishment for her crimes."

"Then in the empress's name, we will take her."

The woman reached for Zarrah's arm, but Bermin didn't relinquish his grip. "I will deliver her myself."

"None who step foot on the island may ever leave," the woman said. "Not even those who guard its shores. If you step onto that dock, the island will claim you, one way or another."

The guard's words chilled Zarrah's blood, because if that was true, then not even the empress would be able to extract her from the prison.

Bermin, however, was unmoved. "Do you know who I am?"

The woman's head tilted. "Yes, Highness."

"Then you know I am above the law."

Not the slightest bit true, and Zarrah could tell from how the guard's eyes narrowed that she knew it, but the woman only said, "It is not the empress's law, Highness. It is the law of the island."

What does that even mean? Zarrah wondered.

Bermin spat on the deck. "Spare me your mutterings. I will deliver the prisoner myself. All who stand in my way will suffer for it."

The guard lifted one shoulder. "So be it."

They forced Zarrah into the waiting longboat, Bermin's grip on her wrists tight enough to leave bruises as the crew released the moorings holding the small vessel in place. No one picked up the oars, but the boat moved swiftly toward the devil's tongue, caught in the current sucked into its maw. Only as they drew close did they run out the oars, steering the boat down the left side of the curved pier to where guards waited next to a ladder with ropes.

Bermin lifted her out of the boat as though she were a child. The waiting guards forced Zarrah to her knees while the rest disembarked, and she took the chance to assess her surroundings. More men and women watched from the fortified guard-posts at the points where the half-moon pier met the island, bows held loosely in their hands, all watchful. Above the guard-posts, steps were carved into the rock, leading a switchback route to the top. The only route onto the island other than into the mouth.

"On your feet!" Bermin dragged her upward, the tips of her boots scuffing on the stone pier as they moved to the center of the half moon and then down the tongue to where a tiny boat was moored.

"You have two choices," the female guard said. "Follow the lanterns to the devil's heart and linger as long as he'll have you, or row to his teeth and allow him to feast. Either way, he will have your soul."

Zarrah didn't bother answering, only stared at the ominous gap in the cliff face. Driftwood flowed into it with alarming speed, the force of the current dispelling any thoughts she might have about rowing against it. Once she was inside the prison, the only way out would be to pledge loyalty to her aunt. If there was a way out at all . . .

Which meant the time to fight was now.

Zarrah slammed her heel down on Bermin's instep and was rewarded with a snarl of pain and a loosening of his grip. Jerking free, she shouldered past the female guard and sprinted up the pier, praying that whatever *arrangements* Bermin had made would keep them from shooting her.

She barely made it a dozen steps before a weight slammed into her back, crushing her against the pier. Zarrah kicked out her heels. Once. Twice. Curses filled the night air, but then hands gripped her legs. Her arms. Her throat.

She tried to suck in a breath, but the hands tightened. Panic flooded her veins and Zarrah clawed at the hands, but others restrained her. She needed to breathe—*God, please help me*—she needed air.

The empress had been lying. Or Bermin hated Zarrah enough that he didn't care about the consequences of defying his mother's orders. The world faded away, but just before blackness consumed her, Bermin said, "You don't deserve my mercy, traitor."

Zarrah only managed to drag in one breath before her cousin lifted her, carrying her to the end of the pier. Then she was flying. Falling.

Her back struck the bottom of the boat, driving the air from her lungs as pain lanced down her spine.

"No!" she tried to scream, but it came out as a wheeze around her gag. "Please!" Zarrah rolled onto her belly, reaching up her bound wrists to the guards, who stared down at her with merciless eyes. Everyone who came to this island was a demon who deserved punishment, and nameless as she was, there was no reason for them to believe her different.

If she went into this place, either it would consume her soul or the empress would.

Bermin unfastened the mooring line, allowing the current to draw the boat away from the pier until he held only the very end of the rope. Screaming around her gag, Zarrah reached for one of the oars with her bound hands, trying to back-paddle, but she only succeeded in swinging the vessel sideways. She needed both oars. Needed both hands.

Reaching up, she wrenched the gag from her mouth, then bit at the knot binding her wrists, but it was tied too tight.

Bermin let go of the rope.

Bending her knees, Zarrah jumped, fingers catching the edge of the pier, the current dragging at her feet and trying to pull her loose.

Zarrah struggled to keep her grip on the wet rock. *Climb,* she ordered herself. *Get your leg up.* But then she felt warm breath against her bare hands. "Bermin," she gasped. "I know you hate me, but think of Valcotta. Think of the lives that could be saved if she were removed from power."

Her cousin's dark eyes regarded her for a long moment, and then he whispered, "I agree, little Zarrah. Valcotta needs fresh blood on the throne to keep it strong." A knife appeared in his hand, and he sliced through the bindings on her wrists before straightening to his feet. Zarrah sucked in a breath of relief as she steadied her grip on the edge, about to pull herself upward.

"But it won't be you." Bermin's boot lifted, then came down with crushing force on her fingers.

Zarrah screamed as she lost her grip and frigid water closed over her head, the current immediately dragging her backward.

Swim.

Her legs churned, driving her to the surface, only for panic to flood her veins as the current took her toward the opening in the cliffs. Her eyes fixed on her cousin, who stood with his arms crossed as she was sucked into the devil's maw.

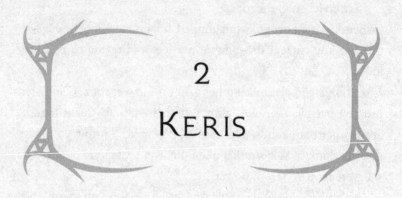

2
KERIS

"WHAT DO YOU MEAN WE CAN'T SET SAIL?"

"There's a typhoon." Dax pointed out the windows of the office. "If you look hard, you can see it."

Keris was perfectly aware of the black skies over the harbor, the gutters of Vencia's streets full of water rushing down to the Tempest Seas. "It's just a squall."

The captain of his guard strolled to the door leading to the balcony and unlatched it, turning the handle. The door immediately wrenched out of his hand, slamming against the wall with enough force that Keris was shocked the thick glass didn't crack. Wind roared into the room, sending papers flying off the desk even as an explosion of thunder caused the whole tower to shudder.

"You're right, Your Grace," Dax shouted. "Just a squall. I'll tell the captain to grow some balls and ready his ship."

Cursing, Keris caught hold of the door, forced to throw his weight against the frame to shut it. The whirlwind of papers slowly settled to the floor. He stared out the window at the crackling lightning, at the spray rising higher than the enormous seawall that protected the harbor from the worst of the surge. A ship-killer, and yet if there'd been a way, he'd have sailed into it.

Cursing again, he twisted away and went to the sideboard, by-passing the wine and going straight for the whiskey. It hadn't been long since word had come of Zarrah's fate, but given the time it had taken the spy to travel from Pyrinat to Vencia, she might already have been delivered to Devil's Island. Might already be in that hellhole filled with the worst of Valcotta's criminals, from which no one had ever escaped. All while Keris stood in the comfort of his palace, drinking his father's whiskey.

A fresh flood of rage surged through his veins, and in a violent motion he hurled the glass against the wall. It exploded, amber liquid dripping down the golden paint.

"You're really embracing your rise in status, Your Grace," Dax commented. "Not just wearing the crown but truly emoting it."

"Fuck off," Keris snarled. "Didn't I fire you?"

"Possibly." Dax picked up the decanter and two glasses, carrying them to the desk. "You talk a lot, and truth be told, I don't listen to half of what you say."

A thousand retorts rose on Keris's tongue, but given that Dax was the only person he could speak relatively freely around, alienating him was not in his best interest. Especially given he actually liked the man.

Keris sat in his father's chair, hating how the stuffed leather molded to him as though he were meant for the seat. Taking a glass from Dax, he stared pensively at the contents, his mind sinking down and down. A typhoon of this size could rage for days, and with storm season in full swing, another could swirl in on its heels, forcing all ships to keep close to the coast. Which meant potentially weeks before he could even hope to secure the assistance of Lara and Aren, if they agreed at all.

You have a navy; go get Zarrah yourself, a voice whispered inside his head. *Every day you delay is a day she remains imprisoned.*

Keris drained his glass, trying to drown the voice because it was starting to grow louder than logic and reason. For one, there was every chance his men would mutiny once they learned where they were going and why. Two, even if he did manage to force them to bend to his will, he'd be playing right into Petra's hands.

The empress wanted war. Wanted war *now,* while Maridrina was weakened from the conflict with Ithicana. Except support for it among her people was flagging, which meant she wanted Keris to make the first move.

Then be clever. Pay a mercenary crew to take you.

That was more tempting, if only because it carried fewer consequences for his kingdom. Except it was also a plan that seemed doomed to fail. An untested crew whose loyalty was to coin was not what he wished to have at his back, especially given that Petra had to be anticipating that he'd come. With his luck, he'd fall right into her trap.

Keris rubbed at his temples. He had one chance to free Zarrah, one chance to get this right, and that meant logic needed to take precedence over his emotions. No mean feat, given that there were moments fear and guilt clamped like a vise around his chest, denying him breath. Moments that made his heart beat so rapidly the world spun and he could scarcely stand, much less think. Just as he couldn't blink, much less sleep, because every time his lids shut, he saw Zarrah's face. Heard her voice. *I never want to see your face again. Never want to hear your voice. And if we cross paths, I will kill you.*

"Why are you so eager to go to Ithicana?" Dax's voice invaded his thoughts, and Keris lifted his head to meet the man's gaze.

"Pardon?"

"What's the hurry? The bridge ain't going anywhere, and allowing the Ithicanians a bit of time to calm their tempers before you go sailing in, making demands, might not be a bad thing." Dax swallowed the contents of his glass, giving an appreciative nod. "That's good stuff."

"Isn't there a rule against drinking while you're on duty?" Keris asked, his tone flat because he didn't have a particularly valid explanation for his plan to go to Ithicana beyond the truth. And the truth wasn't something he had any intention of revealing.

"Could be." Dax scratched his unshaven chin. "But given *you* drink while on duty, I figured it was more of a guideline."

There were several arguments that Keris could have voiced, not the least of which being that he was king and could do as he goddamned pleased. Instead he reached across the desk and refilled Dax's glass. The man had almost single-handedly organized the revolt against Keris's father, spreading Keris's rumors about Aren's treatment that had driven the populace to violent protests and demands for proof the Ithicanian still lived, a critical piece in the plan that had seen Aren liberated. Dax had a strong dislike for both politicians and aristocrats, which was likely why he and Keris got along, never mind that Keris was both. "I need to mend fences with Ithicana and reestablish trade in Southwatch. We lost half our fleet, thousands of men, and famine is once again biting at our flanks. Maridrina is weak, particularly along our southern borders."

"But Nerastis is at a stalemate." Dax rooted around on Keris's desk, looking for the last report, but half the paperwork was on the floor. Giving up, he leaned back in his chair. "There are no signs that the Valcottans intend to move against us."

Because Petra was waiting for Keris to make the first move. Waiting for him to be the instigator so as not to fan the flames of rumor that she was a warmonger. A politician of the first order, because she hid the monster so very, *very* well. So well that only the other monsters had seen her for what she really was.

Monsters like you.

He ignored the whispered voice, turning his mind instead to Petra's strategy. Zarrah had been given no trial, and while rumors she'd been sent to Devil's Island circulated through Pyrinat, no public statement had been made. Certainly no mention of Zarrah's relationship with him, and he had a theory for why that was. The same reason Serin hadn't made it public: Maridrina would have turned on Keris if they learned about Zarrah, executed him without even a thought of a trial, which would've been far too quick a death in Serin's eyes. The Magpie had wanted him to suffer. Petra likely wanted that as well, but there was something she wanted more.

War.

A knock sounded, and Dax, only casual when they were alone, rose to his feet and straightened his uniform. Moving to the door, he opened it and spoke to the guards outside, a loud curse exiting his lips. Slamming the door behind him, he turned to Keris. "There's been an incident at Greenbriar."

That was the name of the estate where the church trained its acolytes. Keris was on his feet in a flash; his blood turned to ice. "Sara?"

Dax's face was grim. "Someone tried to kidnap her."

3
ZARRAH

SWIM!

It was that or drown, and with retreat impossible, the only path to *life* was forward.

Zarrah threw her strength into it, arms cutting the water and legs churning, her eyes fixed on the boat bobbing ahead of her.

The water was frigid and filled with driftwood, the cliff walls towering to either side pressing closer with each passing second. If the water slammed her against them, she was done. Would drown, broken and bleeding, her body food for the fish.

Or whatever else lived in this cursed place.

She needed to catch that boat.

Except, with every second, it drew farther away from her.

Zarrah put her face to the water and swam, feeling as though she hurtled down a swift river, the current giving her momentum.

Something brushed her legs.

Zarrah jerked her knees upward, certain something was in the water with her. Something with teeth.

Then it brushed against her arms, thin and coarse.

Rope.

She managed to snatch the end as it flew past, her arms nearly wrenched from their sockets as she was yanked forward. Coughing and spluttering, Zarrah sucked in a mouthful of air, then hauled herself toward the boat.

Her body trembled with the effort, her burning chest demanding more air in her lungs, and she kicked to the surface. But it was terror, not breath, that filled her as she watched the boat slam against a bend in the cliffs, rebounding toward her.

Instinct drove her beneath the surface.

The boat surged over her head, her shoulders jerked backward by the rope right as her heels struck the cliff. The impact jarred her spine, her knees buckling.

Pain screamed through Zarrah's body, along with the desperate need to breathe.

You can do this, she willed herself. *Fight.*

Hand over hand, she dragged herself along the rope, breaking the surface next to the boat. She caught hold of the edge, then hauled herself upward.

In time for the boat to rotate into the cliff.

Wood crunched, the impact nearly sending her back into the water as the boat spun about.

Clenching her teeth, Zarrah managed to hook an ankle over the edge, and then toppled inside.

Her respite lasted less than a heartbeat, the world spinning around her as the boat twisted on the rushing water.

She needed to get it under control.

Snatching up the paddle in the bottom of the boat, Zarrah braced her feet against the sides, her eyes fixed on the chute of water before her. Only now did she realize *why* sight was possible despite it being night. Overhead, far out of reach, braziers dangled from chains supported by large brackets bolted into the walls of the cliff.

And on the cliff top, archers watched.

They weren't the threat, though. The empress didn't want her dead, just broken enough to be malleable.

She had no intention of conceding to either fate.

Zarrah paddled hard, doing her best to keep the boat from slamming against the cliffs as the water circled ever closer to the heart of the island. Yet the damage to the boat had already been done, the small vessel sitting lower and lower in the water.

And the channel spiraling toward the center of the island seemed unending.

Maybe there was no center. Maybe this was the punishment, to be left on a boat circling around and around, forced to paddle for your life until your strength gave out, your boat gave out, and the water took you.

Or until she begged for her aunt's forgiveness.

"I will not give in," she snarled, then looked up at the watching archers and screamed, "I will not surrender!"

If they heard her over the rush of water, she couldn't tell, for their faces remained impassive. Disinterested, as what they were witnessing was something they'd seen a hundred times before.

The cliff wall on her right abruptly ended.

A surge of water struck her boat from the right, nearly over-turning her. Zarrah clung to the sides, screams ripping from her throat. Not of fear, but of fury.

The boat spun, the light from the braziers above a blur of flame, and then a beach appeared.

The rumors were true.

The water had taken her to the heart of the island. An island within the island, the mass of land encircled by water. Her nails dug into the wood of the boat as she debated what to do. Whether to swim to the beach now or allow the water to take her around the island, giving her a tour of the place.

Except . . .

A fresh rush of fear filled her chest, and Zarrah looked over her shoulder at where her boat had spun. She hadn't been drawn in on a tide but on a current, which meant the water was going somewhere. And that somewhere had to be *down*.

"God spare me," she whispered, realizing that the island truly did have a whirlpool beneath it. If she didn't get onto that beach now, she'd be sucked down to the bottom of the sea. Or to hell itself.

"Die now or die later," a voice shouted from above, and Zarrah looked up to see a smirking guard. "Go past the edge of that beach and the decision is made for you."

Zarrah spared the time to flip her middle finger at the woman, then rowed hard toward the rocky beach, her boat sinking, slowing, even as the water threatened to drag her past the point of no return.

Get out, fear whispered. *Swim.*

Except this boat might be the only chance she had at escape. She couldn't lose it.

"Come on!" Paddling hard, her arms quivered, but panic fueled her strength as she fought the current.

It was a losing battle, the swamped boat too unwieldy. Cursing, Zarrah grabbed the rope still fastened to the front and jumped.

Water closed over her head, the cold a knife to the chest, but Zarrah ignored it and swam. Her boots hit the rocky bottom, but she kept swimming with the current even as she angled up the beach.

Waist-deep.

Thigh-deep.

But she was running out of beach.

"Better hurry," someone called from above, this time a different voice, though the amusement was the same. This was a joke to them. Entertainment to break the doldrums of boredom.

Looping the rope around her hands, Zarrah twisted and braced as the submerged boat floated past. The rope went taut. She heaved, trying to pull it onto the beach, but the current was so strong.

Zarrah screamed, drawing on every reserve of strength as she took one step back. Then two, pulling the boat with her. She was fully out of the water now, heels digging into rocky sand as she dragged the small vessel partially onto the beach.

Sucking in breath after breath, she watched water flow from the holes in the boat, waiting until it was mostly drained before pulling it far enough away from the deadly flow that she deemed it secure. Then she fell on her ass.

And looked up at those who had taunted her.

Across the stretch of water before her rose a cliff, braziers illuminating the water and the beach as though it were a stage and the guards the spectators. "Fuck you," she screamed at them, hating that her people would behave this way. Like she was theater for them. Just like everyone else who'd been brought to the island.

Everyone else . . .

Zarrah's blood went cold. *You idiot. You cursed, loud fool.*

Hand closing on a rock, she slowly turned to look at the island behind her. An island full of the worst criminals in all of the Valcottan Empire.

And found eyes staring back at her.

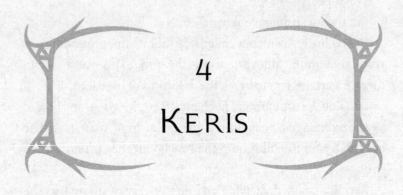

4

KERIS

HE KEPT LOW TO HIS HORSE'S NECK, ONE FIST CLENCHED TIGHT IN its mane to keep him from being blown out of the saddle as his mount struggled its way up the hill. Around him, his guards did the same, the wind as vicious as he'd ever seen it. Only those desperate or mad were out in the storm. Keris was both.

Please be all right.

The guard who'd brought the message hadn't known details, only that something had happened. That someone had tried to steal his eight-year-old sister.

He'd kept her at Greenbriar because it had felt safer. Granting the harem their liberty had meant allowing them to come and go as they pleased, which compromised the security of the inner sanctum. He'd been afraid Sara might be an easy target for anyone who got inside. With everyone around him dropping like flies, keeping the sister he loved best far away had seemed the wisest choice.

He'd been a fool to believe distance would be enough to protect her.

Digging in his heels, Keris urged his mount down the lane lead-ing to the austere building. He dismounted in front of it, drawing his sword as he raced to the doors, finding them barred from the inside.

His stomach clenched, and he hammered on the wood, hearing cries of dismay from beyond.

"Open up in the name of the king," Dax roared, having come up beside him. "You are not in danger from us! Let us in!"

"How do we know this isn't a trick?" a woman called through the latticework on the upper part of the door, only her shadow visible.

Keris's patience snapped. Ripping back the hood of his cloak, he snarled, "Open the door and take me to my sister, or we will break it in."

Her eyes fixed on him, then widened. "It's the king himself!"

Her surprise was warranted because his father wouldn't have come. Would barely have looked up from his desk if he'd learned one of his daughters had been endangered.

There was a shuffle of motion, and then the door eased inward. Ignoring Dax's urging that he hold back, Keris pushed inside. "Where is Sara? Is she harmed?"

The woman bobbed three curtsies in a row, and he was about ready to scream at her to stand up straight when she said, "The princess is unharmed, Your Grace. I'll take you to her. We have captured the perpetrator. He is injured, but alive."

Not for long.

Sword still in his hand, Keris followed the woman, two of Dax's men pushing ahead, their eyes wary. Then they drew to a halt.

Breaking into a run, Keris rounded the corner to find a cluster of women. They stiffened at the sight of armed men, then pulled back to reveal Sara sitting on the ground next to a still woman, a pool of blood around her. "Sara?"

His little sister looked up, face streaked with tears. "Keris?"

He dropped to his knees, blood soaking his trousers as he pulled her against him. "Are you hurt?"

"No," she sobbed. "He dragged me out of my room. When the abbess tried to stop him, he stabbed her." Sara broke off with a choked breath. "She stabbed him back with a knitting needle, and he let me go."

Keris glanced down at the dead woman, recognizing her as the one he'd threatened should anything happen to his sister. His stomach tightened, because he didn't think that it was threats from him that had driven her to protect Sara with a knitting needle.

"Your Grace," Dax muttered, and he pointed to the splatters of blood leading down the hallway.

"Stay here," Keris murmured to his sister, handing her off to one of the women and following the trail of blood, Dax at his elbow. His heart beat with steady thumps fueled by anger, but as he rounded the bend to find two women with heavy candlesticks standing over a prone form, Keris sheathed his weapon and said, "Hello, little brother."

"Keris," Royce said through gritted teeth. "It's been an age."

"That's *Your Grace* to you, you little pissant," Dax growled, but Keris waved a calming hand at him before turning to the candlestick-wielding women. "You have my gratitude for your service, Sisters. Thank you."

The women grudgingly lowered their weapons, dropping into curtsies before retreating down the hall. Keris walked slowly and crouched next to Royce, eyeing his scowling half brother. Royce was years younger than Keris and, last he'd heard, was stationed at one of the garrisons in the southern Kestark mountains. He was also next in line for the throne if Keris didn't produce an heir. Royce was bleeding from a wound on the side of his head, presumably from one of the candlesticks, but the knitting needle jutting out of his side was of more immediate concern. "What brings you to Vencia? Thinking of taking vows to God and joining the cloth?"

"Fuck you, Keris."

"Incest aside, I'm afraid you're not my type."

Royce's glower deepened. "You were always a smart-mouthed little prick. Yapping like a dog about your stupid ideals and then scuttling behind Otis whenever anyone challenged you. The only reason no one killed you was because you weren't worth the effort."

Thud.

God help him, but Keris wished he could burn that sound from his memory. "Hiding behind Otis is no longer an option. So by all means, say and do what you will, brother."

Royce went still, apparently aware of what had befallen their half brother. Beneath his rage, part of Keris recoiled at using Otis's death as a threat. Yet another, far more pragmatic part of him whispered, *Don't pretend that you'd have allowed Otis to survive. He was a dead man from the moment he threatened her life.*

"Well?" Keris asked, feeling his men shift behind him. He glanced over his shoulder at them, then back to Royce. "Prefer to speak in private?" Not waiting for Royce to answer, he said, "Dax, take the men and go watch over my sister. I wouldn't want anything to happen to her while my back is turned."

"Yes, Your Grace," Dax answered, and boots thudded against stone as they retreated.

Once they were gone, Keris said, "There, Royce. We're alone.

What would you like to say to me?" When his brother hesitated, he added, "Let's start with just what, exactly, you intended to do with our sister."

Royce's throat moved as he swallowed, his body flexing as though his instincts demanded that he fight. Or flee. "Nothing. I just came to visit her, and the old bitch took issue with it."

"To be clear, you decided to sneak into an estate dedicated to religious training, in the middle of one of the worst storms Vencia has seen in years, to visit a half sister you've never once spoken to. A conversation"—Keris flicked the knitting needle jutting out of his brother's side—"apparently worth killing an old woman over."

Royce didn't cry out, only clenched his teeth. Which Keris might have given him credit for if not for the fact that the idiot persisted with the lie. "A princess shouldn't be relegated to serving the church. She deserves better. I was going to take her away to give her the life befitting her rank."

Despite himself, Keris flinched. Sara did deserve better. But he knew the blood running through Royce's veins cared nothing for the well-being of little girls. "Cut the bullshit. You learned that she was favored by me and thought to capitalize upon it. Either to ransom her for gold or to use her to lure me into a situation where you might put a knife in my back."

The storm raged outside, the women down the hallway still weeping loudly, but the silence between them muffled it, the tension stiflingly thick.

Royce broke first, huffing out a strangled laugh. "You're being dramatic, Keris. This is always the way it is with Veliant brothers, right? It means everything. It means nothing. We move forward until the next squabble."

Keris laughed along with him, ignoring the part of himself that cringed at the coldness in it. "You're right about that being the way of things. Or would be if I were still only your brother and a prince, not your king."

Royce's laugh faded.

"The rules are different now," Keris continued. "Moves against me are no longer games and brotherly . . . shenanigans, but treason. And all traitors face the same fate in Maridrina."

What color remained in Royce's cheeks drained away. "Ker— Your Grace, please. I wasn't going to hurt her. I—"

"You already did hurt her." Had reminded her that nowhere was safe. That everywhere she went, pain would follow, for no reason other than her name. "Why would I show you any mercy?"

Royce squared his shoulders. "Fuck you, Keris. You can have one of your lackeys cut off my head and spike it on the gate, but know that I'm only the first. Your blood is coming for you. Coming to rip the crown from your pathetic head because Maridrina deserves a warrior on its throne, not a weakling who hid in a library!"

Maridrina did deserve better than him. But Royce wasn't the answer—none of his brothers were. "Let them come."

Boots scuffed behind him, and Keris turned his head to find Dax watching, the man's brow furrowed. "Have a healer see to him; then take him up somewhere secure." Then he locked eyes with his brother. "I am not Father. But that doesn't mean my patience is limitless. Test me again, and I'll drag you out to the Red Desert and bury you alive myself."

Royce gave a tight nod.

"He's right," Keris told Dax once two of his men had dragged a moaning Royce away. "More of my half brothers will come, and not all of them are as stupid as Royce. I want eyes familiar with their faces on all the gates and in the harbor."

"What do you plan to do with them when they show?"

His father's voice echoed in his head. *When you are heir, you are the target of all. You can expect no loyalty from your brothers, and all but the cowards will come for you at one point or another. If you live to inherit, they'll come for your sons. It is the way of it, and it is also the reason you have no uncles still living.*

"I will do whatever I must."

5

ZARRAH

THERE WERE SEVEN OF THEM, THREE WOMEN AND FOUR MEN, ALL wearing worn and dirty clothing that appeared patched together from rags. All had long, unwashed hair, and the men bore thick beards, their bodies thin but hard. Four of the seven had skin a shade of brown, three were paler, all filthy.

And all carried weapons.

Cudgels and staffs and knives that looked to be formed from scraps of scavenged metal. All more than capable of taking a life.

"Welcome to Devil's Island," one of them said, a man as big as Bermin, with a curling black beard that matched his hair. He grinned, revealing an entire mouthful of gold teeth, and stepped closer. "It's been an age since we had any fresh meat."

Meat.

Cannibals.

Zarrah didn't hesitate. Flinging the stone in her hand at the man, she leapt to her feet and broke into a sprint, his cry of pain chasing her up the hill. She could see the shadowed outline of trees and larger boulders ahead, but the rest was lost to shadows.

She stumbled, ankle twisting on the rocks, but managed to

keep her footing. Stone clacked against stone as the cannibals broke into pursuit, the rapid footfalls suggesting they'd not be easily outpaced. "Stop," one of them shouted. "We aren't going to hurt you!"

Just eat me, she thought, then put on a burst of speed.

Small rocks gave way to larger boulders. Zarrah leapt between them, racing toward the tree line, the light from the braziers hanging from the cliffs fading away. The prisoners would know every inch of their island prison. Might well have traps laid or have more of their companions lying in wait to catch her, but the heavy breathing of those in pursuit was loud in her ears. There was no time for caution.

She needed to find a place to hide.

Zarrah reached the trees, the scent of pine thick as her sodden boots crunched the carpet of fallen needles, the cold air burning her lungs. There were well-trodden paths, but Zarrah avoided them. Wove through the blackness between trees and headed to higher ground, banking that being well fed and strong would give her the advantage.

"Stop!" the big man roared, and Zarrah hazarded a backward glance.

He was close enough that she could see the glint of moonlight reflecting off his teeth, others hot on his heels.

"We want to help you!"

Bullshit.

She needed to get farther ahead. Needed a few heartbeats out of sight to hide in the darkness, but the cursed bastard kept pace. Higher and higher she climbed, and it occurred to Zarrah that she had no idea of the size of the island prison. No idea whether she was strides away from reaching the moat of water encircling it or whether it stretched on for another mile.

Icy wind ripped at her hair and clothes as she crested the summit, her heart skittering as she took in the sight. Lit up with end-less braziers was a spiral of water that circled out to the blackness of the sea, all visible from her vantage.

Yet there was no time to take it in. No time to consider escape from the island when it was the prisoners within that she needed to evade.

She sprinted across the top of the summit, her breathing ragged and sides burning.

Only for her feet to snag on something hidden in the darkness.

Zarrah tripped and rolled, body bouncing against rocks and roots until she came to a stop.

Get up! Run!

A groan tore from her lips as she hauled herself back to her feet, her head aching and blood dripping down her cheek. Snatching up a rock from the ground, she whirled—

Only to find her pursuers stopped a dozen paces away, refusing to pass the low barrier of rocks she'd tripped over.

"If you value your life, you'll come back to our territory," the man called. "There is only death to be found where you are going."

"As opposed to the long life awaiting me with you?" Zarrah laughed bitterly, then pressed a hand to her side as pain lanced outward. "My gratitude for the offer, but I'll have to decline."

"They'll kill you, woman! Kill you and—" Breaking off, he took a wary step back, lifting his cudgel.

Zarrah's skin prickled, realization that she might have made a fatal error sinking into her soul a heartbeat before a hand clamped over her mouth.

Zarrah slammed her elbows back, but more hands grabbed her arms. Her legs. Just before they tugged a sack over her head, Zar-rah saw shadowed figures approach the barricade, weapons raised.

And beyond, her would-be saviors retreated from sight.

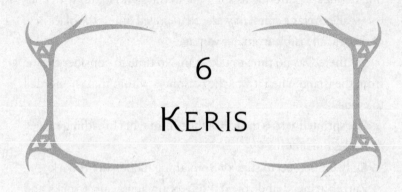

6
KERIS

THERE HADN'T BEEN A CHANCE THAT HE'D LEAVE SARA IN THAT place.

With Dax carrying her meager belongings, Keris had ridden back to the palace with his little sister on the saddle before him, her fists clenching the edges of the cloak to protect herself from the wind. Conversation had been impossible over the noise of the storm, his concern all for guiding his laboring mount and not being blown off in the process.

The horse's hooves made sharp clacks against the paving stones as he rode through the gates into the palace, dismounting first and then lifting Sara out of the saddle. An arm around her back and the other under her knees, he moved to carry her inside, but she jabbed him in the chest with one index finger. "Put me down."

He dutifully set her down. Sara held out a hand, and Dax scurried forward with her cane. "Here you are, Highness."

"Thank you," she said to him, then made her way into the inner sanctum, each gust of wind threatening to send her toppling. Keris kept close, ready to catch her, but his sister only gritted her teeth as the storm lashed at her clothes and hair.

Instead of cutting left into the harem's building, she pressed through the gardens, flowers and leaves from the shredded plants buffeting the group until they reached the shelter of the tower.

Servants immediately descended on them, whisking away sodden cloaks and handing over towels. Keris only wiped at his face, shoving strands of his soaked hair behind his ears before turning to Sara. "You may have your old room back in the harem's house. I'm sure they still have all your dresses and things." He hoped they did, at least. When he'd informed his father's wives that he had no intention of marrying them, as was tradition, he'd also told them that they had the liberty to stay or go live their lives elsewhere as widows. Sara's mother had been one of the first to go. She'd not requested to take her daughter with her, only her jewelry and gowns, and where she'd gone, Keris didn't know. "Sara, your mother—"

"Has left Vencia." Her chin trembled slightly. "Lestara sent me a letter."

Lestara.

The youngest of his father's wives had taken control of the harem after Coralyn's death, and she'd made it clear she had no intention of going anywhere. Much to Keris's dismay.

"It doesn't matter anyway. You said that when you were king, I would come to live with you." Her face was full of accusation. "*You* haven't even visited me once."

Bloody hell. "Because it was safer for you if I stayed away. Safer for people to—" He broke off, having been about to say that it would be better if everyone forgot she existed. Except to her, it likely felt as though everyone had. Including him. "I'm sorry. I should've brought you here straightaway. The servants will have your old room made up now."

"I want to sleep in the tower."

Keris blew a breath out between his teeth. "The tower isn't a good choice. Better to stay in the harem's house."

Her skinny arms crossed. "Because I'm a girl?"

The tower was traditionally reserved for the king and his sons, but Keris hardly cared about that and was stomping all over family traditions anyway. It was the climb that concerned him. "The stairs . . ."

The glare his sister gave him was pure defiance, and Keris trailed off, shaking his head. "Fine. But you should know, I intend to sail to Ithicana as soon as this storm breaks to meet with Aren and Lara."

Her defiance fell away, and tears welled in her brown eyes. "You're leaving?"

Damn it.

Giving Dax a look that said he wanted space, Keris led his sister into one of the rooms that his father had used for meeting with those who couldn't make the climb to the top. Closing the door, he led Sara to one of the chairs and then went to the sideboard, pouring two drinks. He stared at them for a long moment, then gave his head a sharp shake and dumped the contents of one into the other. God, he needed to sleep. What other excuse did he have for nearly serving whiskey to a child?

Going to the door, he leaned out. "A warm milk."

"With honey," Sara called.

One of the servants nodded, and Keris shut the door again. Taking the seat across from Sara, he swallowed a large mouthful of his drink before setting the glass on the table. "I need to travel to Ithicana straightaway. I meant to leave already, but the storm was too fierce." She stared at him silently, so he pressed onward. "I need to speak to Aren. To negotiate."

"Father never went to negotiations himself," she said. "He always sent others. Why can't you send someone else?"

"Because I'm not Father."

Aren't you? his conscience whispered.

A knock sounded at the door and Keris twitched, covering the motion by reaching for his drink. "Come in."

The door opened, but instead of a servant entering, Lestara appeared. His father's wife carried a tray with a steaming glass of milk and a plate of cookies, a throw draped over one of her bare arms. "Your Grace." She dropped into a deep curtsy, the front of her gauzy dress cut low enough that, at this angle, he could see down to her navel. Annoyance flickered through him, and he pointedly looked away.

"Sara, we were so relieved to hear you are all right." Lestara's sandals made soft pats against the floor as she crossed the room, setting the tray down on the table. "And so happy to hear that His Grace has brought you back to live with us."

"I'm going to live in the tower with Keris."

Lestara laughed as though the idea of it were utterly ridiculous, tucking her blond hair behind one ear. "You must refer to His Grace by one of his titles now, darling. Circumstances have changed."

Keris snagged the cookie that Sara's fingers hovered over, giving her a warning glance. She tucked her hands into the fold of her wet dress, the childish greed in her eyes replaced with trepidation as she was reminded that eating in this palace always meant the risk of poison. "It's fine, Keris," she said. "I'm not really hungry."

The faint growling of her stomach belied that statement.

"Sara may call me whatever she wants, because, as you say"—he bit into the cookie, marzipan roses crunching beneath his teeth—"circumstances have changed." Picking up the glass of

milk, he took a long swallow, nearly gagging at the sweetness. He
hadn't the training to taste poison, but it made his sister's importance to him clear to Lestara. "Sara will take rooms in the tower."

The daughter of a king, Lestara had been raised as much on
politics as he had himself, and she switched tactics without blinking. "Of course! It was presumptuous of me to think otherwise. As
most favored sister, Sara deserves every privilege." Slipping the
blanket off her arm, she draped it around the girl's wet shoulders.
"I'll order the dressmakers to come, as I'm sure none of your old
gowns will fit, much less suit."

Straightening, she met Keris's gaze. "I've made arrangements
for Royce's care and eventual imprisonment, as well as ensured his
mother understands that he brought his fate down upon himself,
which she has accepted gracefully. I've also sent compensation to
Greenbriar to pay for the sister's service, as well as to repair any
damages inflicted on the property during the incident."

This had been the way of things since word his father had died
in the battle of Eranahl had arrived in Vencia. Lestara running the
household, much in the way Coralyn once had. It was a monu-
mental task, managing the needs of so many, and not one Keris
was well equipped to do, so he should have been grateful. *Was*
grateful. But he also knew Lestara had an agenda, which meant
every time she did something like this, it put his nerves on edge.
"Thank you, Auntie."

Annoyance passed through her amber eyes, but Lestara inclined her head. "Will you be joining the harem for dinner?"

He considered Sara, who was sipping at her milk, expression
unreadable. "The *family* will have to forgo my presence tonight,
but thank you."

"You will be missed." Lestara curtsied, then swanned out of the
room, the door clicking shut behind her.

Keris slumped back in the chair, resting his drink on his knee. Not knowing quite why, he asked, "What do you think she wants from me?"

Around a mouthful of cookie, Sara answered, "To get in your bed."

He jerked, nearly sending his drink crashing to the floor. "What did you just say?"

Taking a large sip of milk, Sara said, "I'm not entirely certain why, but all the aunties used to say Lestara wanted to get in your bed. I assumed you had a particularly comfortable mattress."

Keris knew as well as anyone that growing up in this palace meant hearing things not intended for the ears of children, but that didn't make it any more palatable. "Such things are not fit for your ears, young lady." Then he frowned, a thought entering his mind. "What else did they say about her?"

"That Aunt Coralyn was grooming her." Sara picked up another cookie, frowned at it, and then put it back in favor of one with more marzipan. "I never understood that, because the aunties have servants to do their hair, so perhaps I misheard."

"No." Keris bit at his thumbnail, more than one piece falling into place as he remembered past events. "You didn't mishear."

Coralyn's strategies for the family, and for him in particular, were likely more far-reaching than he realized. Part of him wondered if he'd be seeing the results of all the little strings she'd pulled for the rest of his life, almost as though she were still here.

Though in fairness, the rest of his life might not be long.

"Do you like being king?" his sister asked, and he focused on her, noting the cookie plate was now empty.

"Not particularly, but it's better than the alternative."

In the way of children, she didn't acknowledge his answer, only asked another question, more softly. "What happened to Zarrah?"

Servants might well be listening. God help him, *Lestara* might be at the door listening, which meant the prudent course would be to shrug. Except he could see the interest in Sara's eyes, knew that she'd been quite taken with Zarrah, who had shown his sister kindness and respect. Rising, he filled his glass and then went to sit next to her. "The empress has sent her to a Valcottan prison."

Sara's eyes widened. "Whatever for? Zarrah is her family."

This was dangerous ground. Sara was a child, and giving her valuable information put her at risk. Except if his enemies ever got hold of her, ignorance would not save her. "Serin told the empress some things about Zarrah that she didn't like. Things she thought made Zarrah a traitor to Valcotta."

His sister's face filled with disgust. "Lies. Zarrah told me of the importance of honor. She'd never do anything to harm Valcotta."

"She didn't betray Valcotta," he said quietly, lifting his glass to hide his lips from anyone peering through a spy hole. "But she did choose to stop seeing the world in the same way as the empress, who saw that as the worst sort of betrayal."

"It's not reasonable for her to expect everyone to think exactly as she wishes." Sara held up her milk glass, mimicking his method. "She is an empress, not a god."

"I'm not entirely certain she agrees, and Zarrah has been made to pay the price." Setting down his glass, he rose, helping her up. "Lestara will have a room made up for you, as well as proper clothing brought so that you might change out of these wet things before dinner."

Sara's jaw worked back and forth. "May I go with you to Ithicana?"

Even if his intent had been to remain in Aren's kingdom, he still wouldn't consider bringing her. The Tempest Seas were too wild, too dangerous, and then there were the Ithicanians themselves . . .

"Not this time. Perhaps during the calm season, arrangements could be made with Lara to visit her."

Sara looked away, chin quivering.

She thought he was abandoning her. Which was fair, because in a way he was. "It's not forever. I'll be back."

He hoped. There was every chance that he'd never step foot in Vencia again.

Guilt twisted in his stomach, along with the rising need to make Sara understand why he had to go. Why it had to be him. Keeping his voice low, he said, "If I explain my plans, will you keep them secret for me?"

"Of course," she said without hesitation. Yet though she'd kept many of his secrets in the past, Keris's throat still constricted. Swallowing hard, he forced himself to speak, his voice still low. "I'm going to Ithicana to ask Aren and Lara to help me rescue Zarrah from prison."

His sister's eyes brightened with delight. "Will you marry her?"

If only that were in the cards. "I will march armies to save her, and that's all you need to know. Now do you understand why I need you to remain here?"

She nodded, and he helped her to the door. "Let us go find Lestara."

"READ SOMETHING TO ME," ZARRAH murmured, her breath warm against his chest. "Something about somewhere else."

Keris blinked against the glow of the sun shining in the window of the stateroom, watching the endlessly rolling waves. "Do you want to be somewhere else?"

Her body shook with silent laughter, and she lifted her head to meet his gaze, her dark-lashed eyes capturing his soul. "No, but last time I let you choose, I was subjected to an hour on the history of coin-making. I'd thought your voice could make anything in-teresting, but you proved me wrong."

"My voice?" He lifted an eyebrow. "I hadn't realized it was so intriguing."

She rolled her eyes. "Please. You know precisely the effect it has." Taking a deep breath, she lowered her voice in mimicry of him and said, "The first known coins were made from electrum, a combination of silver and gold, with trace amounts of other met-als."

"Hmm." He furrowed his brow at her. "I understand what you mean. When you say it that way, it's far more fascinating."

Zarrah gave a soft snort. "I'm going to choose." Rolling off him, she rose naked to walk to the chest of books that sat in front of the stateroom door. The sunlight illuminated the taut muscle and feminine curves of her naked body, and Keris rolled onto his elbow to drink her in. The most beautiful woman in the world trailing her fingers over the spines of his books, searching for the perfect volume.

Why couldn't this be for forever?

A shadow fell over the room, and he glanced from Zarrah to the window to discover the idyllic seas had turned rough, the sky dark with ominous clouds. "I think there's a storm coming. The sky—"

He broke off, for Zarrah had turned, the books in her hands slipping to fall with heavy thuds, her abdomen pierced with a dozen knitting needles. She opened her mouth, and blood dripped down her chin as she whispered, "Why wouldn't you let me go?"

Keris jerked awake, heart hammering and sweat slicking his skin, the room around him dark.

Just a nightmare.

Knowing it was such didn't make him feel any less sick, Zarrah's voice still echoing through his mind, the accusation always the same.

A draft brushed across his cheek.

Had he opened the window? Bloody hell, he needed to ease up on the drinking, because he could scarcely remember going to bed after dining with his sister. Sitting upright, Keris peered at the shadowed drapery across the room, but it didn't stir.

Yet he could've sworn that he'd smelled the salt of the sea and the stink of the city on the air. Keris's skin crawled, and he scanned the room, searching for signs of motion. Signs that yet another of his brothers had come to try to slit his throat. He instinctively reached backward to his pillow, fingers searching for a knife.

A knock sounded on the door.

He opened his mouth to tell whoever it was to go away, but then the door swung open. He'd forgotten to bolt it. What was wrong with him?

A hooded figure stepped inside, and Keris's fingers closed over the handle of his knife, his body tensing.

Only for the figure to draw back the hood, Lestara's face illuminated by the lamp outside the room.

"It's the middle of the night," he said, letting go of the weapon.

"I've been told these are your favored hours." Lestara's voice was a purr as she nodded at whichever of his idiot guards had let her pass and shut the door. She moved to a table and turned up a lamp, then walked to the foot of his bed, unfastening the ties on her cloak.

"Lestara," he protested, but she ignored him, dropping her cloak.

And revealing her naked body underneath.

Shit.

Keeping his eyes fixed on her forehead, he said, "I thought I'd made myself clear, Lestara. I've no intention of marrying the harem, regardless—"

"Of tradition?" She smiled, finishing the sentence he'd said over and over since taking the throne. "I don't blame you. Half of them are old enough to be your mother, and the rest are mothers of your siblings. But not me."

She eased onto the bed, crawling toward him like a cat, her breasts swaying with the motion. Keris shifted backward, his shoulders hitting the headboard as he searched the ground for his discarded trousers, spotting them halfway across the room. *Fuck.*

"I'm the daughter of a king," she murmured. "I was raised to rule, and I'm *very* good at it. Among other things."

Her fingers latched onto the blanket, trying to pull it down, but Keris grabbed hold of the fabric. A battle ensued, which might have been comedic if he weren't on the verge of panicking. "Lestara, you need to leave."

She sat back on her heels, full lips pouting. "I have to say, with your reputation, this wasn't the reaction I expected." Not giving him a chance to respond, she added, "Is it because I'm not a whore that you pay with silver afterward?" Her slow smile returned, and she reached forward to trail a finger down his chest and stomach. "I can play whore; you'll just have to pay me in gold and jewels. And make me your queen."

Anger chased away his panic, and he batted her hand away before she could reach under the blanket. "Get out of my bed, Lestara. I'm not interested."

The seductress vanished, frustration twisting her features. "Why not?"

Because you aren't her. "You're my father's wife."

"Silas is dead," she hissed, "and I have a hard time believing that you care that I'm not a maid, given your proclivities." Her eyes darkened with spite. "Worried you won't measure up? Worried you aren't the man your father was?"

The laugh that tore from his lips was bitter. "Nice try. Now get the fuck out of my room before I have the guards drag you out and put you on a ship back to Cardiff."

Her amber eyes widened. "You wouldn't . . . My father will have me killed for my failures if you send me back."

The statement made him question just what the king of Cardiff had expected Lestara to achieve, but Keris shoved the thought aside. "Then it seems the choice is clear. Get out of my bedroom and go back to your own. Once there, you may choose whether you wish to take your jewelry and leave this palace to pursue your own ends or whether you wish to remain in this household as a favored aunt. But allow me to be abundantly clear, Lestara. You will *never* be queen of Maridrina."

No longer caring that he was naked, Keris slung his legs off the side of the bed and strode to where his trousers lay in a pile on the floor. As he pulled them on, she said, "You're a fool to cast me aside. You need me."

"And why is that?" He buckled his belt, walking to the door because, evidently, words weren't going to get her to leave. But her next statement froze him in place.

"Without me as an ally, you'll return from Ithicana to discover you no longer have a crown."

"Is that a threat?" he demanded, slowly turning.

"No." Lestara lifted her chin, eyes full of defiance. "It's a foretelling. Other than the rabble you dress in uniforms, no one supports you, Keris. Not the military. Not the nobility. Not even the people, who are coming to believe you are every bit the monster your father was. If you turn your back to go on this errand to Ithicana, mark my words, one of your brothers will stage a coup and take the throne."

Nothing he didn't know, yet for some reason, hearing it from Lestara caused his stomach to twist.

"But through me, you have the harem," she said. "The daughters and sisters and nieces of the most powerful men in the kingdom and beyond. Our influence will sway them to support you, to keep your brothers in check, and to ensure the crown remains firmly on your head when you return."

It was what his father had used them for. Why he'd married so many women over the years. Because marriage secured alliances and power. "Why? Why not wait until my back is turned and then choose one of my brothers and make this pitch to them? Why bother with me?"

Lestara slipped off the bed, bending to retrieve her cloak, which she donned before approaching him. "Because you're the best of his sons, Keris. The only one of age who we trust to heal Maridrina and make it strong again."

She was trying to make him believe the harem supported her actions, which Keris doubted. "Am I to assume that the price of this offer is marrying you?"

She hesitated, then said, "In Cardiff, on a child's seventh birthday, a witch looks to the stars and sees the child's fate. The stars said that I would be a powerful woman, a queen, and that my deeds would never be forgotten. They said nothing about living out my days in obscurity as a *favored aunt*."

A story mapped in the stars.

Keris exhaled a long breath. For his kingdom, agreeing to wed her, or someone like her, would be the right thing to do. A strategic choice that any good king would make.

But he wasn't a good king, and never would be.

"Not queen of Maridrina." He twisted the handle on the door, swinging it open. "Please leave."

Lestara stared at him, jaw tight, but instead of obeying, she said, "The book I gave you before you left for Nerastis. I want it back. It was a token of a sentiment I find that I no longer hold for you."

Book? He blinked, then remembered that cursed book about stars and the stories they told. Zarrah had brought it to the dam with her the night they'd first been together. Had she thrown it in the spillway? His mind dredged up the memory of her throwing his coat into the water, but the book . . . That, she'd clutched to her chest. What had become of it after that moment, he had no notion. He'd only had eyes for Zarrah. "It's in Nerastis."

"All your things were brought back from Nerastis."

"I'll look for it tomorrow," he hedged. "It's the middle of the night; I'm not going to go rooting through my library right now." Hopefully he'd get out of having to account for it by boarding a ship to Ithicana.

"If you have it, I want it back. Now."

His temper rose, fueled by lack of sleep and irritation that she'd throw a tantrum over a book because she wasn't getting her way. "I don't know where it is, all right? It's probably lost."

Lestara squeezed her eyelids shut, twin tears flowing out from around them, and guilt instantly replaced his anger.

"I'm sorry. I didn't realize it meant so much to you."

Silence.

"It's fine." Her eyelids opened, and no more tears gleamed within. "It's better that I know the truth."

Without another word, she left the room.

Rubbing at his temples, Keris said to his guards, who were looking everywhere but at him, "No more visitors. I need some sleep."

"Yes, Your Grace," one of them mumbled. "She . . . she said you were expecting her."

"I'm not expecting anyone," Keris answered, swinging the door shut. "Good night."

He stood staring at the door for a long moment, then placed the beam in the brackets, ensuring that he'd have no more unwanted visitors tonight.

Turning down the flame on the lamp, he walked toward his bed, unbuckling his belt as he did. But as he was about to drop his trousers, cold steel pressed against his throat, and a female voice said, "Well, *that* was an interesting conversation."

7

ZARRAH

WOODSMOKE FILLED HER NOSE, AND A MOMENT LATER HER CAP-tors pulled her to a stop, shoving her down to her knees.

"Welcome." The sack was pulled from her head, revealing a woman's face illuminated by dawn light.

Zarrah tried to get to her feet but was shoved back down.

"Relax," the woman said. "We're just going to have a little chat."

Given she'd been forcibly dragged into the camp of a group of criminals, *relaxing* was the furthest thing from Zarrah's mind. Yet there was no threat in the woman's demeanor, so Zarrah risked taking her eyes off her and panned their surroundings. She was in a camp formed of six small buildings made of rough-hewn logs, tarps of what looked like scraps of sail stretched over a handful of small cooking fires. Men and women wandered about, all armed, but it was the two children playing a game with rocks and twigs who caught her eye. Children weren't condemned to this place, which meant . . .

"They were born on the island," the woman said, having followed Zarrah's line of sight. "Common enough, though very few survive. Same for the mothers."

Did her aunt know about this? Did she care?

A thought for later, given that Zarrah remained trussed in a camp full of criminals, the vast majority of whom were likely murderers. "The others said you'd kill me."

The woman chuckled. "Well, we will if you cause trouble, that's true enough. But with a face like yours, Kian's warning was a self-serving one. I'm sure he took one look at you and decided he wanted you in his harem of women. Bastard acts like King Silas Veliant, the way he collects the pretty ones. Treats them like little queens, it's true. Unfortunately, his pecker is filled with disease, so it comes with a cost, if you get my meaning."

Zarrah gagged, then said, "Silas Veliant is dead."

The woman shrugged. "No great loss there, and I'm sure he was swiftly replaced by one of his progeny."

By Keris.

"As fascinating as whatever fresh gossip you bring from the mainland is, you'll find it matters little on Devil's Island," the woman said. "The name is Daria, by the way."

Zarrah focused on the woman, who was perhaps a handful of years older than Zarrah was herself. Of average looks, her dark-brown hair was captured in a long braid down her back, her skin a similar hue of brown to Zarrah's own, and her eyes hazel. Old scars marred her bare arms, the rest of her body covered by patched clothing that needed to be cleaned. "Are you the leader of this group?"

"One of them." Reaching forward, Daria untied Zarrah's bonds. "So what did you do to earn a spot in the Empire's asshole?"

It wasn't an idle question.

What she'd done to earn her spot in this place *mattered* to the woman, though whether her crime would keep her in or out of this camp, Zarrah wasn't entirely certain. What she did know was that telling these people the truth of her identity, the truth of her crime, would see her slaughtered in heartbeats. "Murder."

"Who did you kill?"

It was more a matter of who she *hadn't* killed, but Zarrah shrugged and said, "Superior officer with wandering hands."

"You were a soldier, then? You can fight? I don't mean like a whore in a cathouse brawl, but like a warrior."

Zarrah met her gaze. "Yes."

Daria smiled. "Good. As you've already seen, we don't all get along on this island, and we could use good fighters." Her head tilted. "Name?"

Not only had every person here been sentenced to this prison in the name of the empress, but Zarrah had personally captured several criminals over the years who'd been incarcerated here, so admitting her real identity would be a fool's move. But her name was common in Valcotta—indeed, thousands of baby girls had been named in her honor over the years—so it seemed safe enough. "Zarrah."

Daria's mouth quirked up at the corner. "All right then, Zarrah. We'll give you the tour." She rose to her feet, then reached a hand down to Zarrah, pulling her upright. A sharp whistle had six others, all armed with spears, approaching. "We'll get you a weapon when you've proven yourself trustworthy," Daria said as she led the group out of the camp. "As you might expect, very few who end up in this shithole are deserving of the word."

"Fair." As she spoke, Zarrah felt a wave of déjà vu. A prisoner once more, and again without weapons, again at the mercy of those who controlled the prison, again embroiled in unfamiliar politics and schemes that she didn't quite understand. But Zarrah hadn't been helpless in Vencia, and she wasn't helpless now. "Has anyone ever escaped?"

Everyone in the group laughed, and her cheeks warmed. "I'll take that as a no."

"Don't worry, everyone asks the same thing," Daria answered, still chuckling.

"It's just a matter of when," one of the men added, his teeth bright white against his dark-brown skin. "Name's Saam."

"Quit gaping at her, you jackass." Daria poked the man in the side. "Kian won't be best pleased at losing pretty Zarrah here and might aim to take her back. Which you will make easy, given that you'll never see him coming." She glanced sideways at Zarrah. "Unless you're of a mind to join Kian, don't wander alone, you get my meaning?"

Zarrah nodded, though as she dug through her memory, what she dredged up was that Kian had been more wary of these prisoners than they were of him.

They headed southwest, passing a graveyard with dozens of stone markers of those who had lived and died in the prison. The warriors accompanying them spread out as they walked through the pines, feet silent on the cushioned earth and their eyes constantly roving. Looking for threats.

What were their crimes? Zarrah wondered, for no one ended up in this place without having done something terrible.

You're here, a voice whispered inside her head. *Not because you committed an unspeakable murder, but to teach you a lesson about men.*

I'm the empress's niece, she reminded the voice. *My imprisonment is personal; theirs isn't.*

Are you sure?

Zarrah was forced to abandon the inner argument as Daria said, "People disappear from the island all the time, so it's possible *someone* has escaped, and we just don't know. It isn't as though the guards keep the inmates apprised of current events, you get my meaning?"

"Do the guards converse with you?" There was opportunity there, for it was possible that Zarrah might know one of them. That they might be willing to help her.

"*Converse* is a stretch, but there's a certain exchange of dialogue that occurs," Daria answered, speaking louder as the roar of water grew. "We'll have to see how chatty they are today."

They broke out of the trees, and Zarrah's stomach flipped as she stopped next to a cliff edge. Beneath, the seawater raged in its swirling cycle around the island, but it was to the far side of the murderous channel that her eyes went. About every hundred feet was a stone guard-post, a pair of sharp-eyed soldiers minding each of them, bows in hand.

"Morning, cunts!" Daria shouted across the gap, lifting her hands to flip her middle fingers at the closest guards. "Care to take your best shot?"

Zarrah shifted uneasily because there was nothing to stop either guard from shooting them, no cover to take. And given that the gap between cliff tops was only about thirty feet, it was an easy shot. But the men only gave Daria sour glares, as though this was an old and tired exchange. "They don't ever shoot?"

"Oh, they do." Daria cut left and walked along the edge of the rocky cliff with no regard for the deadly plunge at her right. Casting a vicious grin at Zarrah, she added, "But it gives us something to shoot back, and we've got archers here with better aim. So they only shoot when some fool tries to get across."

"Does that happen often?" Zarrah watched the other woman flip her fingers at the guards at the next post, with a similar lack of effect.

"Every time a tree grows tall enough," Daria answered. "This place does strange things to the mind, and there are some who spend their days nurturing trees, waiting for them to grow tall enough, believing they will be delivered from this horror if only the tree will grow. More still who take great glee in cutting down said trees *just* before they reach that precious length."

Zarrah shivered, for there was a certain madness in both behaviors.

"In truth, those who try are only hastening their end, because there isn't an inch of the cliff tops that the guards don't watch," Daria continued. "Day and night. Night and day. Rain or snow or sun, they watch." Lifting her hands, she screamed "Pig fuckers!" at the next guard-post.

These guards only laughed, and though logically Zarrah knew that most of the criminals in this place deserved to be here, her hands still curled into fists because it felt as though they laughed at her, too.

She moved her attention to the next guard-post. To continue their circuit of the island, they'd have to cross the low wall of stones she'd tripped over in her flight from the other group of prisoners.

The barrier between territories.

Instead of crossing it, Daria cut inland, the wall now on her right rather than the plunge to the sea, but Zarrah didn't miss how the woman's tension grew. As though what lay past that wall was infinitely more dangerous than a fall into a whirlpool down to hell. The other warriors grew equally wary, their weapons held at the ready, eyes skimming the trees on the far side of the cut line.

"How many . . ." Zarrah trailed off as she searched for an appropriate term, then decided on "*organized groups* are there on the island?"

Daria snorted in amusement. "You mean gangs? Two. Though we call them tribes. There are also the lone wolves, who are the true death-dealers on this island. Monsters who do things that would strip the breath from the Devil's chest. You get caught by Flay or Butcher or Ladyfingers, find a way to end things yourself, and quickly."

Zarrah swallowed hard because those names were familiar to her, as was the nature of their crimes. *Monster* was a weak word, and she was now imprisoned on the same island as them.

They'd nearly reached the summit of the island, the trees falling away completely as they approached the barren stretch of land, allowing Zarrah time to truly take in the prison. Her eyes followed the gap of the ocean channel as it spiraled outward in three loops before reaching the sea. Rope bridges connected each ring of rock, allowing the guards to move from the garrison at the pier to the innermost ring, the land naked of trees or brush or structures beyond a few rocky outcroppings. "Is it truly a whirlpool?"

"Yep," Daria answered. "Though it's really more of a drain for those who don't wish to endure their punishment any longer. I'd show you where the water goes under, but it's in Kian's territory. Not another place in the world like it."

Because Devil's Island was not a creation of nature.

No, much like Ithicana's bridge, this island was formed by the giant hands of a god for one purpose and one purpose alone.

To ensure those condemned to its shores would never, *ever* get out.

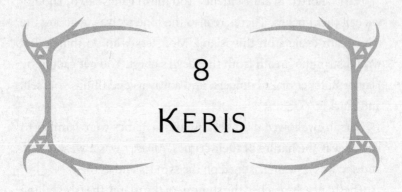

8

KERIS

KERIS FROZE AS THE BLADE ANGLED, PRESSING HARD ENOUGH that blood trickled down his throat but not hard enough to kill. "It's been a long time since I've had so many women in my room. Hopefully this encounter will prove more fruitful than the last."

She chuckled softly. "A foolish hope, Your Grace. I've no taste for incest."

Keris's eyes narrowed. One of his half sisters, then. Undoubtedly one of the ones who trained with Lara in the Red Desert, which meant she was far more dangerous than any of his idiot brothers. His eyes flicked to the mirror, the reflection revealing a fair-skinned woman of average stature, her hair dark as night. Not one of the ones who'd been with Lara the night of the rescue, but given her coloring . . . "It's been a long time, Sarhina."

If it moved her that he'd guessed her identity, Sarhina didn't show it. "Yes, Bronwyn told me that Coralyn had involved you in our plans."

He opened his mouth to point out that it had been *her* who'd been involved in *his* plan, but instead said, "If you wanted to talk, you could have made an appointment. You and the rest of our sisters are in no danger from me."

"What makes you think I wish to talk, Keris?"

"Well," he answered, "there are a limited number of reasons for an individual to sneak into my bedchamber in the middle of the night. We've clearly ruled out an assignation, and, given that I'm still breathing, assassination, which leaves only conversation."

She snorted. "I already dislike you."

Keris shrugged one shoulder, then winced as her knife bit deeper. "Why are you here, Sarhina? Fancy taking the throne for yourself? If so, it appears you need to get in line."

"The last thing I want is to be queen of Maridrina," she answered. "As to why I'm here, it's to determine whether *you* deserve the crown."

"In primogeniture rule, deservedness is not a factor, which means my successor won't be chosen based on merit. So take some time deliberating before you cut my throat."

"All the more reason to bring down the monarchy."

Keris's eyebrows rose, partially for her words and partially for the vehemence in her voice. "And replace it with what? Anarchy?"

Sarhina hesitated, then said, "A council of representatives elected by Maridrinian citizens who will rule for a set term in the interests of the people."

Delight flooded Keris's veins. "I once had too much wine and proposed just such a thing, and Father blackened both my eyes before burning the book I'd quoted from in front of the whole harem to make a point. But I managed to get my hands on another copy a few years ago. It's here. Put down the knife and I'll show you."

"Nice try," she snapped. "Just what kind of idiot do you think I am?"

"If you were an idiot, we wouldn't be having this conversation."

They stood in tense silence for a long moment; then Sarhina said, "Walk. Slowly."

Keris shuffled forward, an ache forming in his shoulder from the way she had his arm twisted behind his back. Reaching the table, which was stacked high with books, he turned up the lamp sitting on it and trailed his thumb down the spines, searching for a title. "This one."

With shocking speed, she moved the knife from his throat and pulled loose his belt. Keris yelped as his trousers nearly dropped, but as he reached to catch hold of them with his free hand, she lashed the leather of his belt around his wrist. She efficiently snaked it around the wrist she still held, cinching them tight. "Sit."

Keris sat.

Extracting the book, Sarhina took the chair across from him and put her knife on the table before opening the volume. "I'd heard you were bookish."

"Used to be," he answered. "Recent events have left me little time to read anything that isn't a report."

Her brow furrowed as she flipped through the pages, the creases deepening. Keris watched his half sister as she read. He had little recollection of Sarhina from before she, Lara, and the others were taken. Coralyn had often groused that she was a foul-mouthed creature, but she'd also said that Sarhina was the undeclared leader among the sisters, despite Lara being a queen. She'd also mentioned that Sarhina was pregnant. That was no longer the case, and as time passed, he noted a dampening of the bodice of her black tunic. But he said nothing, for he knew that any interest he showed in his latest niece or nephew would be perceived as a threat.

And her knife was in easy reach.

Close to an hour passed before Sarhina lifted her head from the book. "You would support these ideas? Despite the fact that if such a change came to pass, you'd cease to hold any meaningful power? Cease to be relevant at all?"

"I like to think that my relevancy isn't merely a function of the blood in my veins," he answered. "As to power . . . it's a burden I'd gladly shirk if not for the fact that doing so would likely require my death."

"What's wrong with you?" she demanded. "You have the capacity to heal Maridrina. To reform it in a better and brighter way, then release it to thrive under a better form of rule. Why would you run from the opportunity?"

He wasn't running from anything. It was only that, above all things, he desired to run toward a woman, and a life, that required him to abandon everything else. "I'm somewhat lazy, I'm afraid. Ideas over execution, if you get my meaning."

Sarhina snorted. "I think you're full of shit." Her eyes narrowed. "Why are you planning to go to Ithicana?"

"To visit Lara."

"You think that wise, all things considered?"

He opened his mouth to retort, then closed it. She didn't mean *wise* in the sense of how Ithicana might respond to his arrival. She meant *wise* in the sense of how Maridrina would fare without him. Which gave him an idea, the *rightness* of it sinking into his soul. "Lestara was correct that everything will go to shit in my absence. No one to keep the harem from pursuing their own goals, no one to keep our half brothers from stealing the crown, and no one to keep the nobility who long supported our father from reaching out their greedy fingers to take more power. Which means I need a *someone*."

Sarhina blinked; then her eyes widened even as she scoffed. "You've lost your mind. Absolutely not."

She's the clever one of the lot, Coralyn had told him while they were planning the escape. *That she wasn't the one chosen to go to Ithicana was undoubtedly by design. Backbone of steel, will not be pushed into anything, and she keeps all your half sisters in line despite them all having Veliant personalities. Tongue like an alehouse bar wench, but I suppose you'd like that about her.*

At the time, he hadn't cared about Sarhina's qualities, as long as she and the rest did their part. But now . . .

"As regent, you'd have the power to begin the process of healing Maridrina." He rested his elbows on the table. "To reform it in a better and brighter way, then release it to thrive under a better form of rule. Why would you run from the opportunity?"

Sarhina's jaw worked back and forth, and Keris could tell that she wanted to say yes. That she'd dreamed about the things she would do, the changes that she'd make, if only Maridrina would accept a woman on the throne. Then she said, "You don't even know me. Why would you trust your assassin half sister with such power when I could just as easily take your crown?"

"Everyone wants to take my crown, Sarhina," Keris answered. "The difference is that while they all want to replace me on the throne, *you* want to replace the throne itself."

Silence stretched, and it was a struggle not to hold his breath.

His half sister finally gave a slow nod. "Fine. I'll hold your crown for you, but it will be on three conditions, the first being that my sisters join me. This role will paint a target on my back, and I do need to sleep on occasion."

Keris shrugged. "Seems like your business, not mine."

Lifting a hand, Sarhina snapped her fingers. Keris tensed as the shadows in the corners of his room moved, a black-clad woman appearing. She lowered her veil, revealing hair so blond it was nearly white and a face he recognized from the night of the escape. He ran through the list of descriptions of his sisters, then settled on a name.

"Good evening, Athena," he said, the dark smile she gave him moderately unnerving. "And the second?"

Hands closed on his shoulders and Keris jerked, twisting his head to find a tall brunette woman smirking where she stood behind him. Bronwyn. "The second is that you get Lara's permission for me to join her in Eranahl," Bronwyn said. "The Veliant sisters take care of their own, and Aren Kertell hasn't impressed us in the past. I want to ensure he's treating her as she deserves."

Keris considered Bronwyn's request for no more than a heartbeat before turning back to Sarhina. "Fine. And the third?"

"You tell us the name of the woman you're risking everything for."

Keris's stomach dropped. Not only because of the accuracy of the question, but because every time someone learned about his relationship with Zarrah, they died. Otis. Coralyn. God help him, even the fucking Magpie.

He chewed the insides of his cheeks, debating how to answer. Easy enough to lie. To say it had nothing to do with a woman or give a fabricated name, except there was something in the tension that sang from Sarhina's form, her hand near the knife, that told him she'd see through every deception. "Zarrah Anaphora. She's been imprisoned on Devil's Island, and I need to break her free."

Sarhina smiled, and then inclined her head. "We have an accord."

9
ZARRAH

FOR ALL THE DANGEROUS MEN AND WOMEN ON THE ISLAND, ZAR-rah swiftly learned that they were not the real reapers.

It was hunger.

"You only eat what you can trap, kill, or forage," Daria instructed. "I catch you taking from anyone else, I'll cut off your hand. Catch you doing it again, I'll cut your throat, understood?"

There was nothing to do but nod. "What is there to hunt?"

"Birds, if you're good with a spear. Fish, once you've made yourself a net to lower into the spiral. Whatever grubs and insects and worms you can dig from the ground, though the season for that is ending."

That couldn't be enough, not for this many people.

"How often do the guards supply us?" Zarrah asked as they re-entered the camp, which was empty but for women with small children and those who stood guard around the perimeter.

The prisoners who'd joined the tour dispersed, but Daria motioned Zarrah to follow and flopped down next to a low-burning fire, holding her hands over the embers. "They send barrels down the spiral. Never the same times or intervals, and they've been known to withhold supplies for weeks if they are in the mood. There's no sport on the island if all are fed."

And all of it had to arrive at the beach. Zarrah's skin prickled as she remembered that amphitheater of horror, and she rubbed her hands up and down her arms, the thin fabric of her shirt doing little to ward off the chill. "Given Kian's tribe holds the beach, I take it that he gets all the supplies, which is why you want fighters? To steal what you need from them?"

"Not just a pretty face, are you, Zarrah?" Daria rested her chin on her knees. "We send watchers and scouts into the north half to keep an eye out for supply drops, but it's dangerous work. Kian's tribe patrols, and there are traps set by Flay and Butcher and Lady-fingers. We prefer to raid when the opportunity allows and take what we can. They used to do the same to us, but the bitch on the throne gave us a fresh crop of rebels, and now we're up numbers on Kian, which is why he didn't cross the border last night despite being better armed."

"Rebels?"

"Nearly every person in this camp, excluding yourself, contests Petra's rule." The corner of Daria's mouth turned up in a half smile. "Many of us were captured spying or in skirmishes and raids in the south. Her soldiers used to just kill anyone they caught, but the bitch figured out quick that it wasn't enough to check defiance, so she started sending us here." She waved a hand around the camp. "Half those they dump in the spiral are just civilians who made the mistake of saying the wrong thing about *Her Most Kind and Benevolent Imperial Majesty*." Daria spat into the flames. "Petra is as cold-blooded as a crocodile, but without its mercy."

Zarrah went still, her mind reeling. Only the worst of criminals were supposed to be sent to this place, and even they had a trial. The idea that her aunt was sending civilians who spoke against her to endure this kind of torture was . . . unconscionable.

Seeming to sense her thought, Daria said, "Didn't know that little tidbit of information, I take it? Valcotta is ruled by a woman who can't stand to hear anything but adoration, so she permanently silences anyone who criticizes her. Those who remain learn to hold their tongues, and the effect is that all come to believe the lie." She huffed out an amused breath. "But not the rebellion. We see her villainy, and she can send as many of us to her hellhole as she wants—we won't stop fighting. Won't stop *surviving*. Not until she's in the goddamned grave."

It was as if the floodgates had been opened on Daria's mouth, and she jumped to her feet, pacing back and forth. "Hundreds of people have been sent here for no other reason but that they spoke their minds, Zarrah. That's on top of the thousands Petra's soldiers have murdered without just cause."

That was impossible. Not because she didn't believe her aunt capable of it at this point, but how could so many have been incarcerated beneath Zarrah's nose? She'd been a commanding officer, a general, privy to all the secrets of the Empire, and she'd never heard a word of this before.

Or had she?

Daria's words unearthed the conversation Zarrah had overheard between Silas and Serin the night she'd intended to assassinate Silas in his tower, the men's voices filling her head.

You promised me an update on the rebels contesting Petra's rule.

Serin's nasal voice had answered, *They've pressed north out of their strongholds in the deep south, though their primary weapon is one Petra uses so adeptly herself.*

Propaganda. Or murder?

She shook her head to clear the memory in time to hear Daria ask, "Where were you stationed?"

"Nerastis."

"So you've been fighting the Maridrinians day in and day out, right? That means you've drunk deepest from her poisoned cup. That you believe the Veliants are the demons all of Valcotta must unite against, and the empress the bastion against them. She needs them to be the villains so that she can be the savior, and she'll sacrifice hundreds of soldiers, thousands of soldiers, to the Endless War to ensure that never changes."

Zarrah drew in a ragged breath, turning her gaze to the embers of the flame because Daria's anger was infectious. Like oil dumped on the fires of Zarrah's own rage. Anger at her aunt, but anger at herself for having been a pawn in her aunt's reign of terror for so long.

"So yes, Zarrah," Daria's voice cut into her thoughts, "we do need fighters to war against Kian and his tribe to stay alive. But it's more than that. The rebellion is going to free us one day, and when that day comes, we need every sword, every knife, every spear we can muster to put Petra Anaphora in the grave."

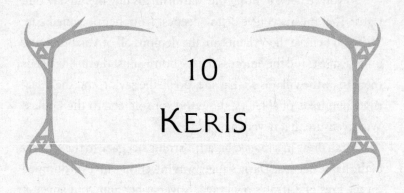

10
KERIS

THE ISLAND WAS FAR LARGER THAN ANY THEY'D SAILED PAST ON their journey through Ithicana.

Yet somehow far smaller than Keris had imagined.

"Eranahl Island, Your Majesty," the captain said. "I'd advise not going closer until the Ithicanians make contact. It's their territory."

Keris glanced up at the white flag flying beneath the Maridrinian banner, the wind snapping the fabric with such violence, it was a miracle neither tore loose. Above both of them flew a narrow strip of purple indicating he sailed aboard the ship. It was meant to be a signal according the vessel right of way, yet it felt something akin to painting a target on his back.

Much as he'd painted one on Sarhina's.

"Our brothers will see you as an easy mark," he'd reminded his half sister before he'd stepped aboard the ship. "Watch your back. And Sara's—if I find out one of our brothers has taken her, there will be hell to pay."

Sarhina had not so much as blinked. "It's not our brothers who concern me." She tilted her head, and his eyes flicked to where the majority of the harem gathered together, seeing him off. Lestara stood at their head, her face the smooth mask that politicians wore only when hiding extreme emotion. "She's going to be a problem."

"I don't see how," he answered, glad that Lestara had dropped the issue of the book she'd given him. "What is she going to say? That I refused to make her queen above the rest? Either way, she's your problem for the time being."

"Along with all the others you've dumped in my lap," Sarhina muttered. "You owe me, Keris."

He struggled not to smile. "I don't owe you anything. You can't wait for me to leave so that you can get to enacting your own personal agenda for the kingdom."

"True." She smirked. "So quit pissing around and get gone."

Given the anticipation thrumming through his veins, Keris didn't bother responding, only turned on his heel and strode up the gangplank.

"Keris!"

Sarhina's voice cut the air, and he paused to look over his shoulder.

"Lara has a tendency of allowing her emotions to take precedence over reason. I'd suggest sending someone who is not you in to smooth her feathers before risking your own neck."

"I can handle Lara," he answered, then boarded his ship.

The bravado he'd felt in that moment had long since disappeared, but there was no turning back now. "Ready a longboat."

"Your Majesty," the captain protested. "We dare not. You can see the shipbreakers and those manning them from here." He gestured to the tops of the cliffs rising out of the sea. "The Ithicanians have very good aim."

"Aren isn't going to throw rocks at me," Keris answered, taking in the swaths of new growth on the slopes of the volcano, the jungle slowly erasing the damage inflicted during the siege.

"Only because he'd rather strangle you with his bare hands?" Dax asked with a laugh.

Keris glared at him, then said, "He's a king, not a wild animal." Though, if he were being honest, killing men with his bare hands was likely something Aren did with regularity.

"He doesn't like you, does he?"

"Not particularly."

"What did you do to him?"

Bad things. Unforgivable things. "I told him he was an idiot."

Dax barked out a laugh. "Will he attempt to strike back at you as punishment for the insult?"

"Unlikely. My father invaded Ithicana and tried to destroy them so as to possess the bridge himself. He betrayed the Fifteen-Year Treaty and stabbed Aren in the back by marrying him to Lara, who was trained to destroy Ithicana, none of which sat well with our people."

Dax nodded. "He earned his death."

"Agreed," Keris said. "I, however, have withdrawn all of our forces and begun the first steps to creating a lasting peace with Ithicana. Our people know that I have come here to make amends. If Aren were to assassinate me, all the goodwill he has with Maridrina would be destroyed, as would any chance at peace. No matter how much Aren personally dislikes me, he won't make that sacrifice."

"Or so you hope."

The crew eased a longboat over the side of the ship, cursing and swearing as it swung on its cables. "We're ready, Your Grace."

Keris gave the captain a short nod. "Let us go see this mythical city Ithicana has kept hidden all these long years."

Dax clambered inside the longboat, along with a sailor who was staring at the island like a man on the verge of pissing himself.

"We should bring more men," Dax advised, but Keris only shook his head as he climbed in.

"The only reason I'm bringing you is that I'm too lazy to row. So get to it."

Dax rolled his eyes skyward as the boat lowered to the waves. "You were insufferable as a prince. Becoming king has only made you worse."

"Row." Keris was in no mood to banter, his nerves rising like bile in his throat as the boat hit the water. Everything felt abruptly more ominous, the volcano looming out of the whitecaps, peak lost in swirling rainclouds.

Rubbing at his temples, Keris forced his attention to the island. Sheer cliffs rose out of the sea, waves exploding against them with each surge, the violence breathtaking. Atop them were stone outposts that almost disappeared into the vegetation, and in each outpost, there was an enormous catapult. As Keris watched, one of the catapults rotated, and his skin crawled as he realized they were taking aim at the longboat.

"Look in the water," Dax muttered, and his attention jumped from the shipbreaker to the waves. To the massive gray dorsal moving past, circling.

It wasn't alone.

At least a dozen fins of varying sizes moved around the longboat, and a cold sweat broke out on Keris's spine, his hands ice despite the oppressive heat.

Crack!

A boulder soared through the air, landing in the water perhaps thirty paces from the longboat. Spray erupted, soaking them, waves rocking the boat and threatening to overturn it.

"We must turn back!" the sailor shrieked. "We are dead men! We must turn around, Your Grace!"

"We are not turning back."

"It was a warning," the sailor wailed, rowing opposite to Dax so that the boat spun in a circle. "The next will crush us! We'll be meat for the sharks! We must go back to the ship!"

Run back to the ship. Run back to Maridrina. Run from the fact that Zarrah was imprisoned on an island full of criminals because she'd made the mistake of loving him.

Keris's temper snapped, and he half rose, looming over the sailor. "You will fucking row," he shouted, "or I will cut your throat and feed you to the sharks, then row myself! Do you understand?"

The man shrank downward, face pale as he nodded. The long-boat resumed its course toward the black opening in the cliffs.

You are your father's son. Veliant to the core.

"The shipbreakers aren't a warning." He adjusted his cloak. "They're a reminder."

"And just what is Aren of Ithicana reminding you of, Your Grace?" Dax called over the growing thunder of the waves striking the cliffs. "Because it ain't to wash behind your ears."

Keris stared at the opening in the cliff, the entrance to Eranahl drawing closer with every stroke of the oars, the scene wholly wild and unfamiliar. "He's reminding me that this is Ithicana." The waves lifted the boat, hurling it into the volcano. There was no turning back now. "And in Ithicana, we play by his rules."

11

ZARRAH

WITH HER EYES FIXED ON THE GRAY GULLS PECKING AMONG THE rocks, Zarrah's arm trembled as she lifted the spear, which was nothing more than a long stick she had sharpened by rubbing it against a rock. *You get one chance,* she told herself. *Get it right.*

She was so hungry. Hungry in a way she'd never known, the endless gnawing in her stomach plaguing her day and night, bad enough that she sometimes doubled over in pain. She was nauseous and dizzy, the few grubs and worms she'd dug up from beneath rocks and then gagged down having done little to sate her.

As Daria had warned her, the tribe gave her *nothing* to eat.

Day after day, she watched them devour what they'd caught, only children and family units exempt from the rule of sharing. Though the smell of the meat they'd caught or stolen from Kian's tribe made her mouth salivate and her eyes burn with need, she didn't begrudge them the rule. Not after hearing their stories. Her aunt taxed heavily to fund the war, and anyone who protested was silenced. Anyone who questioned her changes to the law was silenced. Anyone who questioned her attempts to stymie trade was

silenced. The list of things individuals had been arrested for protesting was as varied as the people themselves, but at their core
was the same crime: speaking out against the empress. They
weren't just fighting to survive; they were fighting for a higher
purpose, and when that day came, it would be the strongest at the
ready.

The gull turned sideways.

Now.

She threw her spear, heart in her throat as it soared through the
air, because she wanted to be the strongest. Needed to be the
strongest, so that she would be in the vanguard of those who
would liberate Valcotta from her aunt's tyranny.

Crunch.

Her spear punched through the gull, both weapon and bird disappearing over the side of the rocks.

Zarrah was already moving.

Bits of rock exploded from her feet as she sprinted, irrationally
terrified that she'd missed, that the bird would be gone, that one of
her competitors for *life* in this cursed place had snatched up her
prey and even now consumed it.

Rounding the rocks, she skidded to a stop, her eyes latching
onto the dead bird, her spear still stuck through its side.

Zarrah fell to her knees, hands shaking as she pulled the creature free, its still eyes seeming to watch her. Blood stained its gray
feathers, and her whole body quivered with the desire to rip into
it, to consume it raw so as to put an end to the grinding pain in her
belly. Her fingers dug in—

Only for a slow clap to capture her attention.

Zarrah snatched up her spear and whirled, bird still clutched in
her hand as her eyes lighted upon Daria, who stood a dozen paces
away, grinning and clapping.

"Well done."

Daria approached, and Zarrah clutched her prize to her chest and lifted her spear, instinct demanding she protect it at all costs. But the other woman only lifted her hands in a pacifying gesture. "Peace, Zarrah. The same rules apply to me as they do to you— I steal, I lose a hand. The prize is yours, but don't allow your hunger to turn you into a beast who devours its prey raw."

Shame burned in Zarrah's chest that her intent had been so obvious, and she lowered the bird from where it was clutched to her chest. "Apologies."

Daria snorted. "No need to apologize—there's not a soul on this island who hasn't considered doing the same." Catching hold of Zarrah's elbow, she tugged her in the direction of the camp. "But to give in is to allow the bitch on the throne victory over us. She wants us to devolve into beasts with no thought for anything but satisfying our own hunger, because it means we are no threat to her. Wants to watch her enemies snapping at one another's scraps while she feasts."

You will starve and suffer while he feasts. Her aunt's words filled her head, and Zarrah shook it sharply to clear it.

"She sent us here to destroy us," Daria said. "What she doesn't realize is that we have taken her punishment and turned it into a training ground to become our strongest. When we are freed, we will be her damnation. But only if we keep our focus, only if we hold on to human purpose, and that"—she patted Zarrah on the back—"means plucking and cooking that bird *before* you eat it."

Zarrah nodded, the other woman's words a balm to the pain in her core, and though hunger still lurked, she found her steps calm and steady as they approached the camp. Some of the prisoners were playing handball, a game that had once been so popular in Valcotta that massive stadiums had been built, with great crowds coming to watch the game masters direct the players on the whispering courts. Zarrah had been to matches as a child, though her aunt had detested the game and banned it not long after her sister, Zarrah's mother, had been murdered by Silas. People still played and bet on the sly, though, and she smiled to see the rebels defying her law by playing it in the prison. "When will the rebels come to liberate you?" she asked. "Have you had communication from them?"

"They'll come when they are ready to make their move against her," Daria answered. "To free us before they are ready would mean drawing her wrath down upon them before they've the strength to defeat her, destroying all that we have worked for. We need to be patient. As to how I know their intentions, every time Petra imprisons one of my comrades, they bring certainty that we've not been forgotten."

Patience had never been her strong suit, but Zarrah had bided her time before and would do it again, so she nodded.

"Here." Daria handed her a knife. "For the bird. Waste nothing, for another will not be swiftly forthcoming."

Stopping at the outskirts of the camp, Zarrah cleaned and dressed the gull before spitting it over a fire, the other members of the tribe applauding her success but keeping a respectful distance. She remained on her knees next to the fire while the bird cooked, her eyes and mind entirely fixated on the meal to come, though she waited until it was fully done. Grease burned her fingers as she pulled loose the first bite, but she didn't feel the heat as her teeth sank into the first real meal she'd had since being taken off the ship.

A whimper escaped her lips at the taste, and her control fractured.

Barely chewing, she swallowed mouthful after mouthful, gnawing at the bones to get the smallest scraps, her belly aching from the onslaught, but she didn't care. Didn't care about anything until the gull was nothing more than a pile of cracked bones in front of her.

Zarrah stared at the mess, cursing herself for her gluttony when she might have stretched the bird into three or more meals. "Idiot," she muttered, picking up the bones to dispose of them outside of the camp.

"Don't be too hard on yourself, Zarrah," Saam said as he walked through the camp, a roughly made handball under one arm. "You'll soon remember how to think of things other than food."

That seemed a dream, but as Zarrah walked away from camp to bury the bones, her belly so full she had to clench her teeth to keep the precious sustenance down, *thought* did return to her head.

What it delivered to her was questions.

Knowing that the island was full of rebels who thought the worst of her, why had her aunt imprisoned Zarrah here? Surely she had to realize that rather than causing Zarrah to rediscover her loyalty, being around these people would only cause her to hate her more. Did she not know they were all alive and, if not thriving, at least surviving?

It didn't make any sense.

She glanced over her shoulder at Daria, who was laughing at something Saam had said to her. Perhaps what didn't make sense was how quickly she'd learned to trust these people, to take them at their word, to see their actions as kindness rather than a form of manipulation.

When she cared for someone, Zarrah was blind to their flaws. To deny that would be to deny her ignorance of how ruthless her aunt truly was. Or how much Keris had been like his father, willing to sacrifice everything to get what he wanted. *I prepared you for life in so many ways, but I neglected to teach you of the devilry of men.* Zarrah flinched as her aunt's voice filled her thoughts.

Was she making the same mistakes again? Who was to say that Daria didn't use this *promise of rescue* as a way to control her tribe? As a mythology that bound them all together and made them strong? Doing so didn't make Daria precisely a villain, but if it was all a lie, then Zarrah needed to seek another way to escape.

Though she'd have to be mindful. Daria was dangerous, and if Zarrah incurred her wrath by questioning her mythology, she might not find herself long for the world. Better to glean what she could from others while pretending to believe every word Daria said, to stay on her good side while she made her own plans. Better to—

A wet crunch filled her ears, followed by a gasp of pain. Zarrah jerked her head up in time to see one of the rebels falling backward, a spear punched through her chest.

Zarrah reached instinctively for her own spear.

Only to find a worn boot standing upon it. Her eyes raced up to find Kian standing next to her, gold teeth glinting.

"Hello, lovely," he said. "We're here to save you."

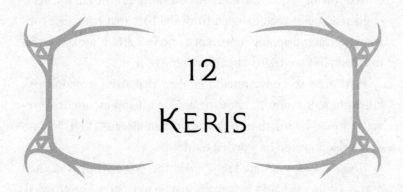

12
KERIS

DARKNESS FELL OVER THEM AS THE BOAT SURGED INTO THE CAVE, the echoes of the surf bouncing off the walls deafening.

Yet the place was not entirely without illumination.

Placed on shelves in the rock were jars of some sort of glowing substance, and Keris curbed the urge to reach out to grab one so that he might discover what was inside.

"We've got company," Dax muttered.

Farther down the tunnel, two figures perched on outcroppings, each holding a bow leveled at the longboat. Their faces, tanned by the sun, would have blended into the masses in a Maridrinian market, and something about that unnerved him. Beyond them, a thick steel portcullis blocked their path, the metal shiny and newly forged.

Pull out the damn gate! Aren's scream echoed through his mind, the memory making Keris shiver as he looked up, seeing deep gouges in the rock from where his father had done just that.

Because you told him to.

The Ithicanian archers remained silent as Dax and the sailor ceased rowing, but a heartbeat later, a rattle cut the air, the port-cullis rising. Seaweed dangled from the bars that had been sub-merged, water dripping in torrents, and to Keris, it looked for all the world like some great beast opening its maw.

He'd been so goddamned confident that Aren wouldn't risk killing him. But now . . . now he couldn't help but wonder if re-venge would be worth it to the other man. Because Keris had no doubt that it would be worth it to his *wife*.

If you're dead, you can't help Zarrah, the voice whispered. *Turn around. Go back to Maridrina and find another way.* "Row," he growled, and the boat moved under the spikes of the portcullis, water rain-ing down on his hood with heavy splats.

More armed Ithicanians watched silently as they passed, and it struck Keris then why he was unnerved by their faces. This was the first time he'd seen Ithicanians without masks. He almost wished they still wore them, for it would hide the anger. The hate.

You deserve it.

Fuck off, he silently screamed at the voice. *The battle had to happen, one way or another. I just changed the ground on which it was fought.*

You set your father on the place where Ithicana was protecting its inno-cents.

"And Ithicana won," he growled, giving his head a sharp shake when Dax shot him a look.

It wasn't lost on him that he was arguing with himself, and part of Keris wondered if he was going mad. If the lack of sleep and the anxiety and the endless, *endless* guilt had broken some critical part of his mind.

Guilt that he didn't entirely understand, because Ithicana couldn't have asked for a better result. One definitive battle, which they won. One definitive battle, in which Lara had killed their fa-ther and regained Ithicana's favor. One definitive *fucking* battle that

had Maridrina removed from Ithicana entirely. None of those out-
comes would have occurred if not for his actions. It would have
been prolonged and bloody, and at the end of it, his father would
have still been king, and peace would have remained a fantasy for
both nations. This was the best possible outcome.

But not the one you anticipated.

Keris clenched his teeth, hating the truth.

You didn't expect them to win, his guilt whispered. *All you cared
about was preventing her treason, saving her, protecting the dream you
shared of ending the Endless War, and if Ithicana burned to achieve it, you
didn't care. Yet for all your plots and plans, Zarrah was still condemned.*

"Fuck me," Dax muttered, tearing Keris from his misery. His
guard had paused in his rowing, the boat drifting as he stared at
the scene before him.

Keris silently echoed the man's words, for they were fitting. The
tunnel had opened up into a massive cavern harbor full of the
ships the Ithicanians favored. Entirely protected from the legend-
ary typhoons of the Tempest Seas and hidden from the eyes of
outsiders, some of the vessels were so large, he wasn't certain how
they got them out of the cavern at all.

Motion caught his attention, drawing it to the far side of the
harbor, where a flat piece of rock jutted into the water. Beyond
rose a flight of stairs. Armed men waited on the platform with
ropes to secure the longboat, which gave him some small comfort that they didn't intend to send him right back the way he'd
come.

As the longboat bumped against the stone dock, Keris pulled
back the hood of his cloak and met the eyes of one of the waiting
men—an older soldier who looked as though he'd faced all the
world had to throw at him and spat every bit of it back.

"I'd ask if you're Keris Veliant," the man said, "but given you

look like Lara with a cock strapped onto her, it seems an unnecessary use of words."

Keris huffed out an amused breath. "Don't forget the balls."

"Nah." The man spat into the water. "Lass has the biggest balls
I've ever seen, whereas you . . ."

"Watch yourself," Dax growled. "This is the king of Maridrina
you're speaking to, and you will—"

"Let it go." Keris waved a calming hand, curiosity drowning his
trepidation as he looked up the stairs. All he could see was the
swirling gray of the cloudy sky. "May we disembark?"

"By all means, *Your Grace.*" The man gave a mocking bow and
several of the other Ithicanians chuckled, their eyes cold.

Rising to his feet, Keris stepped onto the platform, finding little
comfort in having solid rock beneath him. Dax tried to step out of
the boat after him, but the Ithicanian shoved him hard, and Keris's
bodyguard landed on his back in the longboat.

Keris's temper snapped.

He barely remembered reaching for his knife, which meant he
was as surprised as the old soldier to find it pressed against the
man's chest. "Do not harm my people."

"Well, now." The Ithicanian's eyes brightened with interest.
"The wolf finally bares his teeth. Aren said you aren't the sheep
you pretend to be, but I have to admit, I didn't believe him. You're
too pretty." He flipped a lock of Keris's hair back with a flick of one
finger, seemingly unconcerned as Keris's blade dug into his flesh.
"Should've learned my lesson with your sister."

Keris stared him down, allowing the darkness in his core to
peer out.

Silence stretched, but it was the Ithicanian who looked away
first.

"All right. You've made your point. No one will touch your

crew." Slowly reaching up, the man pulled the knife from Keris's grip. "I'll be taking this, though."

"What's your name?" Keris asked. "So I know who to look for when I want it back."

The Ithicanian threw back his head and laughed, teeth bright white against skin tanned dark. "It's Jor. And you'll get it back when Aren says so. Now, if you head up those stairs, you'll find who you're looking for."

Keris climbed the slick steps and out of the cavern into open air. Though the sunlight was watered down by rainclouds, his eyes still stung at the sudden brightness, and he blinked rapidly to clear them as he took in the scene.

It was like stepping into the pages of a book, for it didn't seem possible that such a place could exist.

Covering the steep slopes of the volcano crater, the city's streets and houses and gardens wove seamlessly into the natural vegetation, all of it reflected in a lake in the basin. Trees and vines wrapped around the buildings, their roots digging deep into the earth, everything shades of browns and greens and grays.

In another life, he'd have abandoned duty and climbed the slopes, explored every inch of the city, then gone to the summit to look out over the world. But he'd come here for a reason, and every minute he tarried was another Zarrah remained trapped in that hellhole.

What if they refuse to help?

What if coming here was a mistake?

Keris shoved away the thoughts, focusing on the small group of people standing at the center of a paved pathway, Aren Kertell at the center of them. Aren wore the same drab tunic and trousers as his soldiers, his thick leather boots scuffed and worn, and what looked like a machete strapped to his back. Yet there was no mistaking him for anything other than the king of this place. Whereas in Vencia he'd been a fish out of water, here Aren blended into the wildness of Ithicana even as he dominated it, and Keris found himself grudgingly conceding that he may have underestimated the other man.

"Keris." Aren's eyes were unreadable. "Welcome to Eranahl."

Welcome was a stretch, but given Aren hadn't immediately stabbed him in the chest, it was a start. "I see now why you fought so hard to protect it from the world."

Aren inclined his head but said nothing. At his right, a tall woman with a scarred but beautiful face narrowed her hazel eyes, expression full of distrust. Princess Ahnna Kertell was Keris's guess, and he silently sent his condolences to William of Harendell, because the prince was deeply out of his league.

His skin abruptly prickled, giving Keris a heartbeat of warning before sharp steel dug into his spine.

Because it was his nature, Keris went on the offensive.

"How fitting that it will be a knife to the back, Lara," he said. "It seems old habits die hard."

"Must be in the blood," she answered softly. "For your knife found Ithicana's spine with unerring precision."

"And yet Ithicana still stands."

"Do you think that will save you, Keris?" his sister asked. "Do you think that our victory absolves your betrayal?"

Absolution would ever be beyond his reach, but that didn't mean he'd stand quietly while being accused of crimes he hadn't committed. "Which betrayal would that be? I made no promise to Ithicana, formed no alliance, owed no loyalty. What's more, I'm not the one who is guilty of starting the war—"

He twisted, the knife scoring his back as he turned to face her. Only to find the tip now pressed against his throat. "Just of finishing it."

Lara didn't blink, the hand holding the knife steady and capable of putting him down. Yet no fear pulsed in Keris's veins, only anticipation.

"We'd speculated that you'd come to ask us to help Zarrah," she said. "But it feels more like you've come here seeking your own death."

So they knew about Zarrah. No surprise, given Ithicana's network of spies, but the fact that they'd known and done *nothing* fanned the embers of anger in his heart. Zarrah had risked her life to ally with them, and rather than help her, they'd sat on their asses in their hidden kingdom. "I'm here to remind you that Zarrah helped you. You *owe* her."

Her head tilted. "Do we? Thanks to you, the battle Zarrah agreed to fight never happened. Ithicana fought on its own, without help from anyone."

"Ahh." He curbed the vicious words rising in his throat. "Is that why Ithicana's princess remains? Because the battle Harendell agreed to fight never happened, therefore all vows made are forgotten?"

He heard an intake of breath from behind him, female, and he filed away the princess of Ithicana's reaction for later consideration. If he lived that long.

Lara's gaze had flicked past him, but it swiftly returned as the tip of her knife dug deeper, blood running down to soak his collar. "Our agreements with Harendell are not your concern."

Keris huffed out an amused breath. "You think alliances between nations are private matters? It's all one game, *Your Majesty*, and that means they are *everyone's* business."

"Says the king here on personal business," she answered flatly. "You cannot have it both ways. If you truly meant those words, you'd tell all of Maridrina of your affair with Zarrah Anaphora and take your kingdom to war to win her freedom. Instead you keep your secrets and come here intending to use guilt and obligation to motivate us to do your dirty work, never mind that your actions were nearly Ithicana's ruin. Never mind that involving ourselves in Valcottan matters might well see the empress turn the might of her navy on our shores while we are too weak to defend them. I am sorry for what happened to Zarrah, but she made the choice to involve herself with you and must face the consequences. It's *your* fault she's damned, Keris. Own that."

He owned it every minute of every hour of every day. "So you would leave her to rot to spite me?"

"That isn't what I said."

"Doesn't mean it's not the truth," he snarled. "You're pissed off at me, and like the petty bitch you are, you'll leave the one person on the whole fucking continent who helped you to die just to get your revenge."

"It has nothing to do with you."

Lara shook with fury, and Keris knew he was playing with fire. He didn't care. "If revenge is what you want, then quit pissing around and put that knife in my throat. But after you're done, help her. *Please.*"

The tip of the knife dug deeper, dangerously close to puncturing his windpipe, and Keris could see in Lara's eyes that she wanted to do it. Could see the blistering rage that cared nothing for consequences and everything for having the satisfaction of watching him die, gasping at her feet.

"I stayed at Southwatch after all the soldiers boarded ships to move on Eranahl," he said. "Was there when the Valcottans came to attack, so I saw the moment Zarrah realized what had happened. What I'd done." His throat convulsed as he swallowed. "She was furious. Accused me of betraying her. Told me that she hated me. That she never wanted to see my face or hear my voice ever again, and that if we ever crossed paths, she'd kill me."

Color drained from Lara's face, but she said nothing.

"And then she sailed her fleet into a typhoon to try to come to your aid." His voice cracked. "Would have fought for you to the bitter end, if she'd been given the chance."

"But you took that chance from her, despite knowing it was what she wanted."

Keris's mouth was dry as sand, his chest hollow, because he didn't want to answer. Didn't want Lara to know the truth, for it would only make her think worse of him, which wouldn't help Zarrah's cause. Yet confession rose to his lips. "Every person I've ever cared about has died a brutal death. A violent death."

His mother. Raina. Coralyn. Otis.

His father.

"I . . ." The truth strangled him, but he forced the words out. "I couldn't let it happen. Not to her."

The wind had risen, and it drove droplets of rain against his face. Just as well, for it hid the tears burning in his eyes.

"Yet you could let it happen to *me*," his sister whispered, the wind stealing the words the moment they were spoken.

But not before he heard. The accusation ripped the veil from his eyes, forcing him to *see* past the warrior to the woman beneath.

Grief. Exhaustion. Hurt. Though it hadn't been so very long since he'd seen her on the beach outside Nerastis, Lara was painfully gaunt, her bare arms stick-thin and her face hollow.

Don't look, some awful part of him shrieked. *She's a liar and a traitor. A murderer who deserves no one's pity!*

She was his sister.

You don't know her! She's a stranger! She's nothing to you!

Except every time he blinked, he saw her as a child running through the harem gardens. Chasing butterflies and picking flowers when she thought their mother wasn't looking. A tiny blond girl who sat at his elbow while he read and who'd sneaked into his room at night when she'd been scared by shadows. His sister, who'd screamed for their mother when the soldiers had taken her away.

Who'd screamed for him.

"I—" He bit down on his tongue, silencing explanations. Justifications. "I'm sorry."

It wasn't enough, not after what he'd done, so he added, "You deserved better from me."

No one spoke, the only sound the wind and the rain and the roar of his own pulse.

Her eyes searched his. Then, slowly, Lara lowered her knife. "I already caused one war," she said. "I'll not start another."

Without another word, she turned and walked away, her stride marked with a limp that hadn't been there before. Ahnna glanced at her brother, then followed Lara into the city.

Aren stood unmoving, arms crossed and expression unreadable. Close enough to have heard the entire exchange. To have intervened. Yet he'd kept silent throughout. Keris met his stare, uncertain what to expect.

The king of Ithicana said nothing.

The rain intensified, falling in great sheets, and Keris expected his ship would soon have to retreat to calmer waters, if it hadn't already. Not that it mattered. He wasn't returning to Vencia.

Finally, Aren cleared his throat. "You look like you need a drink."

He needed a whole goddamned bottle. "I need an answer, Aren. Because if it's a no—"

"If it's a no, you're fucked," Aren interrupted. "Valcotta executes traitors, but instead of taking off Zarrah's head, Petra put her on an island as bait for a trap. She wants war with Maridrina. Wants to defeat you. With most of your fleet in ruins on the bottom of the Tempest Seas and a third of your army in the bellies of Ithicana's sharks, if you go head-to-head with her, Maridrina *will* lose. I know you know this. But I also know you'll do it anyway." Aren gave an exasperated shake of his head. "Defeating Maridrina won't be the end of Petra's ambition, so it won't be long until she shows up at Southwatch with all the information I provided Zarrah's sailors about how to get in."

Keris's hands balled into fists, his pulse thrumming with anticipation. *Yes or no,* he wanted to scream. *Give me an answer.*

"There are reasons for and against helping you. Reasons that a good king would think long and hard about." Aren exhaled a long breath. "But what it comes down to is that Petra Anaphora once tried to blackmail me into killing my wife, and I think it's long past time she paid for the offense."

Relief flooded Keris's veins, nearly driving him to his knees. "What makes you a shitty king also makes you a good man."

The king of Ithicana lifted one shoulder in a shrug, gesturing for Keris to follow him up the path. "I'm not a good man, Keris. And if you insult Lara again, you'll find out just how bad I can be."

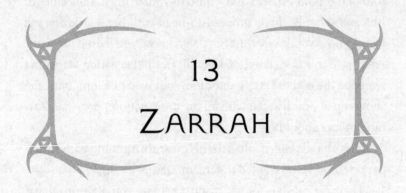

13

ZARRAH

KIAN GRABBED HER ARM. "HURRY! WE DON'T HAVE MUCH TIME!"

Instinct took over, and Zarrah jerked out of his grip, howling, "Attack!"

His eyes widened. "Mad fool!" Then he lunged at her.

Zarrah scrabbled backward. Lashing out with her heels, she caught him in the chest. Kian stumbled sideways, and she rolled, on her feet in a flash with her fists raised. "I'm not going anywhere with you."

"It will be the death of you when they learn your identity," he snarled. "Don't you know what they are?"

Her heart lurched. How did he know her identity? Had one of the guards told him?

"Kill him!" Daria shouted, and Zarrah glanced over her shoulder to see her and Saam nearly upon them, more rebels on their heels.

Spears flew, forcing Kian to dive to the ground to avoid being impaled. "Retreat!" he shouted as his eyes locked on Zarrah. "Get out while you can! We'll protect you!"

Before she could answer, he spun on his heel and joined his men racing up the slope. Seconds later, rebels who'd been away from the camp appeared, summoned by the sounds of alarm.

"Pursue?" Saam demanded, but Daria only shook her head. "No. I'll not go rushing into one of Kian's traps." Her eyes fixed on the body of her comrade, spear still embedded in the woman's chest. "See how many we lost; then call everyone in and double the guard."

Saam moved out to meet the incoming warriors, and Daria rounded on Zarrah. "Told you he wouldn't give you up without a fight, which is why you aren't to go off alone."

"I . . ." What the hell was she supposed to say? Because admitting that Kian claimed he was rescuing her from rebels who'd kill her if they learned her identity wasn't it. "I'm sorry."

Daria knelt to close the glazing eyes of the dead woman, shaking her head. "I wouldn't have believed he'd be that bold just to get his hands on a woman. What did he say to you?"

Kian's words repeated in her head, none of what he'd said making any sense. While he wasn't a rebel, Zarrah highly doubted that Kian was enough of a patriot that he'd risk life and limb to protect a member of the royal family. Which meant she had some other form of value to him—something other than him wanting another woman to have his way with. But what?

Daria was staring at her, and Zarrah realized she hadn't answered the question. "He told me to come with him. Said my life was in danger if I stayed with you."

Daria gave a slow blink. "Did he say why?"

"No." And because Daria still seemed suspicious, Zarrah added, "Maybe because you're going to think I'm more trouble than I'm worth."

The suspicion in Daria's gaze faded, and she gave a sad shrug.

"Death happened before you came, and it will come after. Just . . . just don't wander, all right?"

Zarrah nodded, but her suspicions were piqued. There was more to the island politics than was being admitted, and for some reason, she'd managed to get caught in the middle of it. All she could hope was that it didn't get her killed before she had a chance to escape this place.

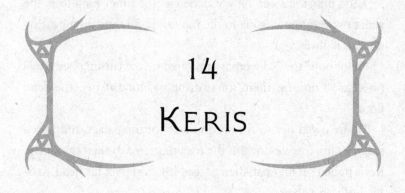

14
KERIS

"Either you've a pair of stones the size of boulders or you're touched in the head, coming into Ithicana like this, boy."

Keris regarded the stout old woman standing in the foyer of the palace like she owned it, hearing Aren exhale a long sigh. "Keris, this is my grandmother, Amelie."

He inclined his head to the Ithicanian matriarch. She wrinkled her nose as though smelling something bad and reached up to tug at the bloodied collar of his shirt, eyes flicking to her grandson. "Your wife's work, I take it? Blades first and her brain second, as always."

Aren tensed with visible annoyance, but all he said was, "Stitch him up, please. We've business to discuss."

She snorted. "Business, you say. I say another king making a mess of things over a woman."

A servant with a tray approached, and Aren snagged both glasses off it and shoved one into Keris's hands. "You might prefer to bleed to death over listening to her acid tongue. The choice is yours." Swallowing the contents of his own glass, Aren set it on the tray. "If you'll excuse me."

Keris didn't answer, only watched as the other king took the stairs two at a time, rising to the top floor and then disappearing down a hallway.

"Idiot boy," the old woman muttered before turning her scowl on Keris. "Come on, then. You're dripping blood all over the clean floors."

He followed her to the second level of the palace and into a small room, the windows at the rear shuttered against the storm. Keris pulled off his coat, then tugged his shirt over his head, tossing both on a chair.

"Not quite as sedentary as the spies claim," the old woman said, looking him up and down in a way that made his cheeks warm. "You seem quite fit for someone who supposedly spends his life hiding in the stacks."

"Books are heavy."

She barked out a laugh. "You are most definitely Coralyn's protégé—she always did love keeping secrets for the sake of it." Rising on her toes, Amelie frowned at his throat. "Already closed itself, so we'll leave it alone. Turn around."

Exposing his back rarely ended well, but there was no helping it, so Keris turned.

"What befell Coralyn?" Amelie asked, hands cool against his back as she assessed the wound. "Our spies have been otherwise focused, but I asked for them to watch for her."

Keris's jaw tightened, and it had nothing to do with the pain of his injury. He debated what to say, the part of him that would never forgive his aunt for what she had done to Zarrah demanding a voice, but he shoved it away. "My father was supposed to die during Aren's rescue. When that didn't happen, someone needed to take the fall. Should've been me, but Coralyn beat me to it and confessed to having orchestrated the whole affair. My father intended to allow Serin to ply his trade on her for more details, but Coralyn was never one to let him have his way. Drank two bottles of his finest and then silenced herself."

"And they say Maridrina has no queens." Amelie immediately segued with "This needs to be stitched. Do you want something to bite down on?"

Keris shook his head, taking a seat on the bench she gestured to. He allowed his mind to drift down into itself, barely feeling the bite of needle and thread as he relived the memories the conversation had brought to the surface. Of Coralyn in the hole beneath the palace, face bruised and gown covered with dirt as she said, *I resolved to kill Zarrah. Aided her quest for vengeance for her mother's death.*

God help him, but he'd hated Coralyn in that moment. Hated how she'd justified her villainy with her desire to protect him. To protect their family. The hypocrisy of his fury was not lost on Keris now, for he'd done the same to protect Zarrah, only to earn her hatred. A vicious circle of behavior where the ends always justified the means, yet he couldn't step clear of it. Couldn't accept the consequences that would come with being anything other than a villain.

You are your father's son. A Veliant to the core.

He tensed, hating that he'd spent his whole life running from something that couldn't be escaped.

"Nearly done," Amelie muttered. "That woman is too quick to violence for her own good."

One of his eyebrows rose. "Not a supporter of Queen Lara's reign, I take it?"

She spat, a glob of spittle striking the smooth tiles of the floor, only for her to immediately curse and toss a cloth over the mess she'd made. "This blasted place grinds my nerves. Give me a good dirt floor, I say."

Possessed of a significant dislike for filth, Keris disagreed but said nothing as he waited for a response to his question.

"You a forgiving man, boy?"

He shook his head.

"Likewise," she muttered. "Not a forgiving bone in my body, especially for those who hurt me and mine."

"Like I did."

He couldn't see her face, but he felt her frown as her hands paused in their motions. "It's different," she finally said. "You attacked from the outside, whereas she struck from within. It leaves a deeper wound, and while I will accept Lara and respect her for what she has done to atone, I will never forgive her."

"Is the rest of Ithicana like-minded?"

"Some," she answered. "And some see her as the one true queen and fall to their knees in her presence, believing her chosen by the guardians of Ithicana. Perhaps even by God himself."

Keris grimaced, having little tolerance for fanaticism.

"But most are so consumed with rebuilding their lives, with surviving, that they do not think of her at all."

Reviled. Worshipped. Or forgotten. A rush of pity filled him that Lara, after all she'd done, was faced with a lifetime of such treatment, and on its heels came anger. "You don't deserve her."

He started to rise, wanting no more part of this conversation, stitches be damned, but quick as a viper, the cursed old woman caught him by the hair and jerked. As his ass smacked back down on the bench, she said, "Aren shares your views. He wanted to abdicate and take her away, but Lara refused. For better or worse, she has chosen this life, so keep your smart mouth to yourself and let me finish. Ithicana will suffer Maridrina's wrath the same whether you die from a festered wound or from Aren tossing you to the sharks."

"My point stands," he said between his teeth as she jabbed the needle into his flesh. "And . . ." He silenced the threat rising to his tongue because it was an empty one. "And while I enjoy hair-pulling in certain circumstances, you have my assurance that those circumstances are not forthcoming."

Amelie cackled and slapped a hand against her thigh. "Must be in the blood. Your grandfather loved having his hair pulled when—"

"There are some things I don't need to know." Though he'd been aware that this woman had once infiltrated the harem as one of his grandfather's wives, Keris still hadn't been ready for such a visceral reminder.

"If it helps, when I was your age, I looked exactly like Ahnna but with bigger tits." She chuckled, fastening a bandage around him. "Smelly old bastard was putty in my hands."

It did not help.

"On that delightful note, thank you for your assistance." Rising to his feet, Keris pulled on his shirt and coat, wanting the security of the leather despite the oppressive heat. "Where can I find him?"

Amelie was focused on packing her supplies into a kit. "Follow the noise. Jor sounds like a braying donkey when he laughs. You may feel free to tell him I said so."

A real laugh escaped his lips, but Keris immediately bit down upon it. *You have no right to laugh,* he snarled at himself. *No right to experience a heartbeat of happiness while Zarrah suffers in that hellhole for your sins.*

Amelie's eyes narrowed, and not wanting to answer any questions about whatever she'd seen on his face, Keris stepped out of the room and into the corridor. The building had an echoing quality to it, much as did the bridge, and he immediately picked up on the sound of laughter, though it was Dax's distinct bellow that drew his attention.

"Bloody bastard is already drunk," he muttered, following the noise down the corridor to the main staircase. Only to slide to a stop as a boy descended, the tail of a long, banded snake in one hand, the hissing creature's head held away by a hook on a long stick.

"Mind yourself," the boy announced. "She's poisonous as they come."

"Venomous," Keris instinctively corrected. "Poison is something you ingest."

The boy gave him a look of disgust. "Don't rightly matter how it got inside of you if you're dead, does it?"

The snake's gaze fixed on Keris, mouth opening wide as it lunged, and he lurched back. "A fair point. Carry on."

Waiting until boy and snake were down the stairs and out the main doors, Keris made his way to the main level, walking down a wide corridor, the doors lining it closed. A pair of servants passed, one girl curtsying and the other crossing her arms, though curiosity filled both their eyes. He nodded at them and kept walking, irritation filling his core as he faintly heard Dax say, "Took nearly an hour to scrape the bastard off the pavement. For such a skinny little fucker, he splattered like a bag of wet mortar."

Someone said something in response, too low for Keris to make out, but Dax was gratingly loud as he said, "They were alone, so no one knows for sure. But given he was also alone with his brother when Prince Otis took his swan dive, I think it's safe to say it's unwise to piss off His Grace when you are in a high place."

Thud.

Keris flinched, retracting his hand from the doorknob and then turning to press his back against the cool wall of the corridor, hunting for his fractured composure. Closing his eyes, he drew in several measured breaths, the last of which filled his nose with a subtle perfume.

"You didn't push him, did you?" Lara asked.

Keris didn't open his eyes, only shook his head. "Serin knew I was going to execute him, so he arranged for a message to be sent to the empress of Valcotta upon his death. Took the opportunity to tell me he knew everything about Zarrah, then jumped. After what happened to Otis, no one believed that I didn't push him."

"Did you kill Otis?"

He hadn't intended for his brother to fall. But that didn't make Otis any less dead. "He discovered what was going on between Zarrah and me. Told me that either I killed her, or he would."

Lara exhaled slowly. "How many people have you killed for her?"

His eyes snapped open, his gaze fixing on hers as he said, "Did the Magpie mean so much to you?"

"No. But Aren does." Her throat moved as she swallowed. "And by involving him in this, you're going to get him killed."

Silence stretched between them, so thick he could hardly breathe, because what could he say? They'd be sailing into a trap set by the most powerful woman on the continent. Infiltrating an island populated by the worst of humanity. The odds of survival were poor. The odds for success even worse. Which had been the reason he'd wanted Lara's help in the first place—she'd spent her life training to find weaknesses where everyone else saw strengths. "He's not the one I need. You are."

The muscles in Lara's jaw bunched, but before she could answer, a deep voice said, "You made a promise, Lara."

Keris cursed, turning to find Aren leaning against the doorway, the big man too stealthy by far.

"Besides," Aren continued, "you *do* need me, because you will need a ship and a crew."

"You can provide those things and remain in Ithicana," Lara answered. "This isn't a good time for you to leave. Everything is too . . . *fragile*."

"Together or not at all." Aren crossed his arms. "You promised."

"As much as I enjoy romantic declarations, she does have a point," Keris said. "There is much to be said for you remaining in Ithicana and securing political stability while—"

"No." Aren stepped into the corridor, facing Lara with his back to Keris. "Even if you hadn't made the agreement, you just crawled out of what everyone thought would be your deathbed. If there is anyone who should stay put, it's you, but I won't ask that of you."

Deathbed? How badly had she been injured?

"Then maybe we both stay put," she snapped. "Let Keris shovel his own shit, because it's not our problem."

"Zarrah doesn't deserve what has been done to her," Aren said. "I owe her. Ithicana owes her."

Lara's blue eyes flashed. "It's as though you *want* to go."

"There is no *as though*, Lara," a female voice called from within the room. "He does want to go. And we can hear this entire conversation, so perhaps bring it inside rather than lurking in the corridor like spies."

If Lara heard the thinly veiled barb, she didn't show it, only limped into the room, leaving Keris to follow. He immediately leveled a finger at Dax. "I didn't bring you here so that you could spill all my secrets after a glass of whiskey."

"Four." Dax belched. "And I ain't told any of your secrets, Your Grace. Everyone in Vencia knows defenestration is your method of choice."

Keris ground his teeth. "That's a big word for you."

Dax laughed. "All these hours around your learned self must be wearing off on me. Won't be long till I start bleeding blue and pissing gold like a Veliant princeling."

Everyone in the room laughed, and Keris rubbed at his temples. "Go find my room and check it for snakes. They're goddamned everywhere."

Dax's eyes widened, all his humor falling away. "Snakes?"

"Take the cat." Aren made a soft clicking noise, and Keris recoiled as a cat larger than most dogs eased out from under the table, stretching its back as it yawned, revealing massive canines. Aren picked up a platter containing what looked alarmingly like grilled serpent and handed it to Dax. "Feed him, and Vitex will stay close and keep the snakes out of his room."

"Right." A bead of sweat ran down Dax's brow as the big cat's eyes tracked the thick coils of meat on the platter. "Where might I find the room?"

"Top floor." Lara settled herself on a chair.

Dax gave a tight nod, then exited the room, the cat following at his heels. The man's boots made increasingly rapid thuds to the point he must have been running, his curses loud until Aren shut the door and plunged all inside into silence.

There were a dozen seated at the table, and other than Aren, Lara, and Ahnna, the only one he recognized was Jor. Most eyed him with curiosity, though one older man's brows were narrowed with distaste. Keris met his gaze for a moment, then took a seat at Ahnna's left, accepting the glass of wine she offered, which was full to the brim. "Thank you."

"Last I drank with a Veliant, I was drugged," she said. "So stay away from my glass."

Yet another barb directed at Lara, and though his sister's face was unmoved, Keris could tell the barb had dug deep. Could tell such comments were endless and relentless, and he rounded on the princess, fixing her with a smile that was all teeth. "Remind me why you're here again, Your Highness? Aren't you supposed to be in Harendell, embroidering the cuffs of William's shirts?"

Ahnna's lips thinned and whitened, but then she inclined her head. "I am, Your Grace. Unfortunately, you've enticed my brother to go on another adventure, which means I must remain in Ithicana because someone needs to run the *fucking kingdom*." Her gaze shot to Aren, who had taken the seat next to Lara and was pouring himself a drink. "That *is* the plan, isn't it?"

"That a problem?"

"Harendell—"

"Has said nothing," Aren interrupted. "No letters, no emissaries, *nothing*, which suggests to me that Edward is content to wait until we are ready to send you north."

"How shocking." Keris took a mouthful of wine, knowing he was being a prick and not caring. "I would've thought that William would be clamoring to get his hands on his oh-so-charming bride."

Ahnna flinched and looked away.

"Leave her alone," Lara snapped, only for Ithicana's princess to round on her.

"I neither need nor want you to fight my battles for me, Lara."

A flicker of hurt passed through his sister's eyes. Lara's willingness to keep *taking* this abuse was like oil on the fires of his anger as Keris locked eyes with Ahnna. "Then why don't you attack *me* with your words rather than punching down at one who won't fight back?"

"She's the queen." Ahnna rose to her feet. "How is that down?"

"A queen who stands alone," he retorted. "Because you goddamned people seem to conveniently forget that if not for her, my father would have redecorated this lovely little palace of yours in red!"

"He would never have had the opportunity to attack Eranahl without her!"

"He would never have realized it was an opportunity without *me!*" Keris twisted to point at Aren. "And I would never have known that pulling out this city's gate was the route in if not for the fact that *your* king blurted it out in front of everyone!"

Not giving Aren a chance to respond, Keris rounded back on Ahnna. "There is endless blame to be cast, Princess, but direct it where it is due, not at the easiest mark. And keep in mind that the man who instigated it all, the one who wanted your miserable bridge and your snake-infested kingdom with its shitty weather, is dead. So quit sniveling over the past and set your eye to the future."

The princess of Ithicana's hands balled into fists, and Keris readied for the blow—

Only to find himself staring at empty space as the woman exited the room.

Silence stretched, broken only as Aren leaned back in his chair and lifted one scuffed boot to rest it on the opposite knee. "I think you need to get more sleep, Keris. You seem a touch more testy than usual."

"Fuck you, Aren," Keris snapped, but his temper was already fading, the endless crawling panic that all of this was taking too long, that he'd be too late, rising to take its place. He drained his glass, then refilled it to the brim and downed it, too. "When do we leave?"

Aren huffed out a breath. "Your mouth is going to get you killed one of these days. Jor, what do we have for stolen ships?"

"Not much readily sailable," the older Ithicanian man answered. "We've got a pair of Amaridian naval vessels, but both need repairs and a good cleaning to get rid of the blood."

"We don't have time for that," Keris said, but both men ignored him, Aren rubbing his chin as he said, "The Valcottans will attack naval vessels of any nation they discover in their waters. Merchant vessel would attract less notice."

"We'll still risk them boarding to check cargo, and we haven't"— Lara glanced at Keris—"the time to secure an appropriate one at Southwatch." She tilted her head, eyes thoughtful. "Petra isn't stupid. She will learn Keris has come to Ithicana and will anticipate we'll assist him, and Ithicana is known for stealth. So we choose something large and obvious and entirely uncharacteristic. A passenger vessel, so the Valcottan navy won't sink us first and ask questions later."

"We aren't in the habit of commandeering passenger vessels," Jor said, "because we aren't in the habit of murdering civilians. As it is, I'm not sold on risking relations with Valcotta for the sake of a woman convicted for treason for banging pelvises with his Royal Prettiness."

"It's not that simple—"

"Unlike your shit-for-brains husband, I'm too old to race off on personal vendettas, girl," Jor said. "Petra might have left us in the lurch with the Maridrinians, but she's not caused Ithicana trouble during her reign except when we started choosing sides. She was close with Aren's mother. I'm going to need more justification that this is warranted before I agree to piss in her porridge."

Keris opened his mouth to tell the old bastard that the decision wasn't his, then thought better of it and switched tactics. "How is this for justification? Petra arranged for Aryana Anaphora's murder." When all eyes moved to him, he added, "At least, according to

Serin. Before he jumped, he told me that Petra leaked information of her whereabouts to him, and he gave them to my father. My father raided across the border and murdered Aryana, cementing the foundation of a twisted sort of trust between Serin and Petra. Which is why she believed his letter about certain"—he gave Jor a long look—"pelvic unions."

Jor smirked, but Lara said, "Serin is a liar. We've no reason to believe anything that passed his lips."

Serin hadn't been lying. Until the last of his days, Keris would remember the delight in that creature's eyes as he delivered the truth, relishing Keris's horror as he fell down and down to splatter against the paving stones. "My father . . . he spoke of Petra in a way quite at odds with how she presents herself to Valcotta." *Petra is a hard woman,* his father's voice echoed up from memory. *If you believe her swayed by sentiment, you are sorely mistaken.* Shaking his head to clear it, Keris added, "And Serin said something else that was interesting. He called Aryana the *true and rightful heir.* If that's true, it means that Zarrah is the rightful empress of Valcotta, not Petra."

The older man who sat at the far end of the table, and who had been entirely silent until now, spoke. "There was a rumor, once, that Aryana had been the emperor's choice." Resting his elbows on the table, he added, "He was sick for many years before he died, and Petra ran the Empire in his stead, as she was the commander of his armies. His general. There was no doubt in anyone's mind that she would be his chosen heir and his champion in the Endless War. Yet after he passed, there were whispers that his dying wish was for a cessation of conflict. Whispers that he'd written the order that Aryana rise as empress."

"I've never heard anything about this," Aren said, then glanced to Jor.

Jor shook his head and said, "You were an idiot child, boy. My every waking breath in that era was dedicated to keeping you alive. The sun could have risen in the west and set in the east without me taking notice."

"Anything else you can remember, Aster?" Aren asked, and Keris's ears pricked at the name.

Where had he heard it before?

Raina's father. It was no wonder he'd been glowering at Keris, given that he'd been culpable in her death.

"The whispers faded," Aster answered. "I'm not sure I heard much of anything about Aryana until years later when Silas cut off her head, turning her into a martyr in the Endless War. Even when Zarrah came of age, it was almost forgotten that she wasn't Petra's own daughter."

Zarrah had loved her like a mother; Keris knew that. Had seen the hollowness left behind when she'd realized Petra was abandoning her for the sake of politics. His father had been a piece of shit, but at least he'd never pretended otherwise. Never deluded any of his children into thinking that he cared, and in Keris's mind, that made him the lesser evil.

"As fascinating as I find rooting through Valcotta's dirty laundry, perhaps you might explain to me why we give a shit," Jor said, crossing his arms. "And the answer had better not be that we intend to meddle."

"Agreed," Lara said. "I'll help get Zarrah out of that place, but no more."

Aren frowned, staring at the liquid in his glass. Then his eyes flicked to Keris's. "What are you planning?"

He had no plans beyond freeing her from that place, everything afterward a dream that he'd never given voice to. "I have no right to plan Zarrah's future. Only the intent to give her a chance at one."

Or die trying.

"Then why bring up her right to the crown?"

"Because he's playing a long game." Lara poured a glass of wine, sniffed the contents, and then wrinkled her nose, setting it aside. "He wants her on the Valcottan throne. Firstly, because he thinks she deserves it, and secondly, because it's the only chance for this war to end in our lifetimes. The only way the Valcottans will support Zarrah's claim is if we reveal the information about Aryana. Except this is *Zarrah*. Her honor will demand vengeance, and her first thought will be to put a knife in Petra's heart, not politics. Her last thought will be to listen to reason from the man who betrayed her trust and destroyed her chance to redeem her honor with Ithicana."

Lara picked up the bottle nearest to Keris and sniffed it, frowning. "All this wine is off. How are you drinking it?" She waved a hand at him before he had a chance to answer. "Never mind. Aren, Keris wants you to temper Zarrah's instinct to race to Pyrinat to try to kill her aunt and then for you to back her bid for the crown, politically and militarily. Have I missed anything, Keris?"

"The wine is fine," he answered, not bothering to hide his annoyance. "There's something wrong with your nose."

"It smells like wet dog, but suit yourself." She flipped her long hair over her shoulder and gave her husband a measured glare. "The worst part isn't that he's trying to manipulate you, but that you are considering doing exactly what he wants."

"I said nothing, committed to nothing," Aren protested. "And this wine is from one of the finest wineries in Amarid. It cost a bloody fortune."

"And you brought it out of the cellar just for *me*?" Keris examined the bottle, which was indeed an excellent vintage. "I'm touched."

"I brought it out for *me*."

"Of course you did, Your Grace. Nothing like a bit of wine to calm your nerves over hosting a king with a bigger palace than yours."

Aren's eyes bulged. "You think I care . . . Why would you think . . . Piss off, Keris."

Amusement rose in Keris's chest, but he caught his laughter before it could escape. *You're drinking fine wine in a palace with all the food you can eat while Zarrah starves on a barren, frozen rock. Focus.*

Lara drummed her lacquered nails on the table. "A passenger ship, Jor."

"Ain't got one."

"That's not entirely true." Aren shifted in his seat. "What about the Cardiffian ghost ship?"

Unease prickled Keris's stomach at the mention of Cardiff, for it made him wonder what Lestara was plotting. All he could do was hope that Sarhina kept her in check.

"No." Jor scowled. "That ship has a hex on it. It's full of ghosts."

"It's not," Aren answered, then looked to Keris. "We found it floating in our waters, all the passengers aboard dead in their beds, crew missing. Nana said they'd all consumed poisoned wine, but Jor here is convinced a Cardiffian witch hexed the ship. It's nonsense."

Keris's unease tripled at the mention of witches. It reminded him of Lestara's prophesy. But it didn't sound like they had any other options. "How soon after the storm can you retrieve it?"

Every Ithicanian looked at him in confusion except for Aren, who chuckled. "This isn't a storm, Keris. Just a bit of rain. But there is a typhoon brewing, and we'll want to get out ahead of it." He nodded to Jor. "I want it ready by morning. You handpick the crew, and keep in mind that we need to pass as Cardiffians, so a bit of sun-deprived skin wouldn't be remiss."

The old Ithicanian rose. "We'll just have His Grace here patrolling the deck. His lily-white ass should do the trick."

The jab went in one of Keris's ears and out the other, his eyes on the contents of his glass. *Tomorrow.* He mentally calculated the days it would take to reach the island prison, the number like a vise around his chest, denying him breath. *Too long.*

The room around him fell away, his mind descending into visions of what Zarrah was enduring at this very moment. Cold. Hunger. A fight for her very life.

"Keris?"

Everyone was standing, Lara holding rolled maps under one arm, her eyes shadowed with exhaustion. "We'll leave at dawn." She hesitated, then added, "I don't suppose there is any chance of convincing you to leave this in our hands? After all, if something happens to you, Ithicana will be blamed."

"Will you do whatever it takes to save her, including sacrificing your own life?" he asked.

"No."

"Then you have your answer."

Shaking her head, Lara exited the room, the other Ithicanians following so that only Aren remained. "Take what you want," the other king said, gesturing to the platters of food. "I'll have someone wait outside to show you to your room when you're ready." Aren hesitated, then added, "Get some sleep, Keris. If your mood stays this bad, Lara is likely to murder you within a day of setting sail."

Keris snorted softly. "She wouldn't be the first to try."

Silence stretched between them, and then Aren said, "She died, Keris. On the heels of the battle, when we were trying to get her past the gate your father had half pulled out, she drowned. We got her back again, but those minutes she was lifeless in my arms were the longest in my life."

Keris sucked in a deep breath, having heard no rumors of this.

"Even then, she'd lost so much blood from her injuries, it was nothing short of a miracle that she lived. Roused long enough a few days later for me to declare her queen, only to fall prey to an infection. Days upon days of fever that stole her strength. That left her gasping for breath, and everyone told me that she was going to die."

"And yet . . ."

"And yet she lived." Aren's hands fisted, then flattened against his thighs. "Lara told you that she won't risk her life for Zarrah, but in the moment, she'll change her mind. She can't keep dodging death forever. So please use this journey south to ask yourself just how much you're really willing to lose."

Everything. If he burned in hell for it, so be it. Yet to Aren, he only nodded. "I understand."

The king of Ithicana left on silent feet, shutting the door behind him and leaving Keris alone with food, maps, and wine. It was the latter two to which he gravitated, but he forced himself to eat. Tasted nothing despite the offerings being of a higher quality than what graced his table in Maridrina, his attention all for the maps. Not that there was anything on them he didn't know. Nothing he hadn't seen on those provided by his own cartographers and spies, the prison holding Zarrah little more than a tiny dot with a label.

Sighing, Keris picked up one of the bottles of wine and opened the door.

To find the boy he'd encountered before, less the snake. "You made quick work of your slithery friend, I take it?"

The boy cocked his head. "Doesn't take long to dump a snake in the jungle."

"You didn't kill it?"

"'Course not," the boy said, giving him a dark smile. "They deal with the rat problem."

"Does that mean I'm going to discover her in my bed when she finds her way back inside?"

The boy shrugged. "It's always a good idea to check your sheets, Your Grace. Never know what you might find between them."

"Truer words never spoken." Keris drank from the neck of the bottle as he followed the boy down the hallway, up the stairs to the top floor, and then down another hall. Though there was a multitude of windows in the palace, all were shuttered, and with the structure being made of the same material, Keris had the uncanny sensation of being back inside the bridge.

Which didn't help his nerves.

Spotting Dax standing outside one of the doors lining the halls, Keris drew up next to his guard. "Find anything?"

Dax made a face. "No. Cat's in there."

"Vitex will keep away the snakes," the boy said. "Not only does his kind eat snake, but they are resistant to most forms of snake"—he looked up at Keris—"*venom*." Then he turned on his heel and walked away.

"Rude little shit," Dax muttered. "One of my sons did that, I'd cuff him upside the head and make him sleep with the goats."

Given that Keris had seen Dax's sons throwing dog shit at carriages, he highly doubted this assessment, but let it slide. "Go get some rest."

His guard frowned. "With respect, Keris, it's you who needs the sleep."

That was true, but he also had a great deal of work to do before morning. "It's fine. Just check your sheets for snakes before you get in."

Dax blanched. "What do I do if I find one?"

"Scream?" Keris suggested. "I'm sure the boy will come help you. Eventually."

"Awful kingdom," Dax muttered. "Between the rain and the people and the snakes, you'd have to be mad to choose to live here."

Keris didn't answer, only watched his friend walk toward the room at the end, wondering how the man was going to take his orders to remain here as his liaison.

Probably not well.

Turning the handle, Keris eased open the door and stepped inside. The room was large, the fine furniture faintly illuminated by costly vases of Valcottan glass containing the same glowing substance he'd seen as they'd passed through the sea gate. The only flame was in a lamp sitting on the desk, turned down low. He started toward it, then tripped over something on the floor, a loud clatter breaking the silence. It was the plate of snake meat that Dax had brought, now empty and discarded.

Biting back curses, he searched the shadows for a cat-shaped form. Unease filled him, and he approached the bed, only to freeze as a pair of glowing eyes appeared over a fold in the blanket. The large cat let out a low growl.

Fixing the cat with a stare, he said, "Apologies for disturbing your rest." The animal eyed him before tucking its head back in the blanket. Bending to retrieve the plate, Keris set it on a table and then went to take a seat at the desk. It held everything he needed—paper, pen, and ink—and he immediately set to writing. First, a note to Lara informing her of Bronwyn's request to join her, which he gave to a servant in the hallway. He then drafted a letter to Sarhina informing her that he'd be remaining in Ithicana for an undetermined length of time, negotiating trade terms, then similar letters to the various ministers and administrators who kept

Maridrina's government running. Setting those aside, he began another set, marking the date in the future and fabricating various terms that he and Aren had agreed to. Then another at a later date still, with more terms and conditions for his government to chew on while he raced south.

By the time he was finished, his eyes burned from writing in the poor light, and his back ached from bending over the desk. *Go to sleep,* he told himself. *You can't help her if you're too tired to think.*

Instead he tossed his coat on the sofa and walked to the set of doors at the rear of the room, unfastening the heavy latches and opening a space wide enough for him to slip outside onto the small balcony. Rain misted his skin, but the wind had died down, and between the clouds, silver stars glowed. There wasn't much of a view in the darkness, the homes covering the slopes of the volcano mostly unlit. The air smelled of rain and wet earth and jungle, along with the ever-present odor of the stone that the majority of the buildings were constructed from. As though knowing that every aspect of their lives was dominated by the bridge weren't enough, the Ithicanians needed to smell it with every breath they took. It reminded him of Raina, who, for all she'd wanted to leave this place, had defended it to her dying breath.

Walking to the railing, Keris stared out into the darkness. He wanted to walk between the homes. To see how this mysterious nation of people lived, what they ate, and what they talked about, because he'd likely never have another chance. Swinging his legs over the railing, Keris looked down to the balcony below to plan his route to ground level.

Thud.

The world swam, the ground seeming to rush up to meet him, and his stomach lurched. *This is nothing to you,* he silently snarled. *A climb a child could make.*

Yet he couldn't move. Couldn't unfreeze his limbs, every instinct in his body screaming that he was going to fall. That he was going to smash into the ground below, gasping out his last while his blood pooled on the damp earth.

Sucking in a ragged breath, he forced himself to climb back over the rail and immediately went inside to retrieve the wine from where he'd left it on the desk. Returning to the balcony, Keris flopped into the wooden chair, water immediately soaking his trousers. *Cursed wet country.*

Drinking directly from the bottle, he stared up at the sky visible between the clouds, wondering if Zarrah was staring at the same stars or whether her view was wholly different. Whether they'd ever look at the same stars again.

Squeezing his eyes shut, Keris drank several long gulps, feeling the alcohol move into his veins. Dragging him down and down.

Only a fool falls into his cup when his back is exposed, Coralyn's voice whispered in his head, but he ignored her and finished the bottle, setting it next to his feet. He needed to sleep, and though this wild and deadly nation was likely the last place he should let down his guard, Keris's instincts for danger were quiet for the first time in as long as he could remember.

Leaning back so that his head rested against the side of the palace, he opened his eyes to stare again at the glittering sparkles of silver. "I'm fixing things with Ithicana," he told Zarrah softly, willing the words onto the wind, hoping they'd carry south. "There will be peace."

Paid for in blood, Zarrah's voice replied. *And your efforts are self-serving.*

His mouth curved up in a smile. "Not entirely." Hesitating, he added, "I have what I need now to come for you and succeed. Please just hang on a little bit longer, Valcotta."

Silence.

"Zarrah?" Keris's voice cracked on her name, his chest tightening as he waited for his imagination to conjure a response so that he might hear her voice. But whether it was the wine or exhaustion or his own mind bent on punishing him, she remained silent, leaving him alone until sleep finally took him.

15
ZARRAH

ZARRAH LAY ON HER BACK, STARING UP AT THE STARS, WISHING that the constellations held less meaning than they did. Wishing she could look at them and see glowing specks of light rather than shapes with stories told to her in Keris's voice.

But no matter how she tried to force him from her mind, thoughts of Keris crept in. His velvet voice filled her head, each blink of her eyes showing images of him reading from a book, every inhalation bringing the phantom scent of spice that she'd recognize for the rest of her life, and in every life to come.

Her aunt's voice rose in response, hissing, *The rat knew you were Valcottan. That you were a soldier. Your speech would have told him you were from a certain class, and therefore a certain rank. All of which made you a challenge worthy of his attention. A prize to be claimed, and a prize to be used once he learned just how valuable you truly were.* The words tarnished her memories, giving them new and darker meanings, and Zarrah bit her lip. Had those clues about her identity been the reason that Keris had continued to meet with her? Had she been a challenge in a sea of women who were no challenge to him at all? Was that what had attracted him to her?

No. She gave her head a sharp shake. *It was because we were like-minded. Because we both saw the same flaws in the world and were impassioned to fix them.*

You are Keris Veliant's victim. Zarrah could almost feel her aunt stroking her brow. Consoling her.

It made her stomach turn.

Scrubbing at her eyes, Zarrah rolled on her side to stare at the flames. Daria and Saam sat on the far side, playing some sort of game with rocks, but she ignored them and pulled the ragged piece of salvaged sailcloth higher on her shoulders against the chill. There was frost in the air. Saam had mumbled earlier about how it wouldn't be long until the snow was thick and food even scarcer than it was now, but Zarrah didn't want to think about that any more than she wanted to listen to her aunt pick apart her time with Keris.

Finding a way to escape. That was what mattered. And not just her, but all these people her aunt had unlawfully imprisoned. Waiting for the rebel commander to decide they warranted the risk of liberation wasn't good enough. That could be months. Years.

It could be never.

Across the fire, she watched Saam lean in to kiss Daria, but she only laughed and shoved him away. "You're not getting out of patrol that easily," she said, and Saam groaned and rose to his feet.

Leaning down, he kissed her again. "Later?"

"If you're lucky." Daria watched him leave, a faint smile on her face. Noticing Zarrah was watching her, she said, "Did you have someone before your murderous ways got you tossed into this shithole?"

"Was already over at that point," Zarrah muttered.

"Who was he? Or she?"

"Doesn't matter."

Daria leaned forward to warm her hands over the fire. "It's important to remember life before you were trapped in this place. To remember who you were, so that when we escape, we can be those people again and not starved animals with no memory of humanity."

"What if I don't want to be the woman I was before?"

Daria tilted her head, considering. "Why not?"

"That woman was a pawn who was endlessly manipulated by those she cared for. I don't want to be her. I want—" She broke off, shaking her head.

"Sounds like it ended badly."

"Yes." Zarrah stared blindly at the embers. "It was always destined to. He . . . he was Maridrinian."

Neither of them spoke for a time. Then Daria said, "Remember what I said about Petra's poisoned cup? She wants every person in Valcotta to hold hate in their hearts for Maridrinians because it serves her purpose. By doing so, you give her what she wants."

"I don't hate Maridrinians." Zarrah sat upright, tucking the sail around her hips. "Far from it. But that doesn't mean I'm foolish enough to think that there is a future for a relationship with one."

Daria burst into laughter, then shouted, "Hey!" at top volume. "Which of you fools has some Maridrinian blood in you?"

A chorus of hoots filled the air, and Zarrah's chest tightened with an emotion she couldn't name.

"You think that out of the millions of Valcottans, no one has swooned over a Maridrinian?" Daria cackled, slapping a hand against her thigh. "Oh sure, it's forbidden in Nerastis and Pyrinat, for those are directly beneath the bitch's eye, but I can assure you that elsewhere—especially in the south—very few care. I expect it's much the same in Maridrina, where those closest to the Veliants spew hate while the rest just pray for an end to the fighting."

Even in Nerastis, Zarrah had seen many who'd clearly come from unions between Maridrina and Valcotta, but that was different. They weren't under the *bitch's eye*, as Daria had so eloquently described it, whereas Zarrah was at the very center of its focus. Which she could hardly explain, just as she could hardly admit that the Maridrinian in question was the current king. "Fair enough, but there were other reasons."

"Do tell. I hope they will be as compelling as the first."

Zarrah snorted at Daria's sarcasm, but the question dug into her soul. "He . . . he loved me in a way that caused a great deal of harm to others. Was so fixated with the need to protect me that he couldn't let me *be* me when being me put my life at risk. He treated me like *his* queen."

"But you want to be empress."

"Yes." Zarrah twitched, realizing how close she was to a very damaging truth, so she laughed and added, "Metaphorically."

"We are all poets here." Daria grinned, then she leaned forward. "But a more important question . . ."

Zarrah tensed, afraid of what the woman might ask.

"Did he have a big cock?"

A laugh tore from her lips, and Zarrah snatched up a handful of dirt and chucked it across the fire at Daria. "That's an important question?"

"A big cock can make up for a small man." Several of the other women in camp shouted their agreement.

Picking up a piece of wood, Zarrah added it to the fire. For all his failings, Keris was a force to be reckoned with. "Nothing about him was small."

"Hmm." Daria gave an approving nod, and then her expression turned more serious. "Some women desire a man who will burn the world to be with her. Some desire a man who will save the world at the cost of her. Which sort of man he is may be beyond your control, but you can choose which woman you wish to be."

Wisdom on a prison island in the middle of nowhere, yet Zarrah couldn't deny the truth of those words. But none of that mattered. It was over between her and Keris. He'd moved on with Lestara, and the chances of her ever seeing him in this lifetime again were small enough to be nonexistent. So instead of looking at the stars, Zarrah met Daria's gaze. "Tell me more about the rebels' plans."

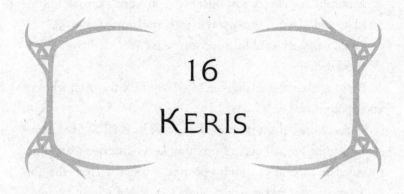

16
KERIS

KERIS WOKE WITH A START AS SOMETHING LANDED HEAVILY ON his lap.

It was Aren's massive cat. The creature yawned in his face, then began grooming itself.

"Off," he said, blinking blearily at the glow of the sun on the horizon as he pushed the cat away. It hopped onto the railing, then leapt into the nearest tree.

It was past dawn. He'd slept late.

Racing into the room, Keris grabbed his bag and the letters he'd written. With rapid strides, he went in search of the room Dax had been assigned. His bodyguard, who'd been sound asleep face-down on the bed, jerked upright and nearly fell off the side.

"I need you to remain in Ithicana until I return," Keris said, tossing the letters on a table. "I need a liaison."

Dax's mouth fell open. "I don't want to stay here," he blurted out. "It's full of snakes. There was one on the floor when I came in last night, and though that boy took it away, I couldn't sleep for fear of one wriggling its way inside my trousers."

A number of choice responses rose in Keris's throat, but instead he said, "I won't order you to stay, but I am asking you."

"Who will watch out for your sorry ass?"

"Lara will."

His guard burst into laughter. "That would be the sister who cut you open yesterday?"

"That's how Veliant siblings show their love. I'll be fine." Spotting the knife Jor had taken from him, Keris sheathed it and then rounded on Dax. "It's a simple yes or no. If it's no, I'll have the Ithicanians arrange for you to be brought to Southwatch, and you can get yourself back to Vencia on a merchant ship and resume your duties in Sarhina's guard."

Dax made a face. "So I have to choose between Sarhina and the snakes?"

"Correct."

"Snakes it is. Sarhina terrifies me."

"I thought you might say that." Swinging his bag over his shoulder, Keris picked up the letters and drew closer. "While you're here, I'd like you to keep your eyes open."

One eyebrow rose, Dax's forehead wrinkling. "You mean for me to spy?"

Keris shook his head. "We have no real understanding of Ithicana or its people. How they think or function. This is a unique opportunity to rectify that limitation, and if we use it to our advantage, so much the better."

Dax stared at him.

Spreading his arms wide, Keris said, "Make friends. It's what you do."

"Yeah, you should try it sometime."

"Kings don't have friends." Keris walked backward to the door. "But if we did, you'd be one of mine." Not waiting for a response, he left the room and walked rapidly to the stairs, descending two at a time. When he reached the ground level, he found Ahnna striding down the hall, the princess wearing the usual drab clothing the Ithicanians favored, though today she was armed with an obscene number of weapons.

"Good, you're here," he said to her, shoving the letters into her hands. "This should give your forgers enough fodder to keep my people convinced I'm enjoying a lovely holiday in this snake-infested mud puddle of a kingdom."

"Kiss my ass, Your Grace." She glanced at the letters. "I hope the cut on your back goes foul and that you slowly rot to death, but I doubt I'll be so lucky."

Keris shrugged. "Dare to dream, Princess." He hesitated, then added, "You're being handed an unprecedented opportunity to negotiate peace between our kingdoms." Pulling his signet ring off his finger, he handed it to her. "Find words that we can all live by."

Ahnna examined the gold ring, the flat surface bearing a V surrounded by a pattern of indentations unique to him, though the methodology behind the identifier was a well-kept secret only a few in Maridrina knew. "My brother might take issue with me negotiating. He doesn't trust me as he once did."

A flicker of pity ran through him, because it had been Ahnna who'd held Ithicana together during Aren's absence. "It's not because of you."

Ahnna glanced at him in confusion. "Pardon?"

"Harendell's silence. It's nothing to do with you." Rocking on his heels, Keris considered his words. "For a very long time, Harendell was something of an obsession for me, so I made an effort to learn everything I could about it, particularly the gossip. Which is why I know King Edward signed the Fifteen-Year Treaty without consulting Queen Alexandra. She's never quite forgiven him for giving up her precious son to be wed to a woman not of her choosing, and I'd bet my kingdom she's the one dragging her heels."

"You'd bet your kingdom on a game of cards," she muttered.

"She didn't choose you," Keris continued, because the princess had the right to know what she was getting into. "Which means no matter what you do, you will never be good enough for William in her eyes."

"Her feelings are irrelevant," Ahnna muttered. "Edward rules Harendell, not Alexandra. He signed the treaty, so she'll have to take me as I am."

Keris snorted softly. "Alexandra is Harendellian to her core. She'll kiss both your cheeks and pour you a cup of tea, then smile prettily with her ankles crossed as you choke to death on the poison she put in your cup." He needed to find Aren before he was left behind but wanted to make peace with Ahnna before he did. "She'll then blame Amaridian assassins so that your brother doesn't come sailing in to avenge your death. So go, but watch your back."

Ahnna's brow furrowed, but if the warning had put any fear into her heart, she didn't show it. Only walked with him out into the rain, the pair of them striding down the path that circled the lake.

"When you weren't up at the crack of dawn, Lara suggested you'd lost your nerve and would leave her to do your dirty work," she said.

"Slept late." Keris kept his eyes on the ground before him. "Too much of your brother's shitty wine coupled with the fact that I hate mornings."

Ahnna lifted her face to the sky, rain splattering her face. "You might come to regret that wine soon enough. Seas are rough." She pointed at the darkness to the west, illuminated every few heartbeats by bolts of lightning. "That's a ship killer."

Unease prickled Keris's skin as he watched the flickers. Not because he was afraid of the storm, but because he was afraid the storm would cage him on this island. That his sleeping late would mean days, even weeks longer that Zarrah would have to fight for her life. "Can we sail?"

She opened her mouth to answer, but a hooded figure approached, and she addressed him instead. "I'm surprised to see you here, Aster. It's not like you to allow Lara out of your watchful sight."

Raina's father scowled. "I don't care for the company she intends to travel with."

Keris didn't have time for this conversation, but old guilt made him pause. "Raina was your daughter, correct?"

Aster stiffened. "Yes. My eldest."

"I had the pleasure of coming to know her," Keris said. "When the attack began, she had the chance to flee. Instead she fought to the bitter end for her kingdom. Died with honor."

Aster's jaw tightened. "Idiot girl should have run. She might have brought the warning that stopped your father in his tracks." Without another word, he turned on his heel and stormed away.

"Prick," Keris growled, though given what Raina had said about her father, perhaps his reaction shouldn't have come as a surprise.

"You have no idea."

They stood in awkward silence, and then Ahnna said, "I don't feel right about this."

"Right about what?" he asked, still glaring at Aster's retreating form.

"Lara convinced Aren to leave without you. I can hear the gate being lifted, so they are underway." Ahnna shot a sideways look at him. "If you run, you might catch them."

Without hesitation, Keris broke into a sprint.

Puddles splashed with every impact of his boots, rain lashing him in the face and the humid air burning in his lungs as he circled the lake. Ithicanians stopped what they were doing to watch him pass, but Keris ignored them, his eyes only for the opening in the rock face that led down to the water.

Faster.

Thunder rumbled, the wind rising, and he knew in his gut that Aren wouldn't wait for him. Or, more accurately, that Lara wouldn't.

Reaching the opening in the rock, he hissed in anger as he saw only a pair of Ithicanians waiting on the platform and no sign of Aren or Lara. Not checking his speed, he jumped down the stairs, landing between them. "Where are they?"

Both men started, one blurting out, "Her Grace said that this task would be easier without you."

"She can kiss my ass," he snapped, and shoved past them.

Ledges were carved into the sides of the tunnel, the rock wet and slick, and his boots slid as he raced down them. The slightest misstep would send him toppling into the water, which surged in and out with each roll of waves battering the island. *Trust your momentum,* he told himself. *It will keep you on your feet.*

Ahead, he heard the rattle of the portcullis. As he rounded the bend, it was to find the thick steel slowly lowering. A small vessel had just passed beneath it, those armed with paddles fighting hard against the surf.

Keris eyed the distance between the last ledge and the bottom bars of the portcullis, and a wave of vertigo slammed into him, the world seeming to twist. *This should be nothing to you,* he silently screamed at himself. *Just do it.*

Water roared, punctuated by thunder from the rising storm, the noise deafening. None of which was loud enough to drown out the memory of Otis hitting the ground, the heavy, wet crunch that haunted him, infecting him with fear that tried to paralyze him.

But not today.

Keris jumped, momentum carrying him through the air. His hands closed around the lowest crossbar of the portcullis, one of the spikes at the base grazing his cheek as he swung beneath it and let go.

Wind slammed against him, the water beneath him deadly, but he kept his eyes fixed on the vessel.

And landed with a thud in the boat.

Falling to his knees, he gripped the sides as it bucked and plunged, water spraying him in the face. Then he turned his head to find Aren grinning. "I told you he'd make it, Lara," Aren shouted at his wife over the roar of the surf. "You owe me three pieces of gold!"

Without having to reach into her pocket, Lara held out a hand holding three glittering circles. They were Maridrinian marks, the faces stamped with their father's image. She dropped them into Aren's hand. "No more secrets, Keris. We need to know the man at our backs."

He gave a tight nod, adrenaline still flooding his veins and his heart a riot in his chest as his eyes fixed on the waiting ship rising and falling in the waves.

We're coming. He willed the words into the wind. *Please just hang on.*

17

ZARRAH

She'd stayed up until the wee hours, picking Daria's brain about the rebels in the south, who were led by someone called *the commander* whose identity was apparently a secret that Zarrah had yet to earn the right to know. Their stronghold was in the city of Arakis, which was close to the border between Valcotta and Teraford. The queen of the Ters kept the rebels supplied with weapons and armor, for she was keen to maintain the buffer between her small kingdom and the Empire.

The rebels were the key to removing her aunt from power and ending the war, and Zarrah tossed and turned for a long time after they'd said their good nights, frustrated with the knowledge that the key was out of reach. "The commander knows we are here," Daria told her with confidence. "He will come for us; have faith in that."

Except all the faith was burned out of her. Too many times she'd passively been a pawn in other people's plans, and Zarrah had no desire to do it again. She was a worthy ally to the rebels, knowledgeable and well connected, and her involvement would give them the legitimacy they needed to take on the empress. She just needed the opportunity to convince them of that.

Which was a challenge, given that she dare not admit her true identity.

As far as these prisoners knew, Zarrah Anaphora was the empress's chosen heir, premier blade in the Endless War, and vocal hater of Maridrinians. Trying to convince them otherwise would seem far too much like she was attempting to save her own skin, or worse, that this was all a ruse by the empress to infiltrate the rebellion.

She finally fell asleep, but just before dawn, the sound of Saam returning from patrol woke her.

More accurately, the sound of him kissing Daria woke her.

There was no privacy in this place. How could there be when the small structures cobbled together with deadfall and nails plucked from supply barrels were shared by all? When wandering outside the glow of the campfires risked an encounter with one of the demons that haunted the prison's shadows? There was safety in numbers, in the combined might of the camp, in the defenses that had been erected, so it was no surprise that she'd witness any and all things that people did.

Even lovemaking.

It wasn't as though Zarrah hadn't seen people coupling before. All of her adult life had been spent in barracks, and she'd long ago lost track of the number of times she'd seen men and women losing themselves in the arms of paid company, or each other, warding off the strain of a life at war with the pleasures of sex.

Daria's laughter was soft and amused, and from the corner of her eye, Zarrah saw the rebel leader straddle her lover, hips rocking against him. Their kisses were long and deep, only the crackle of the fire drowning out the sounds that she knew all too well. The

sucking. The click of teeth knocking together as passion intensified. The moans of pleasure as well-practiced fingers explored
curves and valleys.

Ignore them, she chided herself. *Stare at the fire.*

Yet for all her self-admonishments, Zarrah's eyes drifted to the
pair. Watched as Saam drew off Daria's ragged coat and shirt, exposing her naked torso. His fingers trailed down her back, tracing
over scars that appeared to be from a whipping. Had it been done
to her when she'd been captured? Zarrah didn't know, and knew
better than to ever ask.

The rebel leader whimpered, back arching as she intensified the
rocking of her hips, dragging a groan from Saam's lips. "I need you
in me," Daria whispered.

Saam gave no argument.

Zarrah knew she should look away. Knew that she shouldn't
watch. Except she'd more easily have reversed the sun in the sky
than have drawn her eyes away, because it was not Daria and Saam
she saw, but herself.

And Keris.

Daria's words had triggered a memory, and her mind returned
to the days they'd spent on the ship traveling south to Nerastis. To
their lovemaking.

There'd been a mirror in the cabin. Not cheap polished metal
but glass and silver. More than once, she'd watched their reflection, admiring the rich brown of her arms against his skin, like
strokes of paint over canvas.

"You like to watch, don't you?" Keris's lips had abandoned the
inside of her thigh, his eyes on the mirror.

Zarrah's cheeks burned hot. Watching felt forbidden, like
something only a harlot in a cathouse would enjoy, not a general,
not a woman of the highest birth. "I don't."

Keris's mouth turned up in a devilish smile. "Liar."

Catching hold of her wrists, he drew her upward, guiding her until she knelt on the edge of the bed, her back pressed against his chest and her body in full view of the mirror.

Zarrah looked anywhere but at her reflection. Not because she didn't want to.

But because she did.

"Beautiful." He nipped at her throat. "I can't blame you for wanting to admire yourself."

"I don't." She glared at the floor, knowing her whole body was burning hot. Knowing that with the way she was pressed against him, he'd feel it. "You're being ridiculous, Keris."

His body shook with silent laughter. "Perhaps."

"Go back to what you were doing between my legs," she told him, counting the patterns woven into the carpet to keep her gaze from drifting. "Then order food. I'm hungry."

"So demanding," he murmured, trailing a finger down her throat, between her breasts, over her navel. Stopping just above her sex. "Look, and I'll do anything you want, for however long you want."

"All for a look?" She scoffed. "You're a terrible negotiator, Your Highness."

He kissed her shoulder, breath leaving lines of fire in its wake. "We both know that's not true, General."

She did know it. Knew that he'd find some way to tempt her into giving in, and excitement throbbed through her veins at the anticipation of what he might do. The corner of her mouth curled into a smile; then she closed her eyes.

His breath caught, the hard length of his cock pressing against the small of her back as he leaned into her. A challenge always seemed to entice him more than anything she could do with fingers or tongue, and her body trembled with anticipation.

"I want you to see what I see," he said into her ear, sending shivers through her body. "I want you to worship at your own shrine so that you know what it's like to be on my knees before you."

"Words won't win you this battle," she breathed, tilting her head back to rest it against his shoulder. "I want you in me."

"Then look." His voice was velvet as he closed an arm around her body, hand beneath her breast as he pulled her tight against him. "One look."

Smiling, Zarrah shook her head, and a second later, his free hand captured her own. He lifted it to her face, guiding her fingers over her cheekbones and brow, tangling them in a lock of her hair before trailing them down her throat and over her collarbone. She quivered as her fingertips moved over the scars on her arms, over the peaks of her breasts, the faint lines on her hips. Keris didn't touch her once, yet touched her everywhere, showing her what he saw. Showing her what he worshipped.

Desire burned like an inferno between her thighs, the aching need to be filled by him making her want to weep as she shuddered beneath her own touch. "Please, Keris. I need you in me."

"Then look."

She clamped her eyelids tighter, knowing she was warring against herself, not him, as she rocked against him, relishing his groan as the tip of his cock rubbed against her spine.

"Cruel goddess," he breathed, then pulled her hand down to her sex, sliding her fingers between her aching folds. She was hot and slick, and her body bucked, needing more than this. Needing everything. "Keris . . ."

In answer, he curved his index finger around hers, slipping them into her depths. Using her fingertip to stroke her core until their hands were slick. "Look at what you've done to yourself," he murmured, withdrawing her finger and moving it to her clit, a sob of pleasure tearing from her lips as he circled it.

Tension mounted inside her, her climax rising, but she fought it down. Refused to allow it to claim her until she had what she wanted. Until he was deep within her.

"Look," he said, and she realized that she'd again asked him to fill her. Begged him, the feel of him pleasuring her with her own fingers battering at her will.

Zarrah clenched her teeth, fighting climax, fighting herself. "My own touch is familiar to me," she murmured. "You'll have to try harder if you wish to be victorious."

His hands stilled, holding her fingers in place, and she squirmed against them, cursing herself for speaking.

"Something better than your own touch," he said thoughtfully, then he drew their hands upward. Past her stomach and breasts and throat to pause over her mouth. Then her fingers parted her own lips, and Zarrah tasted herself.

Her lids opened, reflection filling her eyes. The lamp illuminated her sweat-damp skin, casting her in light and shadow, as lovely as she'd ever seen herself. Like passion and desire incarnate, her body quivering as it clung to the edge of climax, wanting to let go and fall forever.

Keris's cheek pressed against the side of her head, his fair hair falling to mix with her midnight curls, his gaze reverent as he watched her watch herself.

"You won," she whispered.

"And yet I serve at your pleasure."

"You know what I want." Just as she knew he was at the limit of his own self-control when he said nothing, only lifted her, his knees spreading hers wide as he lowered her onto his length.

A cry of pleasure tore from her lips as she watched him enter her, claim her, the sight of his cock slamming into her shattering her control. Climax rolled over her in a violent wave, tearing the breath from her chest. Stopping her heart and then making it run wild. The sensation was like starlight, driving all thought from her mind other than that she was his. Would always be his.

Slowly, Zarrah opened her eyes, seeing the fire now burning low, Daria rising for the day while Saam fell asleep in the warmth of her blankets.

A man like him uses seduction with the adeptness of a courtesan, her aunt whispered. *You never had a chance.*

Was it true? Had she been manipulated by something as simple as sex? Had he used it to control her?

All the things he did to make you sing made him king of Maridrina and you a traitor to your people.

A tear trickled down her nose to drip onto the ground beneath her cheek. *This is why you need to banish him from thought,* she told herself. *He's moved on. You are replaced, and with the ease he has done so, perhaps what was between you was not as meaningful as you thought. You are better off without him anyway, for he betrayed your confidence and proved he couldn't be trusted.*

The reasons she shouldn't think of Keris went on and on, but rather than making her feel better, all she felt was hollow and cold.

And so very much alone.

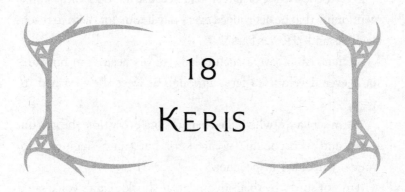

18
KERIS

IF IT HAD BEEN ANYONE OTHER THAN ITHICANIANS SAILING THE ship, the storm would have put them at the bottom of the sea.

They battled the typhoon, the ship bucking and plunging over mountainous waves as Aren and his crew navigated the edges of the storm. Knowing he'd only be in their way, Keris remained belowdecks in his small cabin. He wasn't prone to seasickness, but the endless pitch and roll of the vessel turned his stomach nauseous, though it was nothing compared to how Lara suffered. "She gets seasick on a windless day," Aren had muttered when Keris asked him. "Stay out of her way."

Knowing his sister had a bad opinion of him at the best of times, Keris had taken the other man's advice. Only when they were fully clear of the rough seas did he emerge, blinking at the brilliant sunlight. Rising the steps to the quarterdeck where Aren stood at the helm, he rested his elbows on the railing and stared out over the expanse of sea before them, no land in sight. "Where are we?"

"Nearing Nerastis," Aren answered. "For all it was a miserable journey, we made good time."

Keris made a noise of agreement, because there was little point mentioning that he begrudged every day it took for them to reach Devil's Island. "How is Lara?"

"Better." Aren gave a rueful shake of his head. "I'm not sure she'll ever develop sea legs, although at least she's learned to swim."

"Serin sent a spy who puked her guts out every time she was on a ship and who couldn't *swim*?" Keris burst into laughter. "No wonder you didn't suspect her."

"I'm not sure why that's of any great shock," Lara's voice said, cutting the air. "I was raised in the middle of the Red Desert—it's not as though there was anywhere to learn."

"One would have thought it warranted a few weeks of teaching before you left." Keris leaned his weight on his left elbow. Lara was pale, cheeks hollow and eyes marked with shadows, but otherwise seemed to have survived the journey unscathed.

"Yes, well, it was more critical that I not have any reason to doubt what I'd been taught about Ithicana than for me to learn to float." She gave Aren a soft smile, then joined Keris at the railing. "How did you learn to swim? I assume it wasn't in the fountains of the Vencia palace?"

Her voice and face were indifferent, but he noted how she toyed with a groove in the railing, tracing a fingernail along it while she waited for an answer. Curious, and he couldn't blame her for that. His life had once been her life, but then she'd been stolen away. It made sense that she'd wonder about what she'd left behind. "When I was old enough to start being considered a problem, I was fostered to one of Father's sycophants and went to live on his estate. The man was possessed of both a pond and a son. The latter made it his life's mission to try to drown me in the former. Thankfully he wasn't the fittest boy, so once I learned how to swim to the center of the pond, I was safe enough."

She cocked her head. "I was told you were bookish. That you refused to learn to fight. That you were a spoiled brat of a prince."

"Accurate." He smirked as her frustration rose over not being given the answers she was looking for. "But I also learned very early in life that the world treated me better when I was not myself. I climbed out the windows of my rooms at the estate, and I'd spend the nights being someone else. So while Keris Veliant is devoid of any practical skills, the people he becomes have much more useful abilities."

"Is fighting one of them?"

He didn't answer for a long moment, hating that his value always came back to how well he was able to put holes in other men. But his continued defiance benefitted no one, least of all Zarrah. "To an extent, yes."

"What extent?" Her blue eyes were cool. "I'm not stepping onto that island with a pacifist at my back, Keris. Never mind the Valcottan soldiers we might cross paths with; that island is full of the worst criminals in the Empire. Murderers, every last one of them. I need to know that you'll do what needs to be done. That you'll not hesitate to kill."

Silence stretched as he considered her question, remembered the lives lost as a result of his actions and the marks they'd left upon his soul.

"Killing should be hard." He stared at the ocean before them, the water only a few hues darker than the sky. "But it gets easier, doesn't it? Each life you take counting less and less until one day you find that they don't count for anything at all. At which point you realize that it wasn't just you doing the taking. That each death has stolen a piece of your humanity, and what remains is barely human at all."

"Is that a yes or a no?"

Lara's voice was frigid, which he supposed made sense, given that her hands were soaked in blood. But it was not his sister's past that concerned him—it was his own future. For all his father had pushed him to become a killer, Keris realized now that much of his morality—his identity—had been driven by defiance against that pressure, and with his father gone, there was no one left to defy. It made him wonder who he'd become. *What* he'd become. "I'll do what needs to be done."

"Fine."

Aren cleared his throat. "On that note, it's time we cut in toward the coast like a passenger ship would." Raising his voice, he shouted, "Run up the Cardiffian flag!"

One of the Ithicanian crew members moved to obey the order, a banner of orange and black fluttering into the sky. "Do you keep the banners of all nations in case you need them for random acts of piracy?" Keris asked.

Aren lifted one shoulder. "Came with the ship." Then he bellowed, "Time for a costume change!"

A pair of chests were dragged onto the deck, the Ithicanians rummaging through them and handing out coats made of what Keris guessed was sealskin. Though they'd once been finely made, sitting in trunks in the Ithicanian humidity had rendered them moldy.

Jor rose the steps to the quarterdeck, his arms full of clothing. "Picked out some choice items for you, Your Graces." He dug a headdress made from an animal's skull out of the pile and handed it to Lara. "Every vessel from Cardiff has a witch to spell away the evil spirits, though she was notably absent when we discovered this vessel. If the Valcottans stop us for inspections, wave your hands about and chant nonsense."

He tossed a fur vest at Aren, who pulled off his tunic and donned the garment, seemingly not the slightest bit concerned that his chest was bare to the world. To Keris, Jor handed a moth-eaten coat and a ridiculous fur hat with charms made of rodent skulls dangling from it.

"I am not putting this on my head," Keris said, holding the hat out with distaste. "It stinks."

"It's either that or you stay below," Jor answered. "You're the most recognizable to the Valcottans, and they *are* watching for you."

"It's *hot*. No one in their right mind would wear a fur hat—it will draw more attention than me wearing a fucking crown."

"The Cardiffians are superstitious," Aren said, clearly struggling to hold back a smirk. "They care more about their charms against evil than comfort."

It reminded Keris of when Lestara had first come to Vencia. The other wives had said that she filled her shelves with charms and talismans made of bone, which they'd all found macabre. "Fine."

"Know much about stars?" Jor asked.

His skin prickled. "Yes."

"Good." The old Ithicanian handed him a stick with yet more bones dangling from it, along with a blindfold. "You are now the ship's astrologer."

Keris donned the ratty coat as the ship cut east, the stiff wind doing nothing to disguise the stink of the rotting sealskin, but as the coast came into view, the smell became the least of Keris's concerns. He picked out the distinctive outline of Nerastis, Maridrinian and Valcottan palaces facing off against each other over the Anriot, and beyond, the bluff holding the dam. Though it had not been so very long since he'd stood on the edge of the spillway, screaming Zarrah's name, much had changed. It felt a lifetime ago.

"Valcottan vessel on the horizon!" the lookout shouted from above.

Aren gave a tight nod. "Lower sails as they approach. Everyone else in position."

With flawless efficiency, the Ithicanian warriors donned their costumes, the women in the elaborate robes and headdresses favored by wealthy Cardiffians, the men wearing vests and ceremonial weapons, the garments all courtesy of the dead passengers left on the ghost ship. Anything tying them to Ithicana was well hidden, the scene Aren painted speaking to Ithicana's skill at spying on its neighbors.

Keris took his place next to Aren at the helm, wrapping the blindfold, which was a thin enough weave that he could see through it, around his head. His heart throbbed as the Valcottan ship approached and they dropped sail, listing on the breeze. The other ship ran alongside, the Ithicanians playing their parts by pointing and making delighted exclamations at the Valcottan sailors.

"Destination?" the Valcottan captain called, the markers of rank on his uniform glistening in the sun.

"Pyrinat!" Aren called back, accent flawless. "Eighteen passengers."

The captain's brow furrowed. "Unusual to risk the Tempest Seas at this time of year. What's in your hold?"

"Samples of their wares," Aren called back. "They wish to do business with Valcotta, but the Harendellians are preventing Cardiff's trade at Northwatch. Tolls. Taxes." He spat on the deck. "Ithicana is in bed with the bastards, so we brave the storms."

The captain gave a sage nod, his eyes drifting over their faces. Keris kept his own expression stern, his grip tight on the stick Jor had given him. Then the man said, "May the stars favor your journey to Pyrinat."

Aren nodded, and seeing the captain frown, Keris called, "May they illuminate your path to greatness."

The captain gave him a respectful nod, then ordered his crew to lift the sails.

"Good catch," Aren muttered.

"One of my father's wives is a Cardiffian princess," Keris answered. "She hid their traditions in his presence, but not so around the rest of the family."

"The Harendellians claim Cardiff's women all practice sorcery. That they place love spells on unsuspecting men and then take them for all they're worth."

"If Lestara had that sort of power, she'd have used it," Keris answered, resting his elbows on the railing. "Though perhaps that explains how King Edward sired himself a bastard with a Cardiffian woman while betrothed to Alexandra."

Aren grunted in agreement. "Rumor has it that Alexandra had the woman murdered, but that as the woman breathed her last, she claimed that her son's fate would be revenge upon the one who'd killed her."

Keris whistled through his teeth. "If that's indeed Alexandra, it's no small miracle that James has survived this long. The man must sleep with one eye open."

"What is it the Harendellians say about their yellow eyes?"

"Beware the amber eyes of Cardiff," Keris said, his skin crawling, the sensation making him want to look back in their wake at the kingdom he was leaving behind.

"Full sail south!" Aren shouted. "Let's take advantage of this wind."

19

ZARRAH

THE PASSAGE OF TIME LOST MEANING WITH EACH DAY ZARRAH remained trapped on the island, her waking hours consumed with the endless hunt for food. Stalking birds across increasingly barren terrain. Dropping nets off the cliff into the channel to catch the occasional fish. Digging for anything living under rocks and deadfall. Zarrah came to understand the prisoners who nursed trees. To understand the need to obsess about something so as to have some modicum of hope in one's heart that escape was possible. For though she'd spent hours assessing the perimeter of the prison, watching the patterns of guards, and examining the flow of the water, Zarrah had failed to discover any method of escape that wasn't death.

"Patience," Daria repeated over and over. "They will come for us. Our focus must remain on staying strong and remembering that all we must do to survive will be worth it when we liberate Valcotta from Petra's tyranny."

Yet even Daria had her habits, never missing a morning of visiting each guard tower on the southern half of the island to spit curses at those manning them. "Catharsis," was all she'd say when Zarrah asked why she bothered, though with the way the guards laughed and mocked the woman, Zarrah didn't understand how the routine made Daria feel any better.

Kian's tribe made multiple attempts to *rescue* Zarrah, all of which resulted in casualties on both sides. When she wasn't putting her mind to the challenge of escape, Zarrah questioned time and again why she was of such value to the other tribe leader that he'd risk so much to try to take her. If Daria knew, she wasn't admitting it, and the rest of the tribe seemed equally in the dark.

And much less willing to stay silent about it.

"What about her makes all the trouble worth it?" Zarrah had heard more than a few say. "Give her to Kian so that he pisses off. We don't need this going into winter. How many have been lost just for the sake of keeping one useless woman? She's not even one of us. What would the commander say about us harboring one of Petra's soldiers?"

"You think I hold any love for her?" Zarrah had snapped. "She put me in here, too."

"But you deserved it," the woman retorted. "You're a murderer—the rest of us just had the audacity to speak our minds."

It ground at her nerves not to clap back with the truth, but to these people, the truth would be far worse, so Zarrah bit her tongue. And when Daria assigned her most loyal warriors to watch over her, she didn't argue, understanding the very real risk that one of the rebels might betray her to Kian. Saam followed at her heels everywhere she went, whether it be to hunt or fish, or even to relieve herself in the woods. Oppressive, yes. But better than the alternative.

Except it couldn't go on forever.

"If Kian keeps up with his attacks, your people will revolt," Zarrah said to Daria as they sat next to each other at a fire, eating their respective dinners. "We need to do something to dissuade him, or you may as well hand me over, for that will be the end result."

Daria set her bowl on the ground, and Zarrah glanced at the contents, wondering where she'd found the meat. Stolen from Kian, perhaps, and it made Zarrah wonder if his attacks were also retaliations. Whether she was the scapegoat for the cost of the rebels' thieving. "What do you propose?"

"Go on the offensive," Zarrah answered immediately, for this was the first time the woman had asked for her opinion. "He guards the food, but what we really need is his weapons."

It hadn't taken her long to notice that the other tribe was far better armed, and Saam had told her it was because the other tribe had nets across the channel and salvaged whatever the whirlpool dragged in from shipwrecks, including steel. They'd apparently set up some form of rudimentary forge, which allowed them to create the swords and knives they all carried. That any blacksmith worth his salt would spit at the quality meant little when the weapons were being used against sharpened sticks.

"If we steal enough of them, we might be able to launch an offensive strong enough to take the beach," Zarrah added. "That would change the game, Daria. We'd get the supplies; we'd get first crack at salvaging everything the whirlpool sucks in, most especially the fish! It's not like you aren't raiding him already." She gestured to the bowl.

"Don't get ahead of yourself," Daria muttered, picking up her food and continuing to eat, though she showed little appetite for it. "Kian will fight to the death to keep the beach because he *knows* losing it will only mean a slower death for him and his tribe."

"Your whole tribe survives out here," Zarrah pointed out. "Over a hundred people. I think if push came to shove, he'd concede rather than die."

"Perhaps." Daria shoved a piece of the pale meat into her mouth, chewing mechanically.

She'd pushed too hard—that much was apparent—so Zarrah switched tactics. "If we could steal enough weapons, it *would* be enough to dissuade him from attacking us. We could distribute them to those on watch, and he'd think twice about raiding. Even if we left it at that, it would be something."

"Enough to save your neck."

Zarrah flinched at the sharpness of Daria's voice. "I truly want what is best for all of us, Daria. I understand the sacrifices that have occurred to keep me out of Kian's hands, even if I don't understand why either of you feels so motivated to protect me. If there is something that can be done to end the raids, I'll gladly fight to achieve it. Especially since if I prove my worth on the battlefield, those who think you're better off without me might change their minds."

Daria finished her dinner and tossed the bowl aside.

"Let me prove my worth," Zarrah pressed, desperate to take some form of action to improve their chances. To prove not just to the rebels, but to herself, that their fight to keep her out of Kian's hands was not for nothing. "Let me fight for you."

Daria was silent; then she turned to Zarrah, hazel eyes serious. "Every battle brings risks. You could be killed."

Zarrah knew that better than anyone here, given she'd spent her adult life warring with Maridrina. "I know. But there's a chance lives that might otherwise be lost will be saved, especially if we're clever."

"What are you thinking?"

Picking up a stick, Zarrah scratched a rudimentary map in the dirt. "We know they patrol in three layers. The first along our border, the second in the trees, and the third nearest to their camp." She scratched markings. "The first layer doesn't engage—they serve as lookouts only, using their horns and retreating when they spot a threat, because they know that our target is their supplies. These scouts are young and built for speed, and presumably individuals Kian sees as disposable, because they aren't well armed."

Daria's eyes narrowed. "How does one who has only been on the other half of the island *once* know all this?"

"Saam," Zarrah admitted. "In the moments we haven't been talking about handball, I've been picking his brain about the other tribe." She hesitated, then asked, "Is he wrong?"

Daria shook her head.

"What I propose is changing the targets," Zarrah said. "With a small force of your best fighters, we sneak past the first layer and attack the second, who run in pairs. We take them, stealing their weapons, which is typical. Then an additional force of our warriors attacks the first layer of scouts, but gives them the chance to escape and sound the alarm while the strike force retreats, killing the scouts as we do. We take our prizes and run, and Kian will think it a failed attempt to raid his main camp."

"He'll retaliate."

"Will he?" Zarrah lifted one shoulder. "We have superior numbers. With our fresh supply of weapons, I personally believe he'll think twice, especially if we keep up a strong patrol for the foreseeable future." Seeing that Daria was not quite convinced, she added, "I think there is every chance that when the rebels come for us, we're going to need to help fight our way out of here. We make their lives easier if we are well armed."

Daria leaned back on her hands, eyes on the sky. It smelled of snow, and Zarrah knew she was thinking of a hard winter to come. Thinking of how much easier it would be if they held the beach. Thinking that this proposal might be worth it, even though it would mean losses. "All right," she finally answered. "We'll go tomorrow night."

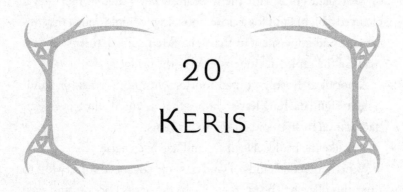

20
KERIS

KERIS SHIVERED, PULLING HIS SEALSKIN COAT TIGHTER AS THE wind ripped at the edges, bits of snow falling all around him.

He was born and raised in Maridrina, where it was always hot; a chilly breeze on a rainy day was the coldest weather he'd ever experienced. He already hated it. Hated how the wind chapped his cheeks and made his fingers ache, how the cold sank into his bones, chilling him from the inside out. Aren muttered something about wind current bringing air up from the frozen south before abandoning his chest-baring vest in favor of a sealskin coat like Keris's. But the miserable weather was the least of his concerns.

They'd reached Devil's Island.

In the darkness of night, they'd circled the ship around the island, crew silent and every light extinguished, only to discover that the place was well worthy of its reputation. There was only one opening in the towering cliffs, the singular pier with accompanying guard towers that were lit up like a street festival at midnight, which allowed them to count well over a hundred soldiers. Too many by far for a direct assault, so they'd risked an inspection of the cliffs themselves in a longboat.

Keris had gone with them, so he'd been there when they'd chanced a bit of light for a closer look. Every single one of the Ithicanians had gone silent at the sight. Aren cursed, then said, "It's made of the same fucking material as the bridge."

Smooth as freshly poured mortar, with not a crack or handhold in sight, dashing Keris's hopes that he could climb even as it had poured fresh trepidation into his veins.

For, like the bridge, Devil's Island had been *made*.

Whether by the hands of God or some advanced society lost to time, this place had been created to be the perfect prison, and even Lara's face had gone grim at the revelation when they'd returned to the ship.

They'd retreated a safe distance to discuss their options, but it was now well into afternoon, and no ideas were forthcoming.

"A barren place."

Keris glanced sideways at Lara, who'd come to stand next to him at the rail. Beyond, Aren paced the deck. "How are you feeling?"

Lara didn't move her eyes from the small rocky island near them, the only life in sight scraggly conifers, the occasional bird, and the seals on the beaches. "Just tired, for the most part." She was quiet for a long time, then added, "This has never happened to me before. I've been injured many times in my life and always recovered swiftly, but this time . . ."

"There's a difference between being injured and dying, only to be brought back and then nearly die again."

Her jaw tightened. "Aren makes it sound worse than it was, and my recovery is hardly our primary concern."

Keris made a noncommittal noise, for he expected Lara's injuries had been every bit as bad as Aren had indicated. But she was right about their concerns, so he said nothing when she switched subjects.

"In a perfect world, we'd have time to learn more about this place before venturing closer," Lara said. "But everything about this prison is well guarded, so even if we had time, we might well have ended up at this point."

"Hopeless?"

She cast him a dark look. "Dramatics won't help. We've been here less than a day—keep in mind that it took weeks of thought and planning and spying to break Aren out of the Vencia palace."

"Zarrah doesn't have weeks," he muttered. "What we need is a stroke of luck, but Lady Fortune rarely favors me."

"Ship off the starboard bow," the lookout shouted. "It flies the Valcottan flag!"

"Shit," Lara hissed.

Keris's stomach sank, and he cursed himself for speaking of luck.

The other Ithicanians donned their costumes and took their places, and Aren motioned to Keris and Lara to join him. "Follow my lead," Aren said once they'd reached him. "I'm going to tell them we hit rocks and damaged the rudder. Buy us some time to linger, though we'll have to do it under their watch. Keris, put on your damn blindfold."

That was the last thing Keris wanted to do, but he dutifully wrapped the linen around his eyes. In combination with the dim light, he could see little.

"Steady," Aren muttered, and Keris heard waves hitting the hull of the approaching ship. Flapping sails and barked orders. "Prepare to be boarded," a deep voice shouted, and moments later, heavy *thunks* of hooks striking wood filled Keris's ears.

"They're boarding," Lara murmured. "And they aren't happy we are here."

"Greetings." Aren's voice again carried the accent of a Cardiffian sailor. "How can we be of service?"

"Passage on these waters is prohibited," the deep voice called, and Keris was struck by its familiarity. "State your business for being here."

"We were blown off course in the night," Aren answered. "Rudder was damaged, and we've dropped anchor to repair it. We carry Cardiffian merchants seeking to form business partnerships in the south. Relationships that do *not* include Ithicana and its bridge."

"You think I'm going to trust your words, you squirrely-eyed warlock?" the Valcottan snarled. "If you're transporting goods from Teraford to the Maridrinians, you're in violation of the empress's blockade."

Aren answered, "You wound me, my friend. We would not dare to cross the empress. Check our hold—we carry no goods from Teraford, only those brought from Cardiff to show Valcottan merchants whose aspirations have been stymied by Ithicana's relationship with Harendell."

Silence stretched, and Keris wished above all else that he could see the Valcottan's expression so that he might judge his intention. But Lara chose to start chanting. It was a nursery rhyme about animals gobbling up other animals, but in the sharp Cardiffian tongue with the bones and skulls on her headdress clattering together, it was eerie and strange.

"What's she going on about?" the Valcottan man demanded.

Aren coughed as Lara repeated the rhyme. "The waters here are cursed. She sings a spell asking them to leave us in peace."

The Valcottans muttered uneasily from their ship.

"We need to inspect your hold," the deep-voiced man said, clearly unnerved by Lara's performance. "Once you've made your repairs, you must leave these waters, or there will be consequences."

"Of course," Aren answered, seemingly nonplussed by the

threat. "Would you like a glass of wine to wet your tongue while you inspect, my friend? We've Amaridian vintage aboard."

"No." The Valcottan ordered his soldiers to move onto the other ship even as Aren ordered his crew and *passengers* to remain above decks. "We aren't here for pleasure."

"Who are you, my friend?" Aren asked. "I am Egil Skallagrims-son, known also as the Iron Fist of Cardiff. This woman is my spellspeaker Grimhilde, known as the Silver Tongue, and my astrologer"—he paused, and Keris sensed eyes on him—"Ulf."

If anxiety hadn't been coursing through his veins, Keris would have rolled his eyes, but the Valcottan leaned closer to him, breath smelling like garlic. "Why is he blindfolded?"

"Because the only light he can see is the stars," Aren answered, and Keris's skin crawled at the verity of that statement. "He is no one."

"He's familiar." The man's face was only inches from his, and it took all of Keris's self-control not to react. "Show your face."

"If he sees light other than the stars, he loses his ability to see the future within them, which will harm my business." Aren's voice turned cold. "I would be entitled to recompense from you, Captain . . . ?"

"Bermin Anaphora." Bermin sneered in disgust. "And I care not for your pagan—"

"Prince Bermin Anaphora?" Aren's elbow bumped Keris's arm as he bowed with a flourish. "Apologies, Highness, we did not know." Then he kicked at Keris's knees. "Kneel before your betters!"

Keris ground his teeth but did so. As did Lara, who fell to her knees, face pressed to the ground, still muttering away in Cardif-fian.

"You are to be the next emperor of Valcotta," Aren said. "It's an honor to have you on my ship, Your Highness."

Even with his eyes on Bermin's boots, Keris could feel the man preening. Had to fight the urge not to stab him in the foot just to wipe that satisfied smile from his face.

"It is right and good that the empress has chosen you, her son," Aren said. "But tell me, what crime did your cousin commit to cause Her Imperial Majesty to execute her?"

Clever.

"Zarrah's fate is not the concern of Cardiff," Bermin answered. "Whereas the contents of your hold are a concern of *mine*."

"Of course, of course," Aren started to say, but then Lara began moaning and swatting at the deck near Bermin's feet, hissing, "I see hands, I see hands!"

"Get away from me, witch!" The prince stepped away, but his back struck the wall, and some of the other soldiers moved close.

"Her spirit is here!" Lara slapped the deck again, then recoiled violently. "Here for vengeance! I see her!"

Though he knew this was an act, chills ran across Keris's skin, and his stomach twisted in knots. *It's not real,* he told himself. *This is all the pretense of a trained spy. An actress.*

"You see nothing," Bermin snapped. "Silence yourself, witch!"

Soldiers moved to drag Lara away, but abruptly, she arched her back. "I see her! Beautiful as the midnight sky, dark of hair and eyes, freckles on her cheeks and fury in her heart. She has been betrayed and will have vengeance!"

The soldiers stirred, one of them muttering, "It's Zarrah. She sees Zarrah."

"She doesn't fucking see Zarrah," Bermin shouted. "Because Zarrah isn't dead."

"Betrayed by the one who loved her like a child," Lara moaned. "She will not rest until she has vengeance."

"Zarrah's ghost is here . . ." One of the soldiers backed away from Lara, the other one wavering. "The empress shouldn't have put her on the island."

"Zarrah was a traitor!" Bermin roared.

The soldier took another backward step. "Then she deserved a traitor's death, not the island. Now the cannibals have consumed her, and Zarrah's spirit has come for us."

Bermin lunged, reaching across Lara to grab the soldier by the front of her uniform, shaking her hard. "Zarrah isn't dead," he roared in her face. "The cannibals won't eat her—they only eat their enemies. This witch is cursed with madness, not truth, and yet you tremble like a child. You are a soldier of Valcotta—behave like one!"

Cannibals.

Horror filled Keris's guts, but Lara's act had rattled the Valcottan prince enough that he was spewing information that he should not. Which begged the question of what else he might say.

Beneath the edge of his mask, Keris watched the wheels turning in his sister's eyes, her lips parting to push Bermin, to see what else she might learn, despite the prince seething with unchecked violence.

"The stars tell a different story," Keris said before Lara could goad Bermin further. "They say the Devils have consumed the rightful heir."

Bermin's whole body went stiff, the flush on his brown cheeks draining, everyone present seeming to hold their breath.

Then, in a burst of motion, Bermin released his soldier and whirled, his boot flying out. Keris could've dodged it, but instead he took the blow in the stomach. The impact slammed him backward against the wall. Bermin was on him a heartbeat later, the tip of his knife puncturing the blindfold over Keris's right eye. "Perhaps it is better you see nothing at all, you pagan piece of shit," Bermin whispered, his breath hot.

Stinging pain seared his eyelid, a trickle of blood running down to pool in the corner of his eye, but Keris kept still. Silent. For though he'd cursed his eyes most of his life, he had no interest in losing one of them.

"Apologies, Your Highness," Aren said. "They are taught to speak of what they see with no regard for whether anyone cares to listen. Ignore their prattling and let us carry on with inspections of our hold and passenger berths."

"I've no interest in your cursed hold, Cardiffian," Bermin snarled. "Get your rudder fixed and remove yourself from these waters, else find you and yours beneath them."

Without another word, Bermin strode toward the ladder, his soldiers following on his heels.

21
ZARRAH

THEY MOVED RIGHT AFTER DUSK, A SMALL FORCE OF TWELVE SPLIT into groups of three. Zarrah was with Saam and Daria. Her only weapons were a spear with a sharpened wooden point and a knife formed of scrap metal that Daria had given her, but Zarrah felt no fear as they crawled on their bellies across the clear-cut at the top of the island, keeping low in the shadows as they slipped between gaps in the rocks that formed the border of the two tribes.

Silence was critical, for if the scouts spotted them and signaled, this would all be for nothing. But Zarrah had spent the last weeks hunting to sustain herself, honing her already practiced skills, and she made not a whisper of sound as she edged over the dead grass.

Daria's hand brushed hers, and Zarrah caught sight of the first scout, nothing more than a shadow in a tree. They gave him a wide berth, not rising to their feet until they were well out of his line of sight, moving quietly down the treed slope in the direction of the beach and Kian's camp.

If past behavior held, there'd be three sets of two guards walking patrol in the second layer, all heavily armed and strong fighters. And they needed to take them down without alerting any of the others that something was amiss. Possible with well-trained archers with well-crafted bows, but all they had was a bow made from the wrong sort of wood and hair from a woman in the tribe who kept it long specifically for this purpose. To go with it, there were only three arrows that had been shot at them by angry guards, which meant the majority of the kills would need to be made at close quarters.

Using her hands suited Zarrah just fine, which was why she'd only shrugged when one of the other groups had claimed the bow.

Her fingers curled and uncurled around the haft of her spear, her breath making clouds in the cold night air. Tiny flakes of snow fell, and at any other point in time, she'd have stopped to catch them on her tongue.

But not tonight.

A belch broke the silence, and Zarrah froze, Daria and Saam doing the same. Her eyes skipped from tree to tree, searching for movement in the shadows, triumph filling her as she spotted two forms moving down a narrow path.

She waited for them to pass, then began her stalk. Already they'd agreed that she and Daria would go for the kills, Saam assisting as required. Daria held the short sword she favored, and she gestured at the one to the left. Zarrah nodded, silently agreeing to take the one to the right.

Daria took three quick steps, then one heavy one.

The men heard and whirled, the one on the left exposing his throat to Daria's already slashing blade. Blood sprayed. The man on the right stumbled back, opening his mouth to shout a warning, but Zarrah lunged, the point of her spear punching through his throat. He gurgled, grabbing hold of the haft and jerking it from her grip.

He wrenched it from his throat, turning it around to slash at her, but Zarrah only backed out of range, watching as he choked to death on his own blood.

"So far, so good," Saam said. "Let's get what we came for."

While Saam kept a lookout, she and Daria stripped the men of swords and knives, as well as the rations of food they found in their pockets. "I'm feeling the fool for not having tried this before," Daria muttered. "But we were so focused on food that—"

A scream split the night. Whether it was one of their warriors or one of Kian's mattered little, for moments later, horns blared.

"Shit," Saam hissed. "Time for us to go."

Weapons were shoved into belts and food into pockets, and then they were on the move, eyes peeled for the scouts who'd be retreating to join their fellows.

Saam caught sight of the scout first and dropped low. Zarrah followed his lead, marking the figure, who moved oddly—as though he were skipping or limping. Easier to allow him to pass, but this was *her* plan, and Zarrah needed to see it through to success. Moving in a crouch, she lifted her spear into position to throw, only for Daria to gasp, "Zarrah, no! It's—"

Her feet went out from under her, only training keeping her from screaming as her body was inverted.

A trap.

She'd stepped into a fucking trap and was now dangling high above Saam and Daria, the blades she'd collected having slipped from her belt to fall in a pile beneath her.

"Flay," Daria said, completing her warning.

Zarrah's heart chilled at the name of one of the most notorious mass killers ever condemned to Devil's Island.

Yet Daria seemed more angry than afraid as she demanded, "Where are you, you sick little piece of shit?"

A giggle sounded from nearby, but Zarrah couldn't see the murderer anywhere.

"Kian's coming with reinforcements," Saam said. "We need to get her down."

"I've a knife in my boot," Zarrah answered. "I'll cut myself down."

"And break your neck when you fall." Daria made an aggrieved noise. "Saam, climb the tree and untie the rope."

The rebel worked his way into the tree while Daria watched for Kian's tribe. There was no mistaking the noise of dozens of warriors racing up the hill, believing themselves repelling an incursion. If they were caught, they were dead.

Saam cursed as he made his way up the pine tree, the dense branches hindering him as he searched for where Flay had fastened the trap.

There was no time for this. She'd have to risk the fall.

Dropping her spear, Zarrah heaved herself up so that she could reach her boot, pulling free the small blade. She caught hold of the rope around her ankles, then immediately let go. "What the fuck is this rope made of?"

The only answer she got was a groan.

Twisting, she looked down and saw Daria sprawled on the ground, a shadow hunched over her. It giggled, patting Daria on the head. "Saam, help her!"

He was already leaping out of the tree. The shadow squealed and ran away in panic. Saam dropped to his knees next to Daria. "She's all right, just knocked out."

"Get her out of here," Zarrah snarled at him. "Go! I'll get myself down and hide if I have to."

"She'll kill me if I leave you!"

"We are all dead if you don't go!"

Saam hesitated, then shoved all her weapons into his belt before lifting the groaning Daria into his arms. "I'll be back with warriors. And Zarrah . . . just stay silent—you're not Flay's type."

What that meant, Zarrah didn't even want to know, so she focused her attention on trying to cut through the peculiar cord binding her ankles. Not one cord, but three, and her piece of scrap metal fitted to a piece of wood held a poor edge. Silently cursing, she sawed at one of the ropes, finally cutting through it.

But she was out of time.

Kian and his warriors were here.

Going still, she prayed that none would look up as the group of men passed beneath her. "Don't pursue past the clear-cut," Kian ordered. "Could be a trap."

Zarrah forced herself to keep breathing, her abdomen quivering with the effort of holding herself upright, one hand clutching the strange ropes. They'd pursue, then retreat. She'd either cut herself down or Saam would return, and she'd get out of this with nothing more than bruised pride.

There was a commotion at the border, shouts and posturing between the two tribes, and she risked sawing at another one of the ropes, only to freeze as footsteps approached. Turning her head, she scanned the shadows, picking out two forms.

"It's her," a strange voice said, a man's, but oddly pitched. "The one you told Flay to watch over. The one Flay must protect in exchange for faces."

"You'll get your faces," Kian answered. "Now piss off, and don't let me catch you listening in."

The smaller shadow scuttled away in that strange skipping stride.

"Recruiting monsters to your cause?" she asked, trying to think of a way out of the situation and coming up empty.

"Flay and his like see things in the woods that we miss, and it's better if they think you're more valuable alive than dead, though you're not Flay's type," he answered. "We've been trying to get you alone to talk."

"Why is that?" she asked. "Who am I to you beyond the niece of the woman who condemned you? Why risk anything to help me?"

"Because you're my ticket out of here."

Zarrah paused in her sawing of the last rope, the answer unexpected. "How so? Who have you been bargaining with?"

"The rebels on the outside. They want you mighty bad, it appears."

"Why would they deal with you when there is a whole camp of their comrades on this island?"

"Isn't the answer obvious?"

She glared at him even though he couldn't see her face, for it was most definitely *not* obvious.

Kian gave a low chuckle. "You don't know, do you?"

"This is getting tiresome, Kian." She sawed harder, wanting to be on her feet for this conversation, not strung up like game. "What don't I know?"

"What they eat."

Gooseflesh crawled its way up her arms, her nerves jangling. "What are you talking about?"

"Your little rebel friends are not the paragons you want to believe," Kian answered. "And it seems their friends on the outside don't want anything to do with those who have turned cannibal."

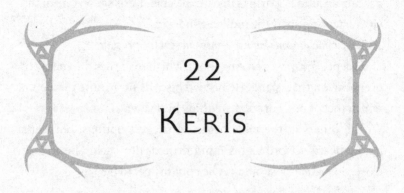

22
KERIS

AFTER BERMIN WAS GONE, KERIS PULLED THE STUPID HAT FROM his head and then removed his blindfold, wiping blood from his eye. When he lowered his hand, it was to find Lara glaring at him. "You should've kept your mouth shut," she snarled at him, the bones and skulls of her headdress bouncing against her cheeks. "He wouldn't have attacked me."

"Because you're a woman?" Keris huffed out an amused breath, then pressed a hand to his stomach as pain lanced outward. "Bermin Anaphora doesn't hesitate to murder *children*, Lara. With my own eyes, I watched him light a house on fire so that the family hiding inside would burn. If you think he wouldn't have put a boot in your stomach, it's because you don't know him like I do."

"I've been kicked before." She crossed her arms, headdress askew. "But this is a waste of breath. Bermin has confirmed our biggest uncertainty but also our greatest fear. Zarrah is alive, but very much in jeopardy. Bermin wouldn't have reacted like that if he were confident she's safe."

They moved into the captain's quarters, one of Aren's crew

passing around hot drinks to ease the cold. Keris sat on one of the chairs, waving away the mulled wine.

The cannibals won't eat her—they only eat their enemies.

Except Zarrah was an Anaphora, which made her the enemy of everyone on that island. He needed his wits now more than ever, which meant not a drop of anything but water.

The others at the table began to suggest options, but Keris barely heard a word as his mind drifted into itself. She was so close. So *fucking* close, and yet he couldn't get to her.

You should have brought an army.

You should have started a war.

You should have set the world on fire.

Shut up, he screamed at the voice. Shoving his chair back, Keris rose and went to the window.

Another chair scraped backward, and then his sister was at his elbow, headdress discarded on the table. "I remember what it felt like to wonder if it is hopeless."

"I know it's not hopeless," he answered. "What I wonder is how high a cost I'll have to pay."

"Is there a limit?"

He hesitated. "If there is, I haven't reached it yet."

Silence stretched between them, and Keris waited for her judgment. Waited for her to say that Zarrah wasn't worth so many lost lives and that it was better to turn back.

A loud thud sounded and Lara twitched. Keris said, "It's just driftwood hitting the hull. The seas around here are full of it, especially close to the island entrance."

Their eyes locked, realization striking at the same time, though it was Lara who spoke. "When we were surveying the pier, did anyone see them making an effort to prevent driftwood from entering the channel into the island?"

Aren frowned, then shook his head. "No."

"If a prisoner is able to pass down the channel, is there any reason a sizable piece of driftwood wouldn't be able to do the same?"

Keris tensed, his heart latching onto this bit of hope even as his head screamed that the solution couldn't be so simple.

"Lunacy," Jor interjected. "Even if you aren't turned to pulp against the channel walls, this isn't Ithicana—the water is freezing. It's snowing, for God's sake."

Lara shrugged. "I didn't ask if it would be easy, only if it would be possible to get past the guards on the pier using driftwood as cover."

"Maybe." Aren rubbed his chin. "I've not ever seen anything like it, but the island draws the current into that channel, along with everything in it. The guards would constantly see driftwood pass—likely enough so that they barely notice it. In the dark, if you kept low, they wouldn't see you."

"You aren't actually considering going in totally blind?" Jor demanded, then threw up his hands in disgust. "All that will happen is whoever goes in will end up as much a captive as Zarrah. This is a prison—the way out is the problem."

"But not the most urgent problem," Keris snapped. "You heard Bermin's soldiers—Zarrah's in the hands of cannibals. Rescuing her from *them* is the foremost concern; getting out of the prison itself is secondary. We wait any longer and all we might rescue is bones! Even if I have to do it alone, I'm going *now!*"

"Then go," Jor shouted at him. "But don't expect a rescue!"

"It's not your call, Jor," Aren said, then jerked his chin at the rest of the crew who were present. "After dark, we'll get as close as we can. The Valcottans won't buy another excuse for us lingering another day in these waters, so we need to move now. Let's go catch ourselves some driftwood."

The other king stood, as did the rest of the Ithicanians, all of them filing out of the room until only Lara and Keris remained.

Lara was quiet, fussing with the buckle on her sword belt. Then she said, "Even if you free her, Zarrah may not be grateful. Aren certainly wasn't. His anger at seeing me came close to hindering our escape more than once."

"I don't expect gratitude. I . . ." Keris scrubbed a hand over his hair. "I . . . I just don't want her to be punished for making the mistake of choosing me."

Silence stretched between them, and he could feel his sister's scrutiny. Then she said, "It wasn't a mistake."

Surprise froze his tongue, and Keris lifted his head to meet her gaze, waiting for the axe to fall. Because Lara disliked him and there wasn't a chance that—

"You are an irritating, egotistical prick." Her breath caught. "But the only flaw in Zarrah's choice in you was that all the world was against it. They never gave you a chance."

Emotion twisted his stomach because what she was saying . . . it wasn't just about his relationship with Zarrah. It was about his relationship with *her*. His sister, who'd been stolen as a child, only to be found, lost again to Ithicana, and then again to the consequences of his actions. Lara's words weren't quite forgiveness, but . . . they were something. A candle in the night. "Lara, I—"

The color in Lara's cheeks abruptly disappeared. "What's that godawful smell?"

Sniffing the air, Keris started to say, "It's"—then Lara lurched and puked on his boots—"dinner."

"Oh, God." She wiped at her mouth with the back of her hand. "I'm so sorry. Normally the seasickness eases after this long on the water, but I can't seem to shake it this time."

More confirmation of what he'd already suspected, so he said,

"Congratulations," hating the selfish part of him that wondered how this would affect Aren's choice to help him with the rescue.

She gaped at him. "What?"

"Congratulations on your pregnancy. I've lost count of my nieces and nephews, but this one will be special."

"No . . . no, I'm not . . ."

"You most definitely are," he said. "I grew up in the harem, sister. You're not the first pregnant woman I've seen vomit over the smell of cooking."

Silence.

"How is this possible?" she finally whispered, turning away from Keris to stare out the window.

The question wasn't directed at him, but he didn't like seeing her this . . . *rattled*. So he said, "I'm not really the ideal messenger for this information, but when a man and a woman—"

"I know how babies are made, Keris!"

He shrugged. "Just checking. There was the possibility that all your training was dedicated to learning how to poke holes into a man and not learning what happens when a man pokes you in—"

"If you say it, I'll stab you in the face."

The unease in his guts faded in the face of her anger, and Keris rocked on his heels, eyeing his sister for a long moment before asking, "You don't want a child?"

"No. Yes." Lara pressed her hands to her face, then dropped them to meet his eyes. "We were taking precautions."

"I've been told the only certain method is abstinence, though I'm not one to judge."

Lara glared at him. "The Ithicanians are going to think I got pregnant to protect myself. To earn their favor."

"Is that such a bad thing?"

"Yes!" Lara paced the room. "To use a child as a shield to protect myself is selfish and disgusting. They already hate me. No need to make it worse."

Keris hesitated, uncertain of whether this was a conversation that he should involve himself in. But he was so weary of good things being soured by circumstances. "And you think *not* having a child is going to change the way they feel?"

Lara went still, her cheeks sucking in as though she were biting them.

"You're the queen," he said. "Which means the vast majority of your subjects don't see you as a person. What you think, how you feel, how you *suffer*? They don't give a shit. All they care about is how the choices you make affect their lives. Putting yourself through hell will change *nothing* for Lara the queen and destroy everything for Lara the woman."

Her eyes went distant as his words sank into her thoughts, likely nothing Aren hadn't already said to her a hundred times before. He watched her see the logic and reject it, frustration building in his stomach because this had nothing to do with what Ithicana thought of her and everything to do with how she felt about herself. "You deserve to be happy, Lara. If this is what you want, please don't allow the joy of it to be destroyed by individuals who don't care about you."

Silence stretched between them, and he didn't break it.

"It's not your problem," she finally said. "Though I'd ask you to keep this development to yourself. Aren needs to be focused on finding a way to get you out once you're in, not on my . . . condition."

Deception had been her downfall, yet it remained burned into his sister's soul. She'd been raised on it, learned to live and breathe it, and though she had to know that it did her no favors, Keris could still see Lara clinging to it like an old friend. "Except it's not just you anymore, is it?"

Lara's gaze sharpened. "Pregnant or not, I'm the one who will figure out a way to extricate you and Zarrah."

He did need her. But that didn't mean he was willing to be used as a tool for her self-destruction. So Keris said, "I'm not going to say a damn thing to anyone, but perhaps remind yourself of the outcome of the last time you kept secrets from Aren."

The blow struck like a knife, and Lara flinched. "You're an ass-hole." She twisted on her heels and stormed from the room.

Sighing, he followed the thud of her bootheels back onto the deck, watching as Lara strode directly to Aren, who was backlit by the setting sun. The other man set down the length of rope he was holding, brow furrowed as he followed her to the empty fore of the ship.

Keris turned his back on them and went to the rail. "How go the fishing efforts?"

"Got what we need, Your Grace," an Ithicanian said, gesturing to the bleached trunks of trees fixed to the ship with ropes.

Keris stared at the driftwood bobbing up and down on the sea, the water dark and frigid and nothing like the turquoise oceans off the coast of Maridrina. As deadly as Ithicana's waters, for the cold was mindless and indiscriminate.

"We'll tow them as close as we can with the longboats," Jor said, scowling. "The less time you spend in that water, the more likely you are not to die. Not that I'd miss you."

Keris was inclined to agree about the temperature. Especially given he wouldn't be climbing out to warm fires and hot drinks, but rather to face frigid night air and the worst criminals Valcotta had to offer.

"No sense delaying," Jor said. "Have something to eat. Take a shit. Do whatever you feel you need to do before you get into the water, because there won't be opportunity later."

"I'm ready," Keris answered, the thought of eating turning his stomach. Lifting his gaze from the driftwood, he stared into the fog in the direction of the island. If all went according to plan, he'd be on the same ground as Zarrah within the hour. Beneath the same set of stars, never mind that they were hidden by mist.

A cough broke the silence, and both he and Jor turned to find Lara and Aren standing behind them. Aren was grinning like a fiend, his arm wrapped around Lara. Her eyes were red and her cheeks damp, but the agitation that had radiated from her moments ago was gone.

"You look awfully tickled, given the circumstances," Jor said. "Why are you grinning like a madman?"

Aren looked down at Lara, who smiled and nodded, and then the king of Ithicana blurted out, "Lara's pregnant. There's going to be another Kertell for you to watch over, you old bastard."

Jor gaped at them, then flung his arms around the pair of them, pounding Aren on the back. "Let's hope the little bugger inherits their mother's brains, because I won't survive another idiot like you!"

Word spread among the Ithicanians, smiles breaking over their faces and soft words of congratulations filling the evening air, and Keris stepped away. This wasn't his moment; it was theirs.

Walking to the front of the ship, he checked that all his weapons were firmly in place. That his boots were tied tight. That his hair was fastened away from his face.

"I'll get you out."

He turned to find Lara behind him, the pieces of blond hair that had escaped her braids blowing in the wind.

"I'm not sure how, yet," she said. "But between Aren and I, we'll get you two out."

They stood in silence while darkness fell and the ship sailed toward Devil's Island. As the glow of its entrance appeared, Keris said, "If things go badly for me, help Sarhina take the throne. She'll be twice the ruler as any of our idiot brothers."

"Does she *want* to be queen?"

"Not in the slightest," he answered. "Which is exactly why she'll do a good job of it."

Aren abandoned the helm and approached. "We're going to stop here and go the rest of the way by longboat. We've got supplies, though there is only so much you can take in. You ready?"

Could one ever be ready for something like this? "Looking forward to it."

Aren handed him a wax-wrapped package. "Once you're in and safe, put some of this into a fire at night and cover your eyes. The glow is bright enough to blind permanently, which is why we'll see it."

"And if I don't survive long enough to do so?"

"We'll do what we can for her, within reason," Lara answered. "I won't promise more than that."

Lara told you that she won't risk her life for Zarrah, but in the moment, she'll change her mind. She can't keep dodging death forever. So please use this journey south to ask yourself just how much you're really willing to lose, Aren's voice said inside his head, and Keris reached out to grip her shoulders. "I'm not willing to lose you again, sister. Don't do anything you shouldn't."

She bit her bottom lip, then nodded. "Good luck."

Keris clambered over the rail and down the ladder, landing with a thud in the now-lowered longboat. He sat on a bench, the wood wet and cold through his trousers, a prelude of what was to come.

Moments later, Aren landed with a soft thud, settling himself next to Keris, eyes on the faint glow cutting through the fog. "Row."

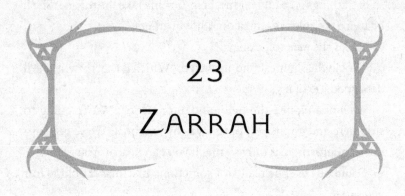

23
ZARRAH

ZARRAH STARED AT KIAN, SKIN STILL CRAWLING. "BULLSHIT. I'VE spent weeks in their camp. Do you think that I don't know what they eat?"

"You tell me," he answered. "You've seen the meat in their pots. Looks like pork, but ask yourself, have you ever seen a pig on this island?"

"They eat birds. Fish. And what they steal from you!"

Kian laughed. "Do you think there'd be a damn bird left on this island if that was what they were putting in their pots?" Resting his hands on his hips, he added, "We hold the beach, and our nets take most of the fish. All of the supplies. You think that what Daria and her ilk steal is enough to fill all those bellies?"

It wasn't, but she'd assumed they had hidden stores.

"They've been feeding you my tribe members, Zarrah. Still feel comfortable in their camp?"

"They don't share." She swallowed hard. "I have to hunt for my own food." A rule intended to keep everyone accountable. A rule intended to ensure that the strong didn't steal the pickings of the weak.

Or was it a rule to keep the prey from discovering they lived within their hunters' camp?

No. No, she knew these people. Would have noticed the smell of human flesh cooking over fire. There was no way they could have hidden such a horrible way of life from her. "You're full of shit, Kian."

He shrugged, then cast out a hand. "Where are the bodies of my men? We found a few of the dead, but we're missing at least two scouts."

"Probably hidden in the bushes." The words came out too quickly, and she knew it. So did Kian, who gave a slow shake of his head. "I could take you by force now, Zarrah. You know that. But I'd rather you see for yourself and choose to come to our camp of your own volition. They'll do their butchering in the graveyard tonight. We'll wait here for you."

"You'll be waiting a long time," Zarrah answered, but the shadow that was Kian only lifted its shoulders.

"Quiet while my men return," he said. "I trust you can get yourself down?"

She fell still as his warriors approached, cursing and swearing and demanding retribution. All Kian said was, "Once we have her, she's our ticket to freedom. The only ticket those fuckers have is to hell."

Then they were gone.

Zarrah waited until their footsteps faded, then cut herself down. She hit the ground hard and off-balance, rolling into a bush, where she took only a heartbeat to let her spinning head clear. Then she was running.

Her pulse throbbed, a stitch forming in her side, but it was what Kian had told her that consumed her brain. It couldn't be true. It had to be some trick. Had to be a lie.

She hit the cut line right as a large rebel force crossed the wall, though they slowed at the sight of her. Daria was with them, and she pushed her way through the others to Zarrah's side. "Are you all right?" she demanded. "I blackened Saam's eye when I realized he'd left you."

"Fine," Zarrah answered, the feel of Daria's hand on her arm making her skin crawl. "They passed right beneath me and didn't even notice. Cut myself down after they left."

Daria nodded, then swayed. Instinctively, Zarrah steadied her. "How's the head?"

"Goose egg the size of a new mother's tit," Daria muttered. "But I'll live. And Flay will regret not killing me when I track that little monster down. Let's head back to camp and assess whether this debacle was worth it."

Zarrah remained silent as they returned to camp, forcing a smile to her face as they examined the fifteen weapons they'd stolen, all of far better make than most in the camp possessed.

"I think this is worthy of celebration," Daria announced. "But some unfortunate souls will have to join me on patrol so that the rest might relax."

Zarrah tensed, knowing full well that the woman had already assigned warriors to guard duty. Taking advantage of the distraction of those celebrating, she went into the woods as though to piss, then picked up Daria's trail. They didn't head to join those guarding the border, but rather to the gully holding the graveyard.

It wasn't true.

It couldn't be true.

Except with every step she took, Zarrah saw clues that she'd previously turned a blind eye toward. Saw how she'd readily accepted Daria's explanations. There was no doubt that Kian was attempting to manipulate her into joining his camp, but that didn't mean that there wasn't a kernel of truth.

Daria's camp *had* to have another source of food beyond what they could steal and forage.

And Zarrah intended to find out what it was.

The carpet of nettles kept her footsteps silent as she traversed the narrow trail, moving slowly in deference to the faint light, but it wasn't long until she could pick out the glow of torchlight.

Daria was no fool, which meant that whatever they were doing, there would be guards. Stepping off the trail, Zarrah moved from shadow to shadow.

There.

Leaning against a tree was a lean form. Saam, she suspected, given the individual was picking at his nails with a knife, the blade catching the faint light. Dropping low, she eased past him and pressed closer to the torchlight.

The scrape of a shovel against rocky soil reached her.

They were digging a grave. Daria hadn't mentioned anyone dying in the raid, but that didn't mean it hadn't happened. Though if that were the case, why be so covert about burying the body? Zarrah crested the lip of the hollow and rested her elbows on the ground as she looked over the graveyard.

Daria and another man were digging, a large pile of rocky earth already piled to one side of the grave. Yet instead of adding to her relief, the sight pulled a frown to Zarrah's forehead, because they weren't digging a new grave.

They were digging up an old one.

There was a loud *thunk* of metal hitting wood, and Daria gave a slight nod. "There it is."

Zarrah watched in silence as they slowed their digging, working their rudimentary shovels around whatever they'd uncovered before Daria dropped to her knees. Reaching into the hole, she grasped hold of something and heaved. Zarrah tensed, but all the other woman removed was what looked like the lid of a supply barrel.

Did they use them as coffins? That made no sense, given there were no animals on this island to dig up a grave.

"Can fit one more. Maybe two, if we're lucky. Get the salt."

Two men came from the opposite side of the hollow, carrying something between them. A corpse. Yet as the torchlight illuminated the form, bile surged up Zarrah's throat.

Not a corpse. A carcass that had been field-dressed like game.

Frozen in horror, Zarrah watched as they stuffed the carcass into the barrel and then dumped in sacks of salt.

Sweat dripped down her brow to splatter against the back of her hand as she watched the other body be carried into the clearing.

"Cut off what we need," Daria ordered. "But chop it up small and cook it here before bringing it back. She can't know, or we'll lose her."

Blood drained from Zarrah's face as realization sank into her soul. They hadn't rescued her from Kian; they'd trapped her. Cared for her like . . . like *livestock*. Kian had been right.

She needed to run. Needed to get away while she could.

There is no escape.

Panic flooded her veins, and Zarrah shifted backward, needing to run. Needing to hide.

Crack! A branch broke beneath her foot.

She froze.

It was too late.

Faces snapped in her direction, Daria's eyes cutting the darkness to lock with Zarrah's, then widening in alarm. "Zarrah—"

She was already hurling herself up the slope.

Branches slapped her face, roots catching at her toes and nearly sending her toppling, but Zarrah didn't slow. Couldn't slow, because now that their secret was out, what were the chances they'd leave her alive?

Given she'd just watched them stuff a butchered man into a barrel to salt cure, her guess was no chance at all.

"Zarrah! Zarrah, wait!" Footsteps pounded behind her, Daria and her warriors pursuing hard. "Let me explain!"

What possible explanation could there be? What words existed that justified what these monsters consumed?

Zarrah put on a burst of speed. The air burned her lungs, a cramp biting her side, but she ignored the pain. Kian was waiting at the border; all she needed to do was make it across. It would be into the arms of a new devil, one whose horrors were yet unknown, but it couldn't be worse than this.

Nothing was worse than this.

Her toe caught.

Zarrah sprawled, her small knife spinning out of her hand and into the darkness. Panicked, she pawed the forest floor, searching for it.

But the footsteps were coming closer.

Were nearly upon her.

A snarl of frustration and fear tore from her lips, but even with the blade, she wouldn't be able to fight them all. Her only chance was to escape.

Hands clawing the dirt, she dragged herself upward. Racing toward the summit of the island.

"Zarrah!" Daria's voice was shrill. "Don't do it! Don't cross over! We won't be able to get you back!"

She didn't waste breath on a response.

Ahead, she spotted the faint light of torches. Kian, now in the company of his warriors, was waiting. And she was almost at the border.

"Zarrah!"

She could feel hands reaching for her. Their breath on the back of her neck.

Screaming, Zarrah flung herself toward the stone barrier. Pain lanced across her kneecaps as they struck, but then she was rolling. Clawing at the dirt to get herself as far from these monsters as she could.

Legs and feet filled her vision, Kian and his men surrounding her.

"Back off, Daria," Kian roared. "If you violate our border, it will be war."

Gasping for breath, Zarrah pushed herself upright and found the two tribes at a standoff to either side of the border, weapons glittering in the torchlight. Daria alone held no weapon, her eyes locking on Zarrah's. "You weren't meant to see that. You were never meant to know."

"No shit." Zarrah spat out the dirt she'd gotten in her mouth. "Those who know they're prey tend to fight back."

"No." Daria gave a rapid shake of her head. "That's never the fate of one of our own, no matter how bad it gets. No matter how hollow our bellies, we'd never do that to one of our own."

"She ain't your own, rebel," Kian retorted. "She's a royal—one of the very people you were trying to overthrow with your little coup down south. It's no wonder you were fattening her up for the grill. Enemies taste twice as sweet, don't they?"

Daria took a step closer to the wall, everyone tensing. She froze, then said, "She was never in any danger from us. You've filled her head with lies when you know that *you* are the reason that we do what we do."

Do what they do. Visions of the slaughtered man being stuffed into a barrel flashed through Zarrah's eyes, and her fury burned hot. "Stay away from me!" She scrambled to her feet. "You eat people. You're a fucking cannibal—a monster!"

Daria flinched. "Not by choice. It was that or starve."

"Better to starve!"

"Says the woman who has never gone without!" Daria's hands fisted. "You know we don't belong here. You know that the empress put us in this place to silence those who contest her tyranny. You know that she relishes the knowledge that we suffer, that we must reduce ourselves to beasts in order to survive."

"They send supplies!" Zarrah took a step forward, only for Kian to catch her arm, giving his head a warning shake.

"Not enough." Daria exhaled a long breath. "Just enough to ensure that we have the strength to turn on each other rather than to turn on the empress. Kian and his tribe purge the children. The elderly. The weak. It is because we refused to do that to our family that we were forced to walk another road, Zarrah. To protect those we cared about, we painted our souls black, but never doubt that it is the empress who handed us the brush."

"There isn't an innocent soul on this island," Kian answered before Zarrah could. "Everyone is a murderer, but there are some of us who have limits to what we will do."

Daria choked out a laugh. "Explain to me how killing your own children is better than surviving on the flesh of the fallen, Kian. Better yet, explain it to Zarrah."

A shiver ran through her, but Zarrah clenched her teeth. She'd seen how Daria could spin words until those who heard them forgot their own thoughts, and she refused to be so manipulated now. "If you really believed your actions were just, you'd have told me the truth. Instead I've lived among you for weeks, trusted your word, only to discover that you've lied to me this entire time. If I must bed down with villains, let it be with those who do not deny their crimes!"

Not giving Daria a chance to respond, she twisted on her heel and strode down the slope.

"Zarrah!" The woman's voice chased her. "We were trying to save you! If you go with them, you are lost! Please!"

"Better lost than whatever you are," Zarrah answered, refusing to look back.

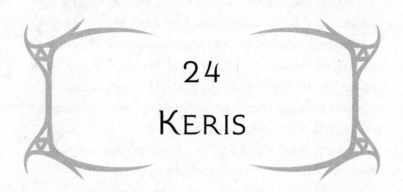

24

KERIS

THOSE AT THE OARS DIDN'T HAVE TO ROW LONG UNTIL THE CUR-
rent caught hold of the longboat and driftwood, tugging them
toward the orange glow of torches illuminating the entrance to
the island. Keris's heart thudded with increasing violence as they
approached, his mouth dry and his hands like ice.

What if this didn't work?

What if he was seen?

Flickers of motion in front of the torches spoke to the number
of Valcottan soldiers guarding the half-moon-shaped pier. Soldiers who'd be armed to the teeth and skilled enough to put a
dozen arrows in his back as he floated past.

"Close enough," Aren muttered, and the oars dipped into the
water, rowing backward to keep the longboat in place. The logs
they towed floated around them.

"Last chance to retreat," Aren said. "Once you're in the water,
there is no turning back."

"My only path leads to her." Flipping his legs over the edge,
Keris slipped into the water.

It felt like knives were stabbing him all over, stealing his breath and sending a slice of panic through his veins. Instinct demanded he climb back into the boat, but Keris forced himself to swim, taking hold of the trunk with the most branches. Water swirled around him, the driftwood jostling, and his breath caught.

"Don't forget to keep your legs moving," Aren whispered. "If you stay still, you're going to freeze."

The crew didn't wait for his response, only released the driftwood. The tree moved toward the glowing pier.

The only sound was the slap of water against wood. The surf should have been loud, but rather than an ebb and surge, it felt as though he were caught in a river flowing silently into hell. All around was blackness, the moon hidden by a cloud.

Trust the current, he told himself. *You know exactly where it flows.*

Yet it felt like he was alone in a vast sea of nothingness, swimming in every direction but none, never reaching his goal.

Splash.

Keris jerked, looking back to the longboat, but it was lost to blackness. What had splashed? What was in the water with him?

Something brushed his leg, and he froze. A shark? Something worse?

The water swirled around him, and Keris heard something take a breath. He swung wildly, his fist finding air, then water, then flesh. A grunt of annoyance, then Aren's voice hissed, "Calm the fuck down. You're panting like a dying dog. They're going to hear you."

"What are you doing here?"

"There is no chance you won't get yourself killed if you go in alone," Aren said. "And I owe Zarrah. Now shut up before someone hears you."

Keris clenched his teeth, willing his breathing to steady, hunting for calmness in the storm of emotion he felt.

"Don't move," Aren whispered. "Keep low."

Voices filtered over the water. It was impossible to make out what they were saying, but the tone was of soldiers bored out of their minds and putting in the least possible effort.

Or perhaps that was just Keris's wishful thinking.

The tree floated into a pool of golden light.

Keeping utterly still, Keris rolled his eyes to the right. Six guards, four men and two women, stood on the pier, all dressed in heavy cloaks of Valcottan violet, weapons glittering at their waists and bows slung over their shoulders. One of them glanced at the tree, and Keris allowed himself to sink beneath the water, the cold making his teeth clench.

His heart throbbed as the tree floated beneath the pier, but he remained submerged until the brilliant glow of torchlight faded before lifting his head and sucking in a mouthful of air. They hadn't been spotted, but they were far from out of danger.

The current picked up speed, drawing the driftwood between the gaps in the cliffs. And into the unknown.

Casting his eyes skyward, Keris marked the glowing basins of oil hanging from brackets and the archers walking the cliff tops, eyes on the water below.

"Hang on," Aren muttered. "This is going to get rough."

The channel of water cut through the rock like a river through a mountain ravine, winding inland. Flecks of spray rose in the air as the channel narrowed, and with every second, they picked up speed.

Crack!

The trunk of the tree struck the bend in the rock, and the whole thing spun. His nails scratched the wood as he struggled to keep a grip, vision filled with light and water. The tree struck the cliff wall again, branches snapping off as the trunk twisted around.

Keris swore and was rewarded with a mouthful of water.

Coughing, he tried kicking to drive the tree away from the cliff wall, but the force of the water was too great.

They were going to hit again, and hard.

He lifted his feet in time to take some of the impact, but his knees buckled. The branches smashed upward, bits of wood striking him in the face as they rebounded off the wall, spinning in a circle.

Crack!

He hissed in pain as the tree struck rock again, his shoulder taking the impact as Aren slammed up against him.

How far had they traveled?

How much farther did they need to go?

Keris hazarded a glance up. Pools of light whipped past, but if archers watched, it was impossible to see through the spray.

Crack!

Horror filled him as the tree split, the half Aren clung to spinning away.

Then a monstrous wave slammed into them from the right, sending the driftwood spinning round and round before the violence of the water eased. Gasping in a breath, Keris fixed his eyes on a rocky beach illuminated by more basins of oil. He couldn't see the cliff tops from this angle. Couldn't tell if the guards were watching.

But they were running out of time.

The current was taking them around the island, and once they reached the end of the beach, there'd be no getting out. They'd be sucked into a drowning machine. They needed to get on that beach.

Then mist began to rise from the water.

In the dim light, Keris saw Aren dumping out the contents of a waxed package, the powder seeming to turn to mist as it mixed with the water. Not enough to cause alarm, but hopefully enough to provide them cover.

Aren abandoned his shattered piece of driftwood and swam hard for shore. Keris clenched his teeth and followed.

There was no point in looking up. No point in looking back. This would work or it wouldn't.

Keris swam like he never had before, panic fueling his strength. Then his hands struck rock, pain slicing up his wrists, which he ignored as he clambered to his feet.

Faster.

Doing his best to remain silent, he waded inland but then hit the beach at a run, chasing Aren up the slope and not stopping until they were into the trees.

Keris dropped to his knees, dragging in ragged breaths. Aren was crouched next to him, equally winded, and Keris asked him, "You all right?"

"I'm fucking freezing. We need to find a way to warm up."

"If you wanted someone to cuddle, you should've brought your wife. You aren't my type."

Aren huffed out a breath. "It's amazing you've lived this long, given the shit that spews from your mouth."

There was no arguing that point, so Keris focused on calming his pounding heart. Wasted effort, for it only hammered faster. Zarrah was here, on this island, which meant he was closer to her than he'd been since that fateful moment on Southwatch. Yet as he took in the shadowed forest, the only sounds the roar of the water and the rustle of the wind through the branches, he felt further from her than he'd ever been. "It feels bigger than I'd thought it would be."

Aren grunted in agreement. "You have that package I gave you? We need to signal the ship while it's still dark."

Keris dug into his coat, then made a face. "It's gone. Lost it in the water."

"Might be just as well. I'm not sure we want to draw attention to the island." Aren rose from his crouch. "My bet is that the prisoners have formed at least one camp. We'll pose as new convicts until we can find Zarrah, then wait for Lara to figure out a way to get us free. Keep your weapons hidden."

Neither of them moved.

For his part, it was because Keris had no clue which way to go.

"Lost already, are you?"

He could *feel* the smirk on Aren's face even if he couldn't see it. "You're the king of the jungle—you lead the way."

Aren laughed softly, then turned on his heel and walked without hesitation through the forest. Keris followed him, trying to curb the anticipation rising in his chest.

How would Zarrah react? There was a chance she'd follow through on her promise and kill him. But she wouldn't want to risk Aren, which he hoped would temper her reaction long enough for him to explain himself.

Just what, precisely, needs explaining? the voice in his head whispered. *What can you say to her that hasn't already been said?*

I'll tell her that I'm sorry, he answered. *That I regret betraying her confidence. That I shouldn't have burdened her with so many lives lost to spare hers.*

The voice cackled in his head, wild and maniacal, like the Magpie's laugh just before he jumped. *A hollow apology, given that you are risking lives for her again.*

It's—

Keris broke off his internal argument with himself as his skin prickled. He glanced over his shoulder, searching the darkness for what had triggered his instincts. "Did you hear something?"

Aren paused. "All I hear is you. Do you think you can take one step without snapping a twig?"

"Price one pays for growing up civilized," Keris muttered even as he hunted for motion. Hunted for eyes watching from the shadows. But there was nothing. "I . . . it's nothing. Keep going."

"I can smell the smoke from their fires," Aren said, starting back down the trail. "*Try* to be quiet so that we can—"

Aren's words cut off as he was jerked skyward, a loud crack filling the air.

Keris stumbled backward, gaping at Aren, who was tangled in some form of net. A trap.

"Cut me down, you idiot!"

Keris moved, grasping the netting and immediately recoiling. "This isn't rope. It's—"

"It's gut," Aren hissed. "Cut it. There's a chance they heard their trap deploy."

Reaching for the knife hidden in his boot, Keris abruptly froze as something sharp jabbed him in the back.

"Pretty faces," a voice lisped. "We'd like to add them to our collection."

25
ZARRAH

"LET'S GET YOU FED, GIRL." KIAN AND HIS SOLDIERS LED HER INTO their camp, which was larger and better appointed than that of the rebels.

No, not rebels. *Cannibals.*

Kian dug into a barrel, discarding sacks of rice in favor of a package of salted meat. The idea of eating made her want to gag, but Zarrah took the jerky she was handed and, after determining it was beef, forced herself to eat, abruptly reminded of how unenthused Daria had always seemed when eating. Why hadn't she seen the signs? Why hadn't she asked questions?

Because you didn't want to know.

"We'll get you set up with your own tent," Kian said. "Ain't no one will hurt you here, no matter what Daria told you. That was one of the conditions—you were to be kept unharmed and well cared for, or the deal was off. You got no reason to trust me, but you can trust *that.*"

A clever plan, using the prisoners' desire for freedom to protect her, and one she wished to know more about. But given the con-

tentious beginnings of her interactions with Kian, going straight
to the topic might not be the right tactic.

Zarrah paused in her chewing, though her stomach growled
for more of the beef jerky in her hand. "How long have you been
on this island?"

"Ten years." Someone threw a log on the fire, illuminating
Kian's face. "Another life. But you'll not be here that long."

He was being kind, but what Daria had told her about him
lurked in the back of Zarrah's mind. This man was very much a
villain, so all she could trust was that he wouldn't jeopardize his
own chance at freedom.

"You're wondering what I did to get here?" Kian grinned, revealing his mouthful of gold teeth. "It's every bit as bad as you
might think, no sense denying that, but . . ." He sighed. "Everyone
on this island has done awful things, Zarrah. The worst of things.
If you put too much thought to the sort of humanity you're now
surrounded with, you'll drive yourself to madness. Better to think
upon how those here act now, as though each individual is an entirely separate person from the one the empress condemned."

There was reason to the advice, but Zarrah couldn't help but
say, "Fair enough, but if what Daria said was true, you and yours
do plenty that's worth judgment."

Kian grunted, then gave a slow nod. "This is a prison, love. To
live as we did before, raising families and caring for our weak, is
impossible. Daria and her lot refused to accept that, choosing instead to resort to the worst means to survive rather than deny
themselves what they felt was their due. Sacrificing their humanity in order to have everything they wanted. Whereas we deny
ourselves and suffer the pain of loss so that we might know ourselves human and not monster."

The old argument of sacrificing the few to save the many that

Zarrah had never much cared for, but having seen the alternative, it was hard to deny. Just as there was no denying that her aunt used this island not just as a prison but as a torture chamber.

Crash!

Zarrah tensed at the noise, which had come from the forest. Shouts emanated from the same direction; then all fell silent. She took a step toward the trees, habit and instinct driving her to investigate, but Kian caught her arm. "Could be a trap. Daria wants you back; she made that much clear. Those on guard will investigate."

Zarrah drummed her fingers against her thigh, the compulsion to go out into the woods, to see who was there, almost more than she could resist, though she wasn't sure why.

"We'll get word to the rebels that we've secured you from Daria and her lot, and they'll likely make their move soon enough." He hesitated, then added, "They know everything that happens on this island through the guards on their payroll. They've washed their hands of Daria because of the choices she and hers have made."

Given the revulsion she herself felt, Zarrah could understand that, but it still jarred with Daria's complete certainty that the rebels were coming for them. Made Zarrah wonder again if it was a myth the woman had created, perhaps motivated by her own delusions, and used to motivate her tribe to remain loyal and strong.

Except . . . There'd been people in Daria's camp who'd been incarcerated less than a year ago. Those prisoners had brought renewed hope, which made little sense if the rebels on the continent had turned their backs on Daria's tribe.

One of Kian's men approached, interrupting her thoughts. "Sounds like Flay caught himself a new look. No one is missing, so it was likely one of Daria's spies."

Who was it? Saam? Bile rose in Zarrah's throat, because she knew everyone in Daria's camp and would not wish such a fate upon any of them. "We should—"

"Whoever he is, he's already dead." Kian gave her a grim smile. "Flay doesn't like his new looks talking back to him, so he cuts their throats right away."

"Why don't you kill him?" she demanded. "Why do you allow such a monster to live?"

"Kill all the snakes, and you soon find your camp infested with rats," Kian answered. "As it is, whoever he caught will satisfy him for a time."

Places like this shouldn't exist.

Kian put a hand on her arm. "Stay strong, Zarrah. Soon we will be free from this place and all its horrors."

There'd be a catch. There was always a catch. But she trusted Kian's self-motivation to get off that island, and that . . . that she could work with.

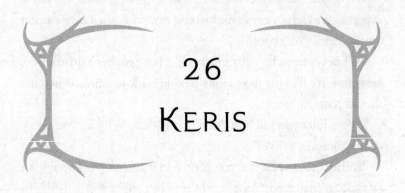

26
KERIS

PULSE ROARING, KERIS SLOWLY TURNED HIS HEAD, BUT ALL HE could see was a small form holding a spear. Alone, as far as Keris could tell, though the man *had* said *we*. "Easy, friend. We only just arrived, so it's too soon to have made enemies."

"We saw," the man whispered, head cocking, though Keris couldn't see his face in the dark. But he could smell him. The man radiated the stink of rot. "We watched."

"Right. So you know." Keris tried to turn to face the man, but the tip of the spear sank deeper, and he went still. Better to keep him talking while Aren extricated himself from the net. "Where are your friends, then? Might we meet them?"

"They are here." The man patted something at his hip. "They are watching."

The man was clearly mad, but that alone wasn't enough to explain the sudden surge of primal dread that poured through Keris's veins.

"It walks." The man poked Keris, sending blood dripping down his back. "It comes with us, soon to become one of us."

Going anywhere with this creature seemed like a quick path to death, but Keris didn't have much choice as the spear dug deeper. Praying to whatever higher power might be listening that Aren would get loose, Keris slowly walked back down the dark trail. "Are you asking me to join your group? Is that how it works on this island?"

The man giggled, and Keris clenched his teeth as the acidic taste of bile burned up his throat.

Thump!

The spear tip disappeared from his back. Keris turned in time to see Aren regain his feet, then charge toward the man, blades in hand. "It has claws!" the creature shrieked, eyes fixed on Aren's knives. Then, with shocking speed, he scuttled into the shadows.

"Where'd the little prick go?" Aren snarled, skidding to a stop next to Keris. "I'm going to fucking kill him." He took a step after the creature, then froze. "There are traps all around us."

A giggle filled the air, and a dozen yards away, a face appeared in a beam of moonlight, head capped with a crown of dark curls. There was something strange about his expression, the woodenness of it at odds with the gleam of his eyes and the delight in his laugh. Then he was lost again to the shadows.

Branches rustled and footsteps pattered, both Keris and Aren rotating with the noise. Another figure stepped into the moonlight. Long hair fell to his shoulders, but his face was equally strange. He pointed at Keris, then faded backward into darkness.

More footfalls, then another appeared. This one was bald and laughing, giving Keris no time to get a good look at him before he ducked behind a tree.

"I can't tell how many there are," Aren said, his knife blade catching the moonlight as he rotated, more and more men appearing, only to swirl away into the shadows. "We need to make a run for it."

Keris eyed the ground around them uneasily, because if they

were caught up in another one of the nets, it was over. The men knew they were armed, and they wouldn't give them a chance to cut themselves loose twice. "Back the way we came. We know it's clear."

"Go!"

Keris broke into a sprint but only made it a few paces before the first man appeared, blocking his path. "We want it," the man crooned, the moonlight falling upon him, revealing a mouth that didn't move with his words. "We shall have it."

"Good God," Keris whispered, despite knowing that God had no power in this place. "He's wearing someone else's face."

Which meant they all were.

"Shit, shit, shit!" Aren hissed, his back against Keris's as he hunted for the other attackers. As he readied himself to fight.

Keris lifted his own knife as the man, the *creature*, stepped forward, snickering and giggling, the sound bouncing off the trees.

Then it froze, head cocked. Listening. It shrieked and Keris jumped, readying for an attack, but it scuttled away into the darkness.

Keris didn't move. Didn't speak. Didn't breathe, as he waited.

A woman stepped into the moonlight.

His heart skipped, and he took a step toward her. "Valcotta—"

He broke off as she lifted her face. Young. Valcottan. But not Zarrah.

"I see you've met Flay," she said. "Not the ideal introduction to the island, but far from the worst."

There was worse than that here?

"He didn't give his name." Keris's fingers tightened on his knife. "And he wasn't alone."

She laughed. "Flay is always alone, but never alone, if you get my meaning."

"I don't."

With complete disregard for his weapon, she came closer. "Flay collects identities, so to speak. What you saw were the many faces of Flay, but he's only one man. If you can call him a man at all."

"Fuck me," Aren muttered. "Someone needs to kill that thing."

"Many have tried," she answered. "But apparently, it's hard to kill a demon. Name's Daria, by the way. Welcome to Devil's Island." She hesitated. "Where did you get the weapons?"

Shit.

"There were men on the beach when we arrived," Aren answered. "They attacked us, but we killed them and took their weapons."

"I see." Daria huffed out an amused breath. "An exciting arrival indeed." She motioned at Keris to follow. "We'll take you back to camp and explain things, all right?"

Keris cast a backward glance over his shoulder. "Isn't camp that way?"

"A camp is that way," Daria answered. "But you boys walk into that camp uninvited, they'll kill you, especially if you've already done in a pair of Kian's men. I'll only kill you if you piss me off, understood?"

"Understood," Aren said, even as Keris fought the urge to ask about Zarrah.

"Good, then let's go. There are worse things than Flay to encounter here if we linger in the dark."

As they followed Daria, more men and women stepped out of the darkness to flank them. All skin and bones. All wearing little more than rags. All armed to the teeth.

But none of them wore human skin, which was a significant point in favor of going with them.

"So," Daria said. "What did you do to end up in this shithole?"

"Bar fight in Pyrinat," Aren lied without hesitation. "Got a bit out of hand, which would have been forgivable if not for the fact one of the men left on the floor was some relative of the empress."

Daria snorted. "Fair enough. And you?" She looked at Keris, then chuckled. "What crime did you commit? Breaking wind in a library?"

Aren guffawed and Keris glared at him, but the other man only smirked and said, "He pushes those who piss him off out of towers."

"Must be a politician, then. Though we don't see many Maridrinian politicos in Valcotta, and most are executed and fed to the dogs, not sent here."

"Lucky me," Keris muttered.

"If you are alive, there is hope," Daria answered. "Can't say the same if you're being pushed out a dog's arsehole."

"Poetic."

Daria shot him a smile, teeth white in the torchlight. "I figured you for a man who appreciates a bit of poetry. Now, walk faster—we need to get back to our territory before they realize we've been here and retaliate."

Keris didn't argue, but as he met Aren's eye, he knew they were thinking the same thing. This island had a war of its own being waged, and they'd walked into the middle of it.

THE GLOW OF DAWN WAS warming the sky as Daria led them into a camp. The few structures were made of wood and scraps of canvas, but the lack of access to proper tools was apparent. The prisoners living within the camp came out at the sound of voices, and Aren's elbow bumped Keris's as he muttered, "There're children."

Though it shouldn't be unexpected, given that there were men and women in the camp, it still hit Keris like a punch to the stomach that children were being born into a prison. That they'd never know freedom, despite having never committed a crime themselves. That Petra allowed this to continue was an atrocity, and he wondered what the rest of Valcotta would think if they ever learned the truth about this place.

But he couldn't focus on that now. If Zarrah sat on the throne, she could put an end to this horror. His eyes skipped from face to face, hunting for the one who haunted his dreams, sleeping and awake.

There was no sign of her.

That doesn't mean she's not here, logic reminded him. *She could be asleep in one of the tents. Could be out hunting. Could be taking a damn piss in the woods.* But Keris was tired of being logical, tired of doing the intelligent thing, tired of making the strategic choice. "We understand there is a group of cannibals on this island. Where might we find them?"

Aren's mouth dropped open with shock, but Daria's eyebrows only rose. "Why?"

"Because they have a person with them whom we are looking for. A woman, mid-twenties, very pretty. Would have been incarcerated relatively recently."

"This was not the plan," Aren said under his breath as he eyed the gathering prisoners, many of whom were armed. "You're going to get us killed."

Daria huffed out an amused breath. "That would be Zarrah."

Keris's chest clenched, the confirmation that she was here, that this woman knew her, making it hard to breathe. "Where is she?"

"Well," Daria answered, rocking on her heels and giving him a dark smile. "She was with us until quite recently, but no longer, I'm afraid."

"We were told by a reputable source that she was being held by a group of cannibals."

"Yes." Daria's smile was all teeth. "She *was.*"

Understanding ricocheted through Keris's core, horror stealing the breath from his chest and making him sway on his feet. He
was too late. Too fucking late, and Zarrah . . . Zarrah . . . They'd—

Daria burst out laughing, slapping a hand against her thigh.
"The look on your face is truly priceless."

Horror turned to rage, and his hands balled into fists. He was
going to kill them. He was going to kill them all.

"Easy!" Daria held up her hands. "We didn't eat Zarrah; she was
stolen from us. Likely as bait for you . . . *Your Grace.*"

27
ZARRAH

ZARRAH SLEPT FITFULLY, WEAPONS GRIPPED IN HER HANDS AND her ears so attuned to sound that she jerked upright at every cough, grunt, or fart that emanated from Kian's camp. When dawn illuminated the scrap of sail that formed her tent, Zarrah was no more rested than she'd been when she laid down her head.

"Hungry?" Kian asked, holding out a bowl of porridge. She greedily dug into the warm oats, having been limited to meat, insects, and mushrooms for far too long. As she ate, Zarrah examined the camp, which was still quiet, the majority of the prisoners asleep. Supply barrels appeared to be the primary building source, forming the walls of several buildings, though there was an incredible amount of ship sail, netting, and flotsam.

"The current drags in all manner of things from the seas," Kian said, retrieving a lantern from a table. "We are rich on the discards of humanity. Come, let me show you."

Zarrah followed him into one of the buildings, surprise filling her chest as she took in the walls, which were entirely covered by artwork, statues and sculptures and glassworks filling the niches formed by the curved edges of the barrels. Much was stained or damaged by submersion in the seawater, but it was still a wondrous display of beauty that had been absent from her life.

"Perhaps a waste of space, but I think it's important to remember who we are," Kian said. "Survival alone isn't enough, for what is the point of surviving if there is nothing in life to enjoy?" He chuckled. "And the gold we've pulled out of the water aided in giving me back my smile."

Zarrah laughed to reward his attempt to amuse her. If he truly was in contact with the rebels, then he was her path off this island, and remaining in his good graces was only to her benefit. But she wasn't going to blindly believe anything Kian said without proof. "Tell me what you know of those who have made these promises. How did they come to be in contact with you? Which guards are on their payroll? And how do they aim to remove us from the prison, given the number of guards on the island and the navy ships patrolling around it?"

Setting the lantern on the small table at the center of the room, Kian motioned for her to take a seat in one of the two chairs, both formed out of barrels cut in half. They were designed so that whoever was seated would lounge backward to enjoy the display, and she wondered how often he sat in here like a king surveying his domain. The reclined position made watching his face difficult, so Zarrah instead perched on the edge of her seat, back straight.

"Message arrived by one of the supply barrels not an hour before your own arrival, hidden in a wax-wrapped package in a sack of rice."

"They ever contact you before?"

Kian shook his head. "It seems you are a prize worth them breaking their cover."

Suspicion rose in her chest. "May I see it?"

Reaching a hand inside his coat, Kian extracted a folded piece of paper. "Seemed too good to be true when it first arrived, but we weren't going to take any chances. That's why we were on the beach when you arrived. We were waiting for a prisoner drop."

It did seem too good to be true.

Unfolding the paper, Zarrah took in the message.

> Greetings,
>
> This message comes from the distant south, where rebellion rises against the empress's rule. It has come to our attention that she has accused her niece, Zarrah Anaphora, of treason and cast her aside like trash, condemning her to Devil's Island. Zarrah is an individual of grave importance to the rebellion, and we will give much to secure her freedom. Those who assist her and protect her from the monstrous villainy of the prison will be rewarded with their own freedom when we come, for we are above the law. Secure her at all costs, or you will be shown no mercy.
>
> The Commander

Zarrah reread the letter, her eyes snagging on *empress's rule*. Not once had she heard anyone in Daria's camp refer to her aunt as *the empress*, only by her name or some slur. Who had written this, she could not say, but not for a heartbeat did she believe it was the rebel commander.

Refolding the page, she handed it back to Kian.

"What do you think?" he asked. "Do you believe it legitimate? And more importantly, do you think the sender will follow through on his promise?"

To say otherwise would compromise her safety, so Zarrah nodded. "I believe it is."

"Do you know why they want you?"

Kian's eyes gleamed with curiosity, and Zarrah was reminded that he hadn't become the leader of his tribe, or survived on this island for so long, by being stupid. But while she'd made her fair share of mistakes, she wasn't stupid either. "Likely for the information I know."

He leaned back in his chair, gaze going to the artwork. But not before she saw the furrow in his brow. Kian had expected an answer from her, but not the one she'd given. Curiosity demanded she press for his opinions, but caution made her ask instead, "Have you received any more communication?"

He nodded. "The guard the rebels have on payroll told us that if we failed and you ended up in Daria's belly, the deal was off. Nothing since, though there might be orders now that we have you." He gestured to the door. "Care to show yourself?"

They left the camp, several of Kian's warriors following at their heels as they went down to the sunlit beach.

It was smaller than Zarrah had remembered, less than fifty paces of rocks mixed with sand, framed by steep inclines. The water flowed swiftly past in its last loop before descending below the island in the mysterious vortex. On the opposite side of it rose the sheer cliffs rimmed with guard-posts, each manned by three soldiers.

"Got yourself a new one, Kian?" one of them called down.

"She got tired of Daria's menu," Kian called back, and the guards all laughed. Zarrah's stomach turned. It appeared the guards were well aware of what the rebels consumed. Her nausea faded as one of the guards rested his elbows on the stone bricks forming the outpost he manned. He glanced sideways at his companions, then lowered one hand, fingers moving in the code used throughout Valcotta's military.

Hold ground.

Rescue coming.

Await signal.

He moved his hands back inside the outpost as Kian called up, "You might send something to reward the lady for making better life choices. Drink, perhaps?"

"The last time we sent you drink, it all went down *your* hatch, Kian," the guard answered. "The memory of you drunkenly servicing your women on the beach is the source of all of my nightmares."

"It is my duty to entertain," Kian cackled, slapping his hand against his thigh, and unease filled Zarrah at the obvious favoritism that the guards showed this tribe over Daria's. Was it because her tribe had resorted to cannibalism?

One of the prisoners approached, smirking as he leaned close to whisper something in Kian's ear that only made the tribe leader laugh harder and shout, "Send us libations, my friend! I promise to make it worth your while."

He then gave Zarrah a lascivious wink.

Despite knowing that this was a show to disguise the real reason they'd come down to the beach, Zarrah gave him a disgusted glare and went back into the camp. Ducking inside the tent she'd been given, Zarrah tucked the canvas under a rock to ensure she was obscured from view before picking up a stick. From memory, she wrote the message Kian had shown her in the dirt, then sat back to stare at the words.

Who had sent it?

Who cared enough, and had power and means, to want to rescue her?

Keris?

Her chest tightened, and Zarrah looked away from the message. Why would he? Not only had she told him that if she ever saw him again, she'd kill him, but the information her aunt's spies had provided more than proved he'd moved on. To Lestara. Zarrah's stomach twisted, her hands balling into fists as she envisioned the beautiful harem wife, though in truth, there were probably others. Keris was the king. He was rich, charming, and more beautiful than any man had a right to be, so women would be clamoring to warm his bed. Why would he risk all of that for her? Besides, the letter's prose was terrible, proving beyond a shadow of a doubt that Keris hadn't written it.

This wasn't his scheme, because it was over between them, what love they'd shared now ash on the wind.

The reminder was a punch to the gut, and she hated herself for caring so much. For having wished that he'd come, despite all that he'd done, because it proved her aunt's words. Proved that she was still under his spell. How could she dream of leading an army to overthrow the empress if the king of Maridrina held so much sway over her? If every time she faced an obstacle, she needed him to provide a solution? A solution that would inevitably be to his benefit.

"Focus," she snarled softly to herself. "It's not him, so who sent it?"

Ithicana? She wouldn't precisely call Aren a friend, but she believed he respected her, as she did him. There was a chance he'd attempt to repay the aid she'd given him, but her heart told her that was a dream. Ithicana had liberated itself, which meant Aren owed her nothing. Even if he felt otherwise, making a deal with murderers and rapists did not strike her as something someone of his morals would do.

The rebels hadn't written the letter. Keris hadn't written it. Neither had Aren.

So who? Who had the desire and means to get a letter into the prison supplies?

Zarrah abruptly went still.

Maybe she'd been thinking about this the wrong way. Maybe the letter hadn't been written by an individual who believed she was worth rescue.

Maybe it had been written by someone who believed she was worth something as bait.

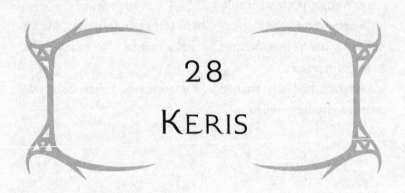

28
KERIS

"A TOUCH FORMAL, BUT I'LL TAKE IT," KERIS ANSWERED, EYEING the warriors who surrounded them. Aren had pulled his knife and appeared ready to single-handedly fight them all himself, and to his credit, not one of them appeared keen to take him on.

Daria rolled her eyes, then sat down on a stump. "Relax, we're on the same side. If things had gone according to plan, we'd currently be keeping her safe while we waited for rescue, but Zarrah didn't take well to learning of our diet and hightailed it over to the enemy's camp." She sighed. "In fairness, it might have been better if I'd been forthright, but I was afraid she'd react as she did."

"How did you know we were coming?" Aren asked, blade still held as though he anticipated one of them would try to take a bite out of his leg at any minute.

"We didn't."

Keris frowned. "Then how do you know who I am?"

"Zarrah told me about you." When he tensed, she said, "Not by name, of course. But enough detail that, in combination with what I'd heard about her time in Vencia, I was able to put two and two together. Especially when daylight revealed those eyes of yours." She leaned forward and scrutinized his face. "The rumors about the color don't lie. Is it true that every Veliant has eyes that hue?"

Before Keris could answer, her attention moved to Aren. "Who's your combative comrade?"

"Family," Aren answered, and Keris glanced sideways at the other man. Though it was technically true, it still surprised him that Aren would refer to him as such.

"Good-looking family." Daria stretched her legs out in front of her. "My name is Daria Retta, and I'm a captain in the true empress's army. Devil's Island might have once been a prison for convicts, but now it's a place the Usurper sends her prisoners of the Silent War, the rebellion against Petra Anaphora's unlawful rule."

True Empress. Unlawful rule. Yet more proof that the rumor Aster remembered was no rumor, nor Serin's final words that Aryana was the true and rightful ruler a lie. Zarrah should be empress, but Petra had stolen her crown.

Daria was watching him with knowing eyes. "Yes. Emperor Ephraim named Princess Aryana as his heir and successor. Rather than bending the knee to her younger sister, Petra destroyed the proclamation and assassinated nearly everyone who knew the truth, using her power in the military to spread the lie that she was named heir. Aryana bent the knee to Petra to protect herself and her young daughter, but secretly spent years gathering support in the south to eventually overthrow Petra's rule. Unfortunately, your father murdered Aryana before her plans could come to fruition, but the cause didn't die with her. We kept up the fight in the name of her daughter and heir even as Petra twisted Zarrah into her own creature."

Daria was quiet for a long moment, and then she continued, "I was captured and imprisoned two years ago. But information comes to me every time Petra imprisons one of my comrades, so I learned that Zarrah came back from Vencia . . . *changed*. Which meant little to me until I received direct word from the commander that Petra had turned on her heir and was sending her to her prison. The idea that Zarrah was no longer Petra's pet gave us hope that she might become the empress we needed her to be. Yet that hope stood on a knife's blade because it resided in this place." She gestured outward. "I was given orders to secure her at all costs and protect her until the commander was able to organize a rescue. In that, I have surely failed."

"How do you communicate with your commander?" Aren asked.

"The commander was able to get one of ours a position as a guard," she answered. "He communicates information to me by signing short messages while I cuss him, and every other guard, out each morning."

"How much of this does Zarrah know?" Keris asked, because if she knew the rebels had concrete plans to rescue her, even the revelation of cannibalism wouldn't have been enough to make her run.

"Some." Daria looked away. "Most of us know Zarrah as Petra's creature, her tool for violence and a proponent of the Endless War, so we were not quick to trust that she hadn't been sent here as an agent to infiltrate the rebellion."

Aren scoffed. "A foolish thought. Why in the hell would Petra risk her heir to discover information about a rebellion that she seems to have well in hand?"

Daria's jaw worked back and forth. "Because Zarrah is unique bait for the commander, and Petra hates him at least as much as she hates *you*." She jerked her chin at Keris.

Keris's eyes narrowed. "Who is this commander?"

All of the warriors surrounding them shifted uneasily, this clearly a secret close to their hearts. Daria bit her lip, then said, "That's a need-to-know. And you don't need to know. But trust that he'll do what it takes to get Zarrah free."

"A task made more difficult by the fact that you lost her," Aren finished. "She's with this other group, led by someone called Kian?"

Several of the other prisoners spat into the dirt at the man's name.

"Kian holds the beach camp," Daria answered. "He knows Zarrah's identity and has been desperate to get his hands on her from the second she stepped foot on the island. I thought it was because she was pretty and he likes his ladies, but he's lost at least twenty men trying to steal her back from us, so I knew it had to be something else. Tried to spy it out with no success. And then bad luck coupled with my mistakes saw Zarrah racing right into his arms."

Keris tensed, and Daria rolled her eyes. "Metaphorically, you idiot."

"From the *moment* she stepped on the island?" Aren asked. "As in, he knew who she was before she was incarcerated?"

Daria went still. "Yes." She was quiet. "Had to be one of the guards who told him."

"To what end?" Righting a stump, Keris sat on it, elbows resting on his knees as he considered what he'd learned. "On the surface, revealing Zarrah's identity to the prisoners would be signing her death sentence—she's the niece of the woman who imprisoned them."

"Worse," Daria said. "She personally captured a handful of them. They have a lot of reason to hate her."

"Which means Kian and his tribe have been given incentive to keep her alive." Keris stared blindly into the distance, then focused on Daria. "Food? Drink? Premium supplies?"

The woman gave a slow shake of her head. "That's a promise easily broken, and Kian's no fool. What's more, he risked his own life to try to take her, and I don't think he'd do that for a few extra bottles of rum."

"Then the incentive must be freedom," Keris said. "And there are very few people who realistically have the gold and the connections to deliver: your rebel commander—"

"The commander would not deal with Kian," Daria snapped. "*We* are his people."

"Perhaps he believes he *is* dealing with his people," Keris said. "Perhaps Kian intercepted a message intended for you."

Or perhaps, Keris thought to himself, *the commander made arrangements with both factions.*

"We must consider that Petra is behind this," Aren said. "There has always been the risk that this was a trap for you. Perhaps she's made an agreement with Kian to double her odds of killing you. A trap within a trap."

It made sense that Petra was behind this. Perfect fucking sense, yet something about it felt *wrong* to Keris. If all she cared about was killing him, that could have been accomplished long ago by an assassin.

Petra's obsession was the Endless War. She wanted glory and the accolades. To go down in the history books as the empress who'd triumphed and expanded the Empire to rule over its ancient enemy. Having Keris killed on this island by nameless prisoners would not satisfy that need.

But capturing him and publicly executing him might.

The thought made him wonder if the teeth of the trap had already closed around him and he just hadn't realized it.

Keris rubbed at his temples, trying to think, trying to come up with a strategy, but he felt sick with fear. Not for himself. But for Zarrah. For Aren. For all of those he'd dragged into this mess with no clear plan to get them out of it.

"So you believe it's *you* Kian needs to deliver to get his freedom?" Daria asked. "Petra was that certain you'd come yourself?"

"She's a monster," he muttered, trying to steady his breathing. Trying to *think*. "But a very clever monster."

"Kian doesn't know we're here," Aren reasoned. "We have time to strategize a way to get Zarrah back from him. Daria, do you have the manpower to retrieve her by force?"

The woman tensed. "We've got more people, but not all are fighters. And Kian has more weapons. We'd take heavy losses. If it's freedom on the line, they'll pursue, which means that whatever plan you have to get yourselves and Zarrah off the island better goddamn include us."

Silence stretched, and Keris exchanged another weighted look with Aren, who said, "When does the commander plan to make his move?"

"I don't know. Days. Weeks. Months, maybe." Daria scowled. "Why? Because you plan to use us to get Zarrah, then leave us to war with Kian until the commander can make it here to rescue us? Half of my tribe will be dead by then. Maybe all."

The warriors surrounding them muttered angrily, and Keris held up a hand. "We ask because we don't have a route off the island, nor the manpower for an outright attack."

No one spoke, the tension thick enough to cut with a knife.

"If you don't have a route off, then you are no rescuers." Daria stood. "You're prisoners, just like us."

She wasn't wrong.

Rising to his feet, Keris walked through the warriors who'd surrounded them, the men and women stepping aside to give him a path. Zarrah was so close. So painfully close, and part of him wanted to break into a run. To race across the island and find her, never mind the obvious consequences.

Instead he forced himself to think, because allowing his emotions to drive strategy was what had gotten him and Aren onto this island with no path for escape.

It might well be true that they had time, that Zarrah would be safe enough in Kian's camp while they were ignorant to Keris's presence. But the longer they were stuck here, the more desperate Lara would become. Perhaps desperate enough to take risks she should not, which could get her killed.

He couldn't leave the problem in his sister's hands. He needed to solve it himself.

Going back to Daria and Aren, he said, "We're going to spring the trap."

"Keris—" Aren started to argue, but Keris cut him off.

"I'm the prize that Kian needs to deliver to gain his freedom. So Daria organizes a trade. Me for Zarrah. She . . ." He swallowed hard. "She was just the bait, so I think he'll agree. If Kian is as smart as Daria claims, he'll demand that he and his tribe be allowed off the island before they give me up. These are dangerous men and women, so the entire island garrison will be required to keep them under control."

Aren's brow furrowed. "They'd have to leave other posts undermanned."

Keris nodded. "If we time it for the cover of darkness, all Daria's man in the guard need do is get a rope stretched between the cliffs. You, Daria, and the rest of the tribe can climb across the water and make your way to the pier to signal the ship. You've enough manpower to take the pier from behind, and then it's only a matter of your ship sailing in to take everyone aboard before the navy is the wiser."

"What about you?"

"Never mind me. Tell Zarrah everything and then get her to the rebel commander. She has the power to rid Valcotta of Petra, and if she does that, Maridrina will be protected."

"We have time," Aren argued. "We don't need to make this decision now. Give Lara a chance to find another solution."

Keris shook his head. "How long do you think Lara will go without communication from you before she gets desperate?" Seeing Aren was going to keep arguing, he added, "Lara asked me if there was a limit to what I'd sacrifice, and this is it. She's the limit. I won't allow my sister to die for the chance of me living— not if my capture will ensure every last one of you gets out alive."

"It's a good plan," Daria said.

"It's a shitty plan." Aren crossed his arms. "And it's not like you to submit, Keris. You're a survivor."

"Then trust that I will."

"That's not good enough. I'm not leaving you to fight this battle by yourself."

Keris's chest tightened with emotion he couldn't quite put words to that the man he'd once thrown to the wolves was willing to risk so much for him.

Even if he wasn't worth it.

So Keris struck the final nail that he knew would secure Aren's cooperation. "It's not just Lara's life that is at risk anymore."

Aren stiffened, then closed his eyes and nodded once.

29
ZARRAH

BAIT.

The word made her lip curl in disgust, her anger rising, because by fleeing Daria and her tribe, she'd placed herself like cheese in a trap.

Her aunt hadn't put her on this island to teach her a lesson; she'd put her on this island to catch someone. Not Keris, for her aunt knew better than anyone that he had washed his hands of Zarrah.

The rebels.

For years, her aunt had been incarcerating the rebels here rather than executing them. Building their numbers and ensuring they suffered, trying to lure the commander who plagued her into an outright attack so that she could crush him. But rescuing his people hadn't been incentive enough for the commander, so to sweeten the pot, the empress had added Zarrah to the mix. Why she was worth so much to the rebels was yet a mystery to Zarrah, but there was no denying that Daria had valued her far more than she reasonably should.

Which meant that somehow, Daria had known her identity from the moment she'd arrived. Had been trying to protect her because she'd somehow known that the commander would feel compelled to make a move on the island.

Clenching her fists, Zarrah bit down on a scream of frustration. Her goal had been to join them, and now she'd discovered she was bait to lure them into a trap and destroy them. Yet again a pawn.

Only . . . something didn't fit.

Zarrah's skin crawled as her eyes skipped over the message, which seemed no more something her aunt would write than Keris. The empress might be a monster, but she was a monster with her own form of honor, and it wouldn't allow her to employ the services of murderers she'd condemned. And it certainly wouldn't allow her to grant them *freedom*. Which meant . . .

The tent canvas abruptly collapsed, crushing her to the ground.

Zarrah snarled, punching and kicking, trying to fight her way loose, but more hands than she could count were holding her down. Yet as she was bound and gagged, one thought played over and over in her head.

There was another player in the game. And she knew exactly who it was.

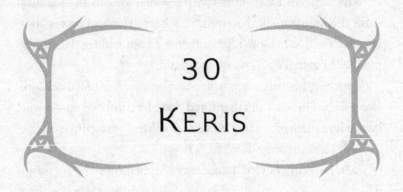

30

KERIS

EVERYTHING WAS IN MOTION.

Daria's contact among the guards was in position, his role made easier by the revelation that members of Daria's tribe were particularly fond of certain trees, nurturing them tall and strong. Even now, those trees were being cut down to form a bridge for Daria's tribe to cross under the cover of darkness.

Which would only be possible if Keris sprung the trap and everything played out as he intended.

"I don't like this," Aren muttered. "It doesn't feel right."

"You're just jealous that I get to be the hero and you're once again relegated to helping people cross a bridge."

Not rising to Keris's baiting, Aren exhaled and rubbed at one temple. "I think we should hold off. Consider other plans that don't involve handing you over to the enemy."

"Only a temporary handover," Keris said. "Besides, it's too late to go back now. Daria's people arranged the trade, which means that Kian knows I'm here. Which means so do Petra's guards. If Daria doesn't go through with the trade, they'll assume that it's because there's a strategy in play and be more mindful of guarding their rear."

"We could lure them onto the island," Aren argued. "Fight them on ground that Daria controls."

Keris huffed out a frustrated breath. "The Valcottan soldiers guarding this prison aren't stupid. If they know that I'm on this island and that they have to come find me, they'll bring enough soldiers to slaughter everyone alive. Quit making bad suggestions; battles are supposed to be your competency."

"This isn't a battle," Aren growled. "It's a fucking sacrifice, and Lara's going to castrate me when she discovers I agreed to it."

"You'll be fine. She'll understand. Though it warms my heart to hear you believe my sister values my life over your balls."

"You two bicker like lovers." Daria caught hold of Keris's arm, pulling him to a stop. "It's time you were silenced, anyway. You're my prisoner. And you"—she pointed at Aren—"aren't supposed to be here. So get to the rear."

Aren's eyes narrowed, but rather than arguing, he retreated.

"He's not used to being ordered around," Keris said. "He'll try to take control so as to do something heroic. If you value the lives of your people, don't let him."

Daria snorted. "Typical man."

"Zarrah trusts that typical man, so it serves your best interests to keep him alive."

Daria didn't answer, only bound his arms behind his back. But then her hands stilled. "Do you love her?"

"Yes."

She made a noise that he couldn't interpret, and, curiosity rising, Keris said, "Why? What did she say about me?" What he wanted to ask was whether Zarrah hated him. Whether she'd forgiven him.

Whether she still loved him as he loved her.

"That you have a big cock."

His jaw dropped, and Daria took advantage, shoving the gag in and tying it around his head so that all he could do was stand there and stare at her.

Meeting his gaze, the woman said, "She said a lot of things, Your Grace, all of which you swiftly proved to be accurate. But on the very small chance you ever get to speak to her again, remember that she is *not* your queen. She is Valcotta's empress. Treat her accordingly. Now walk."

He started up the trail, moving over the bare space at the summit and stepping into Kian's territory. What had Zarrah said that he'd already proven? And what did Daria mean by the comment about him treating Zarrah like an empress and not his queen? And what had he done to give Zarrah cause to believe he no longer loved her?

"Focus, Your Grace," Daria muttered as they descended the hill to the meeting spot. "None of what you are thinking is pressing."

She was right, but it wasn't the threat to his life that made his heart quicken with each step. It was that he was walking toward Zarrah. He'd be in her presence, even if it was only for a moment. A moment that he prayed would undo some of the hurt he'd caused.

Ahead, a clearing appeared, and on the far side of it, a crowd of figures. It was hard to see through the trees, but as they reached the clearing, his eyes found her familiar form.

Zarrah was on her knees, hands bound behind her back, and a gag in her mouth. Thin and dirty, and one of her eyes was swollen. But she was *alive.*

Slowly, she lifted her head, shock filling her dark gaze as she saw him, but it was swiftly replaced with horror. Zarrah screamed around her gag, thrashing and trying to get free of the men holding her arms. A big man with gold teeth kicked her in the back of the knees, the others pinning her to the ground. "Keep her quiet."

Blistering rage filled Keris's chest, his hands balling into fists behind his back, but he held his ground. He was meant to be Daria's captive, and giving any indication that he was otherwise would signal to these prisoners that plots were afoot.

"You break her, we may have to reconsider this trade, Kian," Daria shouted. "You might have a hard time proving His Royal Majesty's identity if we invite Flay over to cut off his face."

Kian reached down to grab Zarrah by the wrists, hauling her to her feet. Her eyes immediately locked on Keris's, and she screamed what sounded like *run*.

"Don't even think about it," Daria snarled, jabbing him with her spear. "Let's get this done, Kian. Hand Zarrah over."

"Run," Zarrah screamed again around her mouthful of fabric. "Fight!"

He wished that were an option, but Daria hadn't been wrong when she'd said that this wasn't a battle they could win. While her tribe had greater numbers, at least half weren't fighters, whereas every one of the men and women behind Kian appeared battle-hardened. This was the only way, and if he died so that Zarrah, Aren, and the rest could live, so be it.

"Meet me at the midground," Kian said. "Then we do the switch."

"Island honor?" Daria demanded.

"Or may the Devil take my soul."

"He already has it." Daria spat into the dirt. "But let it be done."

She jabbed Keris in the spine again, forcing him to walk even as Kian dragged Zarrah, who kept screaming, "Run! Run! Run!" Wrenching free of Kian's grasp, she slammed into Keris.

For a heartbeat, their bodies were pressed together, and time seemed to freeze as he looked down into her eyes. He'd been terrified that all he'd find was hate, but that was the only emotion absent in the liquid depths of her gaze, her words muffled by her gag as she said, "You came for me."

He tried to spit out the wad of fabric Daria had shoved in his mouth, but before he could, Zarrah said around her gag, "Why did you come for me? He's going to kill you!"

A tremor ran down his spine, twisting guilt filling his gut that he was putting her through this. For her once again to be caught blind in one of his plans. *Trust me*, he tried to tell her as he stared into her eyes.

Then Kian had a hold of her again, wrenching her away. Zarrah twisted and thrashed, eyes wild as she screamed and screamed, only for Kian to backhand her hard. "Shut your gob, woman."

The blow stunned her, and Zarrah dangled limply in Kian's grip. Keris's control fractured, and he took two quick steps before Daria jerked on his wrists.

Kian laughed. "Can't say I blame you, Your Grace. She's pretty as they come, and if it hadn't been against the terms of my agreement, I might have taken her for a turn myself."

Don't let him bait you, Keris silently screamed at himself as Kian tossed Zarrah at Daria's feet. *You need him agreeable.*

"Here," Kian said, lifting a cord over his head, from which dangled a key. "I gift you my gallery, old nemesis." He held it out to Daria, but she ignored it, and he let it drop to her feet. "Enjoy the beach."

Daria shoved Keris, and he stumbled, Kian grabbing him by the arm and dragging him back toward his men. Keris risked a backward glance to see Daria lifting a stirring Zarrah, Saam moving to help carry her to safety.

It was done. No matter what happened next, she was as safe as he could make her, so Keris turned his mind to the rest of his plan.

The prisoners dragged him roughly to camp, alternating between crowing insults at him and making suggestions of how best to enjoy their freedom as the sun began to set.

"Didn't go quite according to plan, did it, Your Grace?" Kian said, catching Keris by the hair and pulling loose the gag. "Such hubris to believe you could come onto *my* island and take one of my things. That you could plot, conspire, and machinate, without me knowing exactly what you were up to."

"Character flaw, I'm afraid." Keris smiled. "I've been told time and again that my excessively high opinion of myself will be my downfall, but I never learn."

Kian backhanded him, then hauled him up by the front of his shirt with shocking strength, holding a knife tip above Keris's left eye. "Only need one to prove your breeding, Veliant."

"Willing to bet your freedom on that?" Keris asked. When the man shrugged, he added, "How about your fortune?"

Kian went still, but the knife remained in place. "Fortune isn't on the table."

"Oh, but it is."

Silence stretched, and then Kian said, "I'm listening."

"You know who I am," Keris said. "Which means that you know that I'm very, *very* rich." Utter bullshit, given that his father had drained the coffers in his pursuit of the bridge, but Kian wouldn't know that. "I'd be willing to reward those who help me escape this particular circumstance alive."

The big man snorted. "Gold don't spend on Devil's Island, *Your Grace*. I ain't doing nothing to jeopardize freedom."

"Nor would I ask you to." Keris blinked, feeling the ends of his lashes brush the tip of the knife. "I assume your arrangement included transport back to the mainland."

Silence.

"I see," Keris said. "Doesn't that make you question whether promises will be honored? Doesn't it make you question whether you're just being used?"

Some of the other prisoners heard, and mutters traveled outward.

"Even if you are given a ship to get off the island, all they'll do is drop you on a beach in the middle of nowhere without a penny to your name. So you'll have your freedom, but you'll be destitute."

"We got gold," Kian snarled. "Chests of it."

"You think those guards are going to let you keep it?" Keris scoffed. "You know the men and women who've kept you imprisoned. How well have they treated you? You think they won't steal every penny, including your golden smile, before loading you like cattle onto the ship? You're clearly a smart man, Kian; don't let the scent of freedom cloud your good judgment."

Slowly, Kian lowered the knife. "What are you proposing?"

"Self-interest, my friend." Keris righted himself on the ground, knowing that every one of them was listening. "Make sure you and yours go up first before you bring me up. They know you for dangerous individuals, so they'll have every guard on the island there to assist, which means biding your time. With luck, they will have a ship waiting, and once we are aboard . . . mutiny. Kill them all. Take the ship, your gold, and *me* to ransom back to my country. Or Ithicana," he added as an afterthought. "My sister *is* their queen, and everyone knows how deep the Bridge Kingdom's coffers are."

As he'd expected from a group of criminals, their eyes brightened with greed at the proposition, not a one of them showing any concern about betraying empress or empire. He waited for the idea to circulate, then said, "All I'm saying is that I'm worth a great deal. Why give up such a valuable asset to the woman who imprisoned you if you don't have to?"

There were nods and grunts of agreement, several spitting on the ground and cursing the Empire. To his credit, Kian only smiled and laughed. "You think you have this all figured out, don't you?" Before Keris could answer, he leaned closer. "I'll think about what you've said. But don't get it in your head that I'm risking my life for the sake of your neck." To underscore the point, he kicked Keris in the ribs, sending him sprawling.

Through the pain, Keris said, "Understood." It wouldn't be for his neck that they'd mutiny—it would be for *their* greed—but the results would be the same. He had no doubt in his mind that the guards would provide ample motivation to drive them toward the plan of action.

"Signal the guards," Kian shouted. "Let's get this done."

Several men departed, but the rest scuttled among the shacks and tents, gathering barrels and water-stained chests of what Keris assumed was their treasure. He didn't bother engaging with those who remained to guard him, his mind consumed with replaying the moment he'd seen her.

Alive. Zarrah was alive, and he realized then how much he'd feared otherwise, for it felt like a thousand pounds of rock had been lifted from his shoulders with the disappearance of that uncertainty. Alive and fighting and . . . His throat tightened as he remembered the heartbeat when their bodies had been pressed together, the dark pools of her eyes revealing that she had not entirely forsaken him.

"Kian!" someone shouted. "It's time."

Growling, the big man dragged Keris by the hair down to the rocky beach. Pain lanced through his body as he bounced over the sharp edges, but he refused to cry out. Refused to give these creatures any form of victory.

"Let me see his face!" a familiar voice shouted from above, and Keris found himself stiffening.

Kian pulled Keris's head back so that he was looking at the cliff tops, where Bermin's broad form was outlined by the setting sun. It made sense that the prince was here, that he'd be his mother's agent in this transaction, yet somehow it felt unexpected.

Which made Keris uneasy.

"Keris Veliant," the Valcottan prince crooned. "I'd say that it was a pleasure to meet you, but we've met once before."

Keris's heart skittered, because if Bermin had realized it had been him on the Cardiffian ship—

"In Nerastis."

Relief flooded him, for the vessel's cover hadn't been compromised. "You weren't in a position to say much the first time," Keris called back, distinctly remembering how his shoulder had connected with the other man's throat. "Though I see you've recovered from that particular humiliation."

"It is no humiliation to learn the nature of your enemy." Bermin moved closer to the edge of the cliff. "It brought us to this moment."

Keris's gut soured. What did Bermin mean by that?

"On my honor, the man before us is King Keris Veliant of Maridrina." Bermin looked sideways at the crowd of soldiers lining the cliff. "You'll all swear that it is him?"

The soldiers all nodded, expressions grim. There were dozens of them, all heavily armed in preparation for allowing the scores of prisoners in Kian's tribe free of their prison, exactly as Keris had anticipated. Yet something felt wrong.

Kian shouted, "We captured him for you. Now deliver on your promise and set us free."

Bermin chuckled, then said, "You have served the Empire well," as the sun disappeared behind the cliff, plunging Keris into darkness. "Allow your future emperor to reward you with your freedom."

Taking a torch from a soldier, Bermin flung it across the channel, where it fell among the prisoners. More torches followed,
until the beach was lit up like the sun had reversed its course
around the world. Several of the prisoners lifted the burning
brands, but Keris felt his own trepidation mirrored on their faces.

"Send them to hell!" Bermin roared.

As one, his soldiers raised their bows. The prisoners shouted in
alarm, turning to run, but a barrage of arrows descended in a
cloud. Keris held his breath, fighting every instinct that demanded
he flee the onslaught. Men dropped all around, Kian nearly landing on him as he fell, arrow through his throat. Keris's ears rang
with the noise of their agonized cries for help; then it was nothing
more than moans of dying men and women, his plan to escape
Petra's grasp now smoke on the wind.

Keris gritted his teeth. It didn't matter. The only person this af-
fected was him; everything else was still in play. Aren, Daria, and
her tribe would be escaping across their bridges under the cover of
darkness, would make it to the pier during the time Bermin spent
on these theatrics, and Lara's ship would soon ferry them away.

Lifting his head, he stared at Bermin's outline, illuminated by
more torches. "I think it's safe for you to come down now."

Bermin laughed, then said, "Did you know the guards have a
saying here? They say that the Devil demands the soul of every
person who steps on this island, which is why there is no way
down. No one would ever use it." He took a bow from one of his
men, leveling an arrow at Keris's chest. "Time to give the Devil his
due, Your Grace."

31
ZARRAH

THE WORLD SWAM AROUND HER, FAMILIAR VOICES FILLING HER ears, and Zarrah shook her head to clear it.

"We got you, girl," Daria said, and fingers pulled the filthy gag from her mouth. "Once we're out of harm's way, we'll get those ropes off you."

Harm's way.

Keris.

He'd come for her.

And Daria had betrayed him.

Panic and fury flooded her veins, and Zarrah twisted, falling to her knees. "You bitch," she hissed at Daria. "You gave him to them. You killed him."

"Keris gave himself up," a familiar voice said, and then the ropes around her wrists loosened. "The empress will want him as a prisoner, and he has a plan to get free."

Zarrah whirled to face Aren, shock to find him there mixing with her rising panic. "It's not the empress who made the deal with Kian; it's Bermin. He's been plotting behind the empress's back. The second he has Keris in his sights, he's going to kill him."

"He won't risk crossing Petra," Aren said. "He'll take him prisoner, which gives us time to get him back."

Zarrah gave a wild shake of her head. "The last thing Bermin said before he imprisoned me was that he planned to kill Keris. He swore it to me on his honor."

Unease filled Aren's hazel eyes. "But the navy . . . Bermin couldn't have ordered all those ships here without Petra agreeing to it."

"Because she did!" Zarrah pulled a spear from Saam's grip. "She sent me here as bait for the rebels and their commander." There wasn't time to explain this. There wasn't time to explain her aunt's madness to them when Keris was walking toward death. "Bermin set a trap within a trap, and on my honor, he plans to kill him. We need to go. We need to get him back. We need to fight!"

"Fuck." Aren spun away from her, gripping the sides of his head as he kicked a rock, sending it spinning. "Goddammit, Keris!"

"Gather everyone." Zarrah caught hold of Daria's arm, pulling the woman close. "We'll attack Kian from the rear. But we need to move now!"

Daria didn't move.

Zarrah spun in a circle, realizing that everyone was looking anywhere but at her. They weren't going to help her. "Aren . . ."

"I don't want to leave him," the king of Ithicana said. "But this isn't a fight we can win. Even if we defeat Kian's men, Bermin has the island's entire garrison with him." Aren let out a shaky breath. "Keris knew the risks, Zarrah. Knew that there was every chance he'd be killed, but he chose to do it anyway. Not just for you, but for everyone here. Don't let his sacrifice be in vain."

A scream of rage tore from her lips, and Zarrah dropped to her knees, slamming her fists on the ground.

"Zarrah, listen." Daria knelt in front of her. "Bermin has nearly emptied the guard towers and brought the soldiers to the cliff fac-

ing the beach. This is our chance to get across the channel. Keris
has bought a chance for all of us to be freed."

At the cost of his life.

"You told me it was over between you two." There was desperation in Daria's eyes. "That he wouldn't let you be who you needed
to be."

Daria spoke the truth, yet faced with his death, Zarrah saw now
that her claims had been fueled by her aunt's poisonous words.

"How is he worth risking the chance for you to liberate all of
Valcotta from tyranny? He's given us a chance at peace—don't
throw it away!"

"Peace is a dance," Zarrah said. "It only works when both nations dance to the same music, and without Keris, Maridrina will
keep dancing to the drums of war. He needs to live!"

Daria took a step back, shaking her head, and Zarrah saw that
freedom was worth too much to her to take the risk. That the Endless War was a distant threat to be dealt with another day, not
something to guide her hand.

That Daria was afraid.

Yet it was Aren who broke the silence. "You would defy your
empress?"

Zarrah stared at him in confusion as he surveyed the rebels
with disdain. "You claim to fight in Zarrah's name as the rightful
empress of Valcotta, but she has called you to arms, and you turn
your backs?" He scoffed. "Seems to me you fight only for yourselves, and in Ithicana, we have a word for that. It isn't honor."

Rightful empress?

Then Aren's eyes fixed on hers. "To rule is to lead, Imperial Majesty. Don't let your first and last act be to lead them to certain
death."

She had no time to question why Aren had referred to her as

such, not with Keris's life on the line. Answers would be had after they got out of this alive.

Zarrah swallowed, panic warring with a lifetime of military training. Daria and Aren were right. To attack Kian from the rear would only be delaying Keris's death, not sparing him.

Turning in a slow circle, she let her mind drift, taking in all the variables and considering her enemy, whom she knew better than anyone here. Then she faced her army. "This," she said, "is what we are going to do."

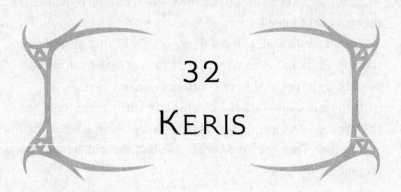

32

KERIS

KERIS'S EYES FOCUSED ON THE TIP OF THE ARROW, FEAR POURING over him like ice water, chilling him to the core. Not only because he was facing his final moments of life, but because the distraction he'd planned to allow everyone else to escape would be far, *far* too short-lived.

Think.

Bermin was a talker. A braggart. If he could draw this moment out even for a few minutes longer, it could be enough for everyone to escape the prison, if not the island itself. "What will your mother say when she learns you killed me and left me to rot in obscurity? Petra doesn't seem the sort to respond favorably to any disruption of her plans, and putting an arrow through my heart just doesn't smack of one of her strategies."

The Valcottan prince laughed, the tip of the arrow shaking. "Because it isn't my mother's, *Your Grace*. It's *my* strategy."

Keris stiffened. He'd believed it was Petra across the game board from him, which meant he'd been playing the wrong enemy.

Time for a change of tactic.

Leaning back, Keris laughed. "You don't take a shit without your mother's permission, Bermin. Do you really expect me to believe you aren't a pawn in her greater scheme? And allow me to remind you—pawns that don't play their roles are swiftly disposed of."

Even across the channel of water between them, Keris could feel Bermin's simmer of rage. Feel the fury that only the truth could provoke. But to his credit, Bermin kept it in check.

"Her scheme is still in play." Bermin held his arms wide, bow in one hand and arrow in the other. "For it was not your capture she sought, but that of the rebel commander. She knew he wouldn't be able to resist Zarrah's plight and would swoop in for the rescue, only to be slaughtered by her waiting navy. You"—he laughed—"were not even a factor, because my mother never once considered that you'd come for Zarrah."

Keris went still, Bermin's words twisting in his mind. It didn't make sense. Serin's revelation of his relationship with Zarrah was what had caused Petra to incarcerate her niece here, so why wouldn't she have thought he would come?

"Looking for the logic?" Barking out another laugh, Bermin lowered the bow to his side. "You will look forever because you are attempting to understand the mind of a madwoman." He took a step closer to the edge of the cliff. "She can't stand that you stole Zarrah's affection from her because she needs to be beloved by *all*. She *needs* Zarrah to come back to her, to love her, to worship her, and in order for her to believe that possible, you needed to become the heartless Veliant who manipulated her precious niece to achieve your own ends. Not just in Zarrah's eyes, but in her own. She convinced herself that you were a demon, and demons don't come to rescue those they've used."

Every word Bermin said sank into his soul, but Keris didn't

allow himself to consider the implications of a madwoman ruling an empire. All that mattered was keeping Bermin talking. Buying more time. "But *you* knew I'd come?"

"My mother doesn't know you like I do." Bermin tilted his head, clearly enjoying the pleasure of being correct. "She thinks you a heartless strategist who murdered his own brother to hide his schemes. Who let his own aunt take the fall for a failed coup to take the crown. Who arranged the death of his own father at the expense of thousands of lives. But I saw you gallop alone into the middle of a raid to aid your people. Watched you climb into a burning home to rescue two gutter-rat children. You are not heartless, Keris Veliant, no, *no* . . . You are a man whose heart decides *all,* even when it risks costing him everything."

"You're more perceptive than I gave you credit for." Keris kept his focus on the prince even as he waited for any sign of commotion. For any sign that Zarrah, and all those with her, had been spotted in their escape. "Though I fail to see what you have to gain from this little side plot to capture and kill me when it will surely infuriate your mother. If she wanted me dead, she'd have sent an assassin a long time ago."

"It's not about *you,* Veliant." Bermin spat in the water below. "It's about Zarrah. She's a traitor to Valcotta, yet my mother still desires her as heir. From Zarrah's own lips, she admitted to giving you our strategies to prevent me from taking Nerastis. She's not your victim but your whore, and yet my mother would set her above me."

The soldiers around Bermin shifted angrily, cursing Zarrah, but Bermin raised his arm to silence them. "She desires Zarrah to be redeemed, but there is only one way for that to happen. One way for my mother to be entirely certain of Zarrah's loyalty, and that's if Zarrah destroys *you.*"

Bermin nocked the arrow, drawing the bow's string. "I don't intend to give her that chance. I will reveal the depths of Zarrah's depravity and treason to all of Valcotta. The empress will have no choice but to recognize me as her heir, and at the head of her armies, I will be the one to burn Maridrina to ash. When the time comes, I will be the Emperor of Valcotta, and all will bend the knee to me." Bermin took aim. "All I need do is kill the Veliant king."

"Like an honorless coward." Keris grinned up at him despite the terror threatening to drown him. "What a legacy, Your Highness. To be remembered for hiding at a safe distance to shoot a man bound at the wrists and on his knees."

Bermin didn't answer.

"Come down here," Keris crooned. "Unless you're afraid to fight me, man to man?"

"You think me a fool to be so baited?"

Yes, Keris thought. And though he knew that the death that would come to him would be far more painful than an arrow to the heart, he said, "I challenge you, Bermin Anaphora."

A smart man would have loosed the arrow and been done with it, but Keris had legions of brothers who thought exactly like Bermin, and he knew that pride would ever trump wisdom.

"You aren't worth a fight, but I will saw off your head myself. Let your rotting eyes serve as more proof." Bermin cast aside his bow. "Get me a rope."

Keris's nerve wavered, because he'd seen his father saw men's heads off. Had listened to them scream, then choke on their own blood until he reached their spinal cord. It was slow and miserable, and Keris was fairly certain that the victims were still able to see when his father finally held up their severed heads.

You can do this, he told himself. *They'll be over the channel by now. Will be making their way to the coast, where Lara's ship is nearby. Just buy them a bit more time.*

Sweat dripped down his spine, his breath coming in rapid pants as the soldiers secured a rope and tossed it over the edge.

This was it. There were no more words to help him escape what was to come.

Heart in his throat, Keris watched as the Valcottan prince climbed down a rope, jumping the last bit to land with a splash in the water. Swimming easily to the beach, he waded out of the channel, clothes clinging to his massive form as he drew his sword. In the shadow of the cliff, Keris could now see the other man's face clearly in the torchlight, feral delight gleaming in his dark eyes.

Bermin was going to enjoy this.

"The arrow would have been more pleasant," Bermin said, stopping before him. "Your desire to live a few minutes more will cost you dearly."

"It would cost me more to die swiftly."

The prince spat into the water. "You will be only the first to fall to my blade, Veliant. Soon all of Maridrina will bleed."

Motion on the cliff caught his eye, and Keris smiled because, of course, she hadn't listened. He'd been an idiot to believe that she would. "If that was your goal, you shouldn't have killed Kian and his men."

"And why is that?" Bermin asked, resting his sword blade against Keris's neck.

A wild laugh escaped Keris's lips as screams filtered down from the cliff tops, but it was a clarion voice from behind him that answered. "Because they might have fought for you, cousin. Whereas now, you must fight me alone."

33
ZARRAH

BERMIN'S EYES LATCHED ON ZARRAH AS SHE WALKED DOWN THE beach toward him, the clash of weapons and screams of the injured as battle raged on the cliff tops seeming distant with her cousin's sword pressed to Keris's neck.

"You honorless bitch," her cousin hissed. "You attack your own people. Does your treason know no bounds?"

Zarrah made a face and swung her spear in her hand, limbering her tense muscles. "Pot calling the kettle black, cousin. You made a deal with these Valcottans"—she gestured to the fallen corpses— "and then slaughtered them."

"They were convicts."

"If they weren't worth giving your word to, you should not have done so." She lifted her chin. "You're the honorless one, Bermin. Proven again by the fact you'd kill a bound man on his knees."

Bermin's face twisted with disgust. "He's the king of Maridrina, Zarrah. Valcotta's mortal enemy. The same blood as the man who murdered *your* mother and my aunt, never mind the countless other Valcottans the Veliants have slaughtered. You swore an oath to fight to the death in the Endless War, but you slaughter Valcotta's soldiers to save your *lover*."

"I swore an oath to defend Valcotta against her enemies," she corrected. "To protect our people and raise Valcotta up high, which is *exactly* what I'm doing. As long as the Endless War rages on, Valcotta suffers needlessly, and there is no sacrifice I won't make to stop it in its tracks."

"Liar," her cousin said with a smirk. "My mother might be insane, but she was right to say that this one"—he tapped the edge of his blade against Keris's neck—"has a hold on you that will never cease until he's dead. You are his plaything, his puppet, and if you ever sat on the throne, he'd rule Valcotta from between your thighs."

Zarrah clenched her teeth, refusing to allow him to goad her.

"Are you that good?" Bermin asked Keris. "Or is she just so desperate for love that she'll take it where she can get it?"

Keris made no response, and Zarrah wished she could see his face so that she might know what he was thinking. What he was planning.

This is your plan, she silently chastised herself. *Quit waiting for Keris to lead.*

She took a step closer, then froze as Bermin said, "Stay where you are, or your lover dies."

Her cousin was stalling; she knew that. Just as she knew that Daria's warriors could not defeat so many heavily armed soldiers, especially if reinforcements arrived. She needed to disarm Bermin and get Keris up that rope while there was still time for flight.

"You afraid to fight me?" she asked, hoping to bait him, but Bermin only laughed. "Fool me once, shame on you, little Zarrah. But fool me twice—"

She threw her spear.

Her aim was true. The weapon shot toward her cousin's face, but for all his failings, Bermin was a warrior through and through. With a snarl, he lifted his blade and knocked the spear from the air before cutting downward at Keris's neck.

To find empty air.

Keris kept rolling as Zarrah charged, snatching up Kian's fallen sword. Her blade met Bermin's with a clash, the strength of his blow making her arm shudder, but she held her ground.

Her cousin did not.

Cursing, he backed away, eyes flicking to the cliff tops. Zarrah barked out a laugh, driving him away from Keris, who was furiously sawing at the rope using a dead man's knife wedged between two rocks. "For all your talk about taking your mother's crown, you're afraid of her," she sneered. "That's why you don't just kill me and be done with that. That's why you need to resort to dishonorable trickery to try to undermine me."

"You undermine yourself," her cousin retorted. "You're a silly little woman who betrayed her empress and nation for a man. My mother might think you redeemable, but I know better. Destroying him won't change anything, because you are weak. Because you are a pawn. Because you were made to be used by others, not to lead."

Zarrah's arm trembled, fury rising in her chest. Except it was being lifted by the fear that he was right.

Silence him, her rage demanded. *Put him in the ground.*

"You never change, little Zarrah." Bermin's eyes flicked to the cliff tops, then back to her. "So high on your own ideals, with no realization that every one of them has been planted in your mind by another."

Something in her mind snapped, and Zarrah attacked.

To fight while she was so angry was the path to an early grave, but Zarrah could no more rein in her sword arm than she could the emotions in her chest. *Silence him!* her wrath shrieked, the intensity of her need giving her strength.

And speed.

Before Bermin could react, she slashed at his ribs, blade cutting deep into the leather of his armor. He hissed but instead of recoiling, swung at her unarmored chest.

But Zarrah was already twisting away.

He stumbled when his blade found empty air, and she stepped past him, the tip of her blade scoring deep into his thigh.

Bermin howled, his toe catching on a rock and sending him sprawling, weapon flying out of his grip. He rolled, reaching for it, but her sword was already cutting down at his exposed spine.

A hand closed around her wrist, stopping the blow. "If you kill him, she'll use him as a martyr," Keris said softly, his breath brushing her ear and making her chest tighten. "He can do more damage dead than alive, and I know that you know that."

"Giving her instructions already?" Bermin laughed, blood trickling from where the tip of her sword pressed into his throat. "Little Zarrah never has a thought for herself. What, pray tell, does the king of Maridrina want her to do?"

Kill him. Kill him kill him kill him.

"Ignore him," Keris said, and she shivered as his unshaven cheek touched hers. "He knows she'll never forgive this. That she'll name a dog her heir before him. That his only chance to be remembered as anything other than a failure is martyrdom."

"So obedient," Bermin said. "That was what she always said about you, little Zarrah. That you listened. That you did as you were told. My mother wanted someone who would follow her instructions even when she was in the grave. Her puppet. His puppet. The rebels' puppet."

Tears ran down her cheeks, her sword arm shaking.

"Zarrah, we need to go. Reinforcements will come."

"Shut up," she snarled. And though she knew it made her sound like a child, she added, "Don't tell me what to do!"

Bermin tilted his head back and laughed. "You might not see the strings attached to you, cousin, but they are there. So many little strings making you dance and dance—"

She screamed and lifted her sword, but instead of slashing it down on Bermin's throat, she drew back a foot and kicked him as hard as she could between the legs.

He squealed in agony, folding in on himself, but she was already turning away. "We need to get up that cliff," she said to Keris, her voice emotionless. "Much of your plan is still in play, only we've lost the element of surprise."

Keris only cast a backward glance at Bermin before heading to the channel. He paused long enough to collect some weapons, tucking them into his boots and belt, then, without a word, swam out into the channel to the floating rope. He climbed, not once looking down.

"You'll be back in his bed before dawn," Bermin shrieked. "You won't be able to help yourself, little Zarrah."

A quiver ran through her body, but instead of allowing her rage to drive her to react, Zarrah stepped out into the icy water, swimming across the channel as the current pulled her toward the rope.

Her body trembled as she heaved herself up, climbing toward the still-raging battle, Keris having already disappeared over the top. But just before she reached the summit, she heard Bermin shriek, "You'll never be your own master, Zarrah! Not while you're Maridrina's whore."

He was right.

Swallowing down the truth, Zarrah rolled over the top of the cliff and, blade in hand, threw herself into the chaos.

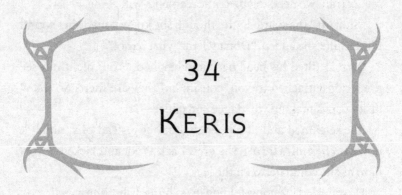

34

KERIS

THE ONLY GOOD THING ABOUT CLIMBING INTO A NIGHTMARE was that it gave him no chance to think about the one left below.

Bodies were strewn everywhere, some still, some screaming and clutching spurting wounds. For a heartbeat, he was frozen; then a man in a Valcottan uniform ran screaming toward him, and instinct took over.

Jerking one of his purloined weapons free of his belt, Keris met the attack with a crash of metal. Only the endless lessons Otis had forced upon him kept the Valcottan from killing him instantly, but for once, Keris didn't hold back.

He couldn't afford to.

There is no sacrifice I won't make to stop it in its tracks. Her words filled his head as he parried blow after blow, then plunged his blade through the man's guts.

Was that the only reason she'd come for him? To end the war?

The man dropped at his feet, screaming, but Keris refused to allow himself to feel anything. Only lifted his weapon to attack another soldier, driving them back to make space for Zarrah to climb over.

If she was even climbing.

Shut up! Her snarl echoed through his thoughts, and he flinched, feeling her rage even as he engaged another soldier. The man was already bleeding from another wound, weak and staggering, and Keris mechanically stabbed him before glancing over his shoulder.

"Keris!" Aren's voice reached his ears over the chaos, and he caught sight of the taller man, Daria defending his back. Both were blood splattered, but very much alive.

"We need to go!" Aren shouted. "We need to get off this island before they signal the naval vessels!"

"Where is Zarrah?" Daria demanded.

She hadn't climbed over the edge. Had she gone back to finish Bermin? What if he'd attacked her? Hurt her? What if she'd fallen in the water?

He needed to go back.

"Keris, we need to go!"

Ignoring Aren, he raced to the edge of the cliff, ready to jump over, but then she appeared.

Rolling over the rocky lip, Zarrah was on her feet, weapon immediately in hand. Without even looking, she raced past him. "Get across the bridge! Go!"

Orders were shouted all around. By Valcottans, by prisoners, by Aren and Zarrah.

It was madness, people rushing every direction. Soldiers and prisoners alike fighting and dying.

He tripped over bodies, fell, then was on his feet. Hunting for her familiar shape, trying to find her in the growing darkness. Trying to find Aren. Trying to find Daria.

"It's the Veliant king," a Valcottan screamed. "Kill him! Kill the rat!"

Keris lashed out wildly, the tip of his blade scoring the man's arm, but he didn't seem to feel it. The soldier collided with him, both of them falling on a carpet of bodies, Keris's sword spinning out of his hand. "Kill the rat!" the man shrieked, swiping at him with a knife.

The tip slammed into the ground next to Keris's ear, and he caught the man's wrist, grappling with him.

They rolled over bodies and rocks, and then Keris's hand found a knife.

He slammed the tip into the soldier's face, the man's scream deafening him, but then another body fell across Keris's shoulders, pinning him as the man beneath him screamed, "My eye! My eye!"

Panic surged, blood soaking his clothes, getting in his mouth. So many screams, so much noise, and he had no idea where anyone was.

Had no idea where Zarrah was.

Keris heaved upward, rolling the corpse off his back and batting away the dying man's hands. Someone dove at him, and he lifted his blade, the tip sinking into flesh and fresh screams rattling his skull.

A blade whistled down in front of his face, and he fell backward, landing on his ass.

Fight, he screamed at himself. *Get up.*

But all he could do was sit in the pile of blood and bodies of men that he'd killed, the battle a swirl of shapes and shadows around him.

Where is she?

"Keris!" Daria's voice jerked him back into the moment, and then the rebel's face was in front of him. "Are you hurt?"

Was he? His eyes skipped over the bodies of his victims. How many? How many lives had he snuffed out in the space of a few moments to save himself?

"Get up!"

He allowed Daria to drag him upward, following as she carved through anyone who stepped in her path, somehow knowing where to go in the darkness and chaos.

Out of the turmoil, Aren appeared. "Get across! We need to cut the ropes so they can't pursue!"

Where is she? His lips felt numb, incapable of speaking, but he must have gotten the words out because Aren shook his head. "I don't know, but there's no more time. We're going to lose this fight."

He couldn't leave her. He wouldn't leave her.

Ripping out of Daria's grip, he screamed, "Zarrah! Zarrah!"

"She's on the other side!" Hands grabbed his arms, and he fought against them. "Keris, it's Daria! It's Daria! Zarrah is across the bridge!"

His arms fell slack at his sides, and he turned in a circle, tasting blood. Spitting, he wiped his sleeve across his mouth, but it was soaked with more of the same. He was drenched in it.

"Go! Go!" Aren shouted.

Hands pulled on the front of his shirt, hauling him onto the bridge. The ropes burned his palms as he clung to them for balance, his toes catching on the boards, threatening to spill him into the water that rushed below.

"Cut the ropes!"

"Arrows! They're shooting! Run!"

He was running, a female hand gripping his own tightly as they stumbled through the blackness. But instead of fleeing the screams, instead of leaving them behind, the piercing wails grew louder. Keris jerked his hand free, stopping to press his palms to his ears, only to cringe because they were sticky with blood.

Where is she?

He turned in a circle, searching the shadows, his head full of fog.

Then an arm slung around his shoulder, tugging him forward. "Night battles are ugly," Aren said, tone as light as though they were abandoning a rowdy tavern for a better location. "But the darkness is going to give us the cover we need to get to the other side of it. Smart thinking getting Bermin to climb down, by the way. I'm convinced you could talk your way into a deal with the Devil and then back out of it again."

"He's still alive."

"The Devil?"

Keris frowned, the fog that had taken hold of his brain clearing. "Bermin, you jackass. Petra doesn't need a martyr to bolster her cause."

"Good thinking." Aren pounded him on the back, then pressed ahead. "Saam? Where do we stand?"

It was Zarrah's voice that responded.

"Bermin's force is regrouping," she called out of the darkness. "Look, you can see the torches. They'll move around the spiral, and we need to stay ahead of them. We cannot linger."

"She's right," Daria said. "There will be no mercy if we're caught, only slaughter. We need to cross the next bridge."

"The next bridge will be guarded," Aren said, "and there's every chance they'll cut the ropes if they see us coming."

"Then we keep going around the spiral," Zarrah suggested.

"More than half my people are injured," Daria answered. "We can't move fast enough."

Keris walked toward their voices, his eyes drifting over the dark shadows huddled on the ground, the air thick with moans of pain and terrified weeping. Children weeping.

He moved closer, recognizing Zarrah's shadow by the way she

moved, his chest constricting because she was so near and yet still so far.

"The remaining guards at the pier will have heard the horns," Aren said. "They'll know that things didn't go as Bermin intended and will have signaled the navy. We have to get to the pier before those ships do, or they'll drive my ship off."

The debate continued, and rather than subjecting himself to the growing certainty that they'd escaped from the frying pan and moved into the fire, Keris walked around the mass of people, heading alone up the pathway to the next bridge.

He increased his stride, the noise of argument and the moans of the injured fading behind him, and he looked up at the sky. With no torchlight, the stars were a sea of brilliant sparks. Stories of the past, if you believed the Cardiffians, and he wondered if new stories were ever added. Wondered if the skies above would change to tell the story of this moment, where they'd come so close to escape only to fail.

Probably not.

The path rose up a slope, and he paused at the summit to survey the bridge that sat a hundred yards away. With the injured in their ranks, the bridge was the fastest route to get everyone across to the steps leading down to the pier, but judging from the glowing torches and mass of gathered soldiers on the far side, they'd get no farther.

Climbing onto a large rock, Keris sat unmoving, and in the darkness and silence, he heard familiar footsteps approach.

35

ZARRAH

SHE LEFT DARIA AND AREN ENGAGED IN AN ARGUMENT OVER what they should do while others tended to the wounded, preparing them to move. She needed to be away from the noise of too many commanders and not enough soldiers, something she'd experienced often in her career. It never turned out well.

Strange as it might seem to some, the battle had given her peace, for it had driven away all thought beyond the fight. Given her clarity of purpose that was now seeping away with what lingered of her adrenaline as she faced the direness of their situation.

Keris had come for her.

He was here.

They were together.

And yet she still felt a thousand miles away from him.

Her breathing accelerated, her mind struggling to sort through the violent twist of emotions. Failing, because she felt *too* much, parts of her at war with themselves so that it felt like she was slipping into madness.

"Breathe," she told herself. "Focus on getting off this island alive."

Wasted words. She was *drowning* in emotion. Zarrah had prepared for a thousand moments on this island, but not one of them had been how she'd react to being back in Keris's presence, because she'd believed what her aunt had said. That he wasn't coming.

But he had.

Keris was here, and Zarrah wasn't sure if she wanted to throw herself into his arms or run as far and fast from him as she could.

Enough! She bit down on the insides of her cheeks hard enough that she tasted blood. *Focus.*

Pausing at the crest of the small slope, Zarrah used the cover of darkness to observe their next obstacle. This was what her mind needed to devote itself to. Coming up with a plan to get as many people as possible off this island alive.

"Thank you."

Zarrah jumped, drawing her weapon as she whirled to attack the shadow sitting on the rock next to the trail. Only to draw her blade up short.

Keris.

Her body trembled with unspent energy, knees feeling as though they might fail her as she took a steadying breath. *Say something. Anything.* "Why are you thanking me?"

"You could already be off the island," he said. "All the dead would be alive, all the injured whole, none of you trapped in this situation. I should probably tell you that you were a fool to come after me, but having faced death, I find I don't have a taste for it. So thank you."

In the time they'd been apart, his voice had haunted her, asleep and awake, but there was nothing like the reality of the velvet tone of it. The voice that had both inspired and destroyed her, and Zarrah's chest tightened painfully even as her pulse roared, panic climbing. For there was no denying that she was drawn to him like iron to a lodestone. While her aunt may have been wrong about Keris coming for her, the way Zarrah felt right now proved her aunt's words that he had a hold on her. "We still face death," she finally said, her voice stilted. "So gratitude is premature."

"Even so."

A response with more than one meaning, and Zarrah's hackles rose with the reminder that words were Keris's greatest weapon, and that he twisted them as readily as he used them to slice. "I want to bring peace to Valcotta, and you are integral to that."

"You say that as though I weren't with you when that dream was conceived. As though we weren't once allies in trying to make it reality."

So high on your own ideals—Bermin's admonition filled her head—*with no realization that every one of them has been planted in your mind by another.*

Zarrah's heart was beating wildly, and she wanted to claw through her skull to extract all the voices inside of her mind screaming that no thought she'd ever had was her own. That her dreams were visions planted in her mind by those who wished to manipulate her. It felt like insanity, but it also felt like the truth. It made her want to fall to her knees and scream for all of them to be silent.

"I'm sorry for all of this," he said. "By the time I learned Serin knew about us, it was too late to stop the message he'd sent to Petra. I didn't know what to do or how to help you, and I . . . I underestimated how angry she'd be. I knew there would be consequences, but . . ." He hesitated. "The moment I knew she'd sent you here, I made plans to go to Ithicana to gain their help."

Zarrah stared at his shadow, so many words needing to pour from her lips that they clogged her throat, and she said nothing at all.

"I know you're angry about how I ruined your plans at Southwatch, but I've made amends with Ithicana. With Aren and with my sister. I've tried to fix things, tried to undo the damage I did." He rose from the rock he was seated upon. "Not that it matters much, given where we stand. I should have waited. Should have trusted Lara to find a way in, but I was afraid I'd be too late."

"My aunt said you were sleeping with Lestara. Revels. Orgies. That you'd forgotten me." Immediately, Zarrah bit down on her tongue. Why, of all the things, had that been what had come from her lips? She knew, of course. Though she'd no right to think of it so, learning he'd been with other women had felt like infidelity, a betrayal of the heart, and it had cut her deep. Not only to be replaced, but to be replaced so quickly, as though what had been between them hadn't mattered at all.

"What? Orgies?" He gave a violent shake of his head. "Either she lied or her spies put stock in untrue rumors." Keris took hold of her shoulders, his hands hot through the fabric of her wet clothes. "There is no one but you. How could there be when you hold my heart?"

A quiver ran through Zarrah's body, the desire to fall into his arms so strong she could scarcely breathe. Instead she stood frozen, trying to unravel the twisted mess of lies and truth, speculation and reality, but it felt tangled beyond salvaging.

"Zarrah, I need you to know that I love you."

"You don't know what love is." The accusation slipped from her lips, more reflex than thought, because she couldn't do this. Couldn't have this conversation while the stakes were so high. "I can't. I can't deal with this right now. I need to be able to think clearly."

Whether she meant about him or the situation, Zarrah didn't know.

Keris stood unmoving. Silent. Then he said, "We should turn our attention to how we are going to get off this island, for it does not appear anyone else has answers."

"Agreed," she rasped, the world swimming in and out of focus.

"I assume the only reason they haven't cut the bridge ropes is because Bermin is over here."

"He's alive," she said, confirming the unspoken question. Her heart steadied as she refocused on strategy. "His soldiers will have pulled him up before they started back around the spiral to pursue us."

"Shame," Keris murmured. "Part of me hoped he'd have to spend time alone on that island with the many faces of Flay."

He was trying to ease the tension, trying to get her to relax, but the fact that he knew precisely how to do so only made her anxiety worse. "The soldiers standing between us and freedom won't know if he's alive or dead, though. Bermin's force has given no signal beyond the horns for a prison break, so if we approach, they'll cut the bridge. Even if they don't, we'd lose half our force to arrows trying to get across."

"Continue around the spiral, then?"

She shook her head. "With the injured, that will take hours. They'll have signaled the navy ships patrolling the island by now. If they reach us before we reach the pier, it's over for us."

"That leaves only retreat in the channels."

She exhaled, shaking her head, because more than half of the prisoners were injured. Between the plunge into the violent rapids, the cold, and the fact most couldn't swim, far too many would die. "No," she muttered, because it *had* to be the bridge. There was no other way to rescue the injured. Her eyes trailed over the soldiers illuminated by torchlight. If escape could not be won by force, it had to be won by duplicity. "Bermin hasn't once tried to kill me, likely because my aunt has given him strict orders that I be kept alive. What are the chances that every guard on this island hasn't been given the same instruction?"

"What precisely are you proposing?"

He'd fight this plan. Do his best to convince her of another route forward, even if it resulted in everyone else dying so that she might live. Zarrah refused to allow that to happen again, so she turned on her heel, walking swiftly to intercept the larger party before they crested the rise. Aren walked with Daria at the front of the group, the tension between the two palpable. "I've a plan," she said, explaining the situation at the bridge and her gambit.

"It's too risky," Daria muttered. "You're banking your life on them not shooting first and begging the empress for forgiveness later."

"I'm only one life."

"A life that everyone here has risked themselves for," Keris snapped.

She turned to see that he had come silently up from behind. His face was hidden by the darkness, but she could feel displeasure radiating from him, and her irritation rose that once again, he was putting her life before others. That once again, he would refuse to acknowledge the merits of her plan because it put her in jeopardy.

Which meant he might well try to sabotage it.

"This isn't Maridrina. Or Ithicana," she added, seeing Aren's shadow cross its arms. "It is Valcotta, and every Valcottan here has recognized my authority. I choose to use that authority to enact a plan that will get my people out alive."

She'd not allow her people to die for the sake of keeping herself out of danger. It wasn't who she was.

"Not minutes ago, you apologized for your actions at Southwatch, yet I can tell you're conspiring to do the exact same thing again," she said, keeping a careful distance from Keris. "Give me your word that you won't interfere."

"No." Keris's shadow shook its head. "I'll not put myself in the position of having to make a foolish decision just to honor my word. We'll try your plan, but as you have said many times yourself, not even the best-laid strategies go smoothly."

He turned back down the path, and once he was out of sight, Daria whistled. "You told no lies, Zarrah. He'll risk everything and everyone but you. It's admirable. And damnable."

"It's fucking infuriating." She looked to Aren. "Don't let him interfere."

He didn't answer.

"We need to move." She gestured to the torchlight moving outward around the spiral. "Bermin and his remaining forces will reach us soon, and we need to be on the other side of that bridge before they do. Gather everyone fit to fight."

There was no hesitation, those who could carry a weapon gathering while the rest assisted the injured.

"Stay out of sight until my signal," she said to the injured, then started down the path, sword in hand.

Her pulse throbbed steadily as she allowed herself to sink into the moment, everything else fading away as she approached the large stone mooring posts to which the bridge was anchored, torchlight glowing atop both of them. On the far side, a mass of soldiers scanned the darkness, expressions tense and their weapons in hand.

"Halt," the leader among them shouted as she stepped into the pool of light, at least a dozen archers training their arrows on her.

"My name is Zarrah Anaphora," she shouted. "Daughter of Princess Aryana Anaphora and niece to Empress Petra Anaphora."

She held her breath, waiting for the soldiers to react. Waiting for the proof that her aunt had given orders that she not be harmed, for if she had not, one of those arrows would swiftly find her heart.

Mutters spread among the men and women, none lowering their weapons. "Where is Prince Bermin?" the leader called. "Why aren't you with him?"

"He was injured," she responded, stopping just before she reached the bridge moorings. "His men are bringing him around the spiral, for the first bridge was cut to contain the prisoners."

Answers that were full of holes. Something all the soldiers realized, given none lowered their weapons. But neither had they killed her, and her confidence grew.

"Put down your weapon," their captain called to her, and when she obliged, he gestured for several of the soldiers to cross.

Zarrah's chest tightened painfully as she watched them cross over the channel. Valcottans, the very people she had sworn to protect. Soldiers who were only following the orders of their empress, who had caused no harm to her, and yet . . .

She lifted her hand.

Arrows shot past her, punching through leather and flesh. The soldiers screamed, several toppling off the bridge to fall into the channel below while others attempted to run back to cover.

Only for arrows to take them in the back.

"Take cover!" the captain shouted. "Cut the ropes."

Zarrah stepped out onto the bridge, walking until she reached the center, where she stopped, the structure swaying beneath her weight. The captain stared at her in horror even as he caught hold of the arm of the soldier who had been about to slice the mooring ropes.

"Put down your weapons, and you'll be spared," she said as her companions raced down to the bridge. "Surrender."

"Are you mad?" he shouted. "The prisoners on this island are more beasts than men. Killers and rapists and cannibals, and you'd set them loose on the world?"

"These people were unlawfully imprisoned by the empress because they dared to criticize her," Zarrah countered as the bridge shook, the rebels pouring onto it. "This is your last chance. Surrender or die."

"The empress was right to send you here," the captain hissed. "You are a traitor to your people, and I will personally throw you back on that island, where if there is justice, you'll spend the balance of your days."

"So be it," Zarrah answered, right as Saam and Daria pushed past her, weapons in hand.

"Kill them," the captain roared, "but leave the traitor alive!"

Archers crouched behind stone barricades loosed arrows, and Zarrah clenched her teeth as screams filled the night, every instinct demanding that she join the fight. Except she was the only thing that was keeping the soldiers from cutting the bridge ropes, so she held her ground as her friends threw themselves into the fray.

Aren passed her, ducking as an arrow whistled past his head. "Bermin is nearly upon us."

Horns sounded, so close it was all Zarrah could do not to look back.

"They're coming!" shouts echoed from behind her, the air filling with cries of terror. "We need to cross!"

"Not yet!" she shouted. "Give them time to secure the opposite side!"

"Shoot them!" the captain yelled. "Secure the traitor!"

Bowstrings twanged, and prisoners screamed.

"Hold your ground!" She half turned to see them massed well within bow shot, the torches held by Bermin's forces drawing closer by the second. The children, the infirm, and the injured were caught between her cousin and the cliff top, pushing closer despite the arrows flying across the channel.

Then she heard Keris shout, "Rocks!"

The rebels behind her all lifted their arms and threw, a wave of small rocks flying overhead to smash into the archers. Many fell short. Others struck the stone barriers. But some aimed true, screams of pain rising from the archers as they were struck.

"Again!" Keris shouted, and more rocks flew. "Go! Hurry!"

No. No no no! They hadn't secured the far side of the bridge. It would be certain slaughter.

"No!" she screamed at the rebels, the children wide-eyed as they clung to the hands of their mothers. "Go back!"

Then a roar of voices filled the air, coming from the far side of the raging battle. "In the name of the True Empress, attack!"

The battle paused as both sides lifted their heads, staring in shock as another force appeared. It was at least one hundred strong, all heavily armed, and for a heartbeat, panic filled her veins that the navy was already here. Except none of them wore uniforms, and fairer-skinned individuals peppered their ranks. Then her eyes latched onto the familiar face of a blond woman running at their head.

It was Lara.

An unfamiliar Valcottan man ran at the Ithicanian queen's side, and he shouted, "Fight for your freedom! Fight for the rightful empress!"

Then all was chaos.

But it was not to the battle that Zarrah looked, but behind. Racing toward them were Bermin and eight soldiers. A paltry force, but more than enough to defeat the one man who stood between them and the escaping prisoners.

Keris.

"Goddammit!" Swinging over the side of the bridge so as not to impede the flow of escaping injured, Zarrah edged back to the cliff top. Leaping the last bit of distance, she raced up the slope and skidded to a stop next to Keris.

"We cannot fight them alone on open ground," she said, hauling on his arm. "We have to . . ." Words stalled on her tongue as she looked backward. The bridge was full of injured who could go no farther, for beyond was a teeming mass of people trapped by the battle. Several tried to press sideways down the cliff tops, only to be jostled, and Zarrah clenched her teeth as they fell, screaming, into the water.

And there was no swift victory in sight.

Everyone is going to die because of you.

Grinding her teeth, Zarrah forced the thought from her head right as Bermin leveled a finger at them. "You didn't get very far, little Zarrah. You never were very good at cutting your losses."

"Retreat to the bridge," she said to Keris under her breath.

Keris didn't argue, walking backward with her as Bermin closed the distance. Her cousin's face was slick with sweat, and given the awkward hunch of his body, it was from pain, not exertion. Yet his voice was steady as he said, "Trapped once again. Makes you wonder if there is some truth to the Devil claiming the souls of all who walk this ground."

"It has certainly claimed yours," she answered. "And it didn't have to be this way. You could've chosen to be better than her."

Bermin huffed out a breath. "Enough stalling, Zarrah. It's over. Surrender and I'll allow you to live."

"You think I care about my life?"

"Surrender, and I'll allow *him* to live," he countered.

"Zarrah," Keris warned as Bermin's men moved to flank them.

"I'll allow the prisoners to go back to the island," Bermin said, moving closer. "On my honor, just lay down your weapons and surrender."

A roar filled her ears, deafening her. "No!"

"Fine," Bermin snarled.

But as he did, Keris caught hold of her arm and hissed, "Run."

There was nowhere *to* run.

Yet as he twisted her around, Zarrah saw the bridge clearing, the injured rebels hurrying through a gap carved in the battle by the newly joined forces.

She and Keris raced toward the bridge, Bermin's boots pounding in pursuit. Ahead, the last few injured were struggling onto the far side. Keris's feet hit the bridge, then hers. They just needed to get across it—

A weight slammed into her back, crushing the thought and what hope she had of escaping this alive.

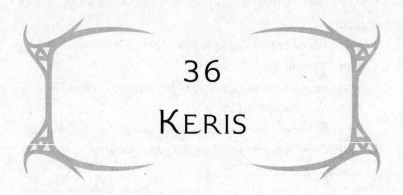

36
KERIS

ZARRAH SLAMMED INTO HIS BACK, KNOCKING HIM FROM HIS FEET and sending the bridge swinging sideways. Keris rolled, and suddenly there were no longer planks of wood beneath his body.

Only open air.

He grasped wildly, hand latching onto a rope and his shoulder nearly dislocating as he fell to dangle from one arm beneath the bridge. Below him was only blackness, but Keris could hear the water. Knew that the prison was doing its best to pull him back to its heart.

It was going to have to try harder.

Reaching up, Keris caught hold of the rope with his other hand. Through the planks, he could see Bermin had Zarrah pinned beneath his tremendous bulk of muscle, close to triple her weight and crushing her.

Anger chased away reason, and reaching up, Keris caught hold of Bermin's sword belt. Then he allowed his weight to drop. The other man grunted in surprise as he was pulled sideways, catching his balance with a rope. But not before Zarrah took advantage.

Wriggling out from under him, she rolled onto her back and kicked, heels catching Bermin in the face even as Keris heaved, using the man's belt to pull himself back onto the bridge.

"You bitch," Bermin shrieked, reaching blindly. Zarrah scrabbled backward.

But not quick enough.

Bermin caught her ankle, spinning her sideways so that she was dangling upside down from the bridge.

"I'll drop her," Bermin said. "Don't think that I won't."

Keris went still.

Behind him, Bermin's soldiers were easing onto the bridge, and once they reached the skirmish, this was over. They'd throw Keris over the edge and take Zarrah prisoner, then cut the ropes to keep the others from coming to their aid.

He needed to take away that option.

Ripping the knife in his boot free, he sawed at one of the mooring ropes. As it started to fray, he shoved the blade between his teeth and swung beneath the bridge.

The mooring rope snapped, the bridge tipping sideways and spilling one of the soldiers into the water. Bermin shouted, scrambling for a handhold.

And letting go of Zarrah.

She screamed, but Keris caught her with his legs, her weight nearly pulling him loose. Her hands clawed at him before latching onto his belt, her ankles hooking around his neck. Upside down, she clung to him. "Hold on," he shouted, the blade between his teeth cutting his tongue.

"As though I have a goddamn choice!"

The bridge swung from side to side as Bermin's soldiers struggled to keep their grip on the tipped planks, Bermin clutching the mooring ropes with one hand and reaching wildly for Keris with the other. Keris edged away from him, his arms shuddering from the strain of supporting his own weight and Zarrah's as the bridge swung back and forth.

Bermin crawled after him. "I'm going to kill you both," he snarled. "Rid the world of you, to hell with what she says. She doesn't control me!"

A thousand quips about mothers, sons, and apron strings filled Keris's head, but he couldn't speak clearly with a dagger clenched between his teeth.

Zarrah abruptly heaved on his belt and unhooked one of her ankles from around his neck. Keris shouted as his trousers edged over his hips, but then she had a leg over one of the mooring ropes, her ass hitting him in the face each time the bridge bounced.

"Climb!" he shouted, again cutting his tongue, blood dripping down his chin. But it didn't matter as Zarrah's body strained upward, fingers latching onto the rope.

"Got it!"

Her weight disappeared from him, and letting go with one hand, Keris took hold of his knife. Spitting blood, Keris sawed at one of the three remaining moorings, laughing wildly as it snapped and the whole bridge twisted, spilling two more soldiers into the water, though the prince held on.

Only two ropes to go.

Bermin's face twisted, seeing Keris's plan, and he crawled along the bouncing length of boards and rope, reaching.

"Get to the other side!" Keris shouted at Zarrah.

But Bermin was moving faster.

Ignoring Keris, he reached for Zarrah's ankle, cursing when she kicked him but then catching hold of her boot.

Keris let go with one hand to use his knife to slash at the prince, but the weapon only glanced off the man's leather armor.

"Cut the ropes!" Zarrah shouted, struggling to get free of her cousin's grip. "Hurry!"

Keris sawed at another rope as above him Zarrah warred with Bermin over her boot, the bridge jerking from side to side, doing its best to spill all three of them into the water below.

The rope abruptly snapped, and everything dropped with a jerk, a single remaining mooring stretched between cliffs the only thing holding them above the water.

And Keris hanging nose to nose with Bermin.

"Stab him!" Zarrah screamed from where she dangled, but his knife had been lost to the water below.

Bermin reached for Keris, fingers catching hold of his sleeve. "You're going to kill us both, you idiot!" Keris shouted, but Bermin only grinned.

"I will go to the Great Thereafter with honor because I do so sending you to hell."

His fingers tightened on Keris's sleeve, clearly intending to use his weight to rip both of them from the bridge and send them plunging to their deaths.

Then an arrow sliced between them, severing the last remaining rope.

For a heartbeat, Bermin's grip on his sleeve kept them together; then the fabric tore.

Keris sucked in a desperate breath as he and Bermin fell away from each other, his fingers squeezing the rope as he dropped with terrifying speed toward the water below.

Zarrah.

His fall ceased with a jerk that nearly pulled his shoulders from their sockets, his body swinging into the cliff wall, the impact almost breaking his grip on the dangling end of the bridge.

Zarrah.

His eyes shot skyward, finding her clinging to the tangled ropes and boards of the bridge just above him.

A roar of fury stole Keris's attention. On the opposite side, Bermin hung from the other half of the bridge. He was climbing, massive arms bulging as he raced toward the top, where his two remaining soldiers peered over the edge.

"Climb, Keris!" Aren yelled from above. "We need to get off this damn island!"

Ignoring the pain in his arms, Keris dragged himself up.

Thunk!

Zarrah cursed, and Keris risked an upward glance to see an arrow embedded in the wood next to her hand.

"Bermin is pulling arrows out of corpses," Aren shouted. "Shoot the soldiers, not the prince!"

Faster.

The rough boards tore the skin from his hands, but Keris didn't feel the pain. Felt only the fear of having gotten so close, only to lose her in a way that there would be no chance of rescue.

Thunk!

Another arrow sank into the planks, nearly striking Zarrah's hand. She lost her grip, dangling from one hand as Keris climbed up beside her. Bracing his shoulders against the smooth rock of the cliff, he twisted the bridge so that the boards obscured their shots. "Climb. Keep behind the boards."

"What about you?"

"I'm right behind you." Every inhale he took was filled with her scent, her wind-whipped hair brushing his cheek. "Your people need their rightful empress."

"Why does everyone keep calling me that?"

"Because it's the truth." But this wasn't the moment for revelations. "I'll tell you why when we're out of the thick of this."

She hesitated, then began climbing.

Thunk!

He gritted his teeth as Bermin tried to shoot them through the planks of the bridge. Above him, Zarrah had reached the top, a Valcottan man holding a shield out to protect her as she climbed over. "We've got you, girl," the man said. "You're safe now."

As Keris neared the top, Aren, who was using a corpse as a shield, reached down to haul him over. "We control this side," he said. "All the soldiers are dead, and we've started moving the wounded. Bermin stands alone—Lara shot the other two dead."

Keris barely heard, his eyes searching for Zarrah. Daria and the Valcottan man had her, were drawing her away, the bodies and shields of their fellows blocking her from Bermin but also hiding her from Keris's sight. Without a backward glance, they started down the path to the stairs that would take them to the guard tower and the pier beyond.

"Lara said he's the rebel commander," Aren said. "They joined forces to take the pier, but that's all I know."

"He's out of arrows," Jor said, jerking his chin across the channel. Bermin stood among the fallen, his face lost to shadows, though Keris could feel the man's rage. Alive, which meant he'd have to face his mother's wrath for his multitude of failures.

Eyes on Bermin, Lara approached, a bow hooked over her shoulder, her face and hair splattered with blood. "Are you hurt?"

"I'm fine."

She gave a tight nod. "Let's go, then. The rebels' other ships lured off the navy, but they'll have seen the signal fires and realized it was a ruse. We need to be gone before they reach the pier."

The Ithicanians backed away from the edge, then turned to follow Lara, only Aren remaining. The other man cast Bermin one last appraising look, slung his arm around Keris, and tugged him forward. "We did it. It's over."

Why didn't it feel like it was over?

Keris's skin prickled.

Turning his head, he watched Bermin's shadow rooting among the corpses. Then the massive man straightened, arms lifting in a familiar form, the outline of a bow just barely visible.

There was no time for thought. Even if there had been, it would have changed nothing. Keris twisted out of Aren's grip and stepped between him and Bermin.

Thunk!

The wet noise filled his ears, and Keris's heart plummeted. He hadn't been fast enough. He'd brought Aren here. He'd put him in danger.

He'd gotten him killed.

Bracing himself, Keris turned to find Aren standing before him, unharmed—

And that was when the pain struck.

Burning agony that raced down to his fingertips, and Keris slowly looked to find an arrow jutting out of his shoulder, the purple fletching stained dark with blood.

"Shit!" Aren snarled, reaching for him. "Lara! Keris is hit!"

"It's fine," Keris muttered. "I'm fine."

He dropped to his knees, only Aren's grip on him keeping him from falling over, his ears filling with Lara's scream. Then his sister was in front of him. "No no no!"

"It's not that bad," he told her. "I just need to pull it out."

"Aren, don't let him pull it out." Lara's eyes were full of murder as she stood, moving past him at a run.

Where was she going?

Blood roared in his ears as he abruptly realized her intent. "Aren, stop her!"

The Ithicanian king was already in pursuit. "Lara, no!"

Keris twisted on his knees, the world swimming as he watched

Lara pull an arrow from the quiver on her back, nocking it in her bow. "Lara!" he tried to scream, but it came out as a croak.

She loosed the arrow.

It soared across the deadly gap right as the moon peeked out from behind a cloud, illuminating the arrow as it sank into Bermin Anaphora's throat.

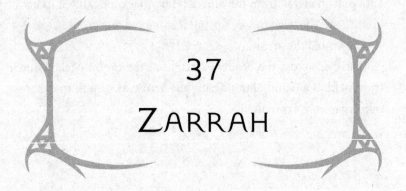

37
ZARRAH

"I'VE GOT YOU, GIRL," A VALCOTTAN MAN SAID AS HE DRAGGED Zarrah over the edge. "You're safe now."

He'd been the one leading the charge at Lara's side. There was something familiar about his voice, his face, but there was little time to think of it as she was drawn away from the ledge. Zarrah glanced backward, but the rebels who'd closed in around her blocked her line of sight.

He came for you, her heart whispered. *He still loves you.*

Instead of filling Zarrah with warmth, that knowledge tightened like a vise around her chest, making it a fight to breathe as her eyes skipped over the bodies of the fallen. He loved her, but it was a love twisted by his blood and upbringing. A love that burned so hot that it destroyed anything that got in its way, leaving ash and death in its wake.

"When our spies learned Petra had sent you here, we made immediate plans for a rescue," the Valcottan man said, his hand pressing against her back as he directed her down the path. "We figured it for a trap, so we came prepared for a fight. Even so, it was good fortune that we crossed paths with the Ithicanians."

Zarrah swallowed the thickness in her throat.

"I'm going ahead to confirm we've started loading the injured, Commander," Daria said, giving Zarrah a grim smile before she jogged forward.

Commander. This man was the leader of the rebel forces.

Yet that revelation went in one ear and out the other as she searched for Keris and found him absent. Zarrah tried to slow her pace, looking over her shoulder, but the press of warriors drove her onward.

The commander gripped her hand. "Once word you are returned to us spreads, warriors will race to join our ranks, and we will rip the crown from the Usurper's head."

Returned to us? She looked at the man's face, again struck by familiarity. "Who are you? What is your name?"

He hesitated, lips opening to answer, but then a distant scream from behind caught Zarrah's attention. Heads turned, but whatever the warriors saw did not cause them to go back. Zarrah tried to see for herself, but the commander's grip on her arm was implacable.

"Commander," a man shouted. "The lights on the navy ships have been spotted, all sailing in fast. We need to hurry."

"There is time for explanations later," the commander said to her. "We need to get on our ship and the Ithicanians on theirs."

They crested the cliff, dark ocean spreading out in all directions. *Freedom.* But that thought vanished as her eyes latched onto the two ships anchored below.

Was this the end?

Not half a day in Keris's presence, and now they'd board separate ships and sail in opposite directions. Would she see him again? Or was this goodbye forever?

Zarrah's feet slowed. There was no future for them together, but she couldn't part ways with him like this. "I need to say goodbye."

The commander looked sharply at her, then pointed out to sea, where glimmering lights drew closer. "Save goodbyes for later or spend eternity together in the grave."

Her eyes burned, but Zarrah wasn't reckless enough to risk more lives for the sake of her sentiments. There was later. There had to be a later.

Moving as fast as they could on the slick steps leading down the cliffs to the guard tower, the group raced through the fortifications and onto the glowing pier stretching out into the ocean. It was littered with corpses in Valcottan uniforms, and her chest tightened.

As though sensing her thoughts, the commander said, "They believe that Petra's reign of terror is inevitable and inescapable, and that is why they keep fighting for her. As the rightful empress, you can give them a different future."

"How am I the rightful empress?"

"Later." Two soldiers caught Zarrah's arms, lifting her into a longboat. "This will all be for nothing if they catch us," one said.

Keris knew. Had said that he'd tell her.

"Everyone in the boat!" Aren's voice reached her, close, though she couldn't see him from this angle. "This is life or death; we have to hurry."

His panic confirmed the rebels' fears, but it wasn't the approaching naval vessels that had her heart pounding. Bending low, Zarrah peered under the pier, seeing the Ithicanian longboat bobbing as they climbed in. Keris had to be less than a dozen feet from her now, but she couldn't see him. "Keris?" she called, but his name caught in her throat, so she tried again. "Keris!"

No answer, only the shouts of Ithicanians and rebels as they filled the boats.

"Row!" the commander ordered, and the boat surged forward.

Zarrah dug her nails into the edge of the boat, her heart beating faster as they drew toward the end of the pier, the Ithicanians rowing hard on the opposite side.

When they reached the end, she'd be able to see him.

The longboat shot out past the end of the pier, bucking and plunging over the waves. Leaning over the edge, Zarrah's eyes locked on the Ithicanian vessel. Much like the one she was in, it was packed with men and women, their faces faintly illuminated by the torches burning on the dock. She found Aren's tall form. He was gesticulating wildly, pointing at the ship, shouting, "Faster!"

Where was Keris?

The vessel drew out of the pool of light, those inside fading to shadowy forms, her chance to see Keris lost.

"We have contacts who do business in Southwatch," the commander said. "We will get word when they return safely. Can send word to them, if you so wish."

Except it wasn't Aren and Lara she was worried about.

She must have muttered as much, because the man said, "The Maridrinian who is with them . . . The Ithicanians didn't tell me who he was, but you called him Keris just now."

Of course Lara hadn't told them Keris's identity. Why would she, given the enmity Valcottans held for her family? But the rebels fought for an end to the Endless War, which had to mean they did not hold such hate for Maridrina. "Your suspicions are correct," she said, watching as Aren's longboat sped toward his ship. "He's Keris Veliant, king of Maridrina." She looked back at the commander. "If you want the Endless War to end, your best chance at achieving it is about to get on that ship."

Everyone who wasn't rowing fell still, silent, the tension ratcheting up higher with each swipe of the oars.

No one spoke, and Zarrah's skin crawled. "What aren't you telling me?"

"He was hit with an arrow," one of the rebels finally said. "I don't think the Maridrinian is long for this world."

Aren's words echoed through her skull even as her chest constricted. *Life or death.*

Zarrah's eyes locked on the other longboat. It had reached the ship, the Ithicanians scrambling up the rope ladder that had been tossed down while others secured lines to the fore and aft of the boat. Only three figures remained inside as it started to rise. Aren's large form. Lara's much smaller one. And . . .

An Ithicanian aboard the ship leaned down with a torch, illuminating the rising boat, and Zarrah's heart stuttered.

Keris's shirt was brilliant red with blood, an arrow jutting terrifyingly close to his throat.

She felt the scream build deep in her core, wild and full of terror as it burst from her lips. "Keris!"

His head lifted, eyes searching the darkness before moving back to his sister. Then he slumped, only Lara's reflexes keeping him from falling.

There wasn't going to *be* a later.

If there were thoughts that came after that realization, Zarrah didn't remember them. Only felt the bite of cold as water closed over her head, the shouts from the rebels a distant drone as she swam toward the Ithicanian ship.

She needed to be away from him to think clearly, to stand on her own feet, but this wasn't what she'd meant. This was a twisting of words, a twisting of sentiment, as though some divine power was mocking her, giving her freedom from love by cutting out her heart.

No! she screamed into the void. *I will not let you have him!*

Waves splashed her in the face, her exhausted body almost spent. "Aren," she shouted, and was rewarded with a mouthful of water. "Lara!"

The longboat had reached the deck rails, Ithicanians lifting Keris onto the ship.

"Aren!"

But Ithicana's king didn't hear her over the shouts of his crew. The noise of the sea. The threat sailing this way.

"Make way," he roared, and panic filled her.

"Keris!" she screamed, reaching for the ship. Knowing this was it, that her chance was slipping through her fingertips.

He turned his head. Searched the water, then pulled from Lara's grasp and fell against the rail, his voice weak as he called out, "Zarrah!"

She had to get to him. Had to help him.

A ladder flew over the edge of the ship, Aren shouting, "Pull her up! They're nearly on us!"

Fueled with a burst of adrenaline, Zarrah drove toward the drifting end of the ladder, reaching fingers snagging the ropes. Her muscles trembled as she pulled herself up it, and as soon as she was clear of the water, the ship lurched.

Gritting her teeth, Zarrah clung to the swinging ladder as those above drew her upward. Then hands had her by the back of her trousers, hauling her over the rail. She landed with a thud on her ass, those who'd lifted her already racing to other tasks.

Zarrah didn't care, not as her eyes found Keris. He was on his knees, Aren holding him upright and Lara shouting, "You have shit for brains, Keris! Why not just throw yourself overboard so I'm spared the trouble of stitching up your idiot self."

If Keris heard his sister's berating, he didn't react. Only pulled against Aren's grip, reaching for Zarrah.

She scrambled on hands and knees, slivers digging into her fingers. But the pain didn't matter as her hands locked with his. "Who did this to you?"

It was Aren who answered. "Bermin."

Bile burned up her throat because she'd had the chance to put her cousin down. Had left him alive for fear of the consequences of killing him, only to pay the price of allowing him to live.

Lara knelt next to Keris, fingers hovering over the arrow where it jutted through the muscle at the top of his shoulder. Another inch to the right, and he'd already be dead. "This idiot decided to jump in front of the arrow."

"Child should meet her father," Keris said between his teeth, swaying sideways as the ship tilted, the sails catching the wind. "If only to better appreciate that her brilliance comes from her mother's side."

Lara is pregnant, Zarrah thought. They'd risked more than she'd realized to help her.

"You're an asshole, Keris," Aren said, but Zarrah didn't miss how his grip on Keris's arms tightened, eyes filled with a mix of gratitude and guilt.

"They're moving to cut us off," someone shouted from above. "Rebels are only raising their sails now—they might not make it!"

Zarrah sucked in a breath, because if the rebels were caught, they'd be executed or imprisoned here. All because they'd risked everything to get to her. All because they seemed to believe she had a claim to the crown, though no one had given an explanation for why.

"Go sail the ship." Keris pushed Aren away from him. "If they catch us only to learn Lara killed their prince . . ."

Bermin was dead?

Zarrah clenched her teeth, cursing the twist of fate that had decided they'd pay for allowing him to live and again for allowing him to die. Yet on the heels of it came the bite of unexpected grief. Bermin was her cousin, and despite their differences, he'd been a near constant in her life. Not only that, he was a victim of Petra as well, her cruelty to him having shaped the man he'd become. Zarrah would have done the same as Lara had if she'd witnessed Keris being shot, but that didn't mean she was without grief that her cousin would never have the chance to redeem himself.

Aren gave Keris a tight nod, then strode to the helm. "No lanterns! We need to lose them in the dark!"

The rest of his orders were a wordless hum. If Lara had killed Bermin, and any witnesses were left alive, it would give her aunt the grounds she needed to one day attack Ithicana.

"What's done cannot be undone," Lara said, as though having heard Zarrah's thoughts. "Help me get him inside before he bleeds to death. Keris, stand up."

Keris said nothing in retort, no quip or rejoinder, and that, more than the shake in his body, filled Zarrah with fear as she slipped under his arm, supporting his weight. The last of the lanterns were extinguished, plunging the vessel into darkness, but above, the moon shone bright, illuminating the ships pursuing them.

She prayed the Ithicanians would live up to their reputation on the high seas, for the navy would not give up easily.

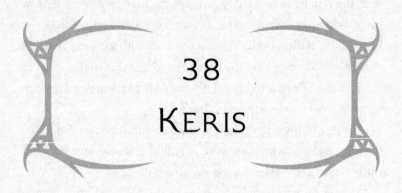

38

KERIS

EACH BREATH HE DREW IN TOOK MORE EFFORT THAN THE LAST, the roar of blood in his ears drowning out the shouts of the Ithicanians. But not the feel of Zarrah against him as she dragged him toward the captain's quarters.

"Why did you leave the rebels?" The expenditure of breath it took to ask left him so lightheaded that stars swam in his eyes.

"Because you—" She broke off, giving her head a sharp shake. "They keep calling me *the rightful empress,* and you said you know why. I need you to tell me."

Lara gave a snort of disgust, but Keris barely heard it over the loud ringing in his ears. When he'd seen Zarrah coming after him, part of him had hoped . . . Keris shoved away the half-completed thought, hiding it beneath forced flippancy as he said, "You needn't have expended the effort. Daria knows the truth, as does the commander."

"They wouldn't tell me, and I . . ." Zarrah averted her eyes. "I'm here, so it might as well come from you."

"Yes, let's interrogate the dying man for information an entire rebellion knows," Lara snarled.

Keris ignored her. "Let's get to it," he said between clenched teeth. "Then you can depart at your earliest convenience."

"Now is not the time!" Lara kicked in the door of the captain's chambers. "I need to get the arrow out and stop the bleeding, or you will die. So shut up."

There was an edge of panic in his sister's voice that told him she wasn't exaggerating, and fear coursed through him. Fear, but also anger. He'd been ready to die to save Zarrah. Ready to die to right a wrong. Hell, he'd been ready to die to save his idiot brother-in-law. But dying now would accomplish nothing and leave so much undone. "She needs to know."

"Later."

"What if I die?"

"Then I'll tell her. Zarrah, help him down."

Zarrah eased him lower, but as she did, the ship switched course, the deck sharply canting in the opposite direction. Pain spidered through him, and the world went dark for a heartbeat. When Keris's vision returned, he was on his side, but what he needed to say was still with him. "Before he died, Serin told me information so that I'd understand why Petra would trust him. The history of their relationship."

"Keris, later," Lara hissed. "Save your strength."

There might not be a later. And he needed to be certain that Zarrah understood that she had a right to the throne. That her legacy had been stolen from her. That she was no one's pawn. "It needs to be now."

"Keris—"

"You have no authority over him, Your Grace," Zarrah said softly. "Nor over me, so be silent."

Lara lunged to her feet, her anger palpable. "I'll get my supplies. Try not to talk yourself to death."

He watched his sister stride to the rear of the captain's cabin and pull the thick drapes before lighting both lamp and brazier. Boots hammered across the deck outside the door, Aren's shouted orders and others calling warnings, making it hard for Keris to focus. The sentences he composed slipping away before he had a chance to voice them. "Before Serin died, he referred to your mother as *the true and rightful heir*. The Ithicanians remember a rumor that your grandfather had come to desire peace between Maridrina and Valcotta in his later years, and that he wished for your mother to take the throne after his death, not Petra. A rumor that went abruptly silent."

"The rebels called her the Usurper," Zarrah whispered, and he nodded.

"The rebels confirmed it." He didn't have the breath to say more. Except that the important part was yet to come. The part that he knew would change everything for her.

The ship rolled, tacking another direction, and outside Aren bellowed, "We'll lose them between the islands!"

"We don't know these waters well enough to sail them in the dark!" Jor shouted back. "You're going to run us up on the rocks!"

Keris squeezed his eyes shut, each bounce over the waves sending a stab of pain through his body.

"Keris?"

The alarm in Zarrah's voice snapped his eyelids open, her dark gaze illuminated by the lamp. The most beautiful eyes in the world. "I'm fine." He was not fine. "It was Petra who told Serin's spies that your mother would be at a villa near the border without a bodyguard. What came next is something you know better than anyone."

Silence.

It stretched on and on, and it was not the reaction he'd anticipated from her. Was not the wrath and promises of vengeance that he'd expected to come flowing forth from her lips. Not able to stand it, he said, "My father might have wielded the blade, but it was Petra who assassinated your mother. Her own sister, and rightful empress of Valcotta. As her named heir, *you* became the rightful empress."

Zarrah didn't respond.

"You've said your piece." Lara knelt next to him, a bag in her hands. "I need to remove the arrow."

It had to come out; Keris knew that. Just as he also knew that it might be the only thing keeping him alive, and once removed, the rest of his life would spill out onto the floor. He couldn't let that happen without certainty that she'd fight for her crown. "Zarrah?"

She didn't so much as blink.

God help him, what if what she'd endured on that island had been too much? What if some critical part of her had been at the breaking point, and instead of giving her strength in anger, he'd broken her? "Zar—"

Without warning, Lara snapped off the arrowhead and jerked the shaft out of him.

Keris bit down on a scream, nails digging into his palms, but his eyes didn't move from Zarrah's. "Promise me you won't let her get away with it," he pleaded, jerking his head from Lara's grasp as she tried to shove a piece of leather between his teeth. "Promise me that you'll fight for your crown."

"Keris, you're bleeding to death!" Lara shouted, the ship rolling sideways, everything on the tables falling to the deck with a crash. "I have to do this now!"

He could smell the smoke of the brazier, see the crimson glow of heated steel. The thought of the pain to come should have terrified him, but it was the thought that he'd pass out and never wake that fueled his fear, because he needed to know that she'd keep fighting. "Zarrah!"

Not a blink. Like her body was there, but not her mind. Desperate, he shouted, "Valcotta!"

Her eyes snapped into focus.

Keris tangled his fingers in her dark curls, pulling her close. "Your mother wanted peace, and Petra killed her for it. Honor her by taking back the crown and liberating Valcotta."

"Fuck honor," she whispered. "I want blood."

"Zarrah," Lara snarled, "unless it's his blood you want, hold him down."

Zarrah didn't move, and Keris swore he felt his heart stutter as it began to fail. Then she was straddling him, fingers digging into his biceps as she threw her weight against him. "Close your eyes."

"I'd rather your face be the last thing I see."

Lara made a noise of disgust. "I should let you bite off your tongue and spare the world your nonsense." She shoved the leather strap between his teeth. "You ready?"

Fire burned in Zarrah's eyes, and he prayed to God and fate and the stars that it would not burn her alive.

Lara gave no warning.

First came the sizzle, then the smell of burning blood.

The pain struck like an avalanche, agony beyond anything he'd ever known, and Keris screamed.

Then there was nothing at all.

39

ZARRAH

KERIS SCREAMED, AND WHAT RATIONAL PIECE OF ZARRAH'S MIND remained knew this moment was cutting a wound in her soul that would never heal. But her anger wouldn't allow the hurt to rise. Wouldn't allow her grief or guilt. Her anger took his pain and used it as fuel for its flames so that all she saw was red.

"Bleeding is mostly stopped," Lara said, and Zarrah saw tears dripping from the other woman's face. Her own eyes were dry as sand. "Let him go."

She couldn't let him go. Couldn't unclench her fingers despite feeling the warmth of blood where her nails had broken Keris's skin.

"Let. Him. Go."

She couldn't let him go because holding on to him was all that was keeping the rage in check.

Steel bit into her throat, just below her chin.

"Let my brother go."

It was only base instinct that finally unclenched her fingers. Zarrah drew back, Lara moving with her.

"Get out," the queen of Ithicana said, the ice in her blue eyes undiminished by the swelling and tears. "Go deal with your thoughts somewhere they can do no harm."

Part of Zarrah wanted the violence. Wanted to spend some of her rage in a fight, lest it consume her entirely. Knowing it was a sort of madness didn't lessen its hold on her.

Then the door to the cabin slammed open, and Aren appeared. "We lost them." His eyes shifted between them. "Is he . . ."

"He's alive," Lara answered. "Barely."

Barely.

Abruptly, Zarrah found she couldn't breathe. Scrambling to her feet, she rushed past Aren. Out onto the open deck and to the fore of the ship. Icy wind ripped at her hair and clothes, and she willed it to cool her anger, but it only flamed hotter.

My aunt murdered my mother.

Her own sister. Her own flesh and blood. And that meant it hadn't just been Zarrah's mother that her aunt had sent Silas to kill; it had been Zarrah as well.

Memory of that moment filled her mind's eye. Of her aunt galloping toward her, face a mask of fury. Fury that Zarrah had once believed fueled by what had been done but now realized was fueled by what had been left *undone*.

Yet instead of finding another way to kill her, her aunt had done something far worse. Had manipulated Zarrah into the exact opposite of what her mother had dreamed for her. Had made her into a tool to perpetuate the war her mother had wanted to end.

Death would've been better.

Death would've spared her this moment of looking back and realizing that Bermin was right. She was a pawn.

A scream boiled up in her throat, and falling to her knees, Zarrah hammered her fists against the deck until her skin split. Then she pressed her forehead to the wood and wept.

A long time passed, and then a voice said, "What do you want to do?"

Lifting her head, she searched the darkness until she found Aren's large outline. "Take me to Pyrinat. I'm going to kill that bitch."

Aren huffed out a breath. "Keris will kill me if I agree to that."

Keris. His name sent a shudder running through her. "Is . . ." She couldn't bring herself to ask the question.

"Still breathing." Aren's shadow settled down on the deck next to her. "He's tougher than he looks. He and Lara are both made of sterner stuff than anyone I've ever met. Something in the blood. Their mother was from one of the desert tribes, so the ability to survive the worst runs in their veins."

Zarrah didn't answer. Couldn't answer, because it felt like none of the air she breathed reached her lungs. .

"He'll want me to convince you to see reason," Aren eventually said. "And I owe him enough to try."

"Why do you feel like you owe him anything?" she demanded. "He stabbed you in the back when he turned Silas on Eranahl."

Aren was silent, the only noise the pounding of surf against the ship's hull. "There are moments in life where one stands at a crossroads, and each path leads to a future so wildly different from the other that it seems impossible they stemmed from the same place. Most of the time, the ripples of those choices touch only a few. But sometimes a choice is made, and the ripples are not ripples at all but rather tsunamis that tear across the world, altering everything in their path." He was quiet again, then said, "I know where I stand now, but I can also see where I would have stood if Keris hadn't chosen you, and for my part, I'm glad he did."

She should be glad they'd reconciled, glad Keris had earned Aren's forgiveness, but that wasn't the feeling that rose in her chest.

"And just what is it that Keris wants me to do?" she asked bitterly. "Tell me, so that I might play my part in his plans to perfection."

Aren took a deep breath, then said, "You are standing at a crossroads now, Zarrah. If what you want is for me to take you back to Pyrinat so that you can attempt to kill Petra, I will. But even if you succeed, I think the only future it will change is your own. Whereas if you walk the path to claim the Valcottan crown"—he rose to his feet—"I think you have the power to change the world."

Zarrah remained where she was for a long time after he left, Aren's words circling her skull. No, not Aren's words—Keris's, for the king of Ithicana had merely played the messenger. It reminded her of the moments they'd spent talking on the top of the dam in Nerastis, when, despite having little idea of how it might be accomplished, changing their world had felt possible. Whereas now she knew what must be done and yet stood frozen at the crossroads, not wanting to take that path.

Wanting instead to race down the familiar trail, weapons in hand, in search of blood.

But if she claimed her birthright and joined with the rebels, she could use their military might and connections to pursue a lawful claim to Valcotta's throne. And with an alliance with Keris, she could end the war. Could give her country a chance to heal from generations of trauma.

It was a good plan. But it was also Keris's plan, and that made her want to run as far and fast from it as she could. *What is to stop you from making the same mistake again?* her aunt whispered. *What is to stop you from being lured back into his bed with sweet words and promises of pleasure?*

Zarrah gave a violent shake of her head. Her aunt was a madwoman and a murderer; nothing she said could be taken as the truth.

But Bermin hadn't been mad, and he, perhaps more than anyone, had seen the truth of the empress's villainy. *You'll never be your own master, Zarrah! Not while you're Maridrina's whore.*

Was an alliance of equals with Keris possible? Or would she ever and always be doing his bidding?

Her aunt was right that Keris had a hold on her, would always have a hold on her, and that terrified Zarrah because he'd proven that he wouldn't always abide her choices. Inevitably, another circumstance would arise where he went behind her back to have things his way.

But to deny this path would mean denying Valcotta peace.

Zarrah rose to her feet, body stiff with cold and all the little injuries she'd sustained in the escape, but she ignored the pain and crossed the dark deck to the captain's quarters. Taking a deep breath, she opened the door and stepped inside.

Like iron to a lodestone, her eyes went to Keris's still form on the floor. Lara had put a pillow under his head and packed blankets around him, but his body still shivered from loss of blood and the cold, his eyes closed.

Zarrah's control wavered, panic rising, but she forced her heart to calm. This was her weakness talking, and she would not concede to it.

A slight cough caught her attention, and she found Aren sitting on the bed, with his wife asleep in his arms. Lara appeared small and fragile in comparison to her husband's large form, but as Zarrah watched, one of the queen's eyes opened. It reminded her of children's stories of sleeping dragons that, once woken, wreaked havoc on those who'd disturbed their rest. Lara's gaze promised violence if Zarrah took a wrong step toward her brother.

"Do we know whether the rebel ships escaped?" she asked quietly.

Aren lifted one shoulder. "No. But I suspect the rebels have some experience evading capture."

Tension eased in her chest, some unconscious part of her having worried about the fate of those men and women who'd risked their lives for hers. "Do you know where to find them?"

"Daria told us that their stronghold is in Arakis. They control the city, so if you go there, they'll find you."

Zarrah gave a tight nod. "If you can get me to the coast, I'll travel there myself."

"We can manage that."

"Thank you." She swallowed hard. "I know I haven't earned a response yet, but if this ... *strategy* comes to fruition and I take on my aunt for the crown, will I have Ithicana's support?"

Aren was silent for a long moment, his hand moving absently up and down Lara's back as he thought. "It's not my support you need."

Keris shifted, muttering something unintelligible, and her eyes snapped to him. But he fell still again.

"Earn the crown," Aren said. "Then we'll talk. But for now, get some sleep. Tomorrow, we'll sail for Arakis."

Keris muttered again, but this time what he said was clear. "Fight, Valcotta."

It was hard to breathe as her chest twisted, the muscles in her legs flexing as she fought the urge to go to him. *You cannot allow him to control you,* she screamed at herself. *You must stand alone if you are to be the master of your own fate.*

"In the morning, then," she said. "Good night, Your Graces."

Turning on her heel, Zarrah stepped back out into the cold.

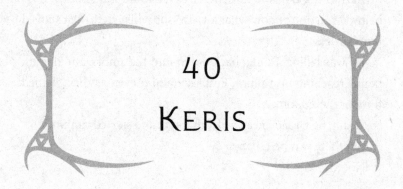

40
KERIS

THE WORLD WAS BURNING.

He ran, trying to escape the flames, but beneath his feet was a sea of corpses. Men. Women. Children. Their eyes like glass, still and unseeing, yet their hands moved. Catching and grabbing at his legs, their nails clawing at his skin.

"Let me go," he screamed, his feet sinking into flesh. Crunching bone.

"Murderer." Their mouths moved in unison, flies spilling outward to darken the air like smoke.

The flames moved closer, burned hotter, the stink of charring flesh filling his nose, but he managed to pull free just before they reached up.

A hill loomed ahead, and he stumbled toward it, climbing. Needing to reach the top, which was above the swarms of flies and clouds of stinking smoke.

His lungs burned, his fingers sliced and bruised by the sharp rocks as he climbed higher and higher.

And finally sucked in a clean breath, blinking back stinging tears.

Zarrah stood before him, her eyes the same still glass as those below. "You don't know what love is," she whispered, then shoved him hard.

He was falling. Falling back down into the smoke and flames, hands reaching up to him. Embracing him even as they blamed him for their doom.

Again, he wrenched away from them, and started running.

But there was no escape.

Not for him.

41

ZARRAH

UNDERSTANDING THAT SHE'D ONLY BE IN THE ITHICANIANS' WAY, Zarrah had retreated into one of the passenger cabins, extreme exhaustion driving her to sleep. But it was a sleep plagued with nightmares, jerking her awake again and again until she could take it no more. Nor could she stomach pacing back and forth across her cabin, worry driving her out to the open air of the main deck.

She emerged right as Aren exited the captain's quarters. "How is he?" she immediately asked, the question that had plagued her dreams tearing from her lips.

The king of Ithicana lifted a shoulder. "Lara says that if the wound doesn't foul, he'll live. She's keeping him unconscious partially for the sake of the pain but mostly because she thinks he'll ignore the need for bed rest if he rouses enough to think for himself. I'm inclined to agree."

"Likewise," Zarrah murmured, pulling the coat Jor had found for her tightly around her shoulders. Though it was more clothing than she'd had on the island, the speed at which the Ithicanians sailed the ship ensured a constant wind, the frigid air cutting through to her bones.

They stood in silence, and then Aren said, "You can go see him for yourself."

"No." The word jerked itself from her lips, and Zarrah tried to soften it with an awkward smile. "Lara knows what she's doing. I'd only be in her way."

A feeble excuse, and both of them knew it, but to his credit, Aren only said, "We're making good time now that we're on a straight course. Won't be long until we're in sight of the mainland."

"The navy has to suspect Arakis is our destination. They'll be in pursuit."

"I assure you," Aren chuckled, "we sail faster."

A variation of a conversation they'd had before, but pursuit was a safer worry to give voice to than the one that lay on the far side of the door. Zarrah had found a level of calm since they'd first escaped the island, but it evaporated whenever Keris entered her thoughts. Whenever she considered the possibility that he might not wake. To look upon him pale and unconscious and still, very much on the brink of death, would undo her, and another outburst on her part might earn Zarrah a knife in the gut.

And she knew exactly who would put it there.

"I'm sorry for my conduct, Your Grace," she said abruptly. "I've been overwrought and ungrateful, especially given the risks you took on my behalf. Please know that I hold you and yours in the highest esteem and will ever consider myself in Ithicana's debt."

Aren's head tilted, hazel eyes considering. "You've nothing to apologize for as far as I'm concerned, Zarrah. You were an ally to Ithicana when we stood alone, and rather than keeping an accounting of debts, perhaps we only commit to continuing to treat each other as friends."

Zarrah pressed a hand to her heart. "It would be an honor to name the rulers of Ithicana as friends. Thank you."

Aren laughed. "Oh, I don't speak for Lara. But I do wish you the best of luck in delivering this particular apology to her ears." Then he turned and walked away.

"Shit," Zarrah muttered under her breath. She squeezed her eyes shut, wanting no part of the conversation to come, though she knew it needed to be had. Her behavior toward Keris had made an enemy out of Lara, though in truth, the distance between her and the other woman predated this moment. And consciously or not, it had been Zarrah's doing, for she'd never felt comfortable around her.

Zarrah had been raised as a soldier. A year ago, she would have said that meant dedicating her life to warcraft and strategy, but now Zarrah realized that it ran deeper. It governed how she viewed others, everyone either a superior, a peer, or a subordinate, and she treated people accordingly. Her aunt had guided her to keep everyone at arm's length, to never allow friendship or sentiment to blur the lines. The only exception had been Yrina, but looking back now, Zarrah saw she'd been no exception at all. Her aunt had chosen Yrina, and for all Zarrah had loved her, she had still treated Yrina more often like a subordinate than a friend.

She had no friends.

Didn't know how to be a friend.

So it was far more comfortable to gravitate toward individuals like Aren and the other Ithicanians. They were also soldiers. She understood them. Understood how to *be* around them.

But not Lara.

Lara was a warrior of rare and dangerous skill, but she wasn't a soldier. She was a queen, but she wasn't Zarrah's queen. And for reasons Zarrah couldn't quite explain, her inability to categorize Lara had left her uncertain of how to behave around the other woman. Especially given Zarrah's initial distaste for Lara's role in the invasion of Ithicana.

But Aren had forgiven her.

Ithicana had accepted her.

What right had Zarrah to continue to hold Lara's actions against her? The answer was that she had no right at all, yet instead of seeking friendship, Zarrah had allowed uncertainty and prejudice to place Lara in the only other category she had: an adversary.

An enemy.

And she'd done a good job of ensuring that Lara shared the same sentiment. Zarrah had erred, and it was past time to stop blaming her flawed upbringing and do something about it.

"Damn it," she whispered, and before she could lose her nerve, Zarrah opened the door to the captain's quarters.

Lara had been curled in a chair reading a book, but at Zarrah's entrance, she lifted her head.

And reached for her knife.

"Your Grace." Zarrah pressed a hand to her heart. "I was hoping to speak to you." Her eyes flicked to Keris's form, the rise and fall of the thick blankets both filling her with relief and stealing her breath. "Alone, if you don't mind."

Azure eyes regarded her for a long moment, and then Lara rose to her feet. She reached a hand to check Keris's breathing, then crossed the room. She had a slight limp that Zarrah hadn't noticed before, though whether it was an injury from the recent battle or from before, Zarrah didn't know. And wouldn't ask.

Wordlessly stepping past Zarrah, Lara called out, "Jor? Would you please sit with my brother?"

The older Ithicanian abandoned the net he'd been untangling, nodding at the pair of them as Lara led Zarrah to the fore, where the galley was located. It was empty, lit only by small windows and the glow of the stove. Lara lit a lamp, then frowned as her boot crunched on something. There were several broken teacups on the floor.

"This ship was found floating in Ithicana's waters," Lara said. "Everyone aboard was dead. Jor thinks it's haunted, as do many of my crew members. Perhaps they are right."

A disconcerting notion, but the revelation that they sailed upon a ship potentially filled with Cardiffian ghosts who smashed teacups somehow broke the tension that was strung between them, and Zarrah said, "I wondered why you were all dressed in sealskin."

"Originally it was for disguises, but it has all come in handy for the cold weather. No one on this ship tolerates it well."

"The Cardiffians certainly know cold."

"None the least from the frosty relationship they have with Harendell. Tea?"

Nodding, Zarrah took a seat at a scarred wooden table. "I want to apologize," she said as the queen filled a kettle with water, then set it on the stove to warm. "For how I behaved when I came aboard, and for all the times before."

A flicker of surprise passed through Lara's eyes. "You helped us when no others would."

"I helped Ithicana and its king," Zarrah corrected. "Not you. Nor have I offered you any real kindness, and I'm sorry for that. You helped me escape Vencia. Helped rescue me from Devil's Island. I . . ." She cringed internally at her awkwardness, unsure of what to say to make this situation better, knowing only that apologies weren't enough.

"In fairness, I had no intention of rescuing you from my father," Lara said, her mouth quirking in a half smile that was eerily reminiscent of Keris. "That was a plan concocted by my husband and my brother, and I clearly recall thinking we'd be better off leaving you behind. So don't place me on too high of a pedestal."

Zarrah laughed softly. For a heartbeat, levity dispelled her anxiety, but then it slipped away. "You risked so much coming to aid me, Lara. Yourself. Your husband. Your people. Your heir." Her eyes flicked to the other woman's stomach, and Lara curled a hand around it protectively. "I am truly grateful. For the rest of my life, I will always come to your aid, if you need it. But—" Her throat clenched, refusing to allow her to speak about the true source of conflict between them.

Lara rose and removed the boiling kettle from the stove. Filling a chipped pot with tea, she added the steaming water and placed two cups between them. As though Lara were equally unwilling to speak of what Zarrah had left unspoken, she did not bring up Keris but rather said, "We didn't do it alone. The rebels were desperate to free you, particularly the commander himself."

Memory of the man filled Zarrah's mind. It had been dark, difficult to see clearly, but she focused on his image. Perhaps twenty years her senior, shaved head, thick beard. Tall and broad. A description belonging to any number of Valcottan men, yet he'd been wholly familiar to her. "Did he give you his name?"

Lara shook her head. "Neither of us was particularly forthcoming as to our identity. We caught sight of their ship doing reconnaissance, knew it was no naval vessel. Jor and I sneaked aboard and overheard their plans, offered an alliance."

Zarrah could only imagine the shock the rebels had endured when Lara had revealed herself. A bold move, and incredibly risky. But Lara had been desperate.

Lara frowned, then added, "I don't know if it matters, but it was only you they cared about rescuing, not the others. From what Aren has told me of the prisoners' . . . *diet*, I believe there might be a desire on the commander's part to distance himself from those who were incarcerated."

Guilt soured Zarrah's stomach, because she remembered the almost religious belief the prisoners held that the commander intended to rescue them. To learn otherwise would be a significant blow, especially if the rebellion refused to accept them back. Yet she also remembered her own visceral reaction to seeing Daria stuff corpses into barrels, the illness she'd felt upon realizing that the meat consumed right in front of her had been the flesh of Kian's tribe members. Expecting the commander and his soldiers to ignore the atrocity and accept the tribe back into the fold was unreasonable.

All of it was unfair, and *all of it* was her aunt's doing.

"They protected me," she said. "Took me in and cared for me, ensured that I never had to endure the horror they faced on a daily basis. I . . . I don't condone what they did, but I also see now that they had no choice if they wished to survive."

Lara took a sip of her tea, expression thoughtful. "Choosing to do the unthinkable to survive is still a choice, and one they made with clear eyes. Only they can say whether the consequences of what they did are worth the life they still possess."

"Well said." Zarrah wrapped her cold hands around her cup. "Yet I feel that I owe them. That I have an obligation to do what I can for them, not just abandon them to judgment."

"That will cost you," Lara said. "What they did is morally reprehensible, and to be seen as supporting them may turn others against you. Politically, it's not a good move."

"What would you do?"

"I'm not known for well-thought decisions," Lara said, chuckling, "so I'm not sure I'm the one to ask. But I will say that I believe there is something to be said in giving people a chance at redemption. What they make of that opportunity is on them."

Zarrah took a too-deep sip of tea, knowing that it was not Daria's tribe Lara spoke of, then winced as the hot liquid burned her tongue. Impossible as it was to believe, given the harm Keris had done to Ithicana, Zarrah could see that he'd earned his sister's forgiveness during their travels. More than that, he'd earned her loyalty. And her protection.

How could she explain her state of mind to Lara when she didn't understand it herself? When she couldn't organize her fractured and ever-changing feelings, over which she had nearly no control? "There are things I must do," Zarrah finally said. "For myself, and for Valcotta, and I'm afraid that if I allow Keris close again, they will not be done my way, but his."

"Because you don't trust him."

Zarrah forced herself to meet Lara's eyes, and it was so painfully similar to looking into Keris's that her tenuous composure shuddered. "Because I don't trust myself."

Lara's mouth tightened with sympathy, and she gave a slow nod. "I understand."

"I know that I'm going to hurt him." Zarrah took a deep breath to steady her voice, despite knowing it to be a lost cause. "And I know that means you and I will never be friends. But I hope that doesn't mean we must be enemies, Your Grace."

Silence stretched between them, the only noise the sea striking the ship's hull as they raced over the waves, the roughness of the water mirroring the turbulence of her thoughts.

Then Lara reached across the table and took hold of one of Zarrah's hands. Her skin was as marked with scars as Zarrah's own, palms rough with calluses, yet traces of pink lacquer still gleamed on a few of her fingernails. The juxtaposition somehow made the queen seem so painfully human, and Zarrah swallowed grief at the friendship that they might have had if circumstances had been different. If they weren't who they were, because Lara knew as well as Zarrah what it was like to be used as a weapon.

"I see why he loves you," Lara said. "You are each everything the other is not, perfect foils, and I fear what he will become without you." She squeezed Zarrah's hand, then let go and rose. "And you without him."

With that, the queen of Ithicana left the room, leaving Zarrah feeling more alone than she had before.

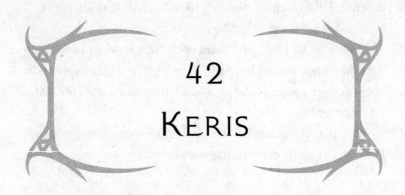

42

KERIS

"KERIS. KERIS, WAKE UP."

He groaned, eyelids peeling open even as pain slapped him in the face, his whole body still feeling like it burned. A face swam above him, and he blinked, focusing on Lara.

"You need to wake up," she said. "We're in sight of the Valcottan coast."

His sluggish mind struggled to process her words, but he finally managed to say, "Whatever you drugged me with, don't give it to me again."

"You needed rest."

"That wasn't rest," he muttered, still feeling the terror of the nightmare that had repeated over and over.

Getting an elbow under himself, he tried to get upright, but pain turned his vision white. "Fuck," he said through his teeth. "It hurts worse than it did before."

"Anything I give you will knock you out," Lara said, easing him up.

"Then pain it is." It took a fair bit of self-control not to scream as she shoved cushions behind his back. "Your nursemaid skills leave something to be desired, sister."

Lara snorted. "You're lucky you're not a ripening corpse."

Visions from his dreams filled his mind's eye, and Keris flinched, covering the motion by guzzling the glass of water she handed him. "Is she . . ."

"She's fine." Lara refilled his glass and then adjusted his blanket like he was some sort of invalid. Which was perhaps accurate. "She just needs space."

Keris's chest tightened, because the person Zarrah needed space from was *him*.

What did you expect? the voice whispered. *For her to be sitting by your side?*

"We're taking her to join the rebels," Lara said. "Then we'll return to Ithicana. We'll make arrangements for you to return to Maridrina, and then I suppose we'll wait to see what strides Zarrah makes with the rebels. You need to rest. Regain your strength."

She was right, but there was too much to do. "I need to speak to Zarrah."

His sister looked away, her jaw tightening. "I don't think that's wise. Better to leave her be."

Keris shoved away the bowl of broth she'd placed in front of him. He realized now that when he'd told Lara that he didn't expect Zarrah to forgive him, he'd been full of shit. That in his selfish and arrogant core, he'd thought that risking everything to rescue her would matter. That it would earn him, if not another chance, then at least some form of . . . of . . . well, he didn't know exactly what.

The door opened, and Jor stepped inside. "We've found ourselves a cove north of Arakis, but we need to be fast. There are patrols, and they're quick to sink those they believe are attempting to avoid port taxes." His eyes locked with Keris's. "The plan is to bring Zarrah to the beach by longboat, then part ways."

Did she even plan to say goodbye?

He'd sailed half the continent, risked life and limb, to haul her ass out of the worst prison in the known world, and he wasn't even worth a goddamned goodbye.

"Aren's asking for you," Jor said to Lara.

His sister made a face, then said, "Stay with Keris. Make sure he doesn't do anything that will aggravate that wound." Then she rounded on him. "You're Maridrina's king. Your kingdom is a mess, yet you've left it in the hands of a half sister you barely know, all the men and women who run it duped into believing you're in Ithicana by Ahnna and her forgers, who will have your people convinced you've agreed to God knows what. You need to go back, and Zarrah needs to press forward. She will need your support, but you can only give it from Vencia. You can only give her what she needs if you are Maridrina's king, and that means you must be apart."

"If I go back and something happens to her, what then?" he asked. "How long until Petra, her rule secure, marches north? Maridrina doesn't have the strength to defend Nerastis when she decides to take it. Doesn't have the strength to stop her if she presses north, taking my territory and slaughtering my people. In going to war with Ithicana, Father played into her plans, because Maridrina is weaker now than it has ever been, and me sitting in his tower in Vencia will not change that. Ensuring Zarrah has the chance to take back the crown *will*."

"Never mind that Zarrah's twice the fighter you are, how do you expect to help her when you're barely out of your deathbed?" Lara threw up her hands. "She doesn't even want you with her, Keris. She wants to do this alone. So let her."

Rather than answering, Keris slowly climbed to his feet. "Take care of yourself, Lara." He caught hold of her chin, forcing her to meet his gaze. "You are the queen Ithicana needs, little sister, and in time, it will become the kingdom you deserve."

Her eyes flooded, though no tears escaped. "You're an idiot." Then she flung her arms around his middle, squeezing him hard before twisting away. "Jor, take care of him."

The old Ithicanian exhaled a long breath after she'd left, then turned to Keris. "Want me to find you something stiff to drink so you have an excuse for doing something stupid?"

"Yes," Keris answered. "Though I suspect it will take more than one drink."

43

ZARRAH

ZARRAH STOOD AT THE RAIL, WATCHING THE COAST OF VALCOTTA grow on the horizon, both counting down the minutes until she could start on the path to ridding her nation of a tyrant and wishing that time would stand still.

The ship cautiously maneuvered its way closer to shore, eventually dropping anchor in a small cove with a rocky beach, steep hills covered in pine trees rising up from the water. There was no reason to linger and every reason to rush, yet Zarrah found herself frozen by the rail.

Lara and Aren approached where she stood, Aren giving orders to his crew to ready a longboat.

Zarrah had a brief internal war with herself, then asked, "Is he awake?"

Ithicana's queen gave a short nod. "Awake and on his feet. He knows your plans. Knows you are leaving."

Yet hadn't come up to say goodbye.

It's for the best, she reminded herself even as she stood motionless. *You need to focus on Valcotta. He needs to return to Maridrina. Everything that needs to be said can be communicated through messengers.*

No, her heart whispered. *Not everything. You need to say goodbye.*

Against her will, Zarrah turned to look at the door to the captain's cabin. *He deserves acknowledgment,* she told herself as she waited. *Deserves a thank-you for everything he's done. Deserves . . .*

"Damn it," she said between her teeth, struggling to breathe, for it felt like a vise had formed around her chest. If she went into that room, words would pour from her lips that would give life to what was between them. Would give hope. And that was crueler than not saying goodbye, because no matter how much her heart might wish otherwise, there was no future between them.

Valcotta couldn't afford it.

Slinging a leg over the edge, she climbed down the ladder into the longboat, Aren following. "We need to hurry," she said to him. "The navy patrols for smugglers, and that's how this will appear."

"You have everything you need?"

"Yes."

A lie, for she found herself looking back at the ship. Hoping to see him on the deck. Through a window.

Nothing.

The boat reached the shallows, the Ithicanians leaping out and cursing the frigid water as they pulled it onto the beach.

"Feels like the last time we parted ways," Aren muttered, eyeing the dense forest. "Watch your back."

Zarrah stepped onto the slick rocks of the beach, patting her bag full of coin and supplies. "Thank you."

Aren hesitated, then said, "I wish there was more I could do for you, Zarrah, but I need to be back in Ithicana."

She smiled. "I appreciate the sentiment, but this is my fight."

Every minute they lingered put them at risk, but Zarrah's eyes still drifted to the ship, searching for Keris's familiar golden hair.

Nothing.

"Goodbye, Your Grace," she said to Ithicana's king, then stood watching as the Ithicanians rowed him back to the ship. Only then did she start walking. Her eyes burned with unshed tears, but Zarrah didn't look back as she climbed the narrow path up the hill, the scent of pine thick in her nose. Up and up, not pausing until she broke out of the trees. There, she stopped to look out over the sea, watching the ship sail toward the horizon.

It's over, she chanted to herself. *It's over.*

It would never be over.

"Don't shed too many tears over their departure," a voice said from behind her. "For all his protests to the contrary, I expect that Aren will be unable to resist sticking his nose into this rebellion. He really does not like your aunt."

Zarrah spun, pulling loose the sword buckled at her waist, the familiar velvet tones of Keris's voice registering a heartbeat before her eyes latched upon him. He sat on a rock, a half-empty bottle of wine and a selection of cheese sitting beside him, a wineglass in one hand.

"What are you doing here?" she shouted before whirling back to the sea. But the ship was too far gone to signal. "They're going to think you fell overboard!"

"I doubt it," Keris answered, sipping at his wine. "Was Jor who rowed me to shore, and it was Aren who took his time dropping anchor to give us the time to do so."

An unjust sense of betrayal filled her that Aren had known and said nothing. "Why? Why the fuck are you here, Keris?"

"Because you and I need to have a conversation."

"Then we should've had it on the ship," she shouted. "I'm grateful for all you've done for me, Keris. Truly, I am. But this is my fight. I need to focus on Valcotta. You need to go back to Maridrina."

Keris took a sip of his wine, then set the delicate glass on the rock next to the cheese. "Are those your orders?"

She didn't answer.

Rising to his feet, Keris walked toward her, the intensity in his azure eyes causing Zarrah's stomach to flip.

He stopped in front of her, and she swayed, uncertain of whether she wanted to step forward or back. Whether she needed to attack or retreat.

"I can be reasoned with. Convinced. Persuaded." He leaned closer, his voice low as he said, "But when it comes to matters of my family, my people, or my kingdom, I will *not* be ordered."

Zarrah lifted her chin, meeting his stare unblinking. "You presume to—"

"I'm not finished." His breath was warm, scented faintly with the wine he'd been drinking. "The reigning empress of Valcotta has her sights trained on my back. Wants to destroy me, my family, and my people. Wants to burn Maridrina to ash, yet you have the audacity to tell me that this is not my fight. To tell me to go back to Vencia to wait for your instructions like I'm one of your soldiers and beholden to your orders. I am not."

"You think—" She cut off as his head tilted, eyes narrowing.

"And this isn't the first time. Despite the fact your plots with Ithicana had a catastrophic impact on my kingdom and people, you didn't involve me. Instead you came to the dam in Nerastis for the sole purpose of telling me how it was going to be." He leaned closer still. "You had no right."

Her heart was throbbing with such intensity that Zarrah swore it might burst from her chest. Countless emotions filled her, but she clung to the one that always served her best. Anger. "But you had the right? You betrayed my confidence and used the information I trusted you with to make your own plans, then stood on Southwatch Island and told *me* how it was going to be. For you to stand here and berate me is hypocrisy. Worse than hypocrisy, because at least I didn't betray you."

"Didn't you?" His voice was cool, but the pulse at his throat was rapid. "We planned together how we'd end the war. How we'd build a peace between our kingdoms so future generations might grow up without the cloud of violence over their heads. If I'd stood aside and done nothing, if you'd taken your ships into legitimate battle to expel my father from Ithicana, it would have been oil on the flames of the Endless War. Not that you'd have lived to see it, because if you didn't manage to martyr yourself in battle, you'd have been executed as a traitor for having failed to follow Petra's orders. I'd have been left alive with a shattered heart in the ashes of a future that you burned, and I challenge you to tell me that's not a fucking betrayal, Valcotta."

She flinched, then erased the slap of his words with vitriol of her own. "You didn't betray me for Maridrina. You betrayed me for yourself. Because you couldn't stand to let me go."

"Hypocrisy abounds, because we both know that you betrayed me not because it was the only path forward, not even because it was the best path forward, but because it satisfied your honor, your need for atonement, and your desire for vengeance."

Zarrah's lips parted to deny deny deny, but no words came because she had no breath. "I . . ." she managed to say, then broke off to gulp in a mouthful of air. "I did it because it was the right thing to do."

Silence.

"I don't know," Keris finally said, "whether you are lying to me or whether you are lying to yourself."

Instinct demanded that she lash out. That she stab the knife of his own failings and twist it deep, but instead Zarrah forced herself to ask her heart that same question. The truth that rose up from the depths of her soul made her eyes burn with tears. "Neither do I."

Keris's throat moved as though he were swallowing hard. "I

told myself I had no regrets for turning my father on Eranahl to keep you out of the battle. That saving your life was worth any price. But . . ." He turned away, eyes fixed on the sea. "There was a moment where we were unified and all things were possible, and somehow I . . . somehow *we* lost that beneath the weight of more selfish motivations. I regret my part. Wish there was a way to find my way back to that place."

Grief settled upon her, drowning out every other emotion and leaving the world faded and gray. Because he was right.

But so was her aunt.

For all they'd been unified in their desires, it was their desire for each other that ensured their dreams would fail. He was the king of Maridrina. She intended to become the empress of Valcotta. For there to be a true and lasting peace, they needed to be wholly dedicated to their people, which would never happen if they spent their nights in each other's arms. "We can't go back, Keris. I won't."

The icy wind pulled a lock of his hair loose from the tie at the back of his head, sending it fluttering like a strand of corn silk across his face as he gave a slow nod. "I love you, Zarrah. You say that I don't know what love is, and maybe that's true. Maybe there is some part of me missing or broken that ensures I don't feel things like a better man would, but I know the way I feel about you consumes me. That it gives me breath even as it steals the air from my lungs. Makes my heart beat even as it cuts it from my chest. What word I give it matters little. What matters is that even after my bones are dust and my name lost to history and history lost to time, I will feel this way for you."

Zarrah's resolve faltered as he scrubbed tears from his cheeks. But before she could speak, he said, "You say there is no going back, and I respect that, but I must ask if there is a way forward. As political allies."

This was what she'd wanted from him, yet Zarrah felt as though she'd been punched in the stomach.

"Petra needs to be removed from power," Keris pressed on, though she didn't miss how his hands balled into fists. Her own nails were also digging into her palms. "Neither nation will know peace if she keeps the crown, and you and I, working together, are best equipped to remove her. So, as Maridrina's king, I'd like to offer a formal alliance to the rightful empress of Valcotta so that our nations might achieve mutually desirable ends." Then he stuck out his hand like a market trader sealing a deal.

Zarrah stared at the hand that knew every curve of her body. That had touched her in ways no one else had. And no one else would.

This is the right choice, the voice in her head whispered. *The right path forward for Valcotta.*

But could she hold to it?

Shoving aside the thought, Zarrah gripped his hand, the heat of it chasing away the chill in her own fingers. "I accept."

Their hands remained clasped for longer than was appropriate; then Keris pulled away.

"Right, then. We should probably start on our way. Jor informed me it's a long walk." He recorked the wine bottle and then stowed it in a pack, which was tossed over his uninjured shoulder. Then, picking up his wineglass and plate of cheese, Keris started down the path.

Zarrah stood frozen, watching him as she came to terms with the situation. It was only as Keris rounded the bend that she jerked into motion, chasing after him. "Do you even know where you are going?"

He took a mouthful of wine, then said, "All paths lead to a road."

"That's not even the slightest bit true." Eyeing the sky, Zarrah took a branch in the path leading off to the right. "Did you even think this through? Rebel territory or not, this is still Valcotta, and you look like . . . like . . . you."

"Your eloquence is inspiring," he answered. "I look forward to the speeches you give from the throne." Casting a sideways glance at her, he sighed. "Blond hair and blue eyes are hardly unique attributes and are most certainly not limited to Maridrinian nationals. As to my particularly striking good looks, that's just a risk of recognition we'll have to take."

She cast her eyes skyward. "It's the ego that will give you away."

"You know how I feel about false modesty." Finishing his wine, Keris tucked the glass into his pack. "Aren told me you have a plan. Care to share it?"

You were made to be used by others, not to lead. Zarrah bit down on the anxiety that rose with Bermin's voice. *You have an agreement,* she reminded herself. *This is a political alliance, nothing more.* "Find the commander," she answered.

She waited for him to point out that was a goal, not a plan, but Keris only pulled the hood of his cloak forward, obscuring his face. "Seems like a good place to start."

44

KERIS

THE PATH HAD, INDEED, LED TO A ROAD, AND THE ROAD TO THE city of Arakis.

What Keris profoundly hoped it led to next was a bed.

Exhaustion blurred his vision, his body ached, his wound itched, and every inch of him felt frozen solid by the cold. It was only force of will that kept him moving, every part of his mind consumed with taking another step.

Which left little energy for him to appreciate the size of the city.

For obvious reasons, he'd never visited Valcotta, his venture to the south side of Nerastis with Zarrah his one sojourn across the border. One night of drinking and reading stories about stars, only to be pursued by soldiers until they could hide on the rooftops. Later, she'd fallen asleep in his arms, and looking back, Keris knew that was when he'd handed her his heart. Days and nights when everything had felt possible and his shoulders light.

Now, venturing into the streets of another Valcottan city with her, Keris felt the weight of all that had happened since pressing him into the cobbles.

Possessed of a large harbor, Arakis was a center of trade, and merchants from every nation crowded the streets. For all he'd been blasé about being recognized, it was no small relief to see that he was far from the only Maridrinian in the city, his people differentiated from those from Harendell and Amarid by the cut of their coats and dresses, the style of the weapons they carried, and the marriage knives belted at the women's waists. The Valcottans seemed unconcerned as they bartered with them at market stalls, showing none of the hate for his countrymen that their empress encouraged. Whether it was because of the distance from Pyrinat or that the rebels held sway in the city, he wasn't certain, but it eased the fear he felt whenever a Valcottan's gaze fell upon him.

The streets were packed with people, and Keris winced every time he was jostled. It took more effort than it should to remain at Zarrah's side as she pressed deeper into the city. "You been here before?" he asked, nearly forced to shout over the din of voices and animals.

"No." Zarrah stepped closer to him to be heard, her shoulder pressing against his arm as a round matron carrying a goat collided against her, the woman cursing them to get out of the way. Instinct demanded he wrap an arm around Zarrah and pull her aside, but Keris only shoved his hands deeper into his pockets.

"I was never sent south." Zarrah twisted sideways to make room for a man pulling a handcart full of dirty straw. "I never questioned it, because my focus was always the war with Maridrina, but now I wonder if it was purposeful on her part."

"Seems likely." He scanned the signs hanging from the fronts of buildings, looking for an inn, only for his eyes to land on uniformed soldiers on horseback, grim eyes scanning the crowd. "Head down."

"I see them." Zarrah maintained her steady pace at his side, allowing the flow of traffic to draw them forward. "I want to get a look at their uniforms."

Breaking away from the crowd would only draw attention, so Keris kept his head down and shoulders slumped as they moved closer to the four horsemen than common sense suggested was wise.

"Move!" one of the soldiers snarled, lashing at the crowd with the ends of his reins. The civilians flinched out of the way, muttering curses and glaring at the soldiers.

"Pig fuckers!" someone shouted. "Go back to Pyrinat! The Usurper misses your ass-licking!"

"Who said that?" The soldier whirled his horse, the animal's hindquarters slamming into Zarrah. She stumbled sideways as the irritated animal kicked out, hooves striking another woman, who screamed. Keris caught Zarrah around the waist, his injured shoulder protesting as he kept her upright. The crowd swiftly turned into a mob, civilians fighting to get away from the horses, only to be shoved back among them.

The animals panicked, eyes rolling as they reared and twisted, hooves lashing out as they fought their riders.

Keris's heart raced; his fingers latched onto Zarrah's clothes as they were shoved from all sides, people falling beneath feet. He tripped over a body, then stepped on another, horror filling him as whoever it was screamed in agony.

But there was no way to help, for to try to drag them up from beneath the weight of so many would only see him pulled beneath the heavy heels of the mob.

Just keep your feet, he told himself. *Hold on to her.*

And then they were out of the thick of it, the street widening and terrified civilians stumbling free, weeping or swearing. Sucking in breath after breath, Keris caught hold of the edge of a building, only for Zarrah to grab his arm, leading him down the street. "Imperial guard," she said. "You can tell from the pattern on the brass on their sleeve."

"Information most definitely worth risking one's life for," he muttered, ignoring her sharp glare.

"They are her most trusted and vaunted soldiers, not a city patrol. They'd have only been sent here for a specific and important purpose."

"Which you nearly handed to them," he snapped. "What if your hood had been pulled back? I can only assume that every single one of those soldiers knows your face."

"Obviously," Zarrah answered. "But it's not me they are here for. At best, word of my escape will only reach Arakis today, more likely tomorrow. Pyrinat is farther away, so she won't yet know. The imperial guard is here for a different purpose."

"Given that man called Petra *the Usurper,* one can only assume that the rebels have been stirring up dissent."

Zarrah's eyes narrowed beneath her hood. "Keep your voice down. If that's indeed why they are here, they'll have men out of uniform serving as eyes and ears."

"I'm aware," he muttered, annoyed at being chastised, given the risk she'd taken, but feeling too ill to fight about it.

They ventured on until they found an inn, Zarrah opening the door to reveal a common room packed with people. Much like in Nerastis, the ceiling was decorated with strings of lamps formed of colored glass, though these were black with soot and neglect. The bar was at the center of the room, low tables stretching out from it like spokes on a wheel, all of them laden with small plates of food and dirty glasses of the dark beer Valcottans favored. There were only two windows, one with stained glass depicting a crowned woman with dark curling hair, though it was hard to see the details through the filth. The other was boarded over. A large stone hearth dominated the wall at the rear; the amount of smoke spewing from it suggested the chimney desperately needed a cleaning, but above it hung a mirror with a gilded frame. A once-fine establishment now fallen into disrepair, the air smelling of smoke, vomit, and bodies deeply in need of a bar of soap.

The people appeared primarily Valcottan, possessed of dark hair and skin of various hues of brown, men and women both dressed in the baggy trousers and loose shirts he'd seen in Nerastis, though there were individuals from other nations as well. Maridrinians sat on the stained cushions used in lieu of chairs, and he heard the accents of Harendell and Amarid, though never together. "Looks like I'll fit in just fine."

"Only if you keep silent." Zarrah approached the bar. "We need two rooms," she said to a woman filling a glass with foaming ale.

"Full up," the woman announced. "Not a room to be had in all of Arakis. Got four to a bed. Try one of the camps outside of the city."

"Why is the city so full?"

The bartender paused in her pouring, giving Zarrah an appraising once-over. "Because of the raids. Whole villages burned to the ground, so people have come to the city for shelter."

"Burned by whom?" Zarrah demanded, but the woman only shrugged, looking away.

She was afraid.

Keris had seen such a reaction countless times before in Maridrina. People afraid to speak out about violence because the instigator was the one who wore the crown. It was Petra's soldiers who were doing the burning, likely on the whispers of rats selling out those who dared to stand against her.

"I see," Zarrah answered, and though her face was unmoved,

the tension in her shoulders revealed that she saw as clearly as he did. "I'll pay double."

The bartender shouted, "Anyone wanting to sell their room for double the price you paid me?"

Keris winced at having so much attention drawn to them, but no one even looked up. "Triple?" the bartender shouted, smirking at Zarrah, who had made no such offer.

"I'll sell you my room," a greasy man with red hair said. "Three silvers for the night, and I'll keep myself warm with the ladies at the Minx till sun-up."

Zarrah's eyes shifted to the bartender, who nodded. "He's got the attic. No hearth, no bed, no blankets, but it's out of the snow." Right at that moment, a gust of wind carrying flakes of white followed the latest patron through the door. "I'll send up a bucket of hot water so that you can wash away the pinch of paying so much for so little."

"Fine," Zarrah answered. "Boiling water, as well as food and drink."

The bartender snorted. "He didn't pay for such."

Shaking her head, Zarrah fished a few coppers out of her pocket and handed them over, then turned to the greasy man. "Key."

The man drained his ale cup, then held out his hand, and Zarrah grudgingly handed over the silver.

"Enjoy," the greasy man said, handing her a key. "I'll put your coin to good use."

Zarrah didn't answer, only headed toward the stairs. They climbed in silence, and for Keris's part, it was because he was out of breath, his shoulder throbbing in time with his rapidly pounding heart. As they reached the top floor, it was to find a footstool against one wall and a trapdoor in the ceiling.

Dragging over the stool, Zarrah stood on her tiptoes to unlock the trapdoor, the fabric of her trousers stretching tight against her bottom as she reached. Keris forced himself to look away, knowing his thoughts should be on how he was going to climb into the attic.

Lowering the trapdoor, Zarrah grasped the edges of the opening, but then paused. "Do you need me to lift you?"

Humiliation turned his cheeks hot, but he was spared having to answer as the bartender appeared, carrying a heavy bucket of steaming water. She set it on the ground, then said, "There's a ladder up there, if you need it. One of the girls will be up with your food." Without another word, she departed.

Zarrah silently climbed through the trapdoor. A moment later, a ladder descended. "You might regret every life choice when you see what our silver purchased for the night," she said as she climbed down to retrieve the bucket of steaming water. "Looks like we'll be sharing with a family of rats."

Sighing, Keris hefted his bag over his shoulder and climbed the ladder.

The bartender had not been lying, for there was no bed, no washstand, not even a mattress on the floor. Which wasn't surprising, given the ceiling was so low he'd be risking hitting his head while on his knees.

The only light was from the setting sun, and it was partially blocked by the filth on the glass of the single small window. A draft of icy cold moaned around its ill-fitting frame. Pulling up the ladder, he set it aside, what warmth he'd gained in the common room rapidly fading.

"Ay!" a girl's voice filtered up from below. "Come get your food."

Zarrah lay on her stomach, reaching down. "Give it here, then."

Keris found his gaze drifting over the length of her body.

Don't, he chastised himself. *Banish the thought from your skull.*

He'd have had an easier time stopping his heart from beating or his lungs from filling with air than quelling his desire for her, but thankfully Zarrah rescued him from his weak will by sitting upright, tray balanced on her lap. Setting it aside, she frowned at the trap. "I don't trust that lock. Give me your belt."

Keris dutifully handed it over, watching her link her belt with his and around the trapdoor before pulling it closed. Dragging the ladder over the top, she threaded the belts through the rungs.

A small lamp burned on the tray, and Keris inspected the offerings. Two relatively clean glasses full of dark beer thick enough to stand a spoon upright, as well as two bowls of something like stew that smelled terrifyingly spicy, plus several pieces of flatbread.

Sitting cross-legged on the floor, he looked for a spoon.

"Like this." Zarrah took a piece of the flatbread and used it to spoon the contents of the bowl into her mouth. "It's good."

He followed suit, ignoring the grime around his fingernails because he was too hungry to wait. The spice was potent enough that his eyes watered, but it was good, so he kept going, pausing only occasionally to calm the fire on his tongue with ale.

Zarrah stacked the dishes on the tray and set the lot aside. Rounding on him, she said, "Take off your shirt."

He choked on the last mouthful of ale. "Pardon?"

"I need to look at your injury." When he didn't move, she crossed her arms. "At the best of times, you've got as much color as a glass of milk, Keris, but at the moment you look . . ." She shook her head. "Your skin is gray."

"Bad lighting."

"Don't be an idiot. You think I can't tell that you're barely able to stand?" Making an aggrieved noise, she scowled at him. "You nearly died from that arrow. Is it bleeding again?"

It was.

But he had no interest in taking off his shirt. Not only was he filthy, but he'd also seen the wound. The cauterization might have sealed it, but it had left behind a burned mess of flesh that seeped fluid. It was disgusting, and he didn't want her to see it. Didn't want her to see him like this, because it would give her cause to question what good his presence was to her.

"It's fine," he said. "I packed bandages and one of Lara's nasty salves. I'll deal with it in the morning."

"If it fouls, you'll die. Take off your shirt."

"What do you know of healing?"

She gave him a flat stare. "More than you. Shirt. Off."

The stubbornness in him wanted to dig in its heels, but Keris reluctantly pulled off his coat, then eased his shirt over his head, grimacing in pain as he did. The bandages beneath were still in place, but the white cloth was soddened with blood and whatever else the cursed injury was leaking.

Zarrah's breath caught, and then she reached for the bucket of water and the cloths the bartender had provided. Keris looked away, staring at the darkness outside the singular window because he didn't want to see her reaction.

"I didn't know you were squeamish," she said, and he noticed a slight tremor in her voice.

"I'm not." He fought the urge to pull away from her. "But I'm spectacularly vain."

A faint laugh exited her lips, and he risked a sideways glance to see her smiling, though it fell away as she unfastened the bandage. An awful peeling noise accompanied the sharp sting of pain as she pulled the fabric away from the wound. Her fingers were warm against his skin. Or perhaps he was just cold.

"Oh, Keris," she said softly, and he hid his cringe with words.

"It's vile. Thankfully I heal quickly."

She caught him by the chin, forcing him to look at her. "You think how it looks is my concern? Do you have any idea how close you came to dying? A finger's breadth to the right, and nothing Lara could have done would have saved you, and I'd be facing this fight alone."

"Not alone," he said. "The rebels will support you. And for all his vagaries, Aren will as well."

"You think any of them can replace you?" The second the words were from her lips, she looked away, the muscles in her jaw tightening as though she hadn't meant to say them, though she swiftly added, "Peace is unlikely without you on the throne."

He didn't answer, and her eyes eventually flicked back up to meet his. The world around them blurred, the noise of the common room below faded away, and the pain in his shoulder became an afterthought in the face of his desire to pull her into his arms. Their connection was endless. Timeless. And though it had been battered and brutalized, the tension between them remained undiminished. As hard to resist as it had ever been.

You gave your word! his conscience screamed at him. *Don't you dare take advantage of a moment of weakness.*

She moved closer, almost an imperceptible shift, but every instinct in his body demanded he close the distance. That he kiss her. Make love to her. Do what it took to make her forget all the hurt, and in doing so, take back all that had been lost.

Don't! His conscience's screams seemed further away with each passing second. *She's the one who has been hurt. The one who has been betrayed by so many. You are supposed to be the one giving her strength, not the one mining beneath all her defenses.*

He forced a smirk onto his face. "If I'm so irreplaceable, then I suppose it's in both our best interests that you ensure this wound doesn't decide a reversal of fortune is in order."

She blinked, a forced smile forming on her lips as she turned her attention to the injury. "Agreed. Did Lara give you anything for the pain?"

"Yes, but I'm not taking it." Her huffed breath of exasperation drove him to add, "It makes me tired and slow to react. I'd rather suffer the pain than sleep through someone slitting my throat."

Zarrah was quiet for a long moment as she used the hot water to clean away the mess, and he gritted his teeth, half from the pain and half from her touch undermining the war his conscience had just won. Catching her wrist, he said, "I can do it."

"Is there a reason you don't want me to?"

Against his will, Keris met her gaze, her large brown eyes illuminated by the lamplight. He was used to them being filled with confidence, even though he knew it was sometimes feigned. But as he stared into their dark depths, it was uncertainty that looked back at him. Hurt.

How had they come to this? How had they gone from being so aligned in thought and feeling and purpose to barely being able to speak to each other?

Keris knew the answer.

Knew that it was trust that had allowed them to speak freely, and it was the trust between them that had suffered the greatest damage.

Which meant that trust was what they both needed to rebuild, and that required a level of honesty.

Letting go of her wrist, he swallowed hard. "I don't want you to touch me, because I made a promise to you, and I'm coming to terms with the amount of willpower it will take to hold to it."

Silence.

Regret threatened to drown him, because when was honesty ever a good idea?

"Do you have enough?" Her eyes flicked to his, then away before he could read their depths. "Of willpower, that is?"

"Yes."

Zarrah's brow furrowed; then she retrieved Lara's salve, smearing it across the injury before moving behind him to do the same on the back of his shoulder. Her fingers brushed his lower back, and he twitched.

"What's this scar from?"

It took him a moment to understand what she meant. "Oh, it's from Lara. We had something of a quarrel when I first arrived in Eranahl. This one is from her, too." He tapped the fading pink mark on his throat.

"Veliants," she muttered as she looped fresh bandages around him, then passed him his shirt.

Though he was freezing from the draft, Keris first availed himself of both warm water and soap to scrub away the worst of the grime. He desperately needed a shave, but with no mirror and his body consumed with shivers, he'd likely cut off half his face in the process. Pulling his shirt and coat back on, he went to the window and dumped the basin of soiled water into the alley below.

"I'll turn around," he told her, taking a seat and rooting his gaze firmly on the wall.

But not watching only heightened his other senses. The whisper of fabric as she disrobed, the splash of water, then the scrub of a cloth against naked skin. Keris squeezed his eyes shut, memory supplying that of which his eyes were deprived.

Were there changes since he'd last looked upon her? New marks and scars from her ordeal to match the wounds inflicted on her heart and mind? He wanted to ask but instead bit his tongue.

"I'm done," she said, going to the window to pour out the basin of water. "You should get some rest."

"Likewise."

She lifted her shoulder in a shrug. "Later."

Was she afraid of lowering her guard around him? Afraid he'd take advantage?

Grabbing his bag, Keris pulled out a brown bottle full of liquid. Icy fear pooled in his hands, because he remembered the dreams that had come the last time Lara had given him this. Dreams he'd been powerless to wake from and that had left him vulnerable to the world.

He took a deep breath, then measured five drops onto his tongue. "You'll have to wake me if there is trouble," he said, then lay on the floor, pulling his cloak over himself against the chill.

Zarrah didn't answer.

With each heartbeat, his pain lessened even as his fear rose, because Keris knew what was coming for him. But blackness descended, and though he clung to the light, it took his consciousness down with it.

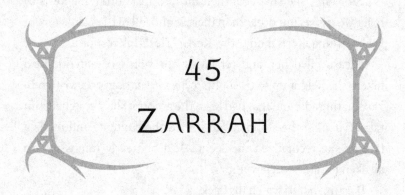

45

ZARRAH

YOU THINK ANY OF THEM CAN REPLACE YOU?

The admission that had slipped from her lips kept repeating inside her head, louder each time, her embarrassment rising with each repetition until she felt like she'd need to claw it out of her skull to silence it.

Why had she said it?

Because it's the truth, her aunt's voice whispered. *I warned you.*

Be silent, she snarled, well aware that arguing with her aunt's specter might well make her as insane as the woman herself. Though insanity was too kind an excuse for her behavior tonight.

Childish. Petty. Insecure. Manipulative.

Zarrah hurled the words at herself, cheeks burning because they were deserved. She'd demanded their relationship be limited to a political alliance, but the moment they were alone, she was the one erasing the lines she'd drawn. Burning hot then cold, tempting him half because she wanted proof that he'd hold to his word and half because she hoped that he wouldn't.

You claim a woman's experience with men but speak of intimacy like a girl.

"Shut up," she snapped, then bit her lip, waiting for Keris to react. To move. But other than the rise and fall of the blanket from his breathing, Keris didn't stir. "Keris?" He didn't respond.

Unease filled her, and retrieving the bottle of narcotic he'd taken, she held it up to the light. *5 drops before sleep* was written in wax on the side, and that had been the amount she'd watched him take. Opening the stopper, she sniffed the contents and made a face as she recognized the scent. He'd be nearly impossible to awaken for at least a few hours.

Trusting her to watch his back.

She *had* betrayed him. Had hurt him. Had threatened his life. If there was anyone Keris should be guarded around, it was her. Instead he seemed hell-bent on protecting her from herself.

Kneeling next to him, she held a hand in front of his lips to feel his breath, her chest tightening at his pallor. Assuming infection didn't take hold, he'd recover, yet when she'd unwrapped the bandage, the sight had nearly doubled her over. So close. She'd been so close to losing him.

Though Zarrah knew she should not, her fingers brushed his hair out of his face. It was longer than it had been before, the texture like silk against her skin. Not for the first time, she was struck by the nearly ethereal quality of his face, it seeming as though every angle had been sculpted by a higher power with the purpose of showing the world true beauty. That the mind behind the face was equally as rare in quality made her half wonder if perhaps darker powers were behind his creation, for no man should be possessed of such advantage.

Sighing, she withdrew her hand and did a pass through the small space to ensure the ladder had the trapdoor held securely, that the window was latched, and that all was well before retrieving her cloak. Wind howled through the cracks in the walls and from around the window, the chill sinking deep into her bones.

Shivering, Zarrah wrapped the cloak around her body, wishing she had a blanket, though there was no chill deep enough to make her retrieve the prior occupant's filthy quilt from the corner.

Keris stirred, muttering something unintelligible, his distress palpable.

Nightmare.

Without thinking, she went to him and shook his shoulder, hoping to rouse him enough to slip the dream. But he only thrashed violently, shouting something about not meaning it and nearly knocking over the lamp. "Keris," she hissed, moving the lamp before shaking him again. "Wake up."

"I'm sorry," he pleaded, eyes pinched shut as if in agony. "I'm sorry."

Her own breath came in rapid pants because she didn't know how to help him. Didn't know what to do to pull him from the depths of whatever horror consumed him because the cursed drug had him in its hold. Desperate, she gripped him tightly, her mouth pressed against his ear. "Keris, all is well. I'm here."

He stiffened, then whispered, "Valcotta," before falling still.

Heart still pounding, Zarrah stayed unmoving, arms braced against the floor and her lips against his ear. *Valcotta.* The name of her empire and all she held dear, but from his lips, it reverberated through to her core in ways Zarrah couldn't explain.

The wind howled, so violent now that bits of snow crept around the window frame and through the cracks, gusting across the floor. Keris's skin was ice beneath her lips, his body shivering, and her stomach tightened. *He's tougher than he looks,* Aren had said. The ability to survive the worst was in his veins, but there were still limits. All it would take was illness striking, taking advantage of injury and cold, and she could lose him.

He's not yours.

Zarrah's eyes stung as she warred with herself, but as the lamp burned low, the oil exhausted, she found herself pulling her cloak over both of them, then curling around Keris's back. Fitting herself against him as best she could, then reaching around his waist to find his icy fingers.

What is to stop you from making the same mistake again? What is to stop you from being lured back into his bed with sweet words and promises of pleasure?

Zarrah pressed her face to Keris's spine. Maybe this was a mistake. Maybe she was going to have regrets.

But he'd trusted her enough to watch his back, and to her, this felt right.

ZARRAH JERKED AWAKE, SURROUNDED BY darkness and unsure of what had woken her. Her body was still pressed against Keris's, her left arm numb from being draped over his waist all night, and she carefully eased it off him before sitting up.

A glance at the window revealed the snow had eased, the faintest glow of dawn pinkening the sky. The ladder and the belts still held the trapdoor firmly in place, but she still scanned the space for intruders.

"Where have you goddamned been?" a woman's shout echoed up from the room below them. "Out all night and stinking of cheap perfume, you think I don't know what you've been up to?"

A man's voice grumbled a penitent response, and Zarrah gave a faint smile as the woman continued to berate him. That had been what had woken her, not a threat.

Another door slammed, and Keris stirred. Not wanting him to realize she'd slept next to him, Zarrah moved away, pretending to fuss with the tray of plates from the prior night while he fully roused. Then she asked, "How do you feel?"

"Like I slept on a cold floor." He cautiously rotated his shoulder. "I was made for feather beds and hot baths, yet last night was the first time I've slept well in . . ." He trailed off, then gave a shrug. "A long time, at any rate."

"Narcotics have their uses," she mumbled, feeling his eyes on her as she unbuckled their belts from the ladder. Had he woken to find her curled around him? Should she say something? Tell him it was because she hadn't wanted him to freeze to death?

Better to pretend it hadn't happened. "Gather up your things, and we'll get something to eat."

"If we're going out, you'll need this."

She looked up to find him holding out her cloak. Bloody hell, she'd left it draped across him, which meant he *knew*.

"It was cold." She reached out to take it from him, and their fingers brushed together, sending a spark jolting through her. "I didn't want you to freeze to death."

"Because I'm irreplaceable?" Humor sparkled in his azure eyes.

"Insufferable is what you are." She fastened her cloak around her neck. "Let me check your bandages."

Keris dutifully pulled off his coat and shirt, and Zarrah's toes curled in her boots at the sight of his chiseled torso, every muscle perfectly defined, down to the V of abdominal muscles disappearing into his trousers. She peeked under the bandages and saw that the wound looked better than the night before. "It's healing."

"More scars for the collection."

His breath brushed her cheek as she tightened the bandages, her pulse accelerating because scars were a mark of survival. A symbol of the strength to endure, and rather than detracting from his appearance, they only made him more formidable. "Shall I find you a handkerchief to dry the tears of your injured vanity?"

He made a noise of amusement, then put his clothes back on. "What's our plan? I assume it isn't to go into the common room and announce that we're looking for the rebel commander."

"Definitely not." Sitting on her heels, Zarrah frowned. "We can assume that word of our escape will soon arrive in Arakis, if it hasn't already, which means my aunt's soldiers will be looking for us. We need to find the rebels before that happens."

"Look for dissenters?" Keris pulled his hair back, tying it behind his head. "Those picking fights with the soldiers, like we saw yesterday?"

Realizing she was staring, Zarrah handed him his belt before fastening her own. "I don't think any well-connected rebel would risk drawing that sort of attention down upon themselves. They've survived this long by being hard to catch."

Rubbing at the scruff on his chin, Keris frowned. "Somewhere we can hear gossip, then." His frown abruptly disappeared. "Bathhouse."

Her cheeks warmed, because while Keris might not know the nature of Valcottan bathhouses, she certainly did. "You're just in want of a razor."

"True, but much like bartenders, barbers know all the gossip. I would know, because I went through Serin's accounts after he took his last flight, and he had at least a dozen of each on the payroll."

"Bartenders seem a better choice," she said, heat moving from her cheeks to her chest. "Drunks talk."

"True, but do you really think the men and women we need to find are alehouse drunks?"

"Probably not." Sighing, she opened the trapdoor. "We'll do it your way, but there's something you should know."

"Oh?"

Forgoing the ladder, Zarrah jumped down and then looked up at him. "In this region of Valcotta, bathhouses are communal."

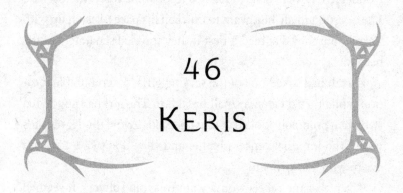

46

KERIS

HE WOULD NOT HAVE SUGGESTED IT IF HE HAD KNOWN.

Stepping over a pool of slush, Keris scowled as a cart proceeded to trundle by and splash him, cold water soaking his clothes. The streets were as crowded as they'd been yesterday, only today he noted how many of the people seemed to be wandering without purpose, more than a few camped in alleys with all their worldly possessions. And he also noticed the drawings. Dozens of walls and fences bore white paint depicting a woman in a crown walking over piles of corpses, cutting the throats of children, and looking up at the sky while starved figures lifted pleading arms to her. Under the scowling eyes of a soldier, two women were trying to scrub paint that said *Death to the Usurper* off a wall, and Keris marked dozens of smaller paintings showing people enacting various forms of violence against a crowned figure.

Though the rebellion had been growing for years, this rise in visible dissent had to be relatively recent, as gossip of this nature traveled far. It suggested the conflict was coming to a head, and he wondered if it was Petra who willed it so, or the rebels themselves. The question made him want to quicken his pace to catch up with Zarrah, but they'd agreed it best if they traveled separately to the bathhouse.

Zarrah had asked one of the serving girls for a reputable location while they'd eaten a small breakfast. The girl had suggested two, then pointedly looked at him and said, "Avoid the Tigress. It's where the imperial officers bathe, and they don't care to share steam with Maridrinians."

Given that the rebels would want to avoid soldiers, it seemed like a good idea to avoid such a place anyway, so Keris had only shrugged.

Ahead of him, Zarrah turned right down a street, and he followed, watching as she entered a building with two massive glass elephants flanking the entrance. Steam poured out each time the door opened to admit a patron, and his step quickened with the prospect of finally being clean, and not at all at the prospect of being naked in the same tub as Zarrah.

Then four soldiers exited a building in front of him, the largest nearly colliding with Keris. "Apologies," he muttered, but the man, who was even larger than Bermin had been, ignored him.

"It's unacceptable," the massive man said, pounding a fist against his thigh. "Those who speak so against Her Imperial Majesty should lose their tongues."

"Agreed," a female soldier answered. "But it's hard to discover who is responsible for the graffiti."

"The whole miserable city deserves to burn," another soldier muttered, rubbing his hands over his arms, and the big man gave him a warning glare.

"Mind your tongue. Our business here will be through soon enough, and then we will turn our eyes toward warmer climes."

Keris stiffened. Arakis was on the southern edge of Valcotta, so nearly the entire empire was warmer than this place, but the intensity of the big man's voice didn't suggest another domestic post. His eyes flicked over their uniforms, marking the same regalia that Zarrah had said signaled the imperial guard. They strode toward another bathhouse along the street, one with glass tigers flanking the doorway.

Keris wavered for only a heartbeat, then followed them, hoping that Zarrah would forgive him for deviating from the plan.

Hot steam rushed over him, and Keris breathed deeply, inhaling the thick smell of scented oils. A young woman dressed in silk trousers and a stomach-baring blouse stood in the entrance behind a glass table balanced on the backs of more glass tigers. She nodded respectfully at the soldiers, more young men and women appearing to escort them into the back.

Then her brown eyes fixed on Keris, glossy lips curling in disgust.

Which was perhaps not unwarranted. Not only was he filthy, but he still wore the moldy sealskin coat given to him on Aren's stolen ghost ship. His cloak and boots were stained, and the knees of his trousers had holes in them.

"This house caters to individuals of a certain class," she said. "Please leave."

He held up a golden coin.

The young woman's eyes settled on it, jaw working back and forth. "Do you want to get yourself beaten?" she demanded. "This house is full of imperial soldiers."

Keris added a second coin.

As always, the gleam of gold blinded eyes to both dirt and nationality, and the young woman smiled. "Perhaps we might take your garments here so that they may be laundered?"

"Past laundering, I'm afraid," he answered. "If you could burn them and provide me with new, it would be most appreciated."

There was no mistaking the relief in her eyes. Snapping her fingers, she waited for a boy to appear, then said, "New garments. Burn the old."

Keris gleefully pulled off the cloak and overcoat and handed them over to the boy. The young woman held out a gilded box, in which he placed his coin and knives. She locked it and presented him with a small key on a chain. He put it over his head.

The boy disappeared with the filthy clothes, another appearing and handing him a cup of wine before leading him into the back.

Unlike Maridrinian bathhouses, which were usually dark, Keris was led into a large open chamber with a ceiling made of glass, though the light was muted by the excessive steam. A dozen pools with colored tiles filled the space, glass tigers spitting steaming water into each to keep it hot for the relaxing patrons. All were Valcottan, the few who noticed Keris giving him dark looks, though none made a move to complain.

The soldiers he'd followed in were already disrobed and in one of the pools, a woman with a stringed instrument singing near them.

"The rest of your clothes, sir," the boy said. Keris pulled off his shirt and trousers, noting the boy's eyes going to the bandage on his shoulder.

"Brigands." Keris pulled loose the wrapping, handing it to the boy.

The boy gestured to a pool near the edge of the room. "The salt will serve you well, then, sir. A selection of clothing will be made available when you are ready to leave."

The thick steam in the room provided a partial cloak as Keris waded into the pool, grimacing as the water splashed his injury.

The soldiers he'd followed were barely visible through the steam, their heads bent together in conversation in the pool they shared on the far side of the chamber.

Retrieving some soap from the selection available, Keris scrubbed away the filth as he considered how to get near enough to overhear. He made himself busy washing grime from his hair, the cloud of grit that floated away to the drain stained slightly red from old blood. God help him, but it felt good to be clean.

But that wasn't his reason for being here.

The pools closer to the officer and his companions were filled with other Valcottan soldiers. Keris wasn't about to test the limits of their patience by joining them, given that the few who'd noticed him had made the same face he would if he found a turd floating in his bath. His eyes fixed on the barber's chair nearest to his target's pool, but there was no way he could get to it without one of them catching sight of his pale ass, which would surely curb their conversation.

Two Valcottans emerged from behind screens of colored glass at the rear of the room, great gouts of steam accompanying them. Doors to the outside, then, likely latrines. Motioning to the boy, he secured two towels, wrapping one around his waist and draping the other over his head. He moved to the rear of the room, keeping as far from the other pool as he could, then stepped behind the screens. There he found a table with empty glasses, pitchers of lemon water, and trays of sliced fruit. On the trays were tiny forks, and he picked one up as he walked to the latrine door. Opening it, he glanced to ensure no one was watching, then jammed the fork tines into one of the hinges, snapping them off with a twist of his wrist.

His skin pebbled with cold as he availed himself of the facilities, returning to discover the boy frantically trying to shut the door, with little success. Keris walked past him, the room now filled with excessive quantities of steam, which more than hid his fair complexion as he made his way to the barber's chair, settling himself into it with his back to the pool just as the boy managed to get the door closed.

"What more can we do? With the commander distracted, we'd thought that we'd gain traction," a woman's voice said. "But no one is taking the bribes. No one is responding to threats. It's time to resort to force. To beatings. To imprisonment. Only fear will loosen tongues on the location of their stronghold."

"Mmmm." Keris recognized the big man's deep rumble. "To do so carries the risk of the people blaming our Imperial Majesty for their suffering rather than them understanding she seeks to protect them. We need to make Arakis see that the rot must be cut out to save the victim."

The barber approached. "How do you wish to be shaved, sir?"

"Get rid of it all," Keris muttered, trying to keep his focus on the conversation while the man sharpened his razor. It had been many years since he'd allowed a barber near his throat.

"How then, Welran?" Anger raised the woman's voice. "While you have been in Arakis less than a month, I've been stationed here for *two years,* trying to catch the wretch and his followers. My patience for coddling the masses thins. Nightly, the rebels splash their slander across the walls and buildings of Arakis, only for all to lift their hands in innocence when dawn brightens the sky. My soldiers are attacked and murdered whenever they are caught alone, forced to take a fellow to guard their back while they squat. The city is against us. They are as much our enemy as the Maridrinians."

The big man that she'd called Welran made a sharp noise. "Keep your voice down."

Chastised, the woman fell silent, and the conversation stuttered as the barber began to soap Keris's face.

"Maridrina is as weak as it has ever been," Welran eventually said. "Fleet lost to the Tempest Seas, soldiers filling the bellies of Ithicanian sharks. The time to take back Nerastis is nigh, but that doesn't mean we turn our back on this threat."

"We know the commander took the bait," the woman said. "Once word arrives that Bermin has killed him, the rebellion will fall to pieces."

They don't know, Keris realized, muttering a negative to the barber's query about a mustache. *Word has yet to come from Devil's Island.*

"He's always been a clever bastard," Welran answered. "And in all these long years, he's yet to put her before his band of rebels. I would not be so quick to think that he will now."

The barber's razor scraped over his skin with expert ease, and Keris's focus on the conversation slipped. He'd never been comfortable allowing another man to hold a blade to his throat, and Keris watched him, looking for any sign of ill intent. Which was why he saw the barber's eyes widen with alarm.

Boots thudded against the glass tiles, and Keris caught hold of the barber's wrist to force the blade away from his throat even as he turned his head. But the soldiers weren't here for him.

Instead they strode to the pool. "General, a ship has arrived with news."

Unable to see what was going on, Keris held his breath, as did the barber, who seemed not to notice Keris's grip on his wrist.

"Well, what is it?"

A scuff of boots, muttered words, but Keris didn't miss *the rebels are allied with Maridrina and Ithicana.*

"Fuck," he muttered, and the barber echoed the sentiment, the rest of the messenger's words hidden beneath the noise of the fountains.

Silence stretched, then Welran said, "There is more. Spit it out."

The messenger heaved in a breath. "It is news of His Highness, Prince Bermin. They say he was slain."

It felt like all the air had been sucked out of the room, and then a bellow of grief and rage shattered the silence. Keris reacted on instinct, diving out of the chair and away from the pool, dragging the barber with him.

Welran surged from the water, manhood slapping against his legs as he gained his footing on the slick tile. The messenger staggered backward, but the big man lunged and caught hold of his cloak. With a howl that seemed more beast than human, he smashed his giant fist into the man's face. Again and again, holding the messenger upright while he shattered the man's skull into bloody pulp, then tossed him into the pool.

"I will have vengeance," he roared, picking up the chair Keris had been sitting in and smashing it against the tiles. "I will have blood!"

Keris and the barber stumbled over each other as they retreated, Welran smashing the bathhouse while patrons and staff screamed and fled, the soldiers staying well out of reach of their general's rage.

"Death to every rebel!" Welran screamed, spinning in a circle. "I will burn you all to ash before I turn on your Maridrinian master!"

His eyes fixed on Keris and the barber, and the barber squeaked, "He's Maridrinian!"

Welran's eyes bulged, and then he was sprinting toward Keris, bloody fists raised.

Keris ran.

Leaping over the divans in his path, he slipped on the wet tile and nearly fell. Catching his balance, he raced to the front door, the glass cracking beneath the impact of his palms as he slammed it open. Slush splashed his legs as he ran into the street, towel clutched in his hand.

It was madness.

People were screaming and running away, but from both ends of the street, soldiers on horseback approached.

He was trapped.

47

ZARRAH

SHE WAS GOING TO KILL HIM.

Wrapped in a robe and staring at her steaming tea, Zarrah did her best to focus on the wrinkled matrons conversing next to her, but her mind kept going to Keris.

This had been *his* idea. His stupid bloody plan to sit in the bath and listen to gossip, but while she'd spent the past hour soaking in a tub, listening to women complain about her aunt's soldiers while their husbands pretended not to stare at her breasts, Keris was nowhere to be seen.

What if something happened to him? fear whispered, but she just made a face and swallowed the rest of her tea. The only thing that had happened was that, as usual, he'd changed the plan with no mind to keeping her informed. He was probably in a bar somewhere, plying customers with drinks to gain information, which he'd subsequently deliver to her as though questioning drunks had been his idea, not hers.

"I'm going to kill him," she said, aloud this time, garnering a few startled glances from other patrons. A heartbeat later, there was a commotion at the entrance to the bathhouse.

Keris, naked as the day he was born and gripping a towel in one hand, sprinted around the corner.

Sliding to a stop, he scanned the steam-filled room until his eyes latched on hers. "Run!" he shouted; then angry bellows shattered the silence.

Zarrah had barely made it to her feet when Keris had her by the hand and was dragging her to the rear of the building. "Another way out?" he shouted at one of the girls who worked there. With wide eyes, she pointed to a door.

Then they were running.

"What is going on?" Zarrah demanded, cold biting her skin as they flew out the back door. "Where were you?"

"Later," he gasped.

Slush splashed her legs, her robe flapping as they ran, the shouts of pursuit loud, but she didn't turn back. Weaponless, their only option was flight, and given Keris was naked and she was nearly so, they needed to get out of sight.

People gaped at them as they raced past, the clatter of horses' hooves deafening as soldiers converged. "What did you do?" she demanded. "What the hell did you do, Keris?"

He didn't answer, only tightened his grip on her hand. "We need to climb. Get to the rooftops."

"You can't!" She risked a sideways glance at him. His unbandaged wound was starting to seep blood. He might be able to get onto a rooftop, but not cross them with the speed it would take to evade capture.

"I'll have to."

A door swung open ahead of them, and a woman dressed in a black leather gown appeared. "In here! Hurry!"

Zarrah hesitated, distrustful of any offer of help, but what choice did they have? Hauling Keris by his hand, she dragged him into the darkness of the building, the latch on the door shutting firmly behind them.

The interior smelled strongly of scented oils, and from somewhere a drummer pounded a rhythmic beat. What was this place?

"Up the stairs, hurry!"

"Who are you?" Keris demanded.

"We've mutual friends," the woman answered, even as a man called out, "Miri, the soldiers are searching every house on the street. Something about a Maridrinian assaulting Welran?"

"Don't impede them," the woman answered. "They need no justification for destruction."

Red glass sconces on the walls provided only minimal light, and Zarrah stumbled twice as they climbed, before her eyes adjusted. "What is this place?"

"Brothel," Keris muttered.

Simultaneously, the woman announced, "A pleasure house."

Reaching the second level, she led them down a carpeted hallway lined with doors. Hedonistic whispers filtered through the walls, but they were dominated by the pounding drum, the rhythm making it seem as though the building had a heart throbbing at its core. They passed an open door, and Zarrah glanced inside, her eyes widening at the sight of a masked woman with three men before Keris pulled her onward.

"In here," the woman—Miri—said, opening the door at the end. The room was nearly filled by a silk-covered bed, cords fastened to the posters, the table across from it covered with things Zarrah had heard of but never seen with her own eyes. Climbing on the bed, the woman opened the window on the wall above it. "Climb across the roofs," she said. "Seek an inn tonight called the Wounded Lioness, and you will find those you are searching for."

Scrambling up next to her, Zarrah looked at the climb that would be required and then back to Keris, who had wrapped the towel around his waist. "Not happening. He's injured."

"I'll manage," he said, but she didn't miss how his jaw tightened as he looked out.

"You'll end up broken on the cobbles." Zarrah pulled the window shut. "We'll hide."

A knock sounded, and a man dressed in silk trousers that left nothing to the imagination appeared. "Miri, they are here to search. General Welran is in the streets, covered with blood. They say he was stabbed by a Maridrinian."

Zarrah felt her eyes bulge. "What?"

"That's a lie." Keris tried to cross his arms, only his towel slipped. "The blood is from the man he beat to death."

"God have mercy on us all." Miri waved her hand at the man. "Slow them down, but don't be obvious about it."

"I'll climb," Keris said. "There's no other choice. There's nowhere in here to hide."

"No." Zarrah scanned the room, but it offered no solutions. "We need to backtrack. Get to the streets."

The moment the words left her lips, the thud of boots on stairs filled the air.

"If you won't climb, you'll need to hide in plain sight." Miri gestured at Keris. "In this house, women are served, not men. She is the patron."

Zarrah's stomach flipped, and Keris gave a sharp shake of his head. "I'll climb."

He moved onto the bed, reaching to unlatch the window, but Zarrah caught his wrist. "Now is not the time to cling to morality. Too much is at stake."

"It won't work," he said. "They saw my face."

"Then I suggest you keep it well hidden," Miri snapped. Going to a closet, she dug through the contents and threw a mask at Zarrah. "Most of the highborn women wear them to hide their identity." Then she went to the hearth, picking up a handful of ash, which she rubbed into Keris's hair, turning it from blond to gray before knotting it behind his head. With a bit of soot, she swiftly rimmed both his eyes. "I could use a pretty face like yours, if you're ever in search of work. We would have you trained, and you'd fetch a fortune."

Zarrah's face burned, but Keris said, "It's always nice to have options." His smirk vanished as Miri ripped away the towel, using it to wipe clean the mud splattered on his legs before tossing it into the fire.

She handed a lace robe to Zarrah, the one from the bathhouse joining Keris's towel. "On the bed, girl. Against the pillows." Heart pounding, Zarrah obliged, allowing the woman to arrange the robe artfully so that it covered her breasts, though her whole body burned as Miri parted her knees.

The tread of heavy boots drew closer, orders to search every room clearly audible, but Keris remained where he stood, eyes on the opposite wall. "Your prudishness will get you killed," Miri snapped at him. "Face between her legs, now!"

A soft growl escaped his lips, but as Keris shook his head, Zarrah said, "We are out of options."

"Fine." He knelt before her. Lowering his head, he rested his cheek against the inside of her thigh. Miri lifted one of Zarrah's legs to wrap it around his neck, murmuring, "To hide the injury."

Stepping back, she straightened her leather skirts as she eyed the scene. "They'll have seen similar in the other rooms. Make it convincing." Then she turned on her heel, the door clicking shut behind her.

Zarrah tried to relax, but her whole body felt stiff as a board, her eyes fixed on the ceiling. "Where did you go?" she whispered, because the thought of remaining in this position in silence was more than she could bear. "What happened? Why did you attack Welran?"

More importantly, why was her aunt's most trusted soldier and bodyguard *here*?

"I saw some officers going into the bathhouse with the glass tigers." His breath was warm against her naked skin, each exhale sending a quiver through her. "I followed them in and was listening to their conversation, their plans, when a messenger arrived with news about what transpired on Devil's Island, including Bermin's fate."

"Oh, God," she breathed, understanding filling her.

"The big one, Welran, lost his head. Beat the messenger to pulp while he cursed the rebels and their *Maridrinian master*. I was attempting to extricate myself when the barber kindly pointed out my nationality to save his own skin. Welran went after me, and I fled. You know the rest."

Zarrah squeezed her eyes shut, horror filling her. "There will be a reckoning."

"You know him?"

"All my life," she whispered. "He's my aunt's bodyguard, and for as long as memory, the rumor has been that it was Welran who sired Bermin."

"Fuck."

"An apt assessment." The boots were coming closer, the drums now silent, and Zarrah stared at the door as she listened to the shouts of protest as trysts were interrupted. The search progressed down the hall, her heart throbbing faster and faster.

"If it doesn't work," Keris said, a loose strand of his hair brushing her thigh, "you get out that window. I'll hold them off."

"We are allies," she answered. "That means we stand together. And if it comes to it, we die together. Now make this convincing."

Threading her fingers through his hair, she pulled him against her right as the door exploded inward.

Zarrah screamed with outrage as two soldiers strode inside. "What is the meaning of this?"

"A would-be assassin attacked General Welran," one of them answered. "A Maridrinian. We are searching the quarter for him."

"Well, he's not in here," she spat. "Get out!"

"We need to search the room."

"Then be quick about it. And you"—her fingers tightened in Keris's hair—"finish what you started. I didn't pay a fortune for your tongue to watch you gape at soldiers."

Said soldiers were staring, obviously considering his fair skin as reason for further investigation, and Keris was not helping the situation. His lips were pressed against her sex, his breath ragged and hot, but he remained unmoving. Unconvincing.

Tightening her grip to the point it probably hurt, she said, "Did you hear me?"

He lifted his head ever so slightly, soot-rimmed eyes meeting hers. Despite their lives being on the line, there was no fear in his blue gaze, only pure masculine lust. Lust that Zarrah knew was only held at bay by the promise that he'd made to her. "Finish me," she ordered, hearing the breathiness in her voice.

His gaze darkened, but for a heartbeat, Keris didn't move. Then he lowered his head between her legs, a gasp tearing from her throat as his lips pressed against her in a kiss that turned the embers in her core to an inferno.

"Your officers will hear of this outrage," she hissed at the soldiers, but they only smirked, one of them leaning forward to catch at the edge of her mask even as Keris parted her with his tongue. "I doubt it," he said. "Will mean you admitting you had a whore between your legs rather than your husband."

Zarrah pushed the soldier's hand away, her other still locked in Keris's hair.

The soldiers laughed, and Zarrah's pulse roared, partially with rising panic that they weren't leaving and partially because of the effect Keris's tongue was having on her body.

He knew her. Knew her body and everything she liked, and on her order, he was making use of that knowledge. Sweat beaded on her brow, tension building as he sucked and teased her, fingers trailing lines of fire along her naked thighs.

The soldiers made a show of slowly searching the room, but their eyes never left her naked body. Keris's naked body. She needed them to leave. Needed them to shut the door, or else . . . or else . . .

"If you wish to watch, you must pay," Miri said from the doorway. "Else it is theft, and I'll report you to the guild."

"Consider it a bit of goodwill toward us, Miri," one of them said, but the house's matron crossed her arms, dark eyes narrowed, and they grudgingly backed out of the room. "Apologies," she murmured, then shut the door.

Keris lifted his face, and a scream of frustration threatened to rise from Zarrah's throat. Like an addict deprived of her drug of choice, her body *needed* him. Needed this fix, and though her mind shouted at her that it was folly, her lips whispered, "Don't stop."

"Zarrah . . ." His voice was strained, as though he battled his own inner war, and she held her breath, eyes squeezed shut, waiting to see what part of him won. Waiting to see if they'd both succumb, proving that what lay between them burned as hot as it ever had. A desire that had always been wrong, always been forbidden, yet left every barrier in ash.

Even those they built themselves.

Her soul felt his will bend to lust a heartbeat before his tongue flicked over her, Zarrah's back bowing as a sob of pleasure tore from her lips. All the world fell away as his fingers pressed inside her, curving to stroke her core even as he sucked her clit. As he pulled her to the edge of climax, every plot and plan and strategy falling victim to her undying need for his presence, his touch, his—

Love.

The word, and all the truths that came with it, pulled her over the edge, only some hidden reserve of self-preservation keeping her from screaming his name as pleasure broke her apart, reforming her heart and soul, only to shatter them again because she had to give him up.

Keris shifted, resting his cheek against her hip, and she moved her hand from his hair to trace a finger down the side of his face. *Say something,* she silently whispered, not knowing whether she was speaking to Keris or herself. "I'm sorry."

The only response was the renewed drumming at the center of the house.

"For what?" he answered. "I'm the one who got us into this mess by following Welran. It's my fault."

"Yes, but I didn't need to . . . I shouldn't have asked . . ." God help her, she couldn't even get the words out. Was proving her aunt right with everything she did. Everything she said. Everything she *didn't* say.

"You think it would have been any different if our roles had been reversed?" His blue eyes flared as he sat upright, revealing that he'd been no less caught up in the moment than she had been. Unbidden, a vision of herself on her knees before him filled her mind's eye, a mixture of memory and imagination that was so vivid her breath caught.

"I hate how right she was." Zarrah squeezed her eyes shut. "She said that the moment I was back in your presence, I'd fall back in

THE ENDLESS WAR   345

your bed. That my loyalty to Valcotta would always come second to my desire for you."

"Petra's a master manipulator," he answered. "She's also a fucking madwoman."

"Yet she saw the truth. As did Bermin." In a surge of motion, Zarrah leaned across the small space, her hands pressed to either side of him. Cheek brushing his as she whispered into his ear, "How can I be the empress Valcotta needs when all I want to do is fall to my knees and suck the king of Maridrina's cock?"

The muscles of his jaw tightened. "That's not what I want from you."

"Because it's all about what *you* want." She moved her head, lips grazing his. "It's all about having things your way, on your terms. I know that better than anyone. Have watched you do it time and again. Watched you do it today. Yet it doesn't seem to matter when I'm in your presence, because all I want is you."

Keris pulled away from her. "There was a time I thought I'd die to hear you say that again, Valcotta, but not like this."

She was furious with herself, but Zarrah found herself turning her venom on him. "So sorry to disappoint."

"Don't." He gave her a warning glare. "There is a limit to the abuse I'll take just because you drank that bitch's poison. It's Petra who deserves your hate, yet you treat her words as though they were delivered by God. Like a fucking mantra."

"I do hate her." Her hands clenched into fists. "I don't want to listen to her. Except to ignore the truth because it came from the mouth of my enemy is just as foolish as believing lies."

"Petra has taken the truth about us and twisted it to the point it barely resembles reality, yet somehow you now hold it as memory. She's undermined your judgment by making you believe that everything you did was motivated by lust."

Nausea swam in Zarrah's gut, her head a mess, no part of her able to focus on a thought. "I'm losing my mind." She stared at her palms, which were marked with bleeding crescents. "I feel like I'm going mad."

"You're not going mad." He gripped her hands. "Petra knows we are stronger united, so it is in her interest to turn you against me even as she turns you against yourself. But ask yourself this: If I manipulated you and used you as part of my scheme to further myself, why am I here now? If all I cared about was gaining the crown, why did I leave it in my half sister's hands to race south to risk my life freeing you from prison? Why am I with you in Arakis, searching for the rebels, if all I care about is a plush life in a palace surrounded by women? Because to be very clear, if that was what I wanted, I could have it in a heartbeat." His eyes searched hers. "Deep down, you must know that what she claims doesn't make sense."

Zarrah didn't know what was real. Couldn't remember. Couldn't think, because it felt as though her mind were unraveling like a spool of thread.

The room spun in a darkening blur of colors as she sucked in breath after breath that didn't reach her lungs. "I feel sick," she gasped, and then everything went dark.

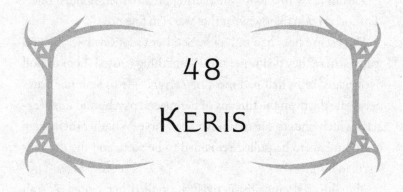

48
KERIS

He caught Zarrah as she slumped sideways, though her loss of consciousness was brief. Gasping, she jerked awake.

"Breathe." He held her steady. "Breathe, or you'll pass out again."

Her dark eyes were full of panic as she fought to get air into her lungs, and Keris wanted to scream in rage at what had been done to her. Petra, with her heartless guile, had turned Zarrah against herself, stripping the woman he loved of her confidence, her fearlessness, her brilliance. And she'd used him to do it.

"I can't . . ." She was shaking like a leaf, tears coating her cheeks. "I don't know who I am anymore. I don't know what I'm doing."

"You are Zarrah Anaphora," he said. "The daughter of Aryana Anaphora, who was the named heir of Ephraim Anaphora. You are a warrior. A general. And by Valcottan law, the rightful empress of this empire. You are in Arakis to join forces with an army capable of overthrowing your aunt, who unlawfully usurped the throne and murdered your mother. And once you have succeeded in liberating Valcotta from her tyranny, you will end the Endless War and bring peace to the Empire."

Zarrah drew in a long, shuddering breath, then nodded once. "I'm sorry. I don't know what that was. I'm fine now."

She wasn't fine, had only wrestled her emotions back behind walls, where they'd simmer until something caused them to boil over again. Petra had had most of Zarrah's life to sink her claws deep. She'd woven the threads of her niece's psyche and knew exactly which ones to tug to unravel the whole. Whether there were more threads to be pulled remained to be seen, and the thought terrified him.

She shivered, and instinctively he pulled her closer. Zarrah molded against him, arms around his waist. She felt limp, exhausted, as though their conversation had stolen every ounce of energy she possessed.

"I can go ask for more wood for the fire." His voice rasped, and he coughed to clear it, painfully aware of the press of her naked skin against his. Of the taste of her still lingering on his lips. "We may be here for a while."

"Not yet," she answered, her head resting against his uninjured shoulder. "The soldiers might still be in the building. Or come back. Better to wait."

"Right."

Reaching down, he pulled the cheap silk sheets over her bare legs, easing her down onto the bed so that they were facing each other. His shoulder felt like it was trying to murder him from within, but Keris ignored the pain to lift his hand and brush her hair from her face.

The corner of Zarrah's mouth turned up, but her eyes were full of sadness. "What are we doing, Keris? How many times will we come together, only for circumstance to pull us apart?"

"I don't know," he answered, pain, old and new, welling in his heart.

"Is there a future for us?" she asked. "Is there a path forward I'm not seeing that allows everything we're fighting for to coexist with us spending our nights in each other's arms?"

The word *yes* tried to push its way from his lips, but he swallowed it down. "No."

"Then why do we keep trying?" Her lip quivered, and he watched her bite down on it, warring with emotions. "Why do we inflict such suffering upon ourselves? Why do we come together, knowing that the wound will inevitably be torn open again?"

He didn't want to answer these questions. Wanted to close his mouth over hers to silence them, because to answer would be to impose logic on matters of the heart. Instead he cleared his throat, voice hoarse as he said, "For my part, it is the absence from you that cuts deepest, the wound growing crueler with every hour, day, week that I cannot see your face or hear your voice. The hope that our separation will end, even briefly, allows me to endure the pain, but if I were to lose that hope, I think the wound would fester until it consumed me entirely."

"Don't say such things," she whispered. "It sounds like prophesy."

Keris looked away, hating that word, though he didn't know why.

"It's what I dreamed about while I was in the bath waiting for you," she said. "A future where all that we desire comes to pass, crowns on our heads and peace between our nations. A world where our union would be accepted. Yet even then, I could not see my way through, as to rule, we must reside in our nations' hearts. You in Vencia. Me in Pyrinat. For you know as well as I do that the moment we turn our backs, darker minds will try to secure power. You risk as much even now by being here."

She was not wrong. There was no doubt in his mind that his brothers were plotting how to be rid of him, and those next in line would all be quick to fan the fires of war.

"And what if we had children. How—"

"Stop." He squeezed his eyes shut. "Please stop."

Zarrah fell silent, the only sound the endless beat of the drum and the faint cries of patrons in the throes of thoughtless pleasure.

"I don't know what is worse," she said. "To stop now and endure the pain of what might have been or to keep going, knowing that there will come a moment when I lose it all."

"You don't need to decide now, Zarrah." Nor did he want her to, because she'd never chosen him. Not once. It was always her people, her honor, her country, which was why he knew she'd be an empress for the ages. He admired her virtue and yet hated it in equal measure, for it hurt them both so deeply.

"I know," she answered. "But until I do decide, I will pursue no intimacy between us. I wish only to take that step with a clear mind and certain heart."

When it came to her, his heart was always certain. Always stalwart in its need to choose her and only her, no matter the cost. But he would not change who she was for the sake of protecting his heart, so Keris only nodded.

They lay in silence, her forehead pressed against his chest, as they waited for Miri to bring word it was safe for them to depart. After a time, he noticed Zarrah's breathing had slowed, a steady rise and fall against him. Asleep.

Keris's chest tightened, sick on the emotions that churned within him, but as the fire burned low, he held her close, warding away the cold even if he was powerless to ward away the doubts that plagued her. Wishing that he could freeze time so as to live in this moment because Keris knew it wouldn't last.

Sure enough, as soon as the thought crossed his mind, the handle on the door twisted and swung open, Zarrah jerking awake as Daria appeared in the entrance. The woman gave them a once-over, then grinned. "Good to see you alive, Your Graces."

49
ZARRAH

Tearing away from Keris, Zarrah straightened the cheap robe she wore, heat burning her cheeks. "Likewise. We weren't certain whether you escaped."

"When you have been the prey as long as we have, you learn a few tricks for evading the predators."

"We are the predators now," Zarrah answered, lifting her chin in defiance against the weakness that had plagued her.

"Says the woman hiding in a brothel." Daria chuckled as she shut the door behind her, tossing garments onto the bed. "Though I'm pleased to see your spirit remains intact." She winked at Keris. "All painted up like a whore. It's a fitting look for you, Your Grace."

Ever nonplussed, Keris only lifted the trousers to inspect them. "How's your stomach handling the change in diet, Captain?"

Zarrah tensed as Daria's jaw tightened, but the other woman only bent to examine Keris's injury. "The Devil must have had his fill of your conversation while you were on the island, for when offered your soul, I see he spat it back out again."

"No accounting for taste," Keris answered, then turned away to pull on the clothes Daria had brought.

Zarrah quickly grabbed the other set, discarding the robe in favor of trousers, a blouse, and a sturdy vest.

"Our people will collect your things from the bathhouse," Daria said to her. "His Grace's belongings are another matter, though. Welran's soldiers took them in the hopes of using them to find you. Is there anything in them that speaks to your true identity?"

"Knives are Maridrinian make," Keris answered. "Coin was a few different currencies, and the clothes were from Cardiff."

"No letters? Jewelry?"

"No. Ahnna Kertell has my signet ring."

Daria's eyebrows rose. "And why is that?"

"She's negotiating peace between Maridrina and Ithicana. My kingdom and council believe me in Ithicana, and I'd like to keep it that way."

"Right."

Daria rocked on her heels, seeming to consider this information, which Zarrah also found interesting. It occurred to her that she was painfully lacking in the details of what Keris had been up to in the time they had been apart, which was something that needed to be remedied. "Do we know what information Welran has about what happened on the island?"

"Some," Daria answered. "There were survivors, and they told those who came to their aid the identities of all the players, including that His Grace was there." She jerked her chin at Keris. "So while they may not know where he is now, a princess with a signet ring certainly won't deceive the Usurper into believing His Grace is in Ithicana."

"Feel free to abandon titles," Keris said, finally turning back around. "Given you've seen me in the nude, I feel we're on a first-name basis."

Daria gave him a dark grin. "You might regret that."

"Undoubtedly." Keris's eyes, still rimmed with soot, flicked to Zarrah.

He's waiting for you to take control. Her cheeks burned, because she'd spent all her life being trained to lead, and it felt like she'd forgotten how. "Are you taking us to the commander?"

"Eventually. His location, as well as the location of the stronghold, is a much-sought-after secret, and tensions are high with today's events. Accommodations need to be made to ensure we aren't followed."

"Does this commander have a name?" Keris asked.

Daria looked at her feet. "Sure. But that's as much a secret as the rest." Rolling her shoulders, she added, "I'll leave him to share what information he sees fit."

Other than rumors remembered in Ithicana and a vague statement made by Serin that she was the rightful heir, the commander appeared to be the only concrete source that Zarrah's claim to Valcotta's throne was legitimate. Who was he to have such information? Why was everyone certain that he was credible? The urge to press Daria was strong, but instead she said, "I look forward to it."

A knock sounded at the door behind Daria. "It's me," a familiar voice said; then the door opened, and Saam stepped inside. He smiled nervously at Zarrah, giving an awkward bow. "Empress." Then his eyes lighted on Keris, awkwardness disappearing as he handed him a pair of boots. "I knew it was you. Soon as I heard that some straw-haired pale-arsed Maridrinian scrapped with Welran, I said, 'Friends, that is Maridrina's king and none other. The man has balls of solid rock and the nine lives of a cat.'"

Keris huffed out an amused breath. "I think only a handful of those lives are left. Good to see you alive, Saam."

"Daria thought you were done for, but I said nah, an arrow won't be enough."

"God spare me, enough already," Daria said, pulling the bag from Saam's hand and handing it to Zarrah. "Your things."

"Right. Sorry." Saam gave another awkward bow. "Empress."

"Zarrah," she swiftly corrected. "One needs to be legally crowned before claiming the title."

"The Usurper is *illegally* crowned and still claims the title," he answered. "So seems just enough for you to, Imperial Majesty." Bowing yet again, he then slung an arm around Keris, hauling him out the door. "Spent the whole of the voyage back telling all who'd listen, which was everyone aboard, about your mad plan on the island."

Their voices disappeared down the hallway, leaving Zarrah alone with Daria, the tension instantly ratcheting higher in Keris's absence. And it was no wonder, given the way she'd treated the other woman after discovering the rebel prisoners' method of survival. Zarrah had been so horrified and disgusted that she'd run into the arms of the enemy instead of pausing to listen to explanation. Whereas Keris had apparently handled it well enough to make jokes about it.

But Zarrah was also reminded of her conversation with Lara. She needed to make a choice about her relationship with the Devil's Island prisoners with a clear eye to the consequences. "How has it been, being back? Have you been treated well?"

Daria was quiet. "Well enough."

Zarrah could guess what that meant. The prisoners were treated with cool courtesy, but it was not the homecoming they'd hoped for.

"You should put your hood up," Daria said. "The search has moved elsewhere, but that doesn't mean they won't be watching."

Pulling on her cloak, Zarrah lifted the hood into place, Daria doing the same. "I'm sorry," she said as they followed the sound of Saam's laughter. "For how I reacted. For not listening to your side of the story." She considered Keris's joke, and added, "For being so self-righteous."

Daria was silent until they reached the stairs. "It was a horrible thing that we did," she finally said. "That's why we kept you out of it, because we knew that we couldn't afford your reputation to be tarnished by such behavior. That we couldn't give the Usurper anything that might be used against you. It's become abundantly clear to me that doing so was the right choice."

Zarrah's eyes pricked, remembering how no one had stood between her and whatever birds landed on the island. In her desperation and hunger, she hadn't questioned it, but now she understood that they'd sacrificed the opportunity of a meal that wasn't salted with immorality for her sake.

"I'll never be the same," Daria said. "I'll never lose the taint of the things that I did, the things I forced my tribe to do, to survive. I'll never not feel filthy. Never not feel sick. Never not wonder if it would have been better to die." She stopped on the steps, staring downward. "Except if we had, then think of how differently things would have gone when you arrived on that island. When Keris and Aren came. When the commander risked the Usurper's trap to free you."

"We'd all be dead," Zarrah said, answering the question, "the rebellion crushed. And the Usurper would continue on as she always has. So it seems to me that the right choice was made, despite the burden you will forever carry." Gripping Daria's arm, she turned the other woman to face her. "On my honor, I do not, and will not, hold what you did to survive against you. And I will have your back in the days to come."

Daria's hazel eyes filled with tears. "Thank you, Empress."

Zarrah didn't correct the title, because to name her so was what Daria and the others had suffered to achieve. She would not diminish that, even if the title was as-yet unearned. "Let's go. If Saam doesn't quit kissing Keris's ass the way he is, we won't be able to get his ego out the door."

Daria laughed, wiping at her eyes. "Truer words never spoken." They continued down the steps, finding the men standing with Miri, who was wiping Keris's face clean with a cloth.

"You know," Daria said just before they reached them, "that's the first time I've ever heard you call her the Usurper."

It was true. Petra had always been her empress, her savior, her aunt. But as the poison the monster had filled her with was slowly expelled, Zarrah found that the Usurper was none of those things to her anymore. "It's time I started calling her what she is to me so that she might learn what I am to her. The enemy." Squaring her shoulders, she said, "Now take me to the commander."

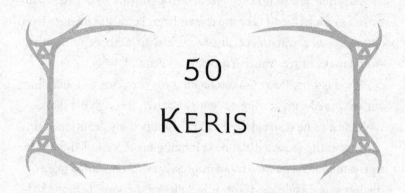

50

KERIS

IT WAS SNOWING AGAIN WHEN THEY LEFT THE PLEASURE HOUSE, Saam talking Keris's ear off as he led them through the sodden streets. Traffic had once again returned, but there was an uneasy edge to the city, civilians eyeing the soldiers on patrol like dogs they thought likely to bite. Keris kept casting backward glances at Zarrah and Daria, whose heads were together in conversation, wishing they'd keep closer.

Not because they weren't more capable than he was of defending themselves if there was trouble but because he knew the weight that was about to be placed on Zarrah's shoulders. The rebels had made her the heart of the resistance, salvation incarnate, destined to achieve all they'd fought for and to change their lives forever. An incredible amount of pressure, and Zarrah had already been pushed past the limits of what anyone should endure. He was afraid that the pressure of the rebels' expectations would push her over the edge. It made his own fear rise, and with it, the desire to insulate her from what was to come. To pull her away from it.

Except that would be a mistake.

Zarrah *needed* to do this. Needed to fight this fight because it wasn't just a battle to take the crown from Petra and liberate Valcotta; it was a war to reclaim her self-worth. To deny her that would make him as much a monster as Petra.

"It's this one," Saam said, reaching for the door of a building with a carved sign of a lioness with an arrow through her flank.

A blast of heat struck him as Keris stepped inside, none of the patrons in the crowded alehouse looking up as Saam led them to a private room separated by an impressive wall of colored glass on the left side. Inside the room were piles of the low cushions Valcottans favored, and equally low tables holding steaming mugs of mulled wine and plates of fried meats.

"This will be the last chance to eat and drink for a few hours," Daria said. "So I suggest we dig in."

Despite his nerves, Keris found himself ravenous, and the four of them all forwent conversation in favor of filling their stomachs. The food was good, but he noted how Daria and Saam ate almost mechanically, eyes staring into the distance as though they needed to disassociate from the act of eating in order to get each mouthful down their throats. As they finished with glasses of dark ale, Daria and Zarrah moved to sit together on a pile of cushions, deep in conversation. So Keris turned to Saam. "I'm glad to see that your commander has taken you back into the fold. I've heard it can be difficult coming back into the world after imprisonment. A challenge to adapt again to the order of things."

Saam pulled a loose thread on a cushion. "It's not been how I envisioned it would. I always thought we'd be hailed as heroes for surviving the worst the Usurper had to throw at us, but instead it feels like we're ..."

"Pariahs?" Keris suggested.

Saam sighed. "They know what we did, and it's as though half of them believe that we wanted to do it. And will continue to do it." He gave a disbelieving shake of his head. "I hate eating now. If there was a way I could go the rest of my life without taking another mouthful of *anything*, I'd do it."

"Understandable."

Saam's eyes lifted to meet Keris's. "Doesn't it bother you?"

"I have to say, it was eclipsed by my face-to-*faces* encounter with Flay. He was a thing of nightmares, while your choice to put your enemies' corpses in a cookpot rather than the ground was merely a footnote in my adventures on the island." Keris rested his elbow on a cushion, leaning into it and then regretting the motion as pain lanced through his shoulder. "Though in seriousness, I've seen true evil enough times to recognize it, and that's not what I see when I look at you."

Saam looked away. "It's all everyone else sees. It's all they think of when they look at me. *Saam the cannibal*." He pressed his fingers to his temples. "Part of me thinks that the only reason the commander has allowed us back into the ranks is because the alternative was to put us all down. We know too much."

"Zarrah won't let him do that," Keris said without hesitation. "And if it comes to it, there will always be a place for you in Maridrina as long as I rule. Ithicana as well, I imagine, though I don't recommend it. Terrible weather and far too many snakes."

Saam barked out a laugh, but then his expression grew serious. "You would harbor Valcottan convicts with a reputation for cannibalism?"

"My reputation is already shit, so I doubt my people would even blink." Taking a mouthful of the ale, Keris added, "You will likely never fully escape this stigma, Saam. Not any of you. But you can overcome it by giving your people something better to remember about you. Great things to outshine dark deeds."

Saam's brow furrowed, and then he nodded. "You're right. Thank you."

Keris shrugged, abruptly aware of Zarrah's eyes on him. Watching. Listening. Yet betraying nothing of her thoughts on her face.

Unease ran through him, because if she'd been listening, then she'd heard him commit her to protecting the prisoners. Which he had no business doing on her behalf, and Keris silently kicked himself for speaking without thinking. Biting the insides of his cheeks, he forced himself to meet her gaze, wary of what he might find there. Afraid that he'd crossed the line.

But Zarrah only gave a slight nod, her mouth curling upward in a faint smile as she turned back to Daria.

Keris had no opportunity to feel relieved as something hammered against the floor beneath his feet. "Shit," he snarled, scrambling backward, but Saam only frowned and dropped to his knees, opening the trapdoor beneath the cushion Keris had been sitting on. In the darkness of the cellar, two faces appeared, both of which he recognized from Daria's camp on the island. "We've got more trouble," one said. "Welran's ordered sympathizers detained. His soldiers are burning their homes and beating them for information on the commander's whereabouts." The man looked past Saam and Keris to Zarrah. "For information on your whereabouts, Empress. We need to get out of here quick."

Keris knew even before Zarrah spoke what she'd say, so it was no surprise when she stood up. "I'm not running while others are tortured for information on my whereabouts. We need to take action."

"We don't have the soldiers," the man said.

Daria added, "It's true. The rebel camp isn't in Arakis. The commander isn't here, only my tribe. We were tasked with securing you because you know us from the island." Daria dragged her hands over her hair, face tight with anxiety. "I don't know where the latest camp location is, but I'd hazard that help is hours away, and we have no way to contact them. We were told to bring you here and that they'd come to us."

Given what Saam had told him, Keris knew there was no chance at all that the commander didn't have his best and most trusted soldiers watching them, and from the way Zarrah's mouth gave an annoyed twist, she was thinking the same.

"The commander will have eyes on the city." Zarrah's voice was steady. "When they see us take action, they'll contact him. He'll have no choice but to come with force, and the rebellion has enough fighters to drive Welran and his imperial guard out of Arakis."

"He won't risk it," Daria argued. "It would be an act of provocation the Usurper couldn't ignore. She'll move against us. Defeat us. Burn Arakis as punishment."

"You think that's not already on the horizon?" Zarrah gave her head a sharp shake. "You think my aunt doesn't already have plans to attack us? Destroy us? Allowing her to kill our allies isn't going to change that! It only means fewer to stand against her when she comes. We must stay, and we must act!"

Zarrah was right, but Keris could see the fear in Daria's eyes. Her tribe had endured horror on Devil's Island, and part of what had kept them going was the dream of challenging Petra. Making her pay for all that she'd done. The moment to act was upon them, but the looming shadow of the woman who'd hurt them so deeply now seemed an impossible adversary to face. "Zarrah is right."

Zarrah's gaze shot to him, eyes filled with surprise.

"Welran either knows or strongly suspects that Zarrah has joined forces with the rebels," he said. "If we do nothing to help those who have supported your cause for so long, if we leave them to be tortured while their homes are burned, he will ensure that the survivors know that Zarrah had the opportunity to act but instead abandoned them. At best it will be seen as cowardice, at worst as betrayal, and even though it is the Usurper's soldiers who have done the harm, it will be Zarrah they blame. We cannot run."

The rebels shifted on uneasy feet, but Keris saw Saam mouth "Great things" to himself before lifting his head. "We faced far worse odds on the island. Now we're fed. We're armed. And we do not abandon our comrades."

All eyes turned to Daria, who gave a slow nod. "All right. We hold our ground and try to come up with a plan that won't get us all killed."

"Send our spies to gather what information they can about where Welran is keeping the prisoners and for a count on how many soldiers he has. Then gather our fighters here," Zarrah said.

The men's faces disappeared back into the cellar, a draft flooding into the room as they exited into the rear alley, leaving the four of them alone again. Daria and Saam bent their heads together, muttering about who was where within the city, but to Keris's surprise, Zarrah didn't join them. Instead she crossed the floor to stand before him.

"If Welran knows I'm here, then this isn't just a gambit to learn the commander's location," she said. "It's a plan to lure me out, for he knows me well. Knows that I won't run."

"Agreed." Every inhalation filled Keris's nose with the scent of her, lavender soap from her time in the baths still clinging to her hair. His eyes went to her bottom lip, caught between her front teeth as she strategized, and it made his heart pound. Swallowing hard, Keris said under his breath, "But he also expects you to be predictable and is unlikely to plan outside of the scope of what he expects you to do. That puts the power back in your hands."

A face appeared in the cellar, a girl who couldn't have been more than sixteen. "Welran's got them in the harbor market square. His soldiers are putting hot irons to their feet to get them to talk."

A torture that Serin had favored, and Keris's stomach curled with disgust to see it deployed on civilians by their own ruler's right hand. It was no wonder that the Magpie had admired Petra— she was the sort of ruler creatures like him thrived beneath.

"How many soldiers?" Zarrah asked.

"I counted sixty," the girl answered. "Most are holding back the crowd of onlookers. Ain't going to be long before someone breaks and talks."

Zarrah's eyes narrowed. "There is no chance that Welran came into Arakis with so few soldiers—there are more. They'll be in the surrounding buildings and on the rooftops. He doesn't know I was separated from the commander during the escape, so he'll speculate that at least some of the rebel fighters are here with me and that I'll come in force. He knows I like to fight from the high ground and will assume I'll begin my attack from the rooftops." Her eyes locked on the girl. "Is Welran addressing the crowd?"

"Seemed like. I didn't stick around."

"Go back and get close enough to listen."

The girl disappeared, and Zarrah pressed her fingers to her temples. Keris could see her coming up with strategies, only to cast them aside as more information filtered in about what they faced, but he said nothing. Only stood at her side, waiting. Waiting for a moment that he prayed would come.

"Welran helped train me," Zarrah finally said, lifting her face to look Keris in the eye. "Half of what I know came from him, and the other half from *her*, which means he knows it just as well. If it comes down to battle, we won't win. But we can't wait for the commander to learn what is happening and bring reinforcements, if he'll even choose to do so."

Keris was very confident, given the risks the commander had taken to free Zarrah from Devil's Island, that he wouldn't abandon her now, but he also suspected that securing enough soldiers for an outright attack against Welran wasn't the solution she was looking for. Suspected that she wasn't looking for a solution at all, but rather for confidence in the one she'd already come up with. "I once heard a wise woman say to a little girl that *not all battles are won with fists and swords. Some are won with words and a clever head.*"

Zarrah smiled, and it was like seeing the woman he'd fallen in love with rising from the ashes, scarred but stronger for it. "I have a plan."

51
ZARRAH

"THIS IS A MAD PLAN," DARIA HISSED IN HER EAR AS THEY WOVE through the streets toward the sound of the crowd. "It has Keris's influence written all over it, and please keep in mind that his last plan did not go at all as he intended."

"It's *my* plan," Zarrah answered, pulling the hood of her cloak more firmly in place. What Keris had influenced was *her*. Though *influenced* was a loaded word, for it implied a level of control. A form of manipulation. What Keris had really done was remind Zarrah not just of who she was, but of who she wanted to be. And who she wanted to be was a woman who had more tools at her disposal than just the weapon in her hand and the violence in her heart. "I'd say blame me if it all goes to shit, but I expect that will mean all of us are dead."

"Oh, that's comforting," Daria said. "Motivational speaking at its finest."

"That's why I'm here and Keris is giving the speeches."

"Don't get me wrong, the man could talk his way out of hell itself, but do you really think this will work? Because I'm going to be angry if I fought my own way out of hell only to die because of a half-cocked plan."

Zarrah ground to a halt, catching hold of the other woman's arms. "No one has to do this. Not you, not anyone in your tribe. You've made that clear to them?"

"Yeah, they know. They agreed to it." Daria pulled free and started walking. "We'll see if they keep their nerve in the moment."

Zarrah bit the insides of her cheeks, because she had the same concern about herself. A growing fear that when it came to it, she wouldn't be able to allow others to take the risk and would leap into the fray. While many would call it bravery, in her heart she knew it was because watching someone else suffer on her behalf was worse than enduring the hurt herself. It was a sort of cowardice, and not one a leader could afford. She needed to be able to trust her comrades. Needed to give them a chance to prove themselves, which was something Daria and her tribe desperately needed as well.

The noise of the crowd grew louder, people shouting, some angry and some pleading, but faintly, above the cries of civilians, she heard sobs of pain.

And Welran's familiar bellow.

"You have brought this upon yourselves," he shouted as she and Daria reached the rear of the onlookers. "Long has Arakis hidden the villains who wish harm upon Her Most Gracious Imperial Majesty. Villains who conspired with Maridrina to unleash the demons of Devil's Island upon Valcotta. Who split and weaken our defenses so that the rats in the north might descend upon us, slaughtering our people and orphaning our children. And to what end? What good has the commander and his band of mercenaries done for you? You hide them, feed them, arm them, and all they bring is suffering."

A shrill scream filled the air, and Zarrah's fists clenched as, through the crowd, she caught sight of one of the soldiers holding a hot iron to the foot of a young man. "Where is the commander?" the soldier demanded. "Where is his stronghold?"

"I don't know," the man screamed. "I swear it! I don't know! I don't know!"

"You were caught painting rebel propaganda on a building," the soldier shouted. "We know you are one of them! Confess, and your life will be spared!"

"I don't know where they are!" His pleas turned to screams again as flesh sizzled, and next to Zarrah, Daria sucked in a breath before whispering, "He doesn't know. Only a select few do, by necessity."

Given that not even Daria knew the commander's current location, Zarrah didn't doubt her words. The crowd was growing, some brave enough to scream demands that Welran cease this horror, that he release those being tortured, but none moved against the spears and swords of the imperial guard holding the perimeter. They were too afraid, too aware that the soldiers would kill them if pressed, but beneath their fear, Zarrah sensed their anger was rising.

"Someone knows!" Welran shouted. "Someone in this crowd has the power to end this man's suffering. Your friend. Your neighbor. Your brother. Anyone could be one of them, and that makes them the cause of this moment. Reveal the truth and we can end this! We can turn our sights on the commander who has caused this!"

"You caused this," someone shouted. "You are the one torturing your own people! You're the one burning the homes of anyone who refuses to kiss Petra's ass!" The crowd roared their agreement, the air reeking of anger and distress, but those who shoved at the soldiers were knocked back with the butts of spears and the flats of blades.

"The commander has Zarrah Anaphora with him," Welran shouted. "Intends to raise her up as a puppet empress, but you should know the nature of the woman. Despite Her Most Benevolent Imperial Majesty raising her as a daughter, Zarrah betrayed all of Valcotta for the sake of her lover, Keris Veliant. The king of Maridrina!"

"Shit," Daria breathed, and Zarrah echoed that sentiment. Grief over Bermin's death was driving Welran's actions, not the Usurper's strategy, and that made him far more unpredictable. Which was not to her advantage.

"The Veliants have been our greatest enemy for generations," Welran bellowed over the clamor. "Have caused the deaths of numbers beyond counting, yet Zarrah does his bidding. That is who the rebel commander allies himself with, and you would protect them?" He circled the perimeter of the square, eyes searching. "They've abandoned you. While you suffer to protect them, the commander and his puppet hide in their stronghold."

"There will be a reckoning," someone shouted. "The Usurper's time is coming to an end! The commander will rip off her stolen crown and put it on a deserving head!"

Zarrah saw anger flare in Welran's eyes, but his voice was mild as he said, "Is that so? By all means, then, let it begin. Let the commander step forward and make his first move, else prove himself a coward. Let Zarrah step forward and claim the crown." Drawing his sword, Welran caught hold of the hair of one of the crying prisoners and held the blade to her throat. "If you are here, then show yourselves!"

He was going to do it. Was going to kill an innocent Valcottan for the sake of luring her out. Zarrah clenched her fists, desperate to act. Desperate to stop this.

The crowd stilled, looking among themselves as though expecting Zarrah to step out of the shadows to end this. Or if not Zarrah, then the commander they'd supported all these long years. "Come on," Zarrah breathed even as fear made her want to scream a warning to Daria's tribe to hold their ground.

Shaking his head, Welran said, "Just as I—"

"I am Zarrah Anaphora," Daria shouted, stepping forward. "I am here to claim my crown!"

Terror flooded Zarrah's veins, and despite this having been her plan, she reached for the other woman to stop her.

Daria was too quick. She shoved through the crowd, a pair of soldiers catching hold of her arms and dragging her inside the perimeter even as Welran strode toward her, righteous fury in his eyes. He drew his blade, and Zarrah pushed against those in front of her, trying to get to Daria in time.

She'd made a mistake.

She should have taken the risk herself.

Welran lifted his sword, then wrenched back Daria's hood. At the sight of her face, he spat on the ground. "You think I don't know Zarrah's face, fool?"

Before Daria could answer, a hooded man stepped forward. "I am the commander! I am here to fight against the Usurper's tyranny!"

Soldiers threw him to the ground, but Welran shook his head as they tore back his hood. "What is this madness?"

"I am Zarrah!" Another woman from Daria's tribe was allowed past the perimeter of soldiers, just as another man shouted, "I am the rebel commander!"

Soldiers dragged them to the center of the square and shoved them to the ground, removing their hoods, only to shake their heads. "It's not them!"

But their voices were drowned out by more shouts as Daria's

tribe members all began to step forward, claiming to be Zarrah. Claiming to be the commander. Claiming to be rebels. The confused soldiers pushing them down next to those who had been tortured, it all happening too swiftly for them to be checked for weapons.

Just as Zarrah had intended.

Except it didn't stop with Daria's tribe. Civilians were stepping up to the soldiers, Zarrah's name on their lips. The commander's. And while there was fear in their eyes, their chins were held high with anger and defiance.

"There is no one a king fears more than his own people," Keris had said to her before they'd parted ways at the alehouse. "And I think no one the empress fears more than Valcottans armed with the truth about who she truly is."

And Arakis had known the truth far longer than Zarrah had. Had known that her aunt was a monster while Zarrah had been staring at her with idolizing eyes, convinced she was a paragon. They'd been poised for a revolt for a very long time; all they'd needed was a catalyst.

And in his grief, Welran had provided it, which, from his expression, he was beginning to realize.

The square was full of civilians now, the soldiers scattered and expressions panicked, because in allowing people past their perimeter, they'd given up their power. Their advantage. There were armed and angry people surrounding them, and all it would take was one lifting a weapon or fist in violence for this to turn from an angry mob into a bloody riot. And the imperial guard was grossly outnumbered.

Back down, Zarrah silently willed Welran. *You can't win this. Retreat.*

She didn't want this day to end in death, especially not Welran's. He'd been like an uncle to her, helping her aunt raise Zarrah and train her, and she knew the grief in his heart. Knew that his soul bled for the death of the son he'd never been allowed to claim, but whom he'd still raised, still watched over, still *loved*.

Walk away, she repeated. *Walk away and live another day.*

Instead Welran's face hardened. Grabbing a girl from Daria's tribe by the hair, he pressed his sword blade to her throat. "Zarrah!" he roared. "Come out, or she dies. I know you are here! I know this is your doing!"

Zarrah grimaced, cursing his pride because it would cause so much death.

"I know you think you can win this without bloodshed," he shouted. "That you believe the whole of Valcotta will come to share your delusion that peace with Maridrina is possible. That both nations will lay down their weapons to make your love affair possible, which makes you every bit as mad as *her*."

He knows she's mad. Zarrah's heart felt like it stuttered, the world swimming around her. She'd been told her aunt was a madwoman by so many. Had told herself. Yet somehow, Welran speaking against the Usurper's sanity made it the truth in a way it hadn't been before.

But unlike her, Welran saw no escape from the Usurper's control, and that was why he hadn't retreated. Why he was antagonizing a mob of people who already had cause to hate him.

"I'll kill her, Zarrah," he roared, and the girl squealed as the blade dug into her flesh. "Don't think that I won't!"

She knew he'd do it. Knew that in another heartbeat, the girl would be breathing her last and that countless more would die as all turned to chaos. So despite it being counter to the plan, despite having committed to remaining hidden, Zarrah stepped forward, pulling back her hood.

Welran's eyes fixed on her.

"Let her go," she said. "I'm here, which means you have what you want. You don't need to hurt an innocent child."

"I doubt she's innocent."

The girl sobbed, trickles of blood running down her brown skin. "Please," she sobbed. "I haven't done anything."

"Let her go."

Welran's hand was shaking, tears gleaming in his eyes. "You killed my boy. You and your *lover*. You're a traitor to your people in every possible way."

Zarrah's heart ached at his grief, the culmination of far more than just Bermin's death. "I didn't kill him, Welran. We fought, and though my heart desired his blood, Keris convinced me to stay my hand. But Bermin wouldn't let it go. Pursued me to the bitter end and made a choice that was his damnation. He chose to make his end on that island."

"He died with honor!" Welran screamed. "Whereas you will die the traitor that you are!"

All around them, the crowd had fallen still, but whispers filtered outward, all of them saying one thing. "It's her. It's Zarrah."

Zarrah's eyes met the girl's, the fear in them reminding her of herself at that age. So quick to throw herself into danger without mind for the consequences. She'd not allow the child to lose the opportunity to learn the wisdom of caution. "Fine. Her life for mine."

His eyes narrowed; then Welran gave a tight nod.

Zarrah wove through the crowd, dropping her weapons on the ground before she reached him, then moving close. "Let her go."

Welran shoved the girl away, then caught hold of Zarrah's arm, pulling her back against his massive chest, blade against her throat. "Walk," he growled. "I won't give you the mercy of killing you myself."

Zarrah took a step but then fell still, a familiar rhythmic tread filling her ears, growing louder by the second. A faint smile rose to her lips, because Keris had not let her down. "Arakis has risen."

Every street leading to the square filled with the glow of torch-light, and then they appeared. Civilians in the hundreds, in the thousands. A few carried weapons, but most were armed with shovels, pitchforks, and sticks. None of them alone could hope to stand against any of Welran's soldiers, but this was an army.

"You can't win this," she said to him. "And killing me won't stop it because they aren't here because of me. They're here because of the Usurper. They're here because they're through with her tyr-anny, through with her warmongering, through with her lies."

Zarrah could feel the heat of Welran's rapid breath on the top of her head as he eyed the mob. Then he shouted, "Imperial guard, to me!"

She silently cursed as the soldiers pushed aside civilians to form up around him, weapons in hand and faces devoid of the fear she knew must have been filling their hearts. They couldn't win this, but the number of people who'd die taking them down would be catastrophic.

"Cutting my throat will only pour fuel on the fires of rebellion, will only make me a martyr," she said. "Stand down and you'll be allowed to board your ship."

"Don't make promises you can't keep," Welran hissed. "A mob is not a thing that can be controlled."

"They aren't looking for violence," Zarrah answered. "They're looking for an end to it. Leave Arakis, Welran. Go back to my aunt and tell her that I'm coming for her."

The mob pressed closer, silently watching. Waiting.

"You cannot win a war against her," Welran finally said. "She will not allow it. And she will make you pay in ways that make

Devil's Island seem paltry in comparison." But he took a step back, then another. And another.

"Retreat to the harbor," he ordered his soldiers, but he didn't let Zarrah go. Kept the blade to her throat as they moved toward the sea, the mob following. But just before they reached the docks, Welran ground to a stop, and Zarrah swallowed hard when she saw that the crowd had closed ranks, denying the imperial guard a path to the ships.

Daria stepped forward. "Let Zarrah go. She belongs to Arakis, and we will not let you have her."

Zarrah said nothing, allowing Welran time for his internal debate. She didn't have to wait long. He shoved her away with such force that she nearly fell into Daria's arms, snarling, "I will not give you the satisfaction of martyrdom."

Daria tensed, but Zarrah said under her breath, "Let him go. We've accomplished what we wished to tonight. Arakis has risen."

"Let them go," Daria shouted. "They have a message to deliver to the Usurper. Arakis bends the knee to Petra Anaphora no longer!"

The crowd roared, chanting "Arakis" as they cleared a path for Welran and his soldiers into the harbor where their ship was moored.

Daria wiped sweat from her brow. "Thank God that's over. My nerves can't handle your schemes."

"It's not over," Zarrah said softly, looking out over the chanting mob. "It's only just begun."

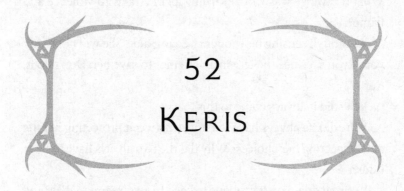

52
KERIS

IT TOOK ALL KERIS'S CONTROL TO STOP HIMSELF FROM INCITING the mob to violence when he saw Welran's blade at Zarrah's throat. Saam caught hold of his arms, holding him back, muttering, "You have to trust her. You have to."

The other man's words felt like madness, for what good was trusting Zarrah when it was Welran who held her life in the balance?

This hadn't been the plan.

The plan had been to get Daria's tribe behind the imperial guard's line and for Keris to provoke the already raging city into marching on the square. To keep the prisoners alive and then force Welran into retreat. Zarrah was supposed to have held back.

"He won't kill her," Saam hissed. "He knows the mob will riot and rip him apart."

But what if that was worth it to Welran? Though it hadn't been by her hand, Zarrah had been complicit in Bermin's death, and Keris had seen for himself what grief could drive Welran to do. What if her death was worth his own life? The lives of his soldiers?

What if revenge was worth turning all of Arakis to violence and flame?

As though sensing his thoughts, Saam said, "She will not thank you if you sacrifice the city in an attempt to save her. Don't do it, Keris."

Why did it always come to this?

Why did he always have to choose between protecting her life and respecting her choices? Why did the two always have to be at odds?

Keris bit down on his tongue to keep from screaming *Why?* and kept within the masses of people following the imperial guard to the harbor, praying that it was the right choice. Begging every higher power to protect her while he chose to do the exact opposite.

They'd nearly reached the harbor, and Keris could see long-boats coming from a ship. They were going to take her. Were going to take her to Petra, and he couldn't let that happen.

But Daria's tribe was already in action, muttering instructions to the crowd to block the path onto the dock, Daria herself stepping up to Welran to say something. Words were exchanged, Keris too far away to hear.

Welran abruptly shoved Zarrah into Daria's arms, and then the rebel shouted, "Let them go. They have a message to deliver to the Usurper. Arakis bends the knee to Petra Anaphora no longer!"

The crowd parted, the imperial guard rushing toward the long-boats, leaving Zarrah and Daria standing alone.

And very much alive.

"It worked!" Saam shouted, slamming Keris on the back hard enough that he staggered. "They're leaving!"

Keris hunted for the sense of relief that should come with victory, but all he felt was a rising tide of unspent adrenaline. Every muscle in his body was tense to the point it hurt, his heart galloping with such violent speed it seemed on the verge of exploding out of his chest.

The mob was cheering now, chanting "Arakis," but through the fists punching the air, his eyes met Zarrah's. She smiled, the embodiment of ferocity and beauty, but his mind juxtaposed a vision of her dead on the ground, blood pooling around her body while she gasped out her dying breaths.

Nausea rose in his throat, and staggering between buildings, Keris vomited up the contents of his stomach.

Resting his hand against the wall for balance, he forced himself to breathe. *It's fine. She's fine. The plan worked.*

"Are you all right?" Zarrah asked from behind him.

Keris straightened and turned, wiping his mouth with his sleeve. "The cost of provoking your people to march was a lot of cheap ale, which my refined palate has no tolerance for."

She watched him with an unreadable expression. "It worked. Whatever you said to them awoke Arakis."

"They were poised to explode," he answered, wishing he weren't so unsteady on his feet. Wishing that his heart would calm, because he felt seconds away from passing out in his own vomit. "And I've a certain amount of experience in stirring up the masses."

"Even so," she answered. "Thank you."

The tension between them made the air thick and unbreathable, as though they both choked on too many things said. Too many things unsaid. Nothing about the moment felt like a victory should, and yet . . .

An unfamiliar man appeared behind Zarrah, and Keris instinctively reached for a weapon, only to come up empty, all his knives lost in the bathhouse. The man regarded them for a moment, then said, "You are to be brought to see the commander now." He nodded to Daria and Saam, who had approached with weapons in hand, though they lowered them upon seeing the man's face. "You two as well. Come with me."

They were brought back to the inn where they'd started the night, then down into the cellar, which was full of barrels.

"In," said the man, who had told them his name was Remy, popping open one of the barrels. "The location of the commander's stronghold is well protected, and your faces are known. We can't risk being followed."

Daria climbed into one of the barrels, Saam getting into another. Zarrah shifted uneasily, reminding Keris that she was no lover of confined spaces, but then she took a deep breath and climbed inside a barrel. Remy pounded the lid back into place. He turned to Keris when he was finished. "You staying or going?"

Cursing, Keris clambered into an open barrel, settling into the damp bottom as the lid was secured over his head. It reeked of stale ale and wet oak, and nausea twisted his stomach as Remy tipped the barrel on its side and rolled it up a ramp, then up another into what Keris could only presume was a cart before righting it again. Pressing his ear to the wood, Keris listened as the rest of the barrels joined him, no part of him liking this. He was blind to what was going on, at the mercy of a man he didn't know, and it wasn't lost on him that Zarrah could be taken to an entirely different location, and he wouldn't know until that lid was opened.

The wagon swayed as Remy climbed aboard, the man shouting commands at whatever creature was harnessed, and they moved forward. Keris rested his head against the side of the barrel as they jolted and bounced, cold swiftly creeping into his bones.

He was exhausted, the weight of injury and events and very little sleep dragging him down and down until the wagon bouncing over a rut jolted him back to the moment.

You need to stay awake, he told himself, knowing he'd fallen asleep and uncertain of how much time had passed. *You need to stay alert.*

Keris forced himself to sit straighter, absently rubbing at the finger on which he normally wore his signet ring. He found himself wondering how his kingdom fared. No information about Maridrina had reached his ears since he'd left Vencia, and at this point, he'd been gone weeks. He could have been usurped and be none the wiser, though news of that magnitude would surely reach even this far south.

Was Sarhina still in control? Were negotiations, led by Ahnna in Ithicana, progressing? Was his nation being fed? Were his endless younger brothers causing trouble?

All significant concerns, yet he'd given them little thought.

You're a shitty king.

Keris rolled his shoulders, wincing as his injury protested the motion. Everything that he was doing was to Maridrina's benefit. With Petra removed from power, the war would end, and trade would thrive, which meant filling both pockets and bellies. What king in the past hundred years could claim as much?

The logic did little to silence the sourness in his stomach, nor did his reasoning that while Sarhina and his advisors could handle the administration of the country just as well as he could, none of them could accomplish what he intended to accomplish in Valcotta. *This is where I need to be, not just for Zarrah but for Maridrina,* he told himself as the wagon bounced its way to the mystery destination. *Some things can't be achieved via letters and messengers.*

Like getting Zarrah back in your arms?

"Fuck off," he snarled at himself, then froze as he heard motion outside his barrel. The wagon was still moving, but he swore he heard footsteps and faint scraping. Then his barrel was moving. Tipping on its side. He shouted in alarm as it rolled, his body tossed about as the speed of rotation increased, only to come to an abrupt stop with a loud crunch.

He groaned, everything aching, his wound screaming, and his head spinning from being tossed about. But all those concerns fell away as voices approached. Wood creaked as a crowbar was fit into the top, jerking loose the lid. The bottom of the barrel tipped upward, and Keris was dumped face-first into snow illuminated by dawn light.

Scrambling upright, he whirled around to find himself face-to-face with a group of armed Valcottans. At their head was the man who'd led the rebel charge on Devil's Island, none other than the commander himself.

The commander inclined his head. "A pleasure to finally meet you, Your Grace."

53
ZARRAH

THE JOURNEY WAS THE PUREST FORM OF MISERY, NOT ONLY BE-
cause of her enduring distaste for enclosed spaces, but also because it reminded her of the night she'd witnessed Daria and Saam
stuffing corpses into barrels to cure. It made it difficult to think,
which was perhaps just as well, because when Zarrah's mind
dwelled too long on what lay ahead, her stomach hollowed.

But there was no going back.

In choosing to act, she had well and truly kicked the hornet's
nest, which meant it was only a matter of time until her aunt took
action.

The Usurper, she reminded herself. *Remember what she is to you.*

Except that was half the problem, for there were moments
when the idea that she would be going to war against the last of
her remaining family made Zarrah's breath catch in horror. If all
miraculously came to pass and the rebellion succeeded, it would
still come at a great cost, for she would stand alone. The last of the
Anaphora line.

Unless she produced an heir.

Her mind recoiled at that thought, and Zarrah pressed her fingers to her temples. Though Keris was in a barrel in the same wagon, she abruptly felt distant from him. Like the claws of fate had dug themselves in deep and were pulling them farther apart with each passing mile the cart traveled. He'd supported her strategy. Had been a true ally in every sense of the word.

But what did that mean?

Her mind circled round and round, the rumble of the wagon eventually lulling her into a dreamless sleep that stretched until the moment the wagon stopped. A crowbar was fitted under the lid of her barrel, popping it open. Fresh air filled her lungs, smelling of snow and evergreens, her breath making clouds of steam. Daria's face appeared, and she reached down a hand to pull Zarrah upright. "Everyone is eager to see you, Imperial Majesty."

A flicker of panic bit at Zarrah's stomach, but she buried it even as she gripped Daria's hand, rising to her feet.

They were in a ravine, cliff walls towering up on either side, but what stole her breath were the dozens of cave openings in the cliff walls, all linked by wooden walkways and ladders. Countless people watched from them, more filling the ravine itself. There were other wagons as well, the remainder of Daria's tribe having been brought by other roads from Arakis to this place.

And every eye was on her.

"The True Empress," someone shouted, and the words spread among the rebels, repeated over and over until the collective noise rose like thunder.

Every man and woman was armed, every person present a warrior. A fighter. A soldier.

This was to be the vanguard of the army that she'd lead against the Usurper.

"They've been waiting a long time," Daria said. "This is a day that will go down in the history of Valcotta as the moment the tides turned and we marched toward liberty."

It was hard to breathe, the weight of Daria's words suffocating. What did Zarrah bring to the table that gave them the confidence to march? To finally go to war?

Legitimacy? People kept telling her that she was the rightful ruler. That her grandfather had named her mother his heir, and that Petra had stolen the crown. But it was all rumor and hearsay.

Experience? It was true that she was trained to lead armies, but so was the commander who had led them all these years.

You're just a figurehead, the Usurper whispered to her. *A pretty face to stand before the crowd while others make the decisions for you.*

Be silent! The words were no longer a plea, but a command, and as the last drops of the Usurper's presence drained from her heart, Zarrah lifted her chin high. More than anyone alive, this fight was hers, for it had touched every aspect of her being. The Usurper had torn apart her world, then rebuilt Zarrah as a villain. Her tool to conquer and control, filling her heart with so much hate that Zarrah forgot herself. Forgot what really mattered, until fate caused her to cross paths with the one person capable of erasing the clouds of anger so that she might see clearly. A victory that had changed her life, yet the war had raged on, and Zarrah had allowed herself to be made a victim by twisted words, her strengths turning to weakness and leaving her a shadow of herself until light appeared to guide her back again.

Some might say hers was a history that proved her unworthy. That proved her fallible. But worthiness was not proven by never falling. It was proven by surviving the impact, learning from the error, and climbing upright again. For it was the struggle to rise from the depths of her own mistakes that had given Zarrah the strength needed to be the victor in this endless war.

And there was one mistake she would not make again.

She turned, searching for the light that had helped guide her through every storm. Only to find him absent. "Where is Keris?"

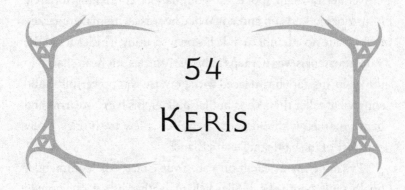

54
KERIS

WEAPONS WERE DRAWN, THE SOLDIERS ACCOMPANYING THE rebel commander moving to encircle him, and Keris was reminded that for all the rebels desired an end to the war, it didn't mean they held Maridrinians in good esteem.

Most especially those bearing his name.

"Likewise, Commander." He lowered his fists, forcing himself to relax despite the adrenaline coursing through his veins. "Though I must say, I expected a meeting at your stronghold, not a private conversation on the side of the road."

The commander chuckled. "You're a Veliant, Your Grace. For all your recent actions suggest that you are a different man than your father, that does not mean I'm fool enough to bring you into my camp without first getting your measure."

"Without your empress present?"

The older man tilted his head. "Why? Do you wish to hide behind her?"

"On the contrary," Keris answered, "I don't wish to do anything behind her back."

Neither of them spoke, the commander continuing to circle him, looking Keris up and down like he was an animal at market. Keris made no attempt to hide his own scrutiny. The leader of the Valcottan rebels was perhaps in his early fifties, his head shaved to the scalp, his dark beard laced with gray. He was powerfully built, somewhat taller than Keris but far bulkier, his bare forearms and hands marked with old scars, as well as a few fresh ones, likely courtesy of the battle on Devil's Island.

"I've done my research on you, Your Grace," the commander finally said. "Ninth son of Silas Veliant, birthed by a desert nomad plucked from obscurity for her beauty."

"Adara," Keris said coolly even as he wondered the last time he'd spoken his mother's name. "Say what you will of my father, but I'll suffer no slander against my mother."

The commander inclined his head. "None intended. Her daughter became queen of Ithicana, her son the king of Maridrina. I think it a shame her life was cut short, though it is said that her murder was what put you at odds with your father."

"People say many things."

"Indeed. I was told you could barely lift a sword without risking your own limbs yet saw otherwise with my own eyes." The man continued to circle. "You are known to be highly educated. Fluent in several languages. A patron of the arts. But also a drinker, a gambler, and a womanizer."

Keris remained silent, some sixth sense telling him that there was something about this exchange that he was missing.

"I have pages upon pages of information about you, Your Grace. Much as I did your father, for while Maridrina is not my enemy, Silas Veliant most certainly was."

Keris tilted his head. "For what he did to Aryana?"

The commander stopped his circling, and in his eyes, Keris

saw anger. Not the hot flood of fresh rage, but an old fury. The kind that had existed for so long that it had become a permanent fixture, its roots dug so deeply into the heart and soul that it influenced every thought, every action. *Who was Aryana to you?* Keris silently asked. *Who are you to have dedicated your life to her cause?*

Who are you to Zarrah that you'd risk everything to rescue her?

"Yes," the commander finally answered. "Though the list of your father's crimes is long."

"You'll get no argument from me on that." Keris briefly considered revealing Petra's complicity but decided against it, for that truth was Zarrah's to tell. That this conversation was happening behind her back was bad enough.

"So imagine my surprise when I arrived on Devil's Island to liberate my empress and my people, only to discover that Silas's son, Maridrina's king, had beaten me to it. Adding to my shock was the discovery that he was in the company of the king of Ithicana, whose kingdom was so recently brutalized in Maridrina's invasion, as well as its queen, who was the instigator of the violence and who also happens to be your sister."

Keris shrugged, then dusted snow off his sleeve, his mind racing. He'd been preoccupied with Zarrah, and with survival, which meant that he'd not given nearly enough thought to the motivations of those he'd deemed minor players in the game. He was discovering now that they weren't minor at all. "I fail to see why this conversation necessitated dumping me into the snow on the side of the road."

Ignoring the question, the commander said, "Daria provided me with some explanation for your motivations on our journey back to Arakis, informing me of the depths of your relationship with my empress, but she knew nothing about your intentions."

"To ally with Zarrah, and with *you*, to unseat Petra from the throne," Keris said, knowing full well that he hadn't answered the man's question any more than the commander had answered his.

"So that's why your army is massing in Nerastis?"

This was the first piece of intelligence about his country that Keris had received since leaving Vencia, and some level of proof that his orders were being followed. "At present, they are there for defense. Petra has made it abundantly clear that she desires to invade Maridrina. A plan made clearer through my own efforts to spy on Welran. But ultimately, when Zarrah makes her move against Petra, I'll commit my own forces to aid her."

"Of course you will. Except answer this, Your Grace: Why do *none* of your soldiers know your plans?"

Keris's hands turned cold.

"We have spies in your palace in Nerastis. Your officers speak freely around paid company, and not one has whispered of your so-called *plan for peace*. Only about continued plans for war. Why is that?"

There was a reason. A reason that terrified Keris so badly that his mind shied away from even considering it, even though it had the power to destroy his plans with Zarrah. "Screaming my strategies for all to hear is a good way to arm my enemies."

"Oh, I know that. Believe that. What is uncertain is who you see as your enemy." The commander resumed his circling. "That is why we stand on the side of the road, away from the presence of the empress, Your Grace. For while she may be blind to the advantages this alliance holds for you in the long run, I am not."

Tension sang through his veins, but Keris allowed none of it to show on his face. "Then allow me to provide clarity. My enemy is Petra Anaphora. Not Zarrah, not the rebellion, and not *you*."

Silence stretched, the only sound the rapid breathing of the soldiers and the wind howling through the surrounding forest.

"You have all the answers, but I see your intentions, Your Grace. You'd pit the rebellion against the Usurper, spend the strength of both forces, then, while backs are turned, take Nerastis. You don't tell your generals of plans for peace because Maridrina's plans are unchanged. The war rages on."

"On my honor, that is not my intent." Keris said the words knowing that this man probably considered him honorless. "I am a true ally to Zarrah. Our goals are shared. And this conversation should not be happening behind her back."

"Baa! Baa!" The commander mimicked a sheep's call, his soldiers laughing. "You want her here so you can cower behind her?"

Keris's fingers curled, his irritation rising. "Do not mistake my respect for her as cowardice."

The commander shrugged. "Perhaps you tell the truth. Perhaps you do desire to aid my empress, to fight for peace, but in that case, you are making promises that you can't keep. Already you are the weakest king Maridrina has seen in generations, so what hubris flows through your veins that you believe you can return to Maridrina and order your army to fight to liberate their mortal enemy? They will laugh in your face and then rip you apart before staking your head on Vencia's gates."

Keris's irritation fled, for this was the fear that lurked deep in his heart. The knowledge that when Zarrah would need him most, he might fail to deliver. Hearing it voiced by this man made that fear a thousand times more intense, for it validated what Keris already knew.

"A weak ally that promises much and delivers nothing is no ally at all," the commander said. "You're a liability that the empress cannot afford, and as such, one we will be sending back to Marid-rina."

Keris's lips parted to protest, but before he could speak, Zarrah's voice cut through the air. "As it stands, Commander, it seems that *you* are a liability that I cannot afford."

55

ZARRAH

GUIDING THE HORSE WITH HER KNEES, ZARRAH KEPT THE ARROW she'd nocked trained on the commander's chest. "Step away from him. All of you. Then put your weapons on the ground."

"You were supposed to keep her at the camp," the commander barked at the mounted soldiers galloping up behind her.

Rather than allowing them to answer, she said, "You cannot have it both ways, calling me Empress but then undermining my authority. You may have wished for a mindless figurehead, but that is not what you'll get with me."

In truth, it had taken some doing to convince the soldiers to give her a weapon and a horse, for they'd been following the commander's orders since the beginning and did not wish to go against him. But Daria and Saam had her back, defending Keris's right to be brought into the camp. The concession had been that close to fifty soldiers had accompanied her.

She could feel their unease, and Zarrah didn't blame them for it. She was a stranger to them. Worse than a stranger, in truth, because what they knew of her was primarily as the Usurper's tool. Whereas the commander had led them all these long years, a stalwart force at their backs. And she had an arrow they'd given her trained on his heart.

The commander alone seemed unconcerned. "You are not a figurehead, Empress, but you must earn the authority to command this army."

"Then quit undermining my ability to do so." Digging in her heels, she drove her horse forward, circling Keris and the commander, her nerves once again jangling with the familiarity of the man. Where had she met him before? Who was he beyond his role as commander of this rebellion? "I would have your name, Commander."

Their eyes locked, but it was his rich-brown gaze that looked away first. "You don't remember, then?" He ran a hand over his shaved head. "I had hoped that you would, but perhaps that was foolish of me, given how much time has passed."

Her heart increased its pace, and she glanced at Keris, but his eyes were on the ground. He knew, but it wouldn't be him who gave her the answer. "Your name, Commander."

"My name is Arjun Retva, consort to the late empress, Aryana Anaphora."

Zarrah swayed in the saddle as though she'd been struck, all the air gone from her chest. *Impossible. It was impossible.* "Retract that lie, Commander, for it was my mother who told me herself that my father had died in battle."

"Your mother was involved in falsifying my death," he said quietly. "One of the hardest things she ever did was lie to you that I was gone, and it grieved us both deeply. But it was a secret too great to be left in the hands of a young child."

Zarrah sucked in a breath, opening her lips to call him a liar. To tell him that she'd kill him for dishonoring her parents' legacy, but nothing came out. All the tiny pieces fell into place, not the least of which was her aunt's certainty that he'd rescue her. Her memory unlocked itself, revealing faded memories of this man as he lifted her into the air, both of them laughing as they spun in circles. "Father?"

"Yes, Zarrah." He met her gaze again. "I have thought of you every day that we have been apart. Not being at your side has been the greatest pain I've ever endured. I will not ask you to forgive the lie, but I hope you will see that all that I have done has been for the sake of not just your mother's legacy, but for you."

"You left me," she whispered. "You left me with *her*."

All around them, the rebels were retreating out of earshot, their eyes low, until only Keris remained. He said, "I never thought anyone would make my father seem a lesser evil, Commander, but I think you have done it." His blue eyes met Zarrah's. "I'll be close by."

Keris strode toward the soldiers, leaving the two of them alone on the snowy field.

"I left you with your mother," her father finally said. "She knew what horrors Petra would bring upon Valcotta, the death that would come as she fanned the flames of war with Maridrina, and she needed me to build her an army so that she could stop her."

"What of after her death?" Zarrah's horse snorted and pranced beneath her, sensing her agitation, so she slipped off and allowed it to trot away. "You left me to be raised by the enemy, to be the victim of her lies and manipulation, to be used in an unrighteous war. You let her turn me into a monster even as you used my name to rally Valcottans to your cause. I was your legitimacy, your figurehead, but not once did you try to liberate *me*!"

"I had to choose between taking you and continuing your mother's fight. It could not be both, for taking you would have drawn Petra's eyes down upon the rebellion before it had the strength to withstand her. We'd have been crushed, and for all her faults, Petra treated you as though you were her own. I thought you'd be safe with her—"

"You left me with my mother's murderer!" Zarrah shouted. "With your wife's murderer!"

Confusion flashed in her father's eyes. "Silas Veliant—"

"Swung the blade. But it was the Usurper who revealed to the Magpie that my mother and I were unprotected and near the border. Knowing what I do now, it wasn't just my mother that the Usurper intended Silas to kill."

Color drained from her father's face, and he slowly dropped to his knees, pressing his forehead to the ground.

Pity softened Zarrah's anger, for her father had believed the lie just like everyone else. "It was you she was supposed to meet in that villa, wasn't it? I've always wondered why she risked traveling so near the border without a guard, but it was because she planned to meet you."

"Yes. I was delayed." The word croaked from his lips, drops of melted snow running down his cheeks as he lifted his head. "And if you think that hasn't weighed upon my soul every day since, you are mistaken. Every day I curse that delay, for without it, Aryana might still live. But we came on the heels of Petra's force, and we had to hold back to prevent discovery." Tears joined the melting snow. "I had to watch Petra's soldiers lift your mother's body down. Watch them put her on the ground and . . . and make her whole."

"If you saw that, it means you watched her take me," she said. "You knew that my mother was dead, and you allowed the Usurper to take me to Pyrinat. Why?"

"We hadn't the numbers to defeat her and take you by force." His throat moved as he swallowed. "Your mother believed it criti-

cal for her to be in Pyrinat. To live under the eye of the people, secure friendships with those in power, because we'd need those
relationships when the day came to move against her sister. I . . . I
hoped that you would pick up where she'd left off."

It hurt, but she'd suffered worse betrayal. That, or she was beginning to grow accustomed to it; Zarrah wasn't certain. Only
that this revelation didn't rattle her in the way learning her aunt
had arranged her mother's murder had.

"On my honor, Zarrah, I had no knowledge of Petra's involvement. We had no reason to believe that she suspected our plans to
take back the crown, for Aryana played her part as a submissive
sister well. For all she'd usurped her, Petra behaved as though she
loved Aryana. I thought she was safe, thought *you* were safe. If I
had known, I'd have risked everything to take you then."

An echo of her conversation with Aren on the ship filled Zarrah's head. *There are moments in life where one stands at a crossroads, and
each path leads to a future so wildly different from the other that it seems
impossible they stemmed from the same place. Most of the time, the ripples
of those choices touch only a few. But sometimes a choice is made, and the
ripples are not ripples at all but rather tsunamis that tear across the world,
altering everything in their path.*

Where would she stand now, if not for the choice her father had
made? How different would her life be? Would fate still have
guided her path to cross with Keris's, or would they always have
stood under different stars? Would she be the same woman as she
was now?

No, she silently decided. *I would not.*

Clearing her throat, Zarrah said, "As much as the truth hurts
my heart, I'm glad you chose as you did."

Shock filled her father's eyes. "Why?"

"The choice you made put me on the path I needed to take to

become a woman capable of taking on the Usurper. I know her better than anyone alive. Her strategies, how she thinks, and what she wants." Reaching down a hand, she waited for her father to take it and then drew him to his feet. "Because of your choice to leave me with her, no one in Pyrinat will question my identity or breeding, though it will be your word against hers about my grandfather's decision to name my mother as heir."

Her father cleared his throat. "Ephraim was no fool. There were two copies of the proclamation signed by him. One Petra destroyed. I have the other."

Her heart skipped, and Zarrah realized that part of her had wondered whether it had been a fabrication. But a signed proclamation . . . that was *proof*.

Giving a slow nod, she started toward the waiting soldiers. "You gave your word to my mother that you'd build her an army. Have you fulfilled that promise?"

"I have. And even now, more flock to our banners."

"Good." She led him toward the waiting soldiers, taking the reins of her horse back from one of them and mounting, so that all might see. All might hear. Because there was a point she needed to make to every one of them. "For long years you have prepared for this moment, gathering the strength needed to stand against the Usurper. At dawn, we will march on Pyrinat to rip the crown from the Usurper's head!"

Silence.

"Where are the shouts of enthusiasm?" she demanded, heeling her horse and meandering through the gathered soldiers. "You have dedicated yourself to the fight to remove the Usurper from the throne. Have stood against her tyranny. Have suffered in your fight to liberate Valcotta from a warmonger. And now you have all that you need. An army. A leader. A just cause. The time to strike is now, yet you hesitate? Why?"

Zarrah scanned their faces, watching them look anywhere but at her, their jaws tight with shame and frustration. "I'll tell you why!" she shouted when not one of them answered. "It is because even with all that, it is not enough! The Usurper commands an army tens of thousands strong, a fleet unrivaled on the southern seas, and coffers as deep as the oceans themselves. To go head-to-head with her now would see every last one of us dead on the ground." She waited a breath. "When will we have the strength we need? In five years? Ten? Twenty?" No one spoke. "Someone answer the question!"

Silence.

Zarrah chose that moment to round her horse on her father. "The answer is *never*. We cannot fight her alone, so it is fortunate that I arrive with the truest ally that I have ever known."

"An ally that makes promises he cannot hope to hold, Empress," her father said as all eyes went to Keris. "I do not doubt his loyalty to you, but Maridrina does not share it. They will not fight for Valcotta."

It was a dream that verged on madness that such a thing were possible, but it had been such dreams that had brought them through every trial and delivered them to this moment. Conviction boiled up from her heart. "If Keris says he will do it, then it will be done. He's proven that to me time and again, and I do not doubt him now."

From the corner of her eye, she saw Keris register the words, though no emotion showed on his face.

"You ask how I have earned the right to call myself Empress?" she shouted. "This is how. While all of you talk of ending the war, of bringing peace to Valcotta, of setting aside enmity, that's all it is. Talk. Whereas I have lived it. Proven it is possible."

Every eye was fixed on her, and it felt suddenly too hard to breathe, her claim too great to justify, even though in her heart, she knew it was true. "I . . ." Words failed her, and Zarrah swallowed hard, the same spiral of emotion that had made her panic in the brothel threatening to rise again. She couldn't let it. Couldn't faint off the side of her horse and expect these soldiers to then follow her into battle.

Countless times in her life she'd rallied soldiers, said what needed to be said to motivate them to fight, always wholly confident in her own leadership. In the righteousness of her cause. Only to learn that she'd been a pawn in a tyrant's game, every goal, every ambition, every desire planted in her mind by the one who'd stolen everything from her. To be freed of her aunt should have been liberating, except Zarrah couldn't help but wonder what she was without Petra Anaphora.

Breathe.

She sucked in a breath, but none of the air seemed to reach her lungs, the world starting to spin.

Then a hand pressed against her leg. Zarrah squeezed her eyes shut, knowing it was Keris without looking down, every part of her responding to his touch, and the next breath of air she dragged in filled her with strength.

Her panic fell away like the deadfall of winter in the face of spring rain. Allowing the bow in her hand to slip from her grip, Zarrah reached down to take hold of Keris's hand.

"Petra Anaphora is a tyrant whose desire to be worshipped by all causes her to turn violence upon any who doubt her. Who question her," she said. "We know this. Know she must be removed from power for Valcotta to ever thrive as it should. Know that she needs to be defeated at all costs. But to defeat an enemy, one must understand the weapons she uses. For the Usurper, her greatest weapon is the Endless War, and the fuel of that war is hate. She needs Maridrina to be the villain so that she might be the savior. Nearly everything she does is with the mind of fueling the belief that every hurt we suffer is at their hands and that we must redeem our honor in vengeance. There is no greater proof of that than in me."

Keris's fingers tightened, and she gave the faintest of nods. "I thought I needed to stand alone to liberate Valcotta," she said, her throat dry from talking but her heart strong in a way it hadn't been in so long. "Except peace wasn't a dream I conceived alone, and if I attempt to achieve it alone, I will fail. As will we all fail if we allow her weapon to hold power against us. We must set aside old hatreds and vows for vengeance against Maridrinians, for if we don't, we give the Usurper power over us. We must join with them and stand united against our common foe in a fight against tyranny. In a fight for a future for our children. Will you lift your weapons and join this alliance? Will you fight for peace?"

No one spoke. No one moved, and Zarrah's heart sank. Most of these soldiers didn't know her, and if they did, they knew her from before. Knew her when she was vengeance incarnate, their enemy's weapon. How could she blame them for not taking the risk of following her?

Then Daria edged her horse forward, shouting, "I joined this alliance back on Devil's Island. I stand by it now, just as I stand by the rightful empress of Valcotta!"

"As do I," Saam declared. "The king of Maridrina has got the biggest balls of any man I've met, and I'll gladly fight alongside him."

Daria's tribe members pressed forward, and Zarrah's throat tightened. They'd proven themselves in Arakis against Welran, shown their bravery and loyalty. Earned a tenuous place back with the rebels, yet they were risking it for Keris. Because he hadn't just proved himself to her; he'd proven himself to them.

She held her breath as they joined her, afraid it would cost them. But then the soldiers she didn't know moved to join them, men and women who were strangers to her and yet somehow had faith that she'd lead them to a better future. Arakis had risen for the rebellion, and now the rebellion would rise for Valcotta itself.

Soon everyone present stood behind her and Keris, leaving only the commander of the rebellion, her father, standing in opposition. Zarrah held her breath, because for all these soldiers had declared for her cause, she knew that if he turned his back on her, as he had so many times before, the support would evaporate.

Slowly, her father stepped forward and inclined his head. "I will join this alliance."

Keris's hand clutched tightly in hers, Zarrah looked out over her army. "Let the Usurper enjoy her crown while she has it, for we are coming to rip it from her head."

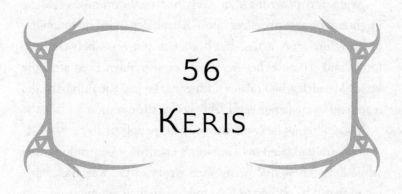

56
KERIS

"I stand corrected on my prior comments about your skills as an orator," Keris said. "That was magnificent."

Zarrah gave him a wry look over her shoulder before turning her attention back to the trail they rode upon, guiding the horse they shared through the narrow ravine. The incline sharpened, and he tightened his grip on her waist, the muscles of her abdomen taut beneath his fingers. So, too, were the muscles in his arms as he fought to keep an appropriate distance between them without falling off the back of the trotting horse.

His words were no lie. Listening to her speak, especially about how their time together had changed her, hadn't just moved the rebels, for Keris had nearly come undone, his emotions still riding high. For a long time, he'd questioned whether he remembered events in Nerastis accurately, or whether he had altered reality to fantasy, a rose-tinted view of the past. Her speech had validated his memories, which should've been a relief.

Instead he felt sick with anxiety that Zarrah's faith in him was misled.

Arjun wasn't wrong that Keris had made promises that he might not be able to deliver upon. Zarrah depended on his ability to bring his army across the border to pin Petra between two forces and secure either her defeat or surrender. Even after the losses Maridrina had taken in Ithicana, he had the numbers and resources to challenge Petra. That wasn't the question.

It was whether he could convince his people to do it.

Valcotta had been his kingdom's enemy for generations, and while Keris knew that many were weary of the war, that didn't mean they'd be willing to fight to liberate their enemy from a tyrant.

His father would have made them do it. Would have put the fear of refusal so deep in their guts that they'd have liberated the Devil himself rather than risk disappointing their king, but they didn't fear Keris that way.

And he didn't want them to.

Using fear to force them to fight a war they didn't want would make him the same as his father. Worse, it would make him the same as Petra. Removing one tyrant only to replace her with himself, and around and around the world circled in the same cycle of horror.

They had to break that cycle, but Keris had no idea how. No idea what he would say, only that the moment was rapidly approaching when he'd have to make his own speeches to his people.

Which, ultimately, meant that he was going to have to return to Maridrina. And leave Zarrah behind.

Keris closed his eyes, listening to the throb of his heart. This was always the way. Walking toward inevitable moments of separation made necessary by duty, circumstance, honor. Every force but their own wills desired them apart, and he'd have given up hope that it would ever be otherwise if not for that hope being what kept his heart beating. What kept him pushing and persevering and fighting for the very things that would again drive them apart. The most vicious of circles, and one from which Keris saw no escape.

"We're here," Zarrah murmured, and Keris opened his eyes, taking in the cliff walls full of cave openings. Ladders and scaffolding lined the cliffs, the armed Valcottans on them watching the party's approach.

"So this is where they've been hiding." Sliding off the back of the horse, Keris reached up to help Zarrah down, caring little when his stupid shoulder screamed in protest. Everyone was watching them, and though life had made him used to scrutiny, Keris still had to fight the urge to move to the shadows.

"The True Empress has joined us," Arjun shouted to the watching crowd. "And with her, she has brought the most mighty of allies, who has agreed to lend us his strength to tear the Usurper from Valcotta's throne."

Keris nearly raised an eyebrow, for Arjun had quite recently referred to him as the weakest king Maridrina had ever known, but then the man grabbed Keris's arm, lifting it into the air. "His Royal Majesty, King Keris Veliant of Maridrina."

Keris braced himself for the ire his name usually brought, but the rebels lifted their hands and shouted, "Arakis has risen!"

"This is a moment for celebration," Arjun roared, "for tomorrow, we make plans to march to war!"

The rebel commander led Keris and Zarrah to a ladder that reached up to the scaffolding. "Can you climb?" he asked Keris. "I know you took an arrow to the shoulder."

"I'll manage." Ignoring the pain, Keris followed him up the ladder to the midpoint of the cliff face, then down the narrow scaffolding running along it. The wood swayed and moved, and Keris caught hold of the rope railing, the ground abruptly feeling far away.

"Unlike you to be troubled by heights," Zarrah said softly from behind him. "I'm sure it's quite secure."

He opened his mouth to deny the flicker of fear in his gut, but instead found himself saying, "It was Otis's fall. The sound of—" He broke off, discomfited. "I've yet to regain my comfort with heights."

Zarrah was quiet as they climbed another ladder, but then she said, "I can't tolerate a certain rhythm of dripping water. Though it was a decade ago, the sound takes me right back to when my mother's blood was dripping down on me. Fills me with the same terror."

She'd never told him that before.

Keris glanced over his shoulder, but her eyes were on the boards of the scaffolding.

"The mind clings to unexpected things," she said, brow furrowed. "Sights. Sounds. *Smells.* But not always in a bad way." The corner of her mouth quirked up, and he fixated on the curve of it, the deadly drop beneath them forgotten as he mused over what she might be remembering.

Arjun stepped off the scaffolding and into a cave entrance, where the ceiling was low enough that Keris had to bend to keep from knocking his head. Rather than dampness, his nose picked up the faint scent of woodsmoke and cooking, the stone beneath his feet dry.

"It's an extensive network of caves," Zarrah's father said. "We have worked hard to keep its existence hidden, though with the increased pressure from the Usurper's soldiers, I'm not certain it will be safe much longer."

THE ENDLESS WAR   405

"The civilians supply you?" Zarrah asked, and her father grunted an affirmative.

"They give up what they can. It's a safer way to support the cause than to pick up arms or raise their voices. Too many who have done the latter have been murdered in their homes or sent to Devil's Island, and they're afraid. Yet the Usurper knows that they are our backbone, and she punishes them. Young people conscripted from Arakis are sent to the worst locations, most lost to battle, accident, or disease within a year. We know it is purposeful, but it's impossible to prove, and anyone who speaks aloud about it disappears, while those known to support her are granted trade licenses and given choice contracts with the crown."

"Subversive," Keris muttered, and Arjun nodded.

"Petra has never been able to tolerate criticism, so she finds clever ways to harm that cannot be traced to her. But let us not tarnish this moment with talk of our enemy. Valcotta is rising, and this is a moment to celebrate!"

The sound of drums and pipes softly echoed down the tunnel, growing louder as they progressed, as did the faint murmur of chatter and laughter of many people. Then the tunnel opened into a large chamber.

Lamps of colored Valcottan glass dangled from the roof, casting a rainbow of light over what appeared to be a communal dining hall. There were many of the low tables the Valcottans favored, cushions and furs used as padding against the stone floor. The tables were laden with jugs of ale and glass decanters of wine, as well as platters of food. Braziers were scattered around the space, the heat putting warmth into Keris's fingers, which had been numbed by the cold. The drummer and the pipe player paused, and heads turned, everyone falling silent.

Zarrah hesitated, then pressed into the chamber, pouring herself a glass of ale. Holding it up high, she said, "I lift my glass to all of you, who have fought so tirelessly and against every odd. Together, we will remake a better Valcotta!"

The rebels all lifted their glasses and roared, "To the True Empress!"

"To the True Empress," Keris murmured, taking a sip from the glass Saam had pushed into his hand, only to nearly gag on the sweetness. "Is this syrup?"

Saam laughed. "Fortified wine, Your Grace. Will put hair on your chest, and soon you'll look like me!" The rebel lifted his shirt, revealing a chest that boasted a full carpet of dark hair.

"You put me to shame, my friend," Keris answered, though his eyes had moved back to Zarrah. Her father had joined her and was escorting her around the chamber, introducing her to his following. Her eyes were bright, the grin on her face authentic and more full of joy than he'd seen in longer than he could remember. Surrounded not just by her people, but by individuals who shared her vision, her dream. Who would help her see it become reality.

Taking another sip of the sweet wine, Keris leaned back against the cavern wall, watching her own the moment. Saam joined him, a bottle in hand, which he used to refill Keris's glass. "How long will you stay?" the rebel asked.

Forever, was the first thought that came to Keris's mind, but he pushed it away. "I'll stay until we have the basis of a plan, an idea of timing, and then I'll need to return to Maridrina."

Saam nodded, then took a mouthful directly from the bottle. "You really believe that your people will fight for us?"

The sweet wine turned sour in Keris's stomach, because that was the question this entire venture depended on. The war between the nations had gone on for so long that it had become a way of life, the enmity his people felt toward Valcottans ingrained in their bones. To ask his army to march into Valcotta not as raiders but as allies would require them to set aside those feelings, which would not be easily done. "If they see that it is in their best interests. The war takes as much of a toll on Maridrina as it does on Valcotta. Endless lives lost to back-and-forth raids that net nothing of value, much of the country going hungry as people fear to farm the best lands north of Nerastis. Peace would bring prosperity and a better future, and that is what I need to make them see."

"Do you think they will?"

"Who can say?" Keris drained his glass. "The war has been reduced to a simmer in recent years, contained to the territory around Nerastis, rather than the all-out conflict that occurred in the past when whole armies and navies collided. The cost of those battles has faded in memory, become less visceral, especially in comparison to recent battles with Ithicana. If there were ever a time to push for peace, now is it."

Saam made a noise of agreement, and they stood in silence. Keris could feel the eyes of the rebels on him, curious but unwilling to approach. Though he knew that he should be putting in some effort to charm them, he didn't move from the wall, content to watch Zarrah in her element. She laughed at something a woman said to her, and though the room was loud with noise, it was all Keris heard.

"Do you enjoy handball?" Saam asked, and the oddness of the question caught Keris's attention. He subsequently realized that the other man was trying to fill what had been an awkward silence, so he asked, "Is that a game?"

"The superior sport," Saam answered. "One day, when all this is over and Zarrah overturns the law forbidding matches, I'll take you to the whispering courts at Meritt, the greatest stadium on the continent."

Saam continued to prattle on about the game, including a

lengthy description of the ingenious architecture the stadium builders had employed in service of acoustics, and the escape tunnels for the game masters when the spectators rioted. Keris only half heard, for at that moment, Zarrah's eyes locked with his. A single look that somehow conveyed a thousand words, and what they said stole the breath from his chest.

Then people moved between them, blocking her from sight, the crowd growing rowdier as they dragged the tables to the sides of the cavern, more musicians joining the original two. As they struck up a swift-paced song, the rebels began dancing, spinning one another around in circles with wild abandon.

Daria appeared in front of him. "People are going to think you strange if you insist on lurking in the shadows, Keris."

"I'm not lurking," he said. "Saam is teaching me the rules of handball, as well as sharing strategies for improving the quality of my chest hair."

She blinked, then shook her head. "That does not help your cause. Come dance!"

A laugh tore from his lips at the idea of it, and he said, "Daria, you would have more luck convincing me to fly than you will trying to get me to dance. Dancing is for—"

"Women?"

He'd been about to say "the entertainment," but both were accurate. "Maridrinian men do *not* dance. I don't even know how."

"Valcottan men do," she answered. "And it is known that if a man is a poor dancer, he is also likely to be a poor lover."

"Ha ha!" Saam shouted, then punched his fist into Keris's side. "A well-landed blow. It's true, though."

The other man writhed his way in among the other dancers, distinctly off-rhythm, and Keris turned to Daria. "My condolences."

She shrugged. "He compensates with enthusiasm." Then her eyes turned serious. "You're supposed to be breaking down the barriers between nations, not shoring them up."

A point he couldn't very well argue, so he held out a hand to her. "Fine. But you must show me how."

Daria grabbed hold of him with an iron grip, dragging him among the dancers. A heartbeat later, he was being spun around and around, new hands, male and female, grasping hold of his, only to pass him on to the next. Shouts of delight over having "danced with Maridrina's king" were loud in his wake.

"Drink!" Saam shouted, pushing a tiny pink glass of spirits into Keris's hand, then linking arms with him to drag him in a rotation.

Keris drank, the world spinning; then Saam let go of him and shoved his back. Keris stumbled a few steps, finding himself standing in front of Zarrah. Her cheeks were flushed, dark curls clinging to her forehead from exertion. "Don't worry," she said. "Valcotta will keep your dancing talents a secret for you."

Because you have to go back, the voice in his head whispered. *Back to Maridrina.*

Keris shoved it away and held out his hand. "Would you honor me, Imperial Majesty?"

Her palm was warm against his as she took it, and then she was spinning him in a circle. No one pulled him away from her, or her from him, the other dancers stepping wide around them as the world fell away. Zarrah's hands were gripped tightly in his as they went round and round, her head tilted back as she laughed.

I don't know what is worse. Her words in the brothel filled his head. *To stop now and endure the pain of what might have been or to keep going, knowing that there will come a moment when I lose it all.*

To have this moment was worth any amount of pain, for this memory would hold him through even the darkest of nights.

410 DANIELLE L. JENSEN

The musicians eased the beat of their music, Daria joining them. Taking a long mouthful of ale, she cleared her throat and began to sing, her voice slow and mournful.

"It's an old ballad," Zarrah said softly, her hand slipping around his neck as she moved closer to him. "A lament for the fallen. It's tradition to sing it on the eve of battle."

Instead of answering, Keris moved his hand to her lower back, drawing her closer. They'd always concealed their relationship, but no longer. No cloaks or shadows or anonymous identities to hide their forbidden union from the eyes of their people. From his periphery, he could see the other dancers watching them, the weight of what they were witnessing slowing their steps.

"Our world is changing already," Zarrah said softly. "I can feel it."

Yet it was the most fragile of changes, easily undone, and Keris pulled her closer even as he heard a faint commotion at the edge of the cavern, tension erasing the moment of quiet calm as Arjun approached, a woman at his side.

It was Miri, the matron of the pleasure house.

"There is news," Arjun said. "We should speak in private."

Unease bit at Keris's skin, and he let go of Zarrah to follow Arjun and Miri out of the gathering. They wove through the maze of tunnels, eventually reaching a chamber barricaded with a wooden door that had been cunningly shaped to fill the opening.

Inside, Keris found a table surrounded by inexpensive stools, though the carpets on the floor were thick. Wooden walls had been fabricated to cover the stone, though not an inch of surface wasn't covered with paper. Maps and reports, sketches of individuals, including one of himself. The artist had filled in his eye color with a paint that was uncannily close to what Keris saw each time he looked in the mirror. There was also a portrait of Zarrah, though it was oil work done with incredible detail. No . . . no, he'd been mistaken. It wasn't of Zarrah, which meant—

"Mother." Zarrah pressed past Keris to stare at the painting for a long moment before rounding on her father. "Where did you get this? My aunt . . . the Usurper removed all portraits of my mother from the palace. Said they were too painful to look upon." Her face abruptly twisted with disgust. "Though in hindsight, I suppose it was because every time she looked upon one, she felt guilty for what she'd done."

"Petra is incapable of feeling guilt," Arjun answered. "She removed them so that she might become your mother figure in Aryana's stead. As to the painting itself, it's my work."

Keris took a seat at one end of the table, content to observe as Zarrah reached up to touch her mother's portrait. She murmured, "I remember the smell of paint in your rooms. That you always had colors on your hands."

"You got into them as a child and painted yourself," Arjun answered. "The servants couldn't get it out of your hair and suggested shaving you bald, but your mother refused. Worked on your hair for days to get the blue paint out of it."

Keris's own father would've beaten him bloody if he'd done such a thing, but there was a faint smile on Arjun's face that suggested the memory was a fond one, even if his tone was gruff as always.

"I remember." Zarrah's tone was wistful; then she rolled her shoulders and moved to sit at the table, drawing a map in front of her. "There will be time for memories later. We need to focus on the present. What news do you bring, Miri?"

Once they were all seated, Miri said, "We've learned that Petra is amassing her army south of Pyrinat. Likewise, her navy. Hundreds of ships crowding the harbor, to the point that merchant vessels are struggling to make port, which isn't sustainable. The only garrison that remains untouched is that in Nerastis."

Arjun nodded. "All the spy reports indicate that with her failure to capture me at Devil's Island, she will now have to move directly against us here."

"Welran spoke of the desire to retake Nerastis," Keris said quietly. "But also an unwillingness to make a move on Maridrina with the rebel threat at its back. It seems to me Petra plans to bring the full weight of her army to bear on the rebellion, and with it crushed, turn her eyes north."

Arjun exhaled a long breath. "Arakis supports our cause, which was made very clear by actions taken last night. To crush the rebellion means—"

"Wholesale slaughter of Arakis and all other southern towns and cities known to support you," Zarrah said. "Cut off the arm to save the life, would be how she'd think of it."

Not even his father would have considered such a move, and Keris began to understand why his father had spoken about Petra with admiration. She was a villain far darker than Silas Veliant could ever claim to be. Clearing his throat, he said, "We've been told you have proof that Ephraim intended Aryana to succeed him."

Arjun nodded, extracting a lockbox that he opened with a key kept on a chain around his neck. Inside was a wax-wrapped document, which he carefully removed and spread in front of them. "I watched him sign this myself."

Keris's eyes skimmed over the document, pausing on the shaky signature of the dying emperor, which he recognized. A large seal in lavender wax was fixed beneath. It appeared authentic to his eyes.

"Then it's true." Zarrah touched the seal, then asked, "How many soldiers can you bring to arms?"

"Five thousand."

No emotion registered on Zarrah's face, but her stillness told Keris that she had hoped the number much larger.

"All trained? All armed?"

Arjun didn't answer, which was an answer in and of itself. "They are committed and will fight to the death, which is more than one can say for the Usurper's soldiers. The queen of Teraford has been supplying us with some weaponry, though it is out of self-interest. She fears that if Petra isn't distracted by rebellion, she'll move to annex choice parts of land along the border."

Zarrah's jaw was working back and forth, and Keris didn't need her to speak to know what she was thinking. Five thousand soldiers, only a portion of which were trained, would not stand a chance against Petra's army, which, last Keris had heard, numbered thirty thousand strong, plus one hundred and fifty naval vessels.

Picking up two pairs of markers, Keris set one on the border. "Your intelligence will be fresher than my own, but there should be five thousand Maridrinian soldiers in Nerastis, a thousand of which is cavalry. All armed, all trained, all experienced fighting men."

Arjun nodded. "Our spies confirm these numbers."

Keris set another marker down on the edge of the Red Desert. "Three thousand, broken into groups, along here. Desert-bred men who can survive on the thought of water alone."

Arjun blinked. "Our spies say a thousand."

"That only means your spies didn't brave the sands. They're there. Plus, I have another thousand who remain in defense of Vencia, along with smaller garrisons to protect the larger towns along the coast. Those I won't touch."

"Navy?"

Keris shrugged. "Beneath the Tempest Seas with my father's

ambition, for the most part. But I've a dozen good ships protecting the border at Nerastis, and another three that manage any pirates who try to attack merchants making the run to Southwatch."

It wasn't enough. While his father had been running his military ragged, Petra had been cooling her heels and building her strength, waiting for this moment. And now it was at hand. From the look in his dark eyes, Arjun was thinking the same things.

Silence stretched, and it was Zarrah who broke it.

"It will do." She rested her chin on her cupped hands, eyes thoughtful as she examined the map and markers. When she realized both of them were staring at her, Zarrah smiled. "It was never about needing large enough numbers to meet her head-to-head. It was about having enough men and women demanding a different future that all the Empire would be forced to listen. All this time, that's what she's been fighting to prevent—voices that demanded something different from what she wanted. Someone different from her. She will silence them no longer, for she will not silence us."

God help him, he loved her.

Didn't know how he was going to live without her.

But if their mutual dream was to succeed, Keris was going to have to bring her the army she needed, which meant leaving her. If he remained in Valcotta with her any longer, he'd be putting everything at risk. Rising to his feet, Keris inclined his head. "It seems that I have my marching orders. Given time is of the essence, if you can arrange a ship north, I'll return to Maridrina to do my part."

Zarrah's lips parted, her eyes widening, but instead of allowing her to speak, Keris turned his back on her and exited the room. More conversation wouldn't change the facts—he needed to resume his role as king of Maridrina once more.

"I need to go outside," he said to Saam, who was waiting near the entrance. "Somewhere high up. Preferably with a stiff drink that doesn't taste like syrup."

"Can do," the man said after Daria nodded. Leading Keris down a tunnel, he asked, "Not go well?"

"On the contrary," Keris answered. "It went exactly as the stars have always said it would."

57

ZARRAH

ZARRAH FELT FROZEN IN PLACE, BOTH HANDS GRIPPING THE table as she watched Keris exit and quietly shut the door behind him. He was leaving. Not just the room, the camp, and Valcotta, but her.

It was necessary.

Inevitable.

But . . .

"The spies say she hates him more than she did his father."

The assertion tore her back to the moment, and she met the commander's eyes. Her *father's* eyes, though she still found herself struggling to reconcile the two. "Pardon?"

"I'll take my leave," Miri said, rising to her feet. "I need to get back to Arakis."

Zarrah waited for the door to shut behind her before saying, "It's because she believes he is the reason I turned from her. She believes he stole my loyalty from her." Pushing the sweat-dampened curls clinging to her face behind her ears, Zarrah shook her head. "When she first learned about us, she flew into a rage against me, and I was certain she intended to see me dead. Especially when she said that I was to go to Devil's Island. But in the time between that moment and the hour before I was incarcerated, something in her mind . . . shifted."

Her father settled back in his chair.

"She seemed to have convinced herself that I was Keris's victim. That he'd manipulated me and used me as part of his plot to take Maridrina's throne. She had a spy report with claims that he'd taken up with one of the harem wives, and while logic suggests that she was lying to manipulate me, I don't think that's the case. I could see in her eyes that she believed everything it said, though it is strange for her spies to pass off rumor as fact. She had convinced herself that Keris had turned on me, which . . ." Zarrah trailed off, ashamed that Petra's delusions had become truth in her own mind. "She made me believe I had been a silly girl. A fool. That I needed punishment to keep me from ever making the same mistakes again."

"She has always been that way," her father answered. "Could never see fault within herself, could never take the blame for anything. And she was a master of finding ways to make others believe that it was their fault."

Looking back, Zarrah could see that now. How Petra never took responsibility for anything that went wrong, not really.

"She adored your mother," he said. "When Ephraim decreed it would be Aryana who took the throne, Petra did not blame her sister, but her father. She told Aryana that she needed to take the crown to protect her, because she didn't believe your mother had the strength for it. The reasons and rationales she gave for her actions grew at a frenzied pace, those who questioned her right to rule dying in accidents, while the military backed her, for she had always been their darling. I challenged her, named her usurper, and the fury that drew from her was a thing to behold. She banished me to the Red Desert to fight in the border wars, where I imagined she hoped I'd make my end.

"It was then we realized that Petra would never give up the crown of her free will, and we made the decision to falsify my death so that I could begin work gaining supporters," he said. "I was young and idealistic, so I thought that support would come easily. Except Petra dedicated the early years of her rule to winning the love of the people, and though there were some who disliked her warmongering, finding those who felt strongly enough to oppose her was . . . difficult. One year became two. Then five. Though I was able to meet with your mother, we didn't dare allow you to see me for fear you might say something to the wrong person.

"At that point, Petra was beginning to show some of her true colors in ways she hadn't since right after Ephraim's death. Excessive punishment for anyone who spoke against her, unfair trials, disappearances, and murders in the night, all while her masters of propaganda tricked everyone into believing her the benevolent ruler, beloved by all. I started making headway, recruiting resistance in Arakis, and we began disseminating the truth about her activities. Rumors that she had stolen the crown. I . . ." He trailed off, eyes distant. "In hindsight, that may have been when Petra realized that Aryana was not on her side, not her supporter at all. When she decided to kill her."

Zarrah took a steadying breath. All of this had been happening right beneath her nose as a child, and she hadn't even known it. Had been blissfully unaware, convinced that all was as it should be as she lived her life as a pampered princess in her aunt's palace. So certain that all was well in her world, the pain of her father's loss a distant memory.

"You saw me once a year before your mother was murdered," he softly said. "She introduced me as a dear friend, and I remember clear as day how you looked at me like a stranger."

A jolt struck Zarrah as the memory was brought forth. "At a handball match in the stadium at Meritt. I remember. Mother loved to watch the matches, but after her death, Petra closed all the stadiums. Something about illegal betting." Or, more likely, because once she'd turned on Zarrah's mother, she'd turned on everything Aryana loved.

Except for Zarrah; instead Petra made her her own.

Her father rose, going to a map cabinet and removing several rolled canvases, which he unfurled on the table before her. They were paintings of Zarrah. Six of them, all at different ages, the latest from when she must have been near twenty. All beautiful work rendered with such precise detail that he must have watched her closely over the years.

"You were always watched. By me, or those close to me," he said. "Only too late did I realize the cost of leaving you in her care. How she changed you, made you into her likeness, her heir in every possible way. Those were dark days, but you found your way out."

"Keris helped me find my way out."

"For which he has my gratitude," her father said. "I know his presence cannot be replaced, but as he travels north, I hope you'll accept me at your side."

Zarrah stared at the paintings of herself over the years, watched as her face hardened under the influence of her aunt, her smile fading. Her aunt had convinced her that to prove her strength, she needed to stand alone. That she couldn't rely on anyone other than herself. Couldn't trust anyone but herself.

And in believing her, Zarrah realized just how weak she'd become.

Pushing back her stool, she rose. "I would be honored to have you walk by my side, Commander. But before we press forward, there is something I need to do."

58
ZARRAH

SNOWFLAKES FLOATED AROUND ZARRAH AS SHE EXITED THE caves and climbed a ladder onto the cliff top. Darkness had fallen, the sky black with cloud cover, but instinct drew her eyes to the rebel on watch duty, the man nothing more than a shadow against the white snow.

"Did you notice which way he went?" Zarrah asked. Light of any form was forbidden, one of the many measures the rebels took to ensure their hideout wasn't discovered.

The shape rose, arm moving to press hand to heart. "Imperial Majesty. His Grace went that way." The man's hand moved to gesture deeper into the canyon. "You should have an escort. It's treacherous ground."

"I'll be fine," she said. "Thank you."

Wrapping her cloak more tightly around her body, Zarrah started in the direction he'd pointed, keeping away from the yawning black space to her right as she followed the faintly visible footprints. The snow seemed to reflect what ambient light filtered through the clouds, making it brighter than it would otherwise be. "Keris?" she called softly. "It's Zarrah."

No answer.

Unease pooled in her stomach. He planned to travel north, but it wasn't like him to just leave without saying goodbye, never mind that he had no supplies. No coin. But she also remembered the grim resignation in his eyes when he'd left her alone with her father. Maybe he'd thought it better to avoid the awkward parting conversation. Maybe he'd thought she would prefer he just disappear north to do his part in the war to come.

"I am going to kill you if you just left," she muttered before calling out, "Keris!"

The only sound was the gusting wind.

What if something had happened to him? Saam had said he'd left with a bottle of whiskey in hand. What if he'd gotten himself drunk and fallen off the bloody cliff? "Keris!"

No response.

Unease turned to fear, and Zarrah stopped in her tracks, wondering if she should return for help.

And then she saw him.

About two dozen paces away, a rocky outcropping protruded from the cliff face, and Keris stood on the very edge of it.

Heart hammering, she broke into a run. "Keris!"

His shadow turned, but he didn't step back from the edge. The outline of a bottle was visible in one hand.

"What are you doing?" she demanded, edging out onto the outcropping, which was slick with snow. "Are you trying to get yourself killed?"

"For most of my life," he answered, "the heights were my escape. Trees and rooftops and the undersides of bridges were the only places I could relax, but now, even that is lost to me." He lifted the bottle and took a mouthful. "Now, whenever I look out over an edge, all I hear is the sound of bodies hitting the ground." Another mouthful. "I used to think that I would never fall, and now some strange part of me wonders what it is like. Wonders what would go through my mind in those few seconds of weightlessness before everything went dark."

A quiver ran through her, and Zarrah moved closer, reaching for him. "Keris, please come back from the edge."

"Regret, I suppose," he said. "For things that I have done. For things that I have not done."

Why was he saying these things? "Keris . . ."

"I cannot change the past, but the future is yet in my hands. I need to go back to Maridrina." The bottle slipped from his hands, falling into darkness. "But there are some things that cannot be left undone."

Zarrah reached for him right as he turned, and then she was in his arms.

She'd come looking for him, looking for this, yet for a heartbeat, the fear that she'd almost lost him held her frozen in place. He reached icy fingers up to cup her cheek, and Zarrah pressed her own palm over them. "I told you that I needed to decide whether to stop now and endure the pain of what might have been or to keep going, knowing that there will come a moment when I lose it all." She sucked in a ragged breath. "I choose you. I want to live every moment with you that I can, no matter that I know circumstance will wrench us apart, because I know we'll fight our way back to each other's arms again."

Keris was silent, wind and snow whirling about them in a wild frenzy, and then his lips were on hers, her desire surging, the chill biting her skin falling away.

She buried her fingers in his hair, tasting the whiskey on his breath as his tongue delved into her mouth, the intensity making her knees tremble.

This was the kiss she remembered. The kiss she'd been craving every second they'd been apart. The kiss she'd needed like breath since she'd been back in his presence. No hesitation. No holding back.

Instead Keris claimed her.

Though in truth, she'd never stopped being his.

A moan dragged from her lips as he ran his hands down her back, over her ass, walking her slowly backward with no care for the fact death reached up at them from all sides. His fingers found the buttons of her coat, pulling it loose and dragging it off her. Her shirt followed, lost to the wind, but Zarrah didn't care as his lips moved down her throat, teeth scraping her skin, and tongue leaving lines of fire in its wake.

His mouth closed over her tight nipple, sucking it deep, and Zarrah cried out even as she pushed his hands down to her belt, feeling him fumble with the buckle and then jerk it free. She stepped on the heels of her own boots to pull them off, Keris dragging her trousers down her legs. Then she was naked but for the cloak fastened to her neck, the fabric floating behind her on the wind.

The air was like ice, but Zarrah barely felt it as he lifted her, her legs around his waist as he walked away from the cliff, laying her down on a flat boulder. She gasped at the chill of the snow against the back of her head, melting into her hair, the wind lashing at her naked sex as he unbuckled his belt, a shadowy god against the snow and night.

She reached for him, but Keris caught her wrists, pinning them to the rock. Zarrah instinctively knew what he wanted, and she spread her thighs wide, a sob of pleasure tearing from her lips as he drove into her slick body.

Always, their lovemaking had focused on her pleasure. On her body. And she realized now that it wasn't out of a desire to manipulate or control her, as the Usurper had claimed, but out of a need to please her. A need to feel worthy of her. She had made a thousand demands of him, and he'd met each and every one.

And all he needed in return was *her*. Proof that she was his, that no matter what obstacles the world pushed between them, every part of her, mind, body, and soul, would always come back to him. Just as he would always come back to her.

That knowledge sent a flood of heat racing through her veins. Made her wrap her legs around his waist to pull him deeper with each thrust.

"Zarrah," he groaned, fingers tightening on hers, the cold burning like fire against her flesh.

"I love you," she breathed, tension building between her thighs, her body tightening around his cock. There was nothing about him that wasn't worthy, nothing about him that didn't deserve what he had. And what he had was her heart. "I love you more than life, Keris Veliant."

His breath was hot against her throat, voice ragged as he said, "You're mine."

"Yours," she gasped, the cold buttons on his coat brushing against her nipples and making her back arch. Each thrust bringing her closer to the edge of climax.

"Forever." He bit her throat, and the slice of pain tipped her over, pleasure shattering her body and creating stars in the midnight sky. "Say it." His voice filled her ears as she rocked her hips against him, tears rolling down her cheeks because nothing in her life had felt this good. "Say it, Zarrah. Say that you are mine forever, no matter where we are."

"Yours," she sobbed, wrenching her wrists from his grip and wrapping her arms around him. "Yours forever. This life and the next, I am yours."

Keris buried his face in her neck and slammed into her, her name repeating over and over as his body shuddered, heat flooding her core as he came in her. It pulled her over the edge once more, pleasure rolling over her body again and again, rendering her boneless and limp in his arms.

The wind howled, the snow beneath her melting to soak her cloak, but all she felt was Keris's breath against her skin, the heat of his body on hers. Slowly, he lifted his head, finding her lips and kissing her. "I love you," he whispered. "No matter what happens, no matter where we both must go, please remember that my heart is yours."

There were no words that could capture what she felt, so Zarrah only kissed him. Drowned in the taste of him until shivers wracked her body and they were forced to retreat inside where it was warm, where they spent the night as though it were the first time.

Not the last.

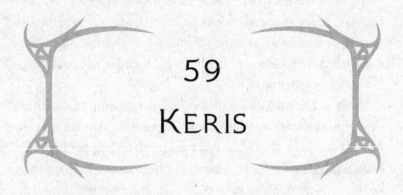

59
KERIS

THOUGH NO NATURAL LIGHT CAME INTO THE CAVERN IN WHICH they slept, some recently developed instinct told him that it was dawn, and Keris opened his eyes. The lamp on the small table next to the bed burned low, illuminating the chamber, and beyond the curtain that served as a door, the rebels stirred as they prepared for the day ahead. But all that mattered to him was that Zarrah was in his arms.

Easing up onto his elbow, Keris watched her sleep, unwilling to wake her. Unwilling to sacrifice this moment.

The lamplight cast dancing shadows over her rounded cheekbones, illuminating the freckles splashed across her skin. Her long lashes moved slightly, as though she were dreaming, though the steady breath through her parted lips told him that whatever visions filled her head, they did not trouble her. His gaze drifted over her dark curls, nearly long enough to brush her shoulders now, then over the long column of her neck to her delicate collarbones. The curve of her breast, and the muscled length of her arm, her fingers loosely interlaced with his.

Why was fate so cruel as to demand he leave her?

A sudden wave of grief passed over him, the intensity so staggering it stole the breath from his lungs. Made his eyes burn so that he had to squeeze them shut. She needed him to do this. Needed him to bring her an army. Needed him to be the king of Maridrina. Yet every part of Keris wished that the only thing she needed from him was himself.

"I love you."

Her beautiful voice filled his ears, fracturing his heart, and when he opened his eyes, it was to find her looking at him. He wanted to lose himself in her dark gaze, to fall down into the depths and forget everything else, but instead he said, "I need to secure passage north."

The faint smile that had been on her lips fell away, and she pressed her forehead against his chest. "Why is it always this way?" Her voice was shaking, as though she were close to tears.

"Star-crossed," he answered softly, feeling a tear drip down his cheek. He wiped it away before it fell on her shoulder.

"I wish I could travel with you," she said. "It's not fair that you have to do this alone."

Keris shook his head, knowing this was her heart speaking, not her mind. Knowing that as she stepped out of his arms and into her role as empress, logic would prevail. "Petra is poised to attack your people. As the rightful empress, you need to be standing at the head of your army. They need to see you present."

Keris felt the dampness of tears on his chest as Zarrah said, "I'm afraid. For you. For my people. For myself." Lifting her face, she met his gaze. "Promise me that this isn't the end."

"I promise," he said, because life was not possible for him without her. He'd come back to her, knowing that they'd again be pulled apart, that he'd again face this grief. Over and over he'd do it, for as long as they both lived, because even stolen moments in her presence were worth a lifetime of pain. "I will come back to you."

She pressed her lips to his shoulder, just below the arrow wound, then moved onto her hands and knees, kissing her way down his chest, then his stomach. Though he'd been in her most of the night, his cock still hardened at her touch. Wanting more. Wanting her.

Zarrah looked up at him then, her large brown eyes framed with endless lashes, anything but innocent as she said, "I'm yours."

He exhaled, relaxing his hold on her, though a groan tore from his lips as she closed her mouth over him. Sucked him deep, her nails trailing over his skin, his heart pounding harder with each passing second. Zarrah knew him in a way no one else ever had, ever would, and part of him would never cease to be amazed that she loved him in spite of it.

Her tongue circled his tip, and he drew in a steadying breath because he was losing control. Though perhaps he was delusional to think he ever had control when in her presence, ever at her mercy. "Zarrah . . . Zarrah, I'm going to—"

She lifted her face for a heartbeat, meeting his gaze, then lowered it again, and the sight of her full lips around his cock was his undoing.

The violence of his climax made him shout her name, bowing his spine, his fingers tangling in her hair as he spent himself. Falling back against the bed, Keris closed his eyes, dragging in breath after breath as she curled around him, one finger tracing over the muscles of his torso.

Marry me, he silently asked her. *Be my wife, the mother of our children*. His lips parted, words rising—

Only for a cough to sound outside the curtain serving as the chamber's door. From the far side, Daria's voice said, "One of our spies has arrived with urgent news. The Usurper has made her first move. We need you both, now."

"Impossible," Zarrah said. "She can't yet know that Arakis has turned against her. Would only just have learned that I escaped the island."

Keris didn't answer, his skin crawling with trepidation because if Petra were merely on the march south, Daria would have said so. It was something else.

It was something worse.

They both swiftly washed and dressed, going into the tunnels and making their way to Arjun's war room. Whispers echoed, the faces of all those they passed grim. Except it wasn't Zarrah they looked to.

It was to him.

They reached the war room to find Arjun and Daria speaking with Miri, who must have turned around to ride back almost as soon as she'd returned to Arakis. At the sight of them, Arjun said to her, "Thank you for bringing us the news so swiftly. Rest before you return to the city."

Miri nodded and departed, closing the door behind her.

"Petra has set sail," he said. "Fifty ships filled with soldiers."

"We have time to evacuate our people from Arakis," Zarrah answered. "We can retreat inland and evade her forces until we're ready."

Keris heard her, but the words sounded distant, barely registering in his ears, because Arjun hadn't been addressing his daughter; he'd been addressing Keris. "She didn't sail south, did she?"

Arjun shook his head.

"She intends to take Nerastis, then?" *Please let it be Nerastis,* he silently pleaded. *Please let this attack fall upon soldiers.*

A fool's hope, because if invasion was her intent, she'd have taken her entire army north.

"It was our spies in Nerastis who sent word," Arjun answered. "Petra's fleet attacked your ships there, damaging or sinking all of them. But instead of disembarking, they sailed north."

Past the army that he'd poised to march to Zarrah's aid, and this news would have taken days on a fast ship to reach them in Arakis.

The world around Keris swam, a roaring in his ears drowning out all other sounds. There were only a thousand soldiers in Vencia to stand against a number ten times that. A thousand soldiers to protect his family. His people. His kingdom.

Sara.

Staggering to his feet, Keris fought for balance as everything spun. "I need to get north," he said. "I need a horse. A ship."

Hands gripped his arms, Arjun's eyes locking on his. "Your armies in Nerastis will know her intent and put on immediate pursuit. And Vencia itself is no easy target, especially if the seas are rough. A thousand well-trained men can defend that city; I'm sure of it."

Keris twisted away, his head throbbing. God help him, he knew how this would go. His armies would abandon Nerastis to race to the aid of the capital, and the rest of Petra's forces would claim Maridrina's half of the contested city.

Falling to his knees, he gagged, bile mixed with fear and guilt rising up his throat.

"We'll get to the coast," Zarrah said. "Send a rider ahead to tell our people to ready our fastest ship."

"Already done," Arjun said. "But ..."

He didn't need to finish, because Keris had already done the math. In the days this message would have taken to reach them, Petra's army would be nearing Vencia.

It was already over.

Zarrah's hands were on him, her voice in his ears, but every time he blinked, he saw Vencia burning. His people dead and dying. And he hadn't been there. Hadn't been focused on them, because he'd allowed Keris the man to make decisions, not Keris the king.

He lifted his head to meet Zarrah's gaze. "Perhaps it is the lot of those who rule to stand alone."

She went very still, then gave a rapid shake of her head. "That is the Usurper speaking, and her words are poison, Keris. You can't blame yourself for this—we were certain her eyes were on the south. Everything told us that she'd move against the rebels before turning north, and even then, we believed Nerastis her target."

Had he been certain of that? Or did he just allow himself to be convinced because it justified his choice to remain with Zarrah? Because it justified him putting his army where she'd need it? His chest tightened to the point he could barely breathe, because he knew the answer. Knew he'd turned a blind eye to anything that might take him away from her, and his people had paid the price. "I need a horse. I need to go."

Go and do what? the voice in his head whispered. *You're too late to make a difference. The dead won't care if you come now, only that you weren't there when it mattered.*

He ignored the admonishment and left the room. Barely seeing anything he passed as he left the cave system and descended the ladders to where horses were tethered. He could feel Zarrah behind him, sense her hunting for words that would offer hope and coming up short. Heard her intake of breath, but before she could speak, he said, "I'm going alone."

"No." She closed the distance between them, though he didn't turn around. Couldn't bear to look at her while he went back on everything he'd ever said. While he ripped to shreds all the promises he'd made with her in his arms, because he would not be coming back.

"I'm not letting you go alone, Keris," she said. "I'm not letting you face this without me."

"It's too dangerous." He slipped the bit into his horse's mouth, then pulled the bridle over its head. "You are Valcottan, and it was Valcottan soldiers that attacked. My people won't care that you're a rebel. They won't care that you hate Petra as much as they do. All they'll see is the enemy, and given how I've failed them, I won't be able to stop them from tearing you apart."

"I'll be careful," she insisted. "Wear a scarf, keep my face concealed."

He lifted the reins over the horse's head, then paused, drawing in a deep breath before turning back to her. "This is where she's turning next, Zarrah. You need to prepare to fight."

Her jaw tightened, beautiful eyes closing as his words struck home.

"What kind of ruler abandons her people on the eve of battle?" he asked. "Not for any valid reason but for the sake of her lover? For the sake of another nation?"

A ruler like him, was the answer, and he was paying the price.

The muscles of her face scrunched like she was in pain, and it was all Keris could do not to pull her into his arms. Instead he kept still, knowing that she'd see the reality of the situation.

"This is my fault," he said. "You pushed me to walk away, to leave the past in the past and set our hearts and minds to defeating our enemy. But I wouldn't let you go. Couldn't let you go, and used words and actions and sentiment to convince you we could have it all because I believed I had the power to remake the world in a way where all was possible. I was wrong, and Maridrina has paid the price of my hubris tenfold."

Her hands fisted. "You act as though I was a passive player in all this, but that's bullshit. If I didn't want you to be here, you wouldn't be. But the truth is that you merely put words to desires that burned in my heart."

"Then we are both fools," he answered, his mouth tasting of bitterness, anger, and guilt.

Zarrah flinched, then whispered, "I don't believe that."

God help him, he wished she were right. But Vencia was half a continent away, and he swore he could taste the ash of its destruction. And their dream was the fuel Petra had used to set it aflame.

Dropping the reins, he cupped her face, using his thumbs to wipe away her tears. And though each word rent his heart, he said, "Some dreams are never meant to be a reality."

She shuddered, the general, the empress, falling away to reveal the woman beneath.

His control crumbled, and he pulled her against him, blind to the rebels looking on as he tangled his fingers in her hair. "You are Empress Zarrah Anaphora, rightful ruler of Valcotta and commander of the army that will liberate it from a tyrant. You need no one, least of all me."

Her fingers dug into his shoulders. "Tell me there is a chance, tell me there is hope, tell me that on the other side of this, we will find a way back to each other."

He wanted to say yes. Needed to. Instead he bent his head and kissed her softly, then swung up onto his horse. "Goodbye, Imperial Majesty."

Digging in his heels, he trotted through camp, following Arjun's lead to the coast, where he'd board a ship to Maridrina, knowing full well that by the time he reached his homeland, he might be a king of nothing at all.

THE REBEL SHIP WAS BUILT for speed, and they made no stops as they sped north, avoiding contact with any other vessels.

Keris barely ate, his stomach in ropes. Barely slept, his dreams plagued with nightmares of what he'd find when he reached Vencia.

"Nerastis, Your Grace," the captain said as they sailed past the contested city. The man handed him a spyglass, and girding himself for the worst, Keris lifted it and turned his eye to the coast.

It was too far to see details. Yet his eyes burned as he remembered his time there, it seeming like both yesterday and a lifetime ago.

He moved his line of sight up the coast, searching for smoke, but there was nothing. Which meant the attack had happened farther north.

The coward deep in his soul crawled upward, whispering that there was no point in carrying on to Vencia. That it was better to fade into the wind than to see the consequences of his distraction.

"You will go," he growled at the coward, not caring when the captain gave him a startled look. "You will face your failure."

Keris shoved the spyglass into the captain's hand, muttering, "Full sail to Vencia."

THE SEAS GREW ROUGH AS they drew closer, the tail end of a storm in the Tempest Seas turning the waves to mountains, though the skies remained clear. Clouds would have been better, because they'd have spared him the hours of watching smoke rise into the sky as they hunted for a cove where he could be safely brought to shore.

"Let us send men with you, Your Grace," the captain said as they rowed the longboat to shore. "After battle, the worst of men come to pillage and loot. It isn't safe."

Keris shook his head. "The empress will need all the ships and men she has in the battle to come. Return to her with news of what you've seen. I'll send word when I can."

The man looked as though he might argue, then eyed the tow-ering plumes of smoke that Petra had left in her wake and instead gave a slow nod. "Condolences, Your Grace. May you find honor in vengeance against the Usurper."

"She'll bleed," Keris answered, stepping into the water. But it wasn't until he was on the beach that he added, "Though not by my hand."

He made his way inland until he reached the main highway that ran down the coast, following it toward the city of his birth. The sides of the road bore the signs of an exodus, broken carts and belongings discarded when it was discovered that survival was worth more than possessions.

Of life, he saw not a single soul, only flocks of ravens soaring in the direction of the jewel of Maridrina.

He saw the first corpse as the blackened and broken walls of the city came into sight. A woman, long dead, an arrow in her back and eye sockets empty, a morsel in the feast of carrion Petra had left behind.

The gates to the city still stood, but the wall to the left and right was crumpled, the massive stones from the catapults sitting like sentries in the ruins.

A gust of wind hit him, and Keris gagged on the stench of rot-ting flesh that rolled over him, bits of ash falling from the sky.

Because Vencia still burned.

As he climbed the ruined wall, Keris stopped in his tracks to look down the hill toward the sea, the white city he both loved and loathed now a ruin of blackened and smoldering rubble, the shat-tered tower of his father's palace poking up from the ashes like a broken spear.

Keris's knees buckled and he dropped to a crouch, knuckles pressed against blood-smeared stone as he took in the broken harbor chain, dozens of burned-out merchant ships listing on the waves. The wharves were gone, markets burned, buildings collapsed into the streets, and above it all, crows circled, bellies fat on Maridrinian flesh.

This is your fault.

He forced himself back to his feet, then his feet to carry him into the streets, picking his way toward his family's home. "Please let them have gotten out," he muttered, visions of his elderly aunts and his youngest siblings filling his mind's eye. But Sara most of all, for she could not run. "Please let Sarhina have gotten you out."

An empty hope, given that his family would've been Petra's primary target, her desire to burn his bloodline from the face of the earth stripping her of mercy.

If she had any at all.

His eyes skipped over the still forms, not as many as had filled his dreams, but somehow worse than anything his imagination had conjured. Men. Women. Children. Eyes gone, bodies bloated, skin rotten.

You were supposed to protect them! the voice screamed. *For all his faults, at least your father did that much!*

Icy sweat dribbling down his back, Keris stopped in front of the palace, his home, staring at the gaping opening where the silvered gate had once been, now twisted and stained with soot on the broken cobbles. It struck him then that this had been what he'd set upon Ithicana. Only the arrival of Lara and a storm had spared Eranahl from this fate.

Is this my punishment? he silently wondered as he stepped into the ruins, eyes skipping to the bodies of dead guards, to bloodstains, to a chest of silk dresses spilled across the courtyard. *Have I finally reaped what I sowed?*

The buildings had mostly collapsed, forcing him to climb the rubble to reach the inner sanctum, and then down into the gardens.

They'd been crushed by the collapse of the top half of the tower. The spread of rocks looked like the remains of a fallen giant, and across the ruins, a message was painted in blood.

Death to all Veliants.

Like a breaking dam, panic flooded his veins, chasing away the numbness of shock, and Keris threw himself at the harem's house, pulling away rocks. Digging. Hunting for the family he'd forsaken.

"Sara!" Sharp edges split open his hands, bruised his fingers, but still he dug, screaming the names of his aunts, of his siblings, needing to find them. Needing to tell them how sorry he was.

"Keris?"

He froze at the sound of the voice, hand finding the hilt of his sword before recognition struck him. "Sarhina?"

His half sister stood alone on the remains of a building. Her black hair was pulled back in a long tail, body encased in the leather and steel armor favored by his people. Her face was drawn with exhaustion, eyes marked with dark circles, but she was alive.

"The family isn't here," she said, and Keris clenched his teeth as he waited to hear that they'd all been taken.

"They are in the mountains," she said. "Along with the rest of the civilians who chose to evacuate."

Evacuate.

The meaning of the word refused to register, and he stared at her, unable to speak.

"Regardless of what the Ithicanian intelligence said about a pending invasion," Sarhina said, "I still knew it was a mistake to deplete the city guard. But no one would listen, given that the order was written in your cursed hand, so the soldiers marched south."

Ithicanian intelligence? He blinked in confusion, unable to comprehend why Aren would abuse his trust by forging such an order. Unless something had happened to their ship? Unless it hadn't been Aren at all, but rather Ahnna, in some form of retaliation? God help him, she had reason enough to do it.

"We learned of Petra's plans to attack Vencia just before her fleet was spotted coming up the coast," Sarhina said. "Too late to call back our soldiers, but we were able to evacuate the people into the mountains."

"Sara?" It was a struggle to get her name out, but she, above anyone else, was his concern.

"She's in our military camp outside the city. As is Lestara." Sarhina's voice soured slightly on the woman's name, but even if it had not, Keris's hackles would still have risen.

"Unfortunately, not everyone would abandon their homes to evacuate." She looked away. "We tried to fight back but were forced into retreat. Petra's army burned the city, wrote their messages, then got back on their ships."

"The territory she wants is Nerastis," he said. "She likely intended to use the attack on Vencia to lure our army back north, then take the city."

"That's what I thought as well, which is why I sent riders south with orders for them to hold their ground. If Petra attacks there, she's in for a fight that won't be easily won."

Keris scrubbed his hands back through his hair, trying to think, but his mind was a mess. "If that was her intent, I should've seen her fleet on my way north. Even if they realized the gambit to lure our army out of Nerastis hadn't worked, they should still have been in proximity. But there was no sign of them." Squeezing his eyes shut, he tried to work out the timeline, but he felt ten steps behind.

Zarrah's prepared, he told himself. *The rebels won't be caught unaware.*

It did nothing to calm the trepidation rising in his chest. All this time, he, and everyone else, had believed Petra's goal was victory in the Endless War, defeating him, and annexing some or all of Maridrina. Had believed that the rebels were an obstacle she intended to remove first before setting her eyes north on her ancient enemy. It was logical. Strategic.

But wasn't what she'd done.

Instead she'd come north and attacked Vencia with no intention of keeping it. But why? Why kick the hornet's nest by delivering a non-fatal blow to Maridrina, only to turn her back on it to go after the rebels, who were, by the numbers, a much smaller threat?

"What was the point of this?" he muttered, sitting on a broken piece of wall and staring at the ground. "What did she hope to accomplish?"

"To undermine you."

Keris lifted his head to meet Sarhina's gaze.

"The economic toll this will take on Maridrina might be a consideration in her mind," Sarhina said, "but the most certain consequence of attack is that the people will blame *you* for leaving the city undefended."

"I didn't write that order."

"But everyone thinks you did," she snapped. "This was your scheme, and I don't know what you did to piss Ithicana off so badly that they'd do this, but I can't see why else it was done. Perhaps Petra made a deal with them. Perhaps she threatened them. Who knows." Her mouth twisted. "But what I do know is that this attack wasn't strategic; it was personal."

Dread pooled in Keris's stomach as all the pieces fell into place. Petra's eyes were no longer on winning the war—they were on winning Zarrah. Killing him wouldn't suffice; Petra needed Zarrah to choose her over him. Needed Zarrah to love her over him. Needed Zarrah to worship her as she had before that fateful night in Nerastis when Zarrah's path had crossed with his and changed them both forever. And Petra believed that the only way to accomplish that was for Keris to fail Zarrah, for Zarrah to perceive that he'd abandoned her when she needed him most.

"She is truly mad," he breathed, horror turning his hands to ice. The cost of lives and gold was beyond measure. All played like pieces on a board, with the end goal of turning Zarrah against him, because in her twisted mind, Petra believed that was all it would take to make Zarrah love her again.

"Mad or not, she accomplished at least part of her goal," Sarhina answered. "You have to let this go, Keris. Let Zarrah fight her own battles. Countless of your people have lost everything because you abandoned them in pursuit of her. You left them vulnerable to the guile of others because you care more about her than you do your own kingdom. Our people believe you left them entirely undefended, and to prove otherwise requires you to admit that you weren't in Ithicana. That you authorized the Ithicanians to forge instructions on your behalf. That you were in the south, freeing your Valcottan lover. That this attack against Vencia was instigated by your illicit affair. That every bit of this is your fault."

All true. It was all true.

"You may not have written the order for the city guard to abandon Vencia," Sarhina said. "But the five thousand men of the Royal Army in Nerastis *are* there on your order. As are the three thousand lurking on the edge of the Red Desert. And it does not take a military genius to know that you didn't send them there to protect our border. You sent them there because you want to give Zarrah the army she needs to overthrow the empress."

Keris said nothing. There was nothing to say, for all her accusations were true.

"Once our people learn the truth, all you can hope for is a quick death." Sarhina looked away. "Better that you run. Falsify your own death and return to your lover's side. Allow someone who will put Maridrina first to lead the kingdom."

Sarhina was right.

Keris turned to stare out over the harbor, the weight of defeat dragging him down as a vision of the future played out in his mind. With no allies, Petra would destroy the rebels, either killing or imprisoning Zarrah. But it would not stop there. She'd once again turn her eyes north, and with victory fresh, would attack Nerastis. Would annex Maridrina bit by bit as she expanded the Empire, eventually reaching her claws out to Ithicana, screaming for revenge for the murder of her son.

In trying to end the war, all he'd managed to do was ensure a future more violent and bloody than the past. Maybe it was better that he disappeared, for Maridrina was better off without him.

Petra had won.

"Did Royce survive his injuries?" he asked, still staring at the fog that concealed Ithicana.

"Yes," Sarhina answered, her voice filled with disgust. "Lestara has ensured he be given the most excellent of care, and in exchange, he has ensured that every person in the kingdom knows that she's responsible for their survival."

Keris's nerves jangled at the mention of the Cardiffian princess's name. "Pardon?"

"She learned of Petra's pending attack via her father's spies. Without her warning, we'd never have been able to evacuate the city, so now the civilians fall to their knees when she passes, calling her the *Savior of the People*."

"Just how," Keris asked softly, "did the king of Cardiff, who is on the far side of the Tempest Seas, know of Petra's plans to sack Vencia?"

"As one who looks every gift horse in the mouth, I have wondered the very same thing," Sarhina answered.

Surely Lestara would not stoop so low . . . Yet on the heels of the thought, he remembered how Zarrah had asked whether he'd taken up with Lestara, a question fueled by a supposed spy report Petra had received. At the time, he'd believed it a fabrication created by Petra to undermine him in Zarrah's eyes. But what if it was more than that? What if it had not been a fabrication, but a plot intended to achieve mutually desired ends: Lestara on Maridrina's throne and Keris forever vanquished from Zarrah's heart? "I assume you investigated her source?"

"She provided the spy's report."

Wheels began turning in his head, a thousand little pieces of information falling into place to form a damning picture. "Where is she?"

"She shares a tent with Sara." Sarhina cleared her throat. "She's kept our little sister very close."

His stomach tightened. "I need inside that tent."

"What you need to do is run before anyone realizes you're here and starts to cast blame."

Keris rose to his feet, meeting her glare. "No."

"Don't say I didn't warn you."

She led him back over the rubble to where a group of Maridrinian soldiers waited on their horses, their eyes widening in shock at the sight of him. "Say nothing of His Grace's presence," she ordered them, and though he could see the blame in the men's eyes, they obeyed. Testament to their loyalty to Sarhina.

One of the soldiers sacrificed his mount to Keris, and then the group made its way through the city. On the eastern half, soldiers worked to gather bodies, loading them into carts to transport out the eastern gates.

To where the mass graves had been dug.

At the sight, Keris leaned over the side of his horse and vomited. Sarhina said nothing, only handed him a waterskin and then led the group onward to the tents in the distance. He pulled his hood up before they reached them, not wanting to be recognized.

Away from the city, the stink of ash and rot was absent, but not the marks of war. Injured soldiers rested on rows of cots, bodies bandaged, many missing limbs. Babies cried, and children, many of them likely orphaned, sat staring with blank eyes as they rode past.

A slow burn of fury filled Keris's chest that this had been done to them, no small part of it directed at himself.

Sarhina dismounted near a tent. "Is Lestara inside?" she asked the guard standing out front, but the man shook his head.

"Just the young princess. The lady Lestara is checking on the welfare of Prince Royce."

"Something she does with regularity, despite his wounds being well healed," Sarhina muttered. "You go. I'll keep watch."

Keris entered the tent, his eyes immediately going to his little sister, who sat reading on one of the narrow cots.

Sara's eyes widened at the sight of him. "Keris! You came back! I knew she was a liar!"

He held a finger up to his lips, then crossed the room to sit on the cot next to her. "Are you all right?"

His little sister nodded. "It's been awful." Her eyes welled up with tears. "The Valcottans destroyed Vencia. The palace is ruined, everyone forced to live in tents or outside. And many died in the attack."

"I'm sorry I wasn't here to keep you safe," he said, wishing there was time to comfort her, but he needed answers. "Has Lestara given you anything to keep for her? Papers? A locked box?" His heart sank when she shook her head. "Has she given you anything?"

"Clothes and shoes." Her eyes brightened. "And a book about stars."

Keris's stomach dropped. Even before Sara reached down to retrieve the book hidden in the folds of the blanket, he knew what volume it was.

With icy fingers, he took the familiar small book from her hand, a tremor running through him as he opened it to flip through the pages of constellations and the stories the Cardiffians believed that they told. The book she'd all but begged him to return despite having had it in her possession this entire time.

But how?

Keris wracked his mind for when he'd last seen it. Zarrah had been holding it when she'd leapt across the spillway. It had been in her hand when he'd fumbled the lock to the room in the inn. And inside, she'd set it on the table.

Where it had been abandoned.

Unbidden, Serin's voice filled his head. *I thought the whore in Nerastis would yield something, but all she could tell me was that you wouldn't touch her and that you'd disappear into the night, returning hours later smelling of lilac. She believed you were visiting a lover, and an innkeeper swore a man of your description rented one of his rooms in the company of a Valcottan woman.*

The very innkeeper who would have found the book when the room had been cleaned for the next customer, later to be given as proof to Serin. Who had subsequently given it to Lestara, sowing seeds that would see to Keris's destruction even after the Magpie was in his grave.

"Keris, are you all right?"

"No." His throat moved as he swallowed hard, his fingers tracing over the inside of the cover, which was bulkier than he remembered. Pulling a knife from his boot, Keris cut open the stitching and extracted a piece of paper with Serin's spidery writing.

> *Lady Lestara,*
>
> *I wish to return to you this book, which you once gifted to His Grace as a token of great sentiment. I regret to inform you that he abandoned the tome in a Nerastis inn, where it was subsequently discovered by the owner. I was told that he had spent the night with a young Valcottan woman, though her identity has yet to be proven. His disrespect of your gift is not surprising, for it is in his nature, but I hope having it back in your care is some comfort to you.*
>
> *Serin*

Keris stared at the letter. Why hadn't Serin revealed Zarrah's identity?

Understanding flowed over him, along with renewed appreciation for the Magpie's cleverness. Lestara wouldn't have trusted anything that came from Serin's lips, but the letter *would* have been enough to spur her to investigate herself. And the conclusions she'd come to had clearly been damning.

Setting down the book, Keris shifted to look at Sara, who was staring at him with wide eyes. "You ruined my book."

His only regret was that Zarrah hadn't thrown this book into the waters of the Nerastis spillway along with his coat. "When I came in, you said something about someone being a liar. Who were you speaking of?"

"Lestara."

"What did she lie about?"

Panic filled her gaze, and Sara looked away, shaking her head. "Not long after you left for Ithicana, Lestara told me you weren't coming back. That you'd told her you were tired of taking care of all of us, especially . . ." She swallowed hard. "Me."

His hands fisted, mind readily supplying a vision of Lestara manipulating Sara's greatest fear.

"I told her she was wrong. That you'd gone to Ithicana to see Aren and Lara to negotiate, but that you'd be back once that was completed. She said, if that were the case, why hadn't you brought me with you?" Sara chewed on her bottom lip.

"You know why," he said. "Because we were going to sail south to rescue Zarrah, which would be very dangerous."

Silence stretched, and Keris fought the urge to drag the details out of her. Except this was his fault. He'd burdened his little sister with the truth and then left her in the clutches of Lestara, a grown woman raised on deception and intrigue.

"She told me that you were angry that I'd returned to the palace. That you'd deliberately left me at Greenbriar because I was too much of a burden, and that you regretted not allowing Royce to take me." Her chin quivered. "She was dreadfully upset, because you'd apparently said you loved her and wanted to marry her, but you'd run away because of me. She said that it was my fault she wouldn't be queen. That's when I knew she was lying, because Zarrah is the one you love."

"Did you tell her that?" he asked, already certain of the answer.

Sara wiped her nose on her sleeve, then nodded. "She called me a liar. Said that you'd never tell me your plans because I'm only a child. That I was making up stories to feel important. She made me so mad, so I told her that Lara and Aren were going to help you rescue Zarrah, and that you were going to marry her. That Zarrah would be queen and that you'd send Lestara back to Cardiff."

Keris squeezed his eyes shut, imagining how well Lestara would have taken that statement.

"She left me alone after that, and has been kind ever since."

Because the princess of Cardiff had gotten what she wanted. "You're right, Sara. Lestara is a liar, and it's time she and I had a little chat."

Rising to his feet, Keris left the tent, finding Sarhina still waiting. Their half sister Athena was with them. "Do you have the supposed order I wrote sending the city guard south? And the Cardiffian spy report Lestara supplied?"

Sarhina's brow furrowed. "Locked in my tent. Why?"

"I'd like to see them."

At Sarhina's nod, Athena departed into the camp.

"While we wait, where might I find Royce's tent?"

"What are you planning?" Sarhina said as she led him through the camp. "What did Sara say?"

Keris didn't answer, his eyes locking on a tent with a purple flag above it. A guard stood before the entrance, from which the squeals and grunts of enthusiastic sexual pursuits emanated. "You might want to wait a few minutes, Your Highness," the guard said to Sarhina. "They're—"

"I think not," Keris said, pushing back his hood. The guard's eyes bulged. "Your Grace. I . . . They . . ."

Keris walked around him, pushing aside the tent flap and stepping inside.

To be greeted with the sight of Lestara on her hands and knees, Royce fucking her from behind. Lestara was gasping Royce's name as though it were the best sex of her life, but the bored expression on her face spoke volumes. As did the shock that grew in her eyes as they latched onto Keris.

"Your Grace!" she squeaked, scrambling away from Royce and

pulling a blanket around her body, leaving his brother naked and gaping at him.

"Keris."

"In the flesh." Keris crossed his arms, giving Royce's rapidly deflating cock a pointed look. "Speaking of which, you may wish to cover yours up."

His younger brother hastily pulled on a pair of trousers. Lestara had taken the opportunity to put on her dress, her long blond hair covering her face as she fastened her sandals. "We didn't know you were back," she said, and Keris could tell it was taking all her effort to meet his gaze. "Or we would have prepared. I . . ." She glanced at Royce. "We . . . You said you were not interested in me, so I hope you won't take offense to me—"

"Fucking the next in line to the throne?" He gave her a smile that was all teeth. "Come with me. We have a great deal to catch up on. You as well, brother."

Offering Lestara his arm, he escorted her out of the tent, Royce following at their heels. There were perhaps two dozen civilians in proximity, mostly women. Their heads turned, a commotion rising as he was recognized, and Keris called out, "You'll all be wanting an explanation for why Vencia was left undefended, why Petra was able to raze it so easily. I have answers, if you care to listen."

"Are you mad?" Lestara demanded, eyes wide. "They blame you, Keris. You're going to get yourself killed."

A wild laugh tore from his lips, and he looked back over his shoulder at the women who followed, fury in their eyes. "You have every right to be angry. Every right to demand answers for why this was allowed to happen. But if you stab me in the back, the truth of who betrayed us all dies with me."

Eyes narrowed, but behind the rage, he saw curiosity bloom. A few women splintered away from the rest, racing into the camp,

and he heard shouts. "The king is here! He says there is a traitor!
He's going to give a speech!"

The crowd behind them grew.

"Keris, this is insanity." Lestara kept glancing over her shoulder
to the mob of women, some holding the hands of their children,
others carrying babies, all with anger in their eyes. All wanting
answers for why their homes had been allowed to burn. "Let us
take a carriage, at least."

"I find myself relishing a walk," he answered, then placed his
free hand on the arm linked with his, tightening his grip as Athena
approached, papers in her hands. She gave him a nod of confirmation, then fell in with Sarhina, who walked silently next to Royce.

Lestara's breath caught, the sound betraying her unease.
"Where are we going?"

"There's something I'd like to show you."

Her steps grew halting as they walked down the road to Vencia,
the stench of smoke and rot growing stronger as the city came
into view. But before they reached the gate where traitors' heads
were typically spiked, Keris cut inland to where the mass graves
were being filled by the unfortunate dead.

The mob kept growing, the tread of their feet a thunder of judgment, but as Keris stopped in front of the largest hole and held up
a hand, they fell silent.

"Why are we here, Your Grace?" Lestara demanded, looking
anywhere but at the bodies. "There are flies everywhere. Flies
spread disease."

"Because I want you to look at their faces."

"No."

"Why?" he said loud enough for the nearest women to hear.
"Does looking at the corpses of your victims make you uncom-
fortable?"

Lestara's whole body stiffened; then she jerked away from him. "What are you talking about? I was the one who brought warning to Vencia about the attack. That they chose not to listen doesn't make their deaths my fault."

"It's true," a woman shouted. "It's because of Lestara that all of us yet live! She is the Savior of Maridrina, whereas you are its curse!"

"It was by your order that we were left undefended!" another woman shouted. "They are your victims!"

Keris held out a hand to Athena, and she handed him two documents. One was on heavy paper and bore a wax seal, the other on cheap scrap. One glance at them confirmed everything that he'd come to believe, but it was the one with the seal that he held up. "This order?"

In his looping, familiar script, the letter claimed that Ithicanian intelligence had learned of Petra's plans to attack the coast south of Vencia and that the city guard needed to travel with haste to bolster the patrols. A single letter that had been the damnation of an entire city, and had thus become his own damnation. It was a fair forgery in both style and content, but there was a fatal flaw.

"Did you know," he said, letting go of Lestara's arm to face Royce, "that each signet ring gifted to a Maridrinian prince upon his coming of age is made of the melted-down gold of those of his ancestors?"

"This hardly seems the time to share scraps of your useless knowledge," his brother hissed, eyeing the mob. "You're going to get us all killed."

Keris smiled at him, feeling strangely calm despite being as close to death as he'd ever been. "Did you know each of them is slightly different?"

His brother blinked at him, then down at the gold signet ring on his hand. Much like the one currently in Ahnna's possession, it was a circle with a V at the center, a pattern of indentations in the gold around the perimeter of the circle. "They are?"

"Yes, one of the benefits of hiding in a library is that I learn things," Keris said. "The pattern of the indentations is a code that represents your birthdate and time, rendering each ring unique." He lifted the order, which bore a red wax seal beneath his signature. "This seal was not made with my ring. This is a forgery."

Before the crowd could react, Athena kicked Royce in the back of the knees, then was on him in a flash, pulling off his ring. "It wasn't me," Royce shrieked. "I swear it, Keris! I've done nothing!"

Keris ignored his brother, holding up the ring to compare it to the wax impression. It was a perfect match. He handed both to Sarhina, who nodded in confirmation. "This was the ring that sealed the forged letter ordering the city guard out of Vencia," she shouted. "Not the ring of your king! We have been betrayed!"

The mob of women stirred, the rising tension rendering the air unbreathable, a single word echoing through the masses. *Traitor.*

Lestara had a hand pressed to her mouth. "I didn't know," she said. "I knew he hated you, but not in my darkest nightmares did I believe he'd betray Maridrina."

"She's lying," Royce shrieked. "I am loyal! Please!"

The mob was pressing toward them, the women without weapons bending to pick up rocks, expressions feral.

"My God, Keris," Lestara cried out. "Why didn't you execute him when you had the chance? You might have saved us all!"

If he hadn't been so angry, Keris might have admired her perseverance.

"Executing my idiot brother would not have spared us," Keris shouted above the noise of the crowd, "because it would not have stopped *you* from conspiring with Petra Anaphora in a twisted plot to make yourself queen!"

His words rippled over the mob, shocked silence following in their wake.

"Lies!" Lestara snarled. "Desperate lies! While you were gone, I watched over Vencia. I am the Savior of the People."

"Tell that to the dead," he said, and when she refused to look at the corpses, he caught her by the hair and forced her to her knees. "Look at them. Look at the people who died because their lives were worth less than your desire to be queen."

"I didn't do anything!" Lestara said between her teeth. "I'm innocent!"

Keris laughed, knowing he sounded like his father and not caring. "There is nothing innocent about you, Lestara. But if you confess, perhaps I'll show mercy." Then he shoved her.

Lestara toppled forward, falling to land on her knees on the pile of bodies. She screamed in horror as her hands sank into rotting flesh, the pile shifting and moving beneath her weight.

"Confess your treason and I'll let you out," he said, watching as she crawled to the sides of the pit and tried to climb out. But the women in the mob surrounding them had been the ones with the shovels, and they'd dug deep.

"I'm innocent! Please, Keris. Please, you know I'm loyal," she howled. "You know I love you."

Keris glanced down at his brother, who was on the ground beneath Athena's booted foot. "Ah, yes. How better to show your love than to conspire with my enemies and then jump into bed with my brother."

"I've conspired with no one." Tears rolled down her cheeks, and she looked to the mob. "He said he didn't want me. Broke my heart and left me alone. What would you have done?"

"I doubt any of them would have picked up a pen to conspire with Petra Anaphora." Keris rocked on his heels, his calmness gone, rage having taken its place. "But that's what you did. When I refused to make you queen, you tormented my little sister until she gave you my plans; then you sent the information to Petra. Forged a letter with orders that would leave Vencia ripe for the taking." Bending down, he met her gaze. "Petra got what she wanted, but given that I still live and breathe, it appears you did not."

"That's not true! Why would I conspire to destroy Vencia and then provide warning that the Valcottans intended to attack?"

"So that you would be named *Savior of the People*?" Keris brushed dust off one of his sleeves, then gave Royce a long look. "Thereby making yourself a valuable ally to the man next in line to the throne just in case your bedroom skills weren't incentive enough."

Royce paled. "Lestara, is this true?"

"It's not true! He's lying because he needs a scapegoat!"

Their conversation was repeated back through the mob, the same accusations and denials over and over, but Keris kept his eyes on his brother. "Didn't you question why one of our father's wives just happened to receive critical intelligence about Petra's *changed* battle plan *just* in time to evacuate?"

"She said her father has spies. That they give her information."

"You really believe that *Cardiff's* spies discovered information that ours failed to learn?"

Royce appeared ready to be sick in the dirt. "Sarhina has the spy report. She can show it to you."

Keris regarded the second document Athena had given him. It was written in the language used in northern Cardiff, so he could only read some of it, but in truth, the language didn't matter.

The handwriting did.

"Petra wrote this herself," he said, handing it to Sarhina. "I've seen her writing before, though there are others who can confirm if you choose not to believe me."

"A forgery!" Lestara shouted.

"Why would one of your father's spies forge Petra's writing in a report to you?"

Lestara didn't speak, but it was far from silent. The mob was in the thousands, perhaps in the tens of thousands, the camps full of the survivors having emptied to come hear the explanation of why their home was ash and rubble.

And they were angry.

"You're a traitor, Lestara." And Petra had wanted Keris to know how she'd gotten to him. Had wanted him to know that it was his choices and missteps that had allowed her to strike this blow. "All those dead beneath your feet are your victims, but so are the living." He gestured at the crowd, which was full of furious faces, marriage knives that had never known an edge until now drawn from their sheaths, the steel glittering. "Perhaps I should allow them revenge."

All the color drained from Lestara's face, but she shouted, "I have done nothing. I am loyal to Maridrina!"

"Enough, Lestara. Confess the truth, and I'll consider mercy. Continue this farce, and I'll listen to your confession as your victims pull you to pieces."

Picking up a shovel, he scooped up dirt from the pile and tossed it at her face. As he did, Keris was suddenly struck with a memory of Raina. Of how she'd told him that there was honor in shoveling cow shit on the bridge because it demonstrated loyalty and a willingness to do what it took. It felt like a lifetime ago that he'd laughed at the idea, yet now he wondered, if he filled enough graves, if he might earn back the trust of his people. He tossed another shovelful of dirt at her, clumps sticking in her long hair. "Confess, Lestara."

The crowd was seething, screaming for blood, demanding their vengeance. "Keris," Sarhina muttered, "we won't be able to stop them."

His heart was hammering in his chest, pulse roaring, because he didn't want to stop them. Didn't want to deny them a chance at revenge. "Confess!" he shouted, throwing another shovelful of dirt in her face.

Lestara's amber eyes met his, and the manipulative, power-hungry viper who'd been told at age seven that she was destined to be queen finally revealed itself. "Fine," she hissed. "I'll confess what I know, Keris. I'll tell them exactly how their king has betrayed them."

He could silence her. Could allow the tide of violence to flow over Lestara before she had the chance to speak the damning truth and allow her death to absolve him of wrongdoing in the eyes of his people.

It was the smart move. The strategic choice.

It was also what his father would have done.

Rounding on the mob, he lifted his hand and shouted, "Listen!"

And his heart skipped in his chest as they fell still, heeding him as their king for the first, and probably the last, time ever.

"The only thing I confess to is trying to rid Maridrina of a traitor," Lestara shouted, voice rising out of the pit as she moved to stand at the center. "Of trying to rid Maridrina of *its king*."

The mob didn't attack, though Keris didn't know if it was on the weight of his command or their desire to hear what Lestara had to say.

"The reason your king has cast aside his good Maridrinian harem is that he's in love with a Valcottan. And not just any Valcottan. The empress's niece, Zarrah Anaphora."

And there it was.

Out in the open in a way that could never be undone, and though Keris knew the revelation might be the death of him, it felt like a weight had been lifted off his shoulders.

"Before your king threw him to his death, the spymaster Serin sent me a message, which I came to understand was his attempt to protect Maridrina from the traitor who'd taken the throne," she shouted. "Serin's message told me that your king, Keris Veliant, took up with a Valcottan woman during his time in Nerastis. Not just once, but night after night, because he was in love with her."

I knew she'd be your damnation, Coralyn's voice echoed through his thoughts. *What you two are doing is forbidden by both your peoples.*

Lestara gave a slow shake of her head. "I didn't want to believe Keris would stoop so low. Refused to believe it, even though Serin offered me proof." She turned to address him. "But when you, who treats his precious tomes like children, could not bring yourself to recall where you'd left my book, I knew Serin spoke true. You abandoned my book, which I'd given to you with love in my heart, in a tawdry inn where you coupled with the enemy."

She lifted her chin, expression full of defiance as she panned the crowd like a queen delivering justice from her throne. Keris held his breath and waited for the judgment that had been held over him for so long. Waited for them to turn their weapons on him. Waited for them to hurl stones for violating an unwritten law that ruled every Maridrinian.

Silence.

"Do you hear me?" Lestara shouted. "Your king is in love with a Valcottan! He hasn't been in Ithicana; he's been in the south, rescuing Zarrah from Devil's Island. He plans to make a Valcottan your queen! The sacking of Vencia was Petra's retaliation for his audacity!"

Her accusation carried over the heads of the crowd, but no one spoke, though tension hummed through the air as everyone waited to see how he would respond. It occurred to Keris, as he listened to the moan of the wind and the shuffle of feet, how exhausting they must all find it to be endlessly at the mercy of those in power. To have their lives torn apart as the result of a petty feud between members of a single family, and to now listen as it was all dragged before them like dirty laundry. He could not change what had been done.

But he could tell them why.

Keris cleared his throat, knowing that his life was very much on the line at this moment, and he'd be lying to say that fear didn't thrum through his veins. But it had always needed to come to this. The truth had always needed to be revealed, else the dream of peace that he and Zarrah had nurtured between them would never come to pass. "It's true. Zarrah Anaphora holds my heart, as I hold hers, and together, we hoped to end the war between our nations. Hoped to bring peace and prosperity to our people. Petra knew our intent, and sacked Vencia because she knew that a union between Zarrah and me was the death knell for the Endless War."

Every muscle in his body tensed as Keris braced for the outburst, but instead the only sound was his words being repeated back to those in the rear.

"What's wrong with you?" Lestara screamed. "Seize him! Kill him! All of this is his fault!"

One of the women watching picked up a handful of mud and chucked it at Lestara. "Shut your gob. He might have shit in Petra's porridge, but it's clear enough that you were the one who opened our back door for her to fling her own mud." Then the woman looked directly at him. "Ain't never thought I'd see the day when a Veliant claimed to want to end the war. War's all your family ever wants, strutting about like peacocks while our men bleed and die. We've been wanting an end to it since it began, but Veliants care only for their pride."

"You've seen the day," Keris answered. "I want the war to end. Though if I've learned anything, it is that *wanting* something will not make it so." Squaring his shoulders, Keris raised his voice so that it would carry out over the crowd. "One must fight for it."

Knowing that he was close to losing them, he shouted, "Petra Anaphora is not the lawful ruler of Valcotta. On his deathbed, Emperor Ephraim voiced his desire for Valcotta to know peace and named his younger daughter, Aryana, heir to his throne because he knew that under Petra's rule, the fires of war would only burn hotter. Instead of acceding to his wishes, Petra usurped the throne . . ." Zarrah's story poured from his lips, the crowd watching with rapt eyes as he unveiled the truth.

"It is true that I was not in Ithicana negotiating terms of trade," he continued. "But it was Ithicana who aided me in sailing south to rescue Zarrah, allowing us to join the rebels who have fought so tirelessly against Petra's rule. Zarrah commands them now, with the intent of challenging Petra for the crown, but they cannot hope to defeat her alone."

Sweat ran in rivulets down his spine as he paused, because this was the moment. This was when he needed to ask Maridrina to fight for the very people who'd just destroyed their homes, whose blades had been the death of those in the grave before them. "You." He pointed at the woman who'd spoken. "You claim that Maridrinians have long wanted this war to end. Have wanted the fighting to cease. Have wanted peace, but my family wouldn't allow it. That it continues only because of Veliant pride. Do others share that belief?"

Nods and shouts of agreement rolled across the crowd, a rising tide of vitriol against his warmongering family.

"What if I told you that Valcottans feel the same way?"

The crowd fell silent.

"Like you, they wish for the end of the war, but under Petra's rule, they are forced to fight. Forced to send their young people to join the Imperial Army's ranks, many of them never seen alive again. And while she wears Valcotta's crown, Petra will never allow the war to end. It is her pride, her identity, her legacy, and to seek peace is beyond comprehension to her. Valcotta is at the mercy of a tyrant, but so is Maridrina. If Petra will not allow her empire to stop warring against us, we are forced to fight back, forced to send the youth to the border to fight and fight and fight. And no matter how much I might wish to do otherwise, I'll be forced into the role of my father, and grandfather, and great-grandfather, for like you, I will have no other choice!"

His mouth was dry, throat hoarse, but it was worth it, because he could see that the women were listening.

"Maridrina did not liberate itself from my father," he shouted. "Ithicana fought that battle for us. Their queen, my sister, defeated him, and in doing so, offered me the opportunity to change this kingdom for the better. And my greatest error has been underestimating the villainy of those like Petra who see the Endless War as a way to maintain their power, even if it means standing on the backs of countless dead. She will not be defeated with passivity, will only grow stronger if our complacency leaves her free to destroy those who rally against her. So I ask you, will you stand not just with me, but with Valcottans, and lift arms to bring Petra Anaphora's tyranny to an end? Will you fight for peace?"

"You'll let us fight?" the woman at the front of the crowd asked. "You'll allow women to defend our families?"

"You have always fought," he answered. "Always defended them. It would be an honor to have you in my ranks as we cross the border to put an end to this war for good."

She stared at him, this woman he'd never met, never seen, whose name he might never know, and Keris's heart felt like it was in his throat. Then she gave a nod. "All right, then. If you say that Petra is the one to blame for this"—she gestured at the smoking ruins of the city—"then I'll gladly march for her blood. Though what about her?" She jerked her chin at Lestara, who was still standing, pale-faced, in the grave.

Keris considered his father's wife, who was a traitor to the nation and who deserved to be executed. But he was trying to take Maridrina down a different path, which meant trying something different than heads on a spike. "Death seems a paltry punishment for what you've done, Lestara, for I don't think you fear it. I think you fear irrelevance. I think you fear powerlessness. I think you fear failing to secure the destiny that a witch whispered in your ear as a child. And there is one place I can think of where you will face all three of your fears day after day after day."

All the color drained from Lestara's face.

"The Harendellians revile your people, Lestara, but none more than Queen Alexandra herself. So I think I'll ask a favor of my friends in the north and request they take you into their care, where you will be fed and clothed like a lady but looked upon as one does shit discovered on the sole of one's shoe."

"No!" Lestara dropped to her knees, tears flooding down her cheeks. "Please, Keris. Just kill me. I'd rather die than go there!"

"Which is why it is the perfect punishment."

Lestara screamed and screamed, but her shrieks were drowned out by the sea of voices, all declaring that they'd march. That they'd fight.

That they'd bring Petra Anaphora to her knees.

"Ithicana stands with you as well," a familiar voice said from behind him. "We will join this alliance against tyranny."

Keris turned, his chest tightening as he found Aren standing behind him, Lara at his side.

Farther down the slope from them stood Dax and Jor at the head of hundreds of armed Ithicanians. As Keris's eyes moved over them, the winds gusted, clearing fog out over the water and revealing dozens upon dozens of ships. Fishing boats and merchant vessels and naval vessels that Ithicana had collected over the years, few of which would be good in a fight but all of which were capable of carrying an army south.

Turning back to his people, Keris said, "Let us to war. And by God, let's make it the last war fought in our lifetime!"

60
ZARRAH

NOT KNOWING WAS THE PUREST FORM OF TORTURE.

Every minute that passed since Keris had left was filled with preparation for the conflict to come, but as she helped train fighters, secure supplies, and rally more to the rebel cause, Zarrah was screaming in wordless fear. Every messenger who arrived sent a bolt of terror down her spine that word had come about what had happened in Vencia. That it had been sacked, the hundreds of thousands of civilians living there now dead. That those who'd survived had turned on Keris, blaming him for their ruin.

That he was dead.

And for all her certainty and faith in Keris himself, her hope that he'd be able to deliver an army to join the rebellion's fight dwindled with each passing day.

"You keep lowering your guard," she said to one of the women she was instructing, a baker who'd lost her husband because he'd been vocal against the Usurper. She'd never held a sword until now, wouldn't last a minute against a trained soldier, but Zarrah was in no position to send her away. For this was the sort of soldier joining her ranks. Civilians who'd been pushed too far or lost too much and who *needed* to fight back. There was power in that. Strength in having an army that wasn't just being paid to fight, but that wanted to fight. Whose very survival depended on victory.

A party on horseback appeared, and Zarrah stepped away from those she was training when she saw her father in their midst. He broke from the group and trotted in her direction, nodding at those who saluted as he passed. "Imperial Majesty," he said, dismounting. "A word?"

The title still felt unearned at best, at worst stolen, but she understood the importance of using it. "Of course."

She followed him a distance away, Daria and Saam, her ever-present shadows, standing with their backs to them to give a semblance of privacy.

"Vencia has been sacked," he said softly. "Our spy approached the city right after Petra abandoned it, took stock, then headed south at all speed to give us the news. Nothing left but rubble and ash, the Veliant tower a broken ruin."

The muscles in her jaw worked as Zarrah fought to maintain composure. "Casualties?"

"The regent, Sarhina Veliant, was able to evacuate the city in advance of the attack. It appears she had some level of warning, which saved countless lives."

Zarrah let out the breath she'd been holding. Buildings and towers could be rebuilt, but lives could not. This sacking would have long and catastrophic consequences, but it could have been far, far worse. "The Usurper left after the city fell? She made no attempt to go after the evacuees?"

Her father turned to stare in the direction of the coast. "This was not an attempt to capture Maridrinian territory, not an invasion at all. It was a strike intended to hurt the spirit of the nation, slaughtering civilians but leaving the armies untouched. To ensure their blood boils at the mention of Valcotta, so when they have finished licking their wounds, they bring the fight that she wants, not the fight that we want." He cast a sideways glance at her, eyes full of pity. "She knew Keris's plans, Zarrah. Knew that he intended to aid you. This attack was perpetrated to ensure he wouldn't be able to do so."

To ensure that he wouldn't even try, for Zarrah couldn't even begin to imagine how the Maridrinians would respond if Keris asked them to march to liberate Valcotta from their tyrant empress now.

Except that she knew he'd have done it anyway.

"There's more," he said. "Petra's fleet is now sailing to make war upon us in Arakis. Even if by some miracle Keris manages to convince his army to march south, they will never make it to us in time."

The Usurper was ten steps ahead of them.

"We need to abandon Arakis," her father continued. "Move farther inland, or even consider seeking sanctuary in Teraford until we have the numbers we need to fight her."

The hundreds of civilians training had stopped and were watching them, sensing the gravity of the conversation even if they couldn't hear the words. For most, these were the lands they'd been raised on, and to flee would mean abandoning their homes.

Potentially forever.

For two decades, her father had fanned the flames of rebellion. Recruited and trained fighters. Spread propaganda to undercut the Usurper. Struck at her soldiers in skirmishes and raids. Always preparing for some moment in the future when the stars aligned, and the rebellion could be assured of victory.

Except if there was anything that Zarrah knew, it was that the stars rarely aligned, and that one could not stand paralyzed, waiting for them to do so. Her father would never choose to attack the Usurper. Would never hold his ground against her. Because the rebellion would never have the strength he needed to take that first step forward.

But she did. "Ready everyone to march. If there is to be a chance of the Maridrinians reaching us in time, we need to move the battleground closer. We choose the ground, and I say, that ground is Pyrinat."

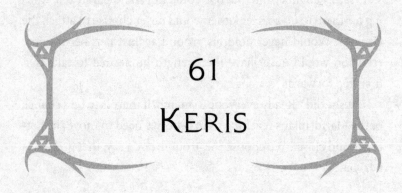

61

KERIS

"We'll be in Nerastis in a few hours," Aren said from the doorway, his dark hair plastered to his head from the heavy rains that had assaulted the fleet on the journey south. "You'll want to prepare yourself."

"I'm prepared," Keris said, not looking up from the game board that rested on the table between him, Sarhina, and Lara.

Aren didn't move from his spot, wind gusting in past him. "What is your plan? It's one thing to sway civilians with promises of a brighter future, quite another to convince hardened soldiers to fight on behalf of those they've spent their lives fighting against."

A fact of which Keris was painfully aware. "I'll give a speech, I'm sure."

"Saying what?"

He'd written countless attempts on the journey south to Nerastis, every word of which he'd tossed in the trash. "Something that will be transcribed into the history books, no doubt."

"Keris—"

"You focus on getting us to port. I can't very well give a speech if I'm on the bottom of the sea because you were too busy advising me on speeches when you should've been steering the ship."

"The ship isn't going to sink, whereas you—" The vessel abruptly tilted sideways at such an angle that everything on the table slid to the floor save the game board, which was mounted to the table itself. Aren cursed, the door slamming shut as he departed.

"I've no taste for sea travel," Sarhina muttered, moving their pieces back into their places. It was a game of strategy that Keris had been forced to learn as a child. He was good. Lara was better. Sarhina kept beating both of them. The eldest of his warrior sisters added, "I thank every higher power daily that it was you who were sent to Ithicana, Lara."

"*You* were the higher power that ensured that." Lara pushed her braid back over her shoulder. His sister was visibly pregnant now, stomach swollen, but the malaise that had plagued her on the journey to Devil's Island had disappeared. Her blue eyes flicked to Keris. "She had the uncanny ability to be middle of the pack on every test, never the best and never the worst."

Keris snorted. "I would not have been so easily fooled."

Both of his sisters rolled their eyes; then Lara rose and came to his side. "Aren's right. Winning one battle is not winning the war. If you don't think of a way to convince these men to fight for Zarrah, we will sail no farther than Nerastis."

He gave a tight nod, and though he knew his sister was less than satisfied with the response, she left the room.

"I don't suppose you have any ideas?" Keris asked Sarhina.

She frowned at the game board. "None. If I were any of your commanders, I'd refuse the order to march. Petra's army is massive, well supplied, and rested. Even in conjunction with the rebels, we are outmatched." She moved a piece, then met his gaze. "Your turn."

It felt like it was always his turn. His move. And Keris couldn't help but wonder if this one would be his last. "Before we reach Nerastis, I want to change a law."

Sarhina blinked. "There is already a law that your subjects must obey you. Another that they can't kill you. They'll happily break both, knowing there will be little consequence from Royce when he takes the crown." She made a face. "He's such an imbecile, I almost hope someone sneaks into camp and kills him."

"Do you know who is next in line after him?" he asked, suddenly curious. Veliant princes were notoriously good at getting themselves killed, and he'd lost track of which of his younger half brothers came after Royce.

"Parix."

A laugh escaped Keris, stealing some of the tension from his chest, for the last thing he'd heard about Parix was that he'd been caught having inappropriate relations with a sheep and been banished to the middle of nowhere by their father. "Then it's a good thing it's the law of succession that I wish to amend."

Resting his elbows on the table, Keris explained what he wished to do. Sarhina was silent for a long moment, then she exploded to her feet and paced the rocking deck. "No. This is absolute lunacy, Keris. It won't work."

"I disagree." Rising to his feet, he glanced out the window at the passing coastline, barely visible in the haze of wind and rain. "Either way, I'm the king, Sarhina. While the crown sits on my head, my word is law. Have one of the scribes aboard draft it, and I'll sign before I disembark. I want it done now, just in case this goes poorly."

Her hands had balled into fists, pale cheeks red with color. "Maridrina will never accept this, Keris."

"I don't intend to give them a choice." Going to the door, he paused before opening it. "We cannot hide, sister. Even after destroying the rebel forces, Petra's armies will *still* be massive, well supplied, and rested, and we have always been her target. We fight now with allies, or we fight alone."

Pushing her dark hair behind her ears, Sarhina scowled at him. "If you're looking for speech ideas, I'd start there."

Keris nodded and left the room. A very wet Dax stood outside, though his bodyguard said nothing as he followed Keris to his cabin. "I need you to help me with something," Keris said once they were inside and standing before a chest on the floor.

"I told you, I ain't carrying your goddamned books again," Dax groused. "They're too bloody heavy, and I don't see why you need them where we are going, anyway."

Most of his library had been lost to the fire that destroyed the palace. "It's not books."

Kneeling, he flipped open the lid, revealing the shining metal and thick leather of the armor inside.

Dax whistled between his teeth. "Well, that's a fancy bit of work."

"Yes." The chest had apparently been in Coralyn's rooms, discovered by those salvaging the ruins. The note inside said, *Since I am no longer there to guard your back.* ~C

It made him wonder what Coralyn would have said if she had lived to see this moment.

"You ever worn armor before?" Dax asked, and Keris shook his head. Much as he'd refused lessons with all the arms instructors or any tuition in battle strategy, Keris had dug in his heels over wearing armor. "I drew a line in the sand many years ago," he said, more to himself than to Dax. "Refused to cross it no matter how much pain it caused me, because I believed my defiance meant something. And perhaps it did, though the one who cared is now dead. So by remaining on this side of the line, who am I defying? What victories can I hope to win?"

Dax shifted restlessly, then shrugged. "I'm not the one to ask."

Keris barely heard the answer as he knelt to touch the crest embossed on the breastplate. He wished she were here. Wished that it were Zarrah he posed these questions to, but she was somewhere south of here and in dire need of his aid. So Keris answered the question himself. "None. For the dark truth of the world is that peace must be paid for in blood."

Straightening, he met Dax's gaze. "Will you please help me put it on?"

"That I can do," Dax said, the relief at being asked something he could finally answer palpable as he pulled the armor out of the chest. "Turn around."

Keris stared at his reflection in the mirror while Dax strapped the armor onto him. It felt as though, with each piece of metal that was attached to him, he was letting go of a piece of the mask he'd worn all of his life. Casting off his last protection against a world that stood at odds against him, for he could no longer hide behind it.

Not if he was going to change the world.

Belting on his sword, Keris clapped his friend on the shoulder. "Thank you." Then he went back on deck.

Eyes moved in his direction as he strode through the rain and up the stairs to the quarterdeck, where Aren stood at the helm. The king of Ithicana's eyebrows rose. "Nice outfit."

"Kiss my ass."

Keris moved to rest his elbows on the railing, surveying the storm-tossed sea ahead of him, Nerastis faintly visible on the horizon.

"Her blockade still holds," Aren said. "Reports say there are ten ships on patrol, though Maridrina still holds the harbor."

"Can you sink them?"

Aren snorted. "Of course I can. But are you sure you want to? It's a declaration of war, and as yet, you have no army. Only holds full of civilians willing to fight."

"Sink them."

Aren was silent. "Are you sure? If we leave them be, we still have the option to back away from this conflict if we need to. There is no turning back if we sink ten of her ships."

"When I step onto that dock, I want my army to have only one path forward," Keris answered. "There can be no other choice after what Petra has done."

All that remained to be seen was whether it would be an invasion or a liberation. If it was the former, he was unlikely to be alive to witness it.

Aren's eyes went to the seas. He was under no obligation to do what Keris wanted. The fleet was Ithicana's, as were most of the trained soldiers, and doing this would also be a declaration of war on his part. A war he couldn't really afford, given his nation was battered and healing from the last.

Aren cleared his throat. "Put every one of those vessels under the waves."

The order echoed over the ship, the Ithicanians moving without question. While those in the main fleet lowered sails to slow their pace, over two dozen tiny vessels broke ahead, splitting off in different directions to disappear into the storm.

"Now we wait."

Keris's heart throbbed a steady beat, his eyes moving over the gray horizon. No one spoke, the world seeming to stand still despite the violence of the seas and fierce snapping of the banners above his head.

Brilliant light bloomed on the horizon, only to disappear.

Keris blinked, for a heartbeat thinking that he'd imagined it, only for another ball of light to bloom. Then another.

Aren made a noise of approval. "They're only putting holes in the hulls. Most will stagger back to shore before they sink."

Most. But not all. Keris felt queasy witnessing the ease with which they had extinguished lives. A few words spoken, some explosives, and hearts ceased to beat. Men and women who had families. Friends. Who, a matter of minutes ago, had believed their whole lives ahead of them. "Make port."

Motion caught his eye. Sarhina stood glaring at him from below, and she lifted her fingers to beckon him. Keris made his way down, following her out of the rain, Dax on his heels.

"Will this do?" She gestured to the large piece of parchment on the table, ink still glistening wet.

His eyes drifted over the words. "Yes."

But as he picked up the pen to sign, his half sister caught hold of his wrist. "This is folly that you can't afford."

Keris didn't answer, only prized her fingers off his wrist and signed his name. Pulling the ring Aren had returned to him off his finger, he sealed the order in red wax. "Dax," he said. "If it comes to it, you must swear that you watched me sign and seal this with my own hand, understood?"

His bodyguard leaned forward to read the alteration to a Maridrinian law that was old as time. "Bloody hell, you do like to kick the hornet's nest." Then he huffed out a breath. "You won't need a witness. Everyone will know you're behind this."

"Because it's stupidity," Sarhina snarled, sprinkling sand over the wet ink to dry it while blowing on the wax. "And it will be the death of me." She carefully packaged the document. "Excuse me, Your Grace, I need to leave before I succumb to my burning desire to remove your heart."

She stormed away, law in hand. Keris gave a faint smile at her back because he'd seen the care she'd taken with the order, the paper carefully rolled up in a waxed wrapping to keep it safe from the weather. No matter what happened here, Sarhina would see it through.

Out the window, Nerastis appeared in his line of sight as Aren captained the vessel into the harbor, and Keris returned to the quarterdeck. The docks were filled with soldiers in Maridrinian uniforms, cloaks hanging sodden in the rain, which fell harder now, pinging against his armored shoulders.

He'd won them over once before when he'd refused his father's orders to abandon Nerastis, but what goodwill had been earned then would be vanquished by the sacking of Vencia, for there was little doubt that the news had traveled ahead of him.

He'd left openings for those like Lestara to make their moves. His misstep had cost many of them their homes. Lives of friends and family. They had no reason to follow him anywhere, and he didn't think speeches would work on these battle-hardened men.

Keris didn't know what he was going to do. Didn't know what he was going to say.

The sails lowered, the ship drifting toward the dock. Keris recognized some of the men waiting, helmets tucked under their arms, hair plastered to their faces. How would he convince them to do this?

Needing to move, he made his way down to the main deck, where the Ithicanians were tossing lines to those on the docks and readying a gangplank. His own few soldiers massed on deck behind him, their faces unreadable, although he could smell the sweat of nerves. Had heard the whispered comments between them on the journey south that this would result in a coup against the crown. That he'd be deposed. That he'd forever be known as the Veliant with the shortest reign in history.

Keris swallowed hard, the slam of the gangplank against the

dock making him twitch, though a lifetime of practice kept his nerves off his face. "You will remain with Princess Sarhina," he said to his soldiers. "She and her family are to be protected at all costs. Am I understood?"

The men blinked in surprise, one of them saying, "But, Your Grace—"

"Sarhina is your charge," he repeated, then stepped onto the gangplank and strode down to the dock.

Captain Philo stepped out to meet him, bowing. "Your Grace."

"Captain."

"We received word about Vencia." Philo's throat bobbed as he swallowed. "We were prepared for an inland incursion to take the land north of Nerastis, which has long been the region Valcotta coveted. Not . . ." He swallowed again. "We were not prepared, Your Grace."

"I have learned that it is difficult to prepare against the mind of a monster," Keris answered. "Petra Anaphora attacked a city full of civilians. A city of little strategic value. A city she knew she couldn't hold, which is why she didn't bother to try. But she was not without her reasons for doing so." His throat tightened, but Keris forced himself to add, "Our enemies exploited my distraction, which means the fault is mine, not yours."

Philo gave a slow blink, and then his mouth twisted into a grimace.

Blame had already been cast.

A bead of sweat rolled down Keris's spine, swiftly followed by another, because he deserved to be blamed. It had been his fault, and he deserved their ire. But he couldn't allow it to fall down upon him now, not when Zarrah was marching to war and expecting him to have her back. Without his army, it would be lambs to the slaughter for the rebels against the full weight of Petra's army.

Think.

Say something.

"The Valcottans sent an emissary yesterday," Philo said, breaking the silence. "He told us that the attack on Vencia was retaliation for your involvement with plots to release dangerous criminals imprisoned on Devil's Island into the civilian population of Pyrinat and your support of a coup in the south." The captain's jaw tightened. "The emissary committed to a truce in Nerastis on the condition that we refrain from raiding. And from meddling with Valcottan affairs. The emissary warned that if we violated the terms in any way, the full might of the Valcottan army would be brought to bear upon this garrison."

That fucking clever—

"We agreed to it, though with this attack on their fleet"—he gestured to the burning ships in the distance—"I think it fair to say the truce is over."

Keris exhaled slowly because the alternative was to scream. And scream and scream because Petra had outmatched him, again. Outplayed him, again. And it would be Zarrah and the rebels who paid the price, though it would not stop there . . . "There won't be a truce," he said. "It is merely a stratagem to keep Maridrina from retaliating while she deals with the rebels contesting her rule. By agreeing to it, we would be playing into Petra's hands. What we need to do is—"

"Support a coup to put your lover on the throne?" a familiar baritone called out from behind the ranks of Keris's soldiers.

Slowly, the men parted, though they did not need to do so to reveal Welran, Petra's bodyguard a head taller than all those around. Unarmed, and wearing only a Valcottan uniform, Welran strolled through the Maridrinian soldiers, expression amused. He was the emissary, the one who had duped Keris's army into believing Petra would hold to a truce. "So we meet again, Your Grace."

I should have killed you in Arakis, was the first thought that came to Keris's mind, but he kept the fear from his face and instead dusted an invisible piece of lint from his cloak. "Well, if it isn't Petra's inamorato in the flesh. I was so dreadfully sorry to hear of the fate of your progeny, though in fairness, Bermin was a few stones short of a load, so it's no one's loss. Shame Petra's past her prime, else you might have tried again. That was my father's strategy."

Welran's jaw tightened, but he didn't rise to the bait. "Indeed. Yet for all the warriors Silas fathered, it was you who took the crown. The brilliant, bookish genius who, rather than raising Maridrina up high, has brought it to ruin."

"It's—"

"Because," Welran continued, cutting Keris off, "you are also a whoremongering, womanizing philanderer."

Keris knew the direction Welran was going, yet there was no point in denying his words. His reputation was known across Maridrina, and the soldiers in Nerastis had seen it with their own eyes. In and out of pleasure houses, courtesans brought into the palace, parading up and down the stairs to his rooms with no regard to propriety. He hadn't cared. Or rather, he'd cared so much about being everything his father hadn't wanted him to be that he'd delighted in his infamy. Coralyn had always told him that there'd be a cost, and Keris had laughed.

He was no longer laughing.

Not as his army shifted restlessly, having no reason *not* to believe everything Welran had told them, because the lies were hidden within damning truths.

"A bacchanal," Welran spat, "who was content to use his kingdom in the pursuit of his own pleasure, no matter the cost to innocent civilians. A debauched gutter rat who left his capital defenseless so that he might use his army to gift his harlot a crown."

Anger boiled up and burned away Keris's fear. "Say what you will about me, but speak ill of the empress again and I will have your tongue."

Welran roared with laughter. "And who," he demanded, wiping away tears of mirth, "will do the cutting? You?" He slapped his thigh as though the idea of it was the purest form of comedy. "You stand alone, Your Grace, with no one left willing to do your dirty work. Even your demon of a sister is having second thoughts, which is why she and her uxorious husband are hiding on their ship. Look. Look!"

Keris refused to turn. Knew that there was nothing but empty dock behind him.

"Admit it, Your Grace," Welran said. "Admit to your army that you put a woman before them. Admit to them that you sacrificed their homes and families in a fool's attempt to put a crown on Zarrah's head. Admit that you want them to march toward a battle where most of them will die, all on the chance of keeping your *whore* alive to warm your bed again."

In three strides, Keris was on him, Welran's eyes widening in shock. Warm blood slicked his fingers as he plunged the blade into the bigger man's throat. He followed as Welran staggered several steps, falling on his back. Keris's armor creaked as he knelt on the man's chest. "I told you if you insulted Zarrah again that I'd have your tongue," he said, then reached into the hole his knife had made and pulled out Welran's tongue, slicing it free at the base. "Now I have it."

Keris blinked away the vision, Welran's smirking face coming back into focus before him, the blood and violence nothing but a short-lived fantasy.

God help him, but Keris wanted to make it reality. Knew that for all of Welran's insults, he *could*. But the world had enough men who reached for blades first. Men like his father, and all the Veliant kings who'd come before him.

I swore to be different.

Keris squared his shoulders. "Zarrah Anaphora is the rightful empress. She is the future of Valcotta, a leader and a peacemaker, and whether I remain on the throne of Maridrina has no bearing on that. She will find a way to end the war that has ruled us for generations, a way to rip the crown from the tyrant usurper who stole it, and there will soon come a day when men such as you are given less space than an ink splotch on the history books. I will bet my crown, my kingdom, and my very life upon it."

Welran gave a dismissive snort, but Keris didn't miss the unease in the man's eyes as he said, "Your crown and kingdom are already lost to you, Your Grace. Your life will soon join them." He turned to Philo. "I know that the attack on the fleet was not your doing. Give Keris Veliant over to us, and we will hold him to account. Then you will be free to choose a king fit for the throne of Maridrina."

Philo gave a sharp shake of his head, then fixed his gaze on Keris. "You were supposed to be different. Instead you are the same as your father, tramping over our backs in pursuit of your obsession. Maridrina needs a ruler who will put the people first, and that ruler is not you."

Philo was not wrong.

Keris drew in a breath, knowing that it was over. That he'd failed her. He only prayed that Ithicana would go to Zarrah's aid, and that it would be enough. That she'd keep fighting and achieve everything they'd dreamed of, and that the stars would one day tell the story of a love that changed the world for the better. "Peace is not a product of complacency, Captain. It is won by those who look at the past and the present and say, we can do better."

"Pretty words will not save you, Your Grace. Put down your weapons." Philo started toward him, then stopped, his gaze fixing on something behind Keris. "Why are they here? What have you done?" he demanded, even as Welran's brow furrowed first with surprise, then concern.

Heart in his throat, Keris slowly turned, his mind taking far too long to grasp the enormity of what he was witnessing.

When it did, the breath disappeared from his chest.

62

ZARRAH

It was not Zarrah's first hard march, but never in her life had the stakes been so high, the ceaseless worry exhausting her far more than the riding and walking. It was certainly what kept her awake every night.

But they'd made it. Had reached the place where she'd hoped to stand her ground, the midday sun shining down upon them.

Dismounting her horse, she handed the reins to a groom, her father doing the same. Together, they waited while the camp formed around them, taking reports in the open air until the command tent was raised. "We moved faster than expected," her father said. "Our spies may be having difficulty finding us, which is why we've not received news."

Zarrah gave a short nod, her eyes on the horizon. It was too distant yet to see, but Pyrinat, Valcotta's capital and largest city, was within a day's march. They had made good time, for everyone near Arakis who could give up horses and oxen to the cause had done so, even as they made preparations to evacuate the city. She'd been confident that the Usurper would choose to redirect her army to protect the capital, yet it had still been a relief to learn that plans to attack Arakis had been abandoned and the Imperial Army was gathering near Pyrinat. Only a small relief, though, for it meant the full weight of the Imperial Army was waiting to face her.

Outnumbering her force, six to one.

"He may yet be coming," her father said, knowing the direction of Zarrah's thoughts. "I've sent out scouts to look for signs the Maridrinians are marching, but they have to proceed with caution to avoid the Usurper's soldiers."

Zarrah didn't answer, as they'd had this conversation many times before. The report she'd received yesterday was that Keris remained in power and had been joined by Lara and Aren, the intent to sail to Nerastis. There'd been no news since. No word of whether his army had agreed to march in support of the rebellion, or whether they'd killed him for having the audacity to ask such a thing. *Aren and Lara are with him*, she reminded herself. *If it comes to the worst, they'll get him out alive.*

Or so she hoped. For all the strength of Ithicana's rulers and their soldiers, they were in no position to take on the might of Maridrina's army in Nerastis, which was well equipped to repel sea attacks. Especially if the Valcottan garrison there chose to engage.

There were so many unknowns. Too many, and though no one said so to her face, Zarrah heard the whispers among the rebels. *Maridrina isn't coming. They've abandoned us.*

We stand alone.

If Keris didn't come, it meant he was dead. Or imprisoned. Because even if his army refused to follow him, he'd have returned to her. There was no doubt of that in her heart.

So Zarrah watched the horizon, waiting, waiting, even as she quietly planned for what would have to be done if his familiar form never appeared.

"Tent's up," Daria said as she approached. The other woman's presence was an endless comfort to her. Their friendship had grown during the journey, Daria taking on the role of captain of Zarrah's bodyguard, with Saam as her lieutenant, and most of the individuals she chose to fill the ranks being survivors of Devil's Island. Zarrah had made the choice partially to counter the negativity they faced as a result of their choices on the island, but also because they were the only ones who never whispered, never doubted. While some might accuse Zarrah of surrounding herself with sycophants who didn't challenge her, that couldn't be further from the truth. She surrounded herself with those from the island because they alone knew and understood what sort of man they'd allied themselves with, which meant their faith that Keris would come was just as strong as hers.

She, her father, and Daria went inside the tent to silently eat their rations, the elephant in the room growing larger with each passing second that no more scouts arrived, no messengers with news that the Maridrinian army was on the horizon.

"You have a decision to make," her father finally said. "We need to accept that for all they might be on the march, the Maridrinians are not here *now*. The Usurper will make a move soon enough, and though we have the high ground here, victory is not in the cards. We need to consider retreating until we have more information about what occurred in Nerastis. Buy ourselves time."

Zarrah exhaled, then drew in another breath, trying to calm her thundering heart. If they retreated, the Usurper's army would put on the chase, driving them farther and farther south. If the Maridrinian army was on the march, they would have to pursue, every day a drain on resources and morale, and she wondered how long they'd last before digging in their heels.

"This was always a leap of faith, Zarrah," her father said softly. "But we must now face reality. Retreat, so that we might fight another day."

A leap of faith.

The tent faded away, and Zarrah saw herself standing on the dam outside of Nerastis, facing the gap in the spillway, Keris on the far side. Death rushing between them. She'd made that leap, and countless more since, and she refused to turn back now.

There was a commotion outside, and Zarrah tensed, eyes going to the entrance.

"I'll see what it is," Daria said, exiting.

Zarrah held her breath, letting it out in a rush as her friend stepped back inside, shaking her head. "It's a messenger from the Usurper under a white flag," she said. "Here to offer terms of surrender."

Her father cursed under his breath, and Zarrah felt frustration seething out from him. Half his lifetime had been spent in pursuit of the Usurper's downfall. He'd led the rebellion, made it strong, then handed the reins to her, only for it to come to this. "Bring them in."

Daria nodded, and a moment later, she and Saam returned with a female soldier.

"Captain Sephra," Zarrah said, inclining her head. "It has been a long time."

"Zarrah." Sephra's gaze was cold beneath the halo of her graying hair. She'd been a member of the imperial bodyguard as long as Zarrah could remember, and other than Welran, no one was more loyal to the Usurper than her. "You should have allowed yourself to fade into oblivion, but instead your legacy will be bringing the first civil war to Valcotta in two hundred years."

"What are her terms?" Zarrah asked, not rising to the bait.

"Her Imperial Majesty Empress Petra Anaphora offers the following terms," Sephra said. "If her niece, Zarrah Anaphora, agrees to surrender herself to the empress's care, those who have unlawfully risen against rightful rule will be granted exile and allowed to retreat south into Teraford."

"Lies," her father spat. "If you surrender, she'll put you in irons and then turn her army on us. She won't suffer those who have slandered her name for so long to live—it's against her nature."

Zarrah knew that as well as she knew that the sun rose in the east. But she also knew that it was a risk they needed to take. They could not win this fight on the battlefield, outnumbered as they were, and Keris . . .

Is not coming.

She squeezed her eyes shut, struggling against the rising tide of anguish that threatened to drown her with each breath she took, only for his voice to echo in her thoughts. *Fight, Valcotta.*

Except how could she fight when the plan she'd created was in shambles? Everything had hung upon having the numbers, and the strength, to give Valcottans the truth. She hadn't needed soldiers to fight the Imperial Army; she'd needed them to elevate her voice. She'd needed them to amplify her words so that she could pull back the curtain and reveal the monster wearing the crown, allowing all the men and women wearing imperial uniforms to see who, and what, they were fighting for.

There was a reason the Usurper was so desperate to silence anyone who spoke the truth. She knew that if it were to spread, it would be her damnation.

Yet despite everything she, Keris, and the rebels had done, her aunt had once again managed to silence them.

Tyranny had won.

Zarrah's eyes skipped over those in the room, knowing she'd failed them. Her father. Daria. Saam. Her chest tightened, for her friend had spent the entire journey begging her to make abolishing the ban on handball her first act as empress. Such a stupid, in-consequential thing to focus on, yet knowing she'd failed to deliver even that made her eyes burn.

Handball . . .

Zarrah stiffened, an idea slowly forming in her mind as she stared at Saam, jerking back into the moment only when he frowned at her scrutiny.

Zarrah wheeled on Sephra. "Tell her I agree to the terms."

The other woman blinked, clearly surprised. "You will come with me now?"

Zarrah shook her head. "I will surrender to my aunt, and only my aunt. Tell her to meet me in Meritt. Not the town itself, the stadium."

"The handball court?" Sephra's nose wrinkled, clearly sharing the Usurper's disgust for the game. "You'd make a spectacle of it, then."

"Those are my terms," Zarrah said. "Do you agree, or will it be war between us?"

Sephra was silent for a long moment; then she shrugged. "Perform all you want, Zarrah. Your name will be soon forgotten."

I doubt it, Zarrah thought to herself as Saam escorted the woman out, waiting until she'd be well out of earshot before rounding on her father. "Make ready to retreat. Show no hesitation."

"She offers only lies, Zarrah," he snarled. "She will take you in irons even as she orders pursuit. Will chase us south and into Ter-aford. Might well cross the border rather than allow us to live."

"If my plan works, it won't come to that. But if it does, the Ter queen will have no choice but to raise arms, and she is not without allies in the south. That may be where you find your victory against the Usurper."

"At what cost?" her father shouted. "And to what end, if you are dead at her hands?" Catching hold of her shoulders, he shook her. "This is the last thing Keris would want you to do. We will retreat, but it will be with you at our head, Empress."

"This is not about Keris," she said, not sure if that was truth or lie, for her heart was his, every aspect of this fight twisted into her feelings for him. "As it is, the Usurper will not kill me."

"How can you believe that?" he demanded. "You have done more to harm her than anyone alive. Turned thousands against her. Betrayed her by siding with her greatest enemy. She hates you, Zarrah, and the best you could hope for is a swift death."

"She doesn't hate me." Zarrah pressed a hand to her heart, shocked to discover that she still cared what her aunt thought of her.

How much easier would it be if she could erase the years since her mother's death and forget how her aunt had stood by her? How she'd held her while tears drenched her cheeks and sobs wracked her body? How she'd trained Zarrah to fight and be strong, to defend herself and her country? But every memory remained. "She loves me."

"That mad bitch doesn't know how to love!" her father shouted. "She's a monster!"

"Perhaps not love as you and I know it," Zarrah answered, "but it is the best word for how she feels about me. And it is not so much how she feels about me that ensures my safety, but her need for me to love her as I once did. Her need for me to worship her as a savior, as a *mother,* as I once did. Her obsession is *me,* and even if she needs to keep me locked up until the end of my days, she'll do so because she's incapable of accepting that I'll never be hers again."

"This is lunacy." Her father pressed his fingers to his temples, twisting away from her. "I can't agree to it. I *won't.*"

"It's not your choice."

She met Daria's gaze, the other woman having stood silently in the corner of the tent the entire conversation. "Make ready."

Daria clenched her teeth. "Goddammit, Zarrah." She gave a sharp shake of her head. "Keris would beg you not to do this, and I wish he were here, for he would convince you to see reason."

"I am the Empress of Valcotta," Zarrah answered. "My will is my own, not the king of Maridrina's."

Unlike my heart.

Silence stretched, and fear rose in Zarrah's chest that they would not abide. That despite all her plans, it would still come to battle and death, as it always had. She wanted to tell them to trust her, but this was her leap of faith, not theirs, and she needed them to retreat without hesitation.

Daria slowly inclined her head. "If this is your will, then so shall it be, Your Imperial Majesty." She started to leave, but Zarrah caught hold of her friend's arm, pulling her close. "Take care of them for me. Don't give up."

Scrubbing at her eyes, Daria nodded, then left the tent.

"Please don't do this."

At her father's words, Zarrah turned around. "I'm not giving up," she said. "This isn't the end."

"Then why do I feel as though I'm losing you?" His shoulders slumped, and for the first time since they'd been reunited, Zarrah saw her father's age. Saw the weathered skin and gray hair, the age spots on his hands. The exhaustion.

"I let her take you from me once," he said. "Now I am to let her take you again?"

Zarrah felt the weight of the same loss. He was her father, yet all she had of him were faded memories from her childhood. To her, he was a ghost and the commander, not yet her father, and she wished with all her heart that there had been time to change that.

Prayed that there still would be.

"She's not taking me this time," Zarrah finally answered. "I'm choosing to go of my own volition, because I believe it the right choice for our people. I . . . I still believe I can win this, Father."

"How?"

She hesitated, not wanting to give false hope. "I believe in Valcotta. In the people. I believe that if given the choice, they will make the right one for the future."

Her father looked away, and Zarrah's chest sank. After all these years of fighting, he had no faith in the people he fought for.

"I'm going with you."

"No, you are not," she retorted, more startled than anything. "Not only do I need you to lead the rebels free of this, but coming with me would be suicide. You, she won't hesitate to kill."

"I chose the rebellion over you twice," he said. "I won't do so a third time."

Zarrah's eyes burned. "And if I order you?"

"You will have to have me tied up and put on a horse," he said. "Even then, it would only be a matter of time until I came after you, daughter."

It was true she couldn't stop him. The rebels might call her Empress, but it was her father they'd followed all these years, and she wasn't fool enough to think they wouldn't set him free. "Only if you promise to stay hidden once we reach the stadium. And swear you won't involve yourself."

His jaw worked back and forth, but he nodded.

Zarrah took a deep breath. "Then let us ride. We don't have much time."

THEY LEFT BEHIND A CAMP scrambling to load carts and horses, captains and lieutenants shouting orders under Daria's watchful eye, and it killed Zarrah to leave them. She'd led them to this place with the promise of victory, only to have them turn tail before the battle even began.

I believed he'd come.

I was wrong.

A shuddering breath left her chest, and Zarrah urged her horse to more speed, heading down the road toward the stadium in the late afternoon sun.

"Why Meritt?" her father called, reining his galloping horse alongside her mount.

"She'll appreciate the spectacle of it," she called back. "Will enjoy taking my surrender with all to see."

And I want her to relish that moment, she thought silently to herself.

In the distance, a towering structure appeared, and Zarrah guided her horse down a side track in the direction of the abandoned handball stadium. It was formed of two tall parallel walls with triangular pavilions on either end. It had been an age since she'd sat in those bleachers at her mother's side, watching the game masters call commands to the players from the pavilions, their voices so loud it seemed like a game played by gods. She remembered the magic of it. Remembered the delight on her mother's face as she had cheered, able to find joy despite all the challenges she faced.

It was right that the end should come here.

Reining her horse next to the eastern pavilion, Zarrah dismounted. Her father did the same, and together they climbed the steps and entered the massive pavilion. Dirt and debris had collected in the corners of the stone room she stood in, the only furniture the stone table on which the game masters would rest the pages of their strategy, all the other trappings that had once decorated this place long ago stolen.

"I need the document in which my grandfather declared Mother his heir," she said, knowing her father had kept it on him at all times during the journey.

"Why?"

"Because when she sees it, she'll know that she can lie to me no longer."

He hesitated, then extracted the wax-wrapped paper from his inner pocket, handing it to Zarrah. "Keep it safe. It is the only proof we have of the truth."

She tucked it into her own pocket, then placed the small lamp she'd brought with her on the table and swiftly lit it.

"They're coming," her father said, though the warning was unnecessary, for Zarrah could hear the Imperial Army marching. Her hands were icy, but sweat beaded on her brow. "You need to leave," she said. "Before they arrive and it's too late." Seeing he was ready to argue, she added, "You either believe I am empress or you don't, Father. What you say now will demonstrate how much faith you have in me as a ruler."

Her father huffed out an aggrieved breath. "You are like your mother. Just like her."

Zarrah didn't answer, only waited.

"I have faith in you," he finally said, closing the distance between them and pulling her into a tight embrace. "And I love you dearly, daughter. Know that."

Zarrah bit her lip to contain her emotions. "Hurry."

He pressed his hand to his heart. "Good luck, Imperial Majesty."

The army grew closer, and Zarrah moved to attach a white scrap of fabric to one of the sconces on the front of the pavilion while her father hurried down the steps to retrieve the horses. Mounting one, he took the reins of the other and galloped out of

the stadium. Relief flooded her chest with the last uncertainty removed, and she went to the midpoint of the stairs to wait.

It did not take long.

Scouts moved warily into the stadium, eyes roving as they
searched for threats. One cautiously approached, stopping his
horse at the base of the steps. "Lay down your weapons and surrender," he shouted.

Pulling out her knife, Zarrah pressed the razor tip to her jugu-
lar. "I will surrender to the Usurper and none other."

The man's jaw tightened, but he backed his horse away, confirming Zarrah's belief that her aunt had ordered she not be
harmed.

More of the army moved into the stadium, men and women
casting long shadows as the sun began its descent in the west. Zarrah's hand trembled from holding the knife in place at her throat,
but she was afraid to move it lest the soldiers get their hands on
her. Which would make all of this for naught.

What if she doesn't come?

What if I'm wrong about how she feels?

Thoughts raced through Zarrah's skull, and it wasn't long until
her clothes were damp with sweat and her stomach twisted into
knots of anxiety. This wasn't how she fought her battles. Her
strength was combat and killing, not subterfuge and manipulation, but if Keris had taught her anything, it was that sometimes
there were better paths to victory than violence.

I wish you were here, she silently whispered, allowing her gaze to
flick briefly to the sky. *I need you.*

No, you don't, the sky seemed to answer, and her eyes burned.

Drumbeats abruptly filled the air, and Zarrah tensed. *She's coming.*

The ranks of soldiers parted to allow the drummers through,

and then the Usurper appeared. Riding a large white horse capari-soned in silver and lilac, her aunt slowly approached the pavilion, expression unreadable. She wore armor, a sword at her waist and a small shield hanging from a hook on her saddle. Ever the warrior who led armies to victory.

The Usurper drew her horse to a stop at the base of the stairs. "It pleases me that you've come to see reason, dearest. Put down your weapons and come here so that we might put all of this be-hind us."

"No."

The Usurper tilted her head, eyes narrowed. "You cannot win this, Zarrah. You placed your faith in a man, in a Maridrinian, in a *Veliant*, and you must now see the consequences of doing so. You stand alone because you put your faith in one who did not deserve it. One who did not even deserve his own crown, for it was his own army, his own people, who gave him over to Welran in Neras-tis. Keris Veliant failed you, dear one."

Oh God, no. Grief filled her chest, threatening to drown her, but Zarrah forced her spine straight. The time to weep, the time to hurt, was later.

"My faith was not misplaced," Zarrah called out. "To die fight-ing for one's cause is not a failure."

"He isn't dead." The Usurper's mouth quirked into a half smile. "Welran's orders were to bring him to me alive."

Zarrah's heart gave a rapid skitter, then plummeted into her stomach. Keris was alive. Alive, but this creature's prisoner. Death might have been a greater mercy. "To what end?"

"*His* end, once you come to realize that all the pain you have suffered is because of him."

Horror flooded Zarrah's veins, because she knew what was coming even before the Usurper said, "My army has surrounded the rebel forces. Every last one of them is a traitor to the crown, a Veliant pawn, but I will forgive their transgressions once you condemn their master. Once you condemn *your* master."

A choice between Keris and the rebels. His life for theirs. "And if I refuse?"

"Then the rebels will be executed," the Usurper answered. "And the rat will be kept a prisoner until such day as you are willing to cast off his control over you."

Zarrah swallowed the burn rising up her throat, her knees feeling abruptly too weak to keep her standing. A sting of pain burst on her neck, and she sucked in a deep breath, realizing she'd nicked herself. Tiny droplets of blood ran down her throat, but rather than lowering her knife, she took a deep breath to steady her hand. Her plan was still in play. "How do I know you even have him? How do I know that you aren't negotiating with an empty hand?"

"You don't, but why does that even matter? Choosing between your people's lives and that of your puppet master should be easy, dear one."

It should have been, but it wasn't.

"Choose now," the Usurper said. "Or the choice will be made for you, and it will be *both*. Prove to Valcotta that you value your nation and your people over your lover."

Zarrah stiffened, for it was as though the Usurper had read her mind. If she chose Keris in front of so many witnesses, she'd lose all credibility. For who would want an empress who valued her lover's life over that of her people?

She couldn't save everyone. She had to choose.

Her throat tried to strangle the words, her tongue to freeze in place, but Zarrah's voice was clear as she said, "I choose my people."

The Usurper dropped her reins and pressed a hand to her heart. "I knew you would make the right choice." Turning her head, she gestured to Sephra. "Send riders on the north road to meet Welran. Tell him to gut the rat on the side of the road, then stake him out as carrion for the scavengers to feast upon."

Sephra saluted, and the Usurper's attention moved back to Zarrah. "I will not be so cruel as to make you watch. The rat will disappear from existence, and in time, it will be as though none of this happened."

A hot tear slipped down Zarrah's cheek as she watched Sephra leave the stadium. She'd killed him. Killed him, and in doing so, cut out her own heart. Honor and duty might carry her forward, but she'd never recover. And she'd certainly never forget.

"Put down the knife," the Usurper said. "Come to me, and we shall heal from this ordeal together."

"Not yet," Zarrah answered. "First there are matters you and I need to discuss."

Silence stretched, the only sound the shuffling of the soldiers. The stomping of horses' hooves. The Usurper exhaled, and it was written all over her face that this was not a conversation she wished to have. But then she inclined her head. "As you like. Put down the knife and I will come up."

"Trust needs to be earned, Auntie," Zarrah answered. "Tell your soldiers to back up and I'll throw down my knife."

A huff of annoyance pulled from the Usurper's lips, but she made a sharp gesture. "Retreat a dozen yards but"—she gave Zarrah a long look—"be wary of a trap."

"Farther," Zarrah demanded, heart pounding because her aunt sensed she was up to something, her eyes gleaming with suspicion. "This conversation is between you and me."

The Usurper hesitated, then gave a curt nod, and soon the

ranks of soldiers were retreating down the pitch. Close enough for them to come to her aunt's aid if there was an attack but far enough away that her aunt could speak freely without fear of being overheard.

Zarrah smiled, then tossed her knife onto the stadium turf, along with her staff. Holding up her hands, she said, "I'm unarmed."

"You're too well trained to ever be unarmed," the Usurper answered. "Move to the far side of the table, dear one."

She's afraid of me.

Nodding, Zarrah climbed the steps into the pavilion, circling into the position of the game master, then waited for the Usurper to come and stand on the opposite side of the stone slab.

The trap was sprung, the steel claws descending, but the Usurper was not caught yet.

"If there is to be trust between us, Auntie, there must be honesty. Which means that I need to hear the truth from your lips."

The Usurper's eyes narrowed. "Just what truth do you think I'm withholding?"

"The truth about my mother's fate."

Silence.

The Usurper's face was unmoved, but Zarrah could feel the wheels turning in her head. The calculation. Monster she might be, but a brilliant monster who'd hidden her true nature for a very long time. She would do everything in her power to keep it that way. Which meant that Zarrah had to be wary.

"You were there, Zarrah. With your own eyes, you watched Silas Veliant slaughter Aryana. Watched him put her up on a cross for the carrion crows to feast upon while her blood rained down upon you at its base. Watched me gallop into the villa. Watched me untie you. Heard me promise you vengeance."

"True," Zarrah answered, forcing herself to keep her eyes on the Usurper's and not look beyond. "But how did Silas know we were there?"

"The Magpie's spies. For all he was a disgusting little creature, Serin was a worthy spymaster."

"Indeed. Although from his own lips, Serin told Keris that it was you who revealed that my mother and I were at the villa without a bodyguard. You used Silas as your assassin, which he was more than glad to be."

"Lies!" The Usurper slammed her palms down on the stone slab, and despite herself, Zarrah flinched. "Lies! Time and again, you take everything the rat said as truth rather than open your eyes to his manipulation."

"Keris wasn't lying."

The Usurper snorted. "Believe that if you must, but if that's the case, then he was deceived by Serin."

"I don't think so." Zarrah pressed her sweat-slicked palms to the tabletop. "That was why you believed him when he sent word that Keris and I were lovers. You and he had an understanding, a trust cemented by complicity."

The Usurper's voice shook with rage as she said, "You have been misled. I loved my younger sister. Love you, with all my heart, despite all the villainy you've enacted against me. What cause would I have to see you both killed? What did I stand to gain?"

Lifting her hand from the table, Zarrah reached into her cloak pocket and removed the duplicate proclamation her grandfather had written naming her mother as heir, keeping her voice low as she placed it on the table. "Because my mother was the rightful heir to the Valcottan Empire."

The Usurper's eyes raked over the aged document. The signature. The seal imprinted with the Emperor's ring. "You've been given a forgery."

She belied her words by reaching to take the page, and Zarrah drew it away. "I don't think so, Auntie."

Fury flared on the Usurper's face, only to vanish in a heartbeat. "Did you come here to surrender or not, Zarrah? For this feels very little like surrender."

"I came for the truth."

"And yet you seem content to believe lies."

Zarrah stared at this woman she'd once loved like a mother. Her savior and salvation. For the first time, it occurred to her that the Usurper believed her own lies, lived in her own delusion of the truth. "Near the end of his reign, my grandfather, Emperor Ephraim Anaphora, voiced his desire to see an end to the Endless War. To work toward peace with Maridrina, for he was tired of the slaughter. Tired of thousands of children growing up as orphans. Tired of the violence. So rather than naming you, the daughter who lived and breathed the war to the point it had become her identity, as heir, he named his younger daughter. My mother, Aryana, was like-minded to him and desired peace above all else. Yet rather than acceding to your father's wishes, when you learned of his intent, you rallied the officers in the military loyal to you and usurped the crown. When he died, you arranged for the assassination of all witnesses to the signing of the declaration, then destroyed the document itself, not realizing that my mother was in possession of the second."

The Usurper did not react, only stared her down, eyes cold and calculating. "Are you finished with your little story?"

"No," Zarrah answered. "I am not. My mother knew you were willing to kill to keep the crown, so she pretended to accept your rise to power, supporting you publicly. But in private, she and her husband, my father, took the first steps in gaining supporters. Together, they falsified his death so that he could go to the south and rally those who desired an end to the war, sowing the first seeds that you were not the rightful ruler of Valcotta. Somehow, you learned of her plans, and you made arrangements for her assassination. And mine, because I was her named heir. You supplied the Maridrinian spymaster with details of when and where my mother and I would be near Nerastis, knowing full well that Silas Veliant would not miss the opportunity for blood."

The Usurper shook her head. "These are lies told by Keris Veliant to turn you against me."

"It is the truth that turned me against you." Zarrah lifted her chin. "You rode into that villa believing we would both be dead, but what a shock to discover that I still lived. You couldn't very well kill me with your soldiers watching, but in truth, I don't think that's what stayed your hand. I think it was the way I looked at you when you rode through the gates, like there was no one in the world but you. And you realized that you could make me yours. Could raise me in your image, fighting your battles and defending your honor, worshipping you like a goddess and therefore blind to your every flaw. That you could make me the perfect heir, for not only was it my birthright, but when the day came for me to ascend, it would be as though a second coming of you sat upon the throne. I was your *fucking immortality*!"

The Usurper flinched, and Zarrah bared her teeth. "But then I met Keris. You knew something was drawing me away from your way of thinking, and you tried to fight it. Forbade me to have anything to do with it. But it was too late. My mind had been unleashed from your control. You knew it, which was why you didn't attempt to rescue me, likely thinking Silas would kill me the moment I walked through the gates of his palace. But Silas Veliant was a game master as well, *Auntie,* and I see why he kept me alive. Not because he was afraid of provoking your ire, but because he knew that you were *pissing yourself* that he'd tell me the truth."

The army was shifting restlessly, but Zarrah didn't take her eyes from the Usurper's face, for she couldn't risk her aunt turning around to see the claws of the trap descending.

Not yet.

"Silas alluded to it so many times, knew that my father was the commander of the rebellion in the south, and now, looking back, I think he never intended to kill me. That it was his plan to eventually have me learn the truth about you, then unleash me to join my father, for what better way to strike a blow than to have Valcotta turn to civil war."

"And you have realized his dream for him," the Usurper spat. "Valcottans against Valcottans, when we should be united and looking north to honor and glory. If we fall to Maridrina, it will be *your* doing, dear one."

"I am not your dear one!" Tears poured down Zarrah's cheeks. "I am not yours, and I will die a thousand times over before ever being yours again. We had a chance for peace. A chance to end the war, because that was what Keris was fighting for, and you killed him."

"No, Zarrah," the Usurper answered. "*You* killed him."

She had. And her soul would never recover from it.

Zarrah finally allowed her eyes to break from the monster's.

She looked out over the sea of imperial soldiers and knew that, for all her heart would never be whole, she had made the right choice. That losing him would not be in vain.

"An inventive story you have spun," the Usurper said. "But to what end? You have lost. Keris Veliant will soon be meat for the crows. Your pitiful army is in my grasp. What do you have to gain from all of this?"

"I want you to admit to me that it is the truth," Zarrah said. "Admit it to me, and I will burn this piece of paper, this last bit of concrete truth of your crimes. Refuse, and I will run into your army and scream my story and show as many of them the proof as I can before you put me down."

The Usurper cast her eyes skyward. "You think they'll believe you, girl?"

"Some of them will," Zarrah answered. "And they will be the ember that slowly flares into the inferno that will destroy you. So choose, Auntie."

Silence stretched, and Zarrah swore that no one in the stadium stirred. That no one breathed.

"Fine," the Usurper answered. "Have it your way. It is the truth. All that you say is the truth." Pulling a knife, she added, "Now burn it, or I will cut your throat before you make it two paces."

Drawing the small lamp in front of her, Zarrah pressed the corner of the document to the flame. Watched as fire consumed it until all that remained was ash and melted wax, along with the smile on the Usurper's face. She leaned across the table, and with the last proof of her crimes destroyed, the monster's voice was unleashed. "I was raised to rule. Eldest and strongest, yet in his final days of his life, my father turned against me and named your mother his heir. Said that she was the empress Valcotta needed— *balm to the fucking wound,* he called her. But I saw the truth. Saw that she'd make us weak, and I refused to let that happen. I should have killed her then, but I loved her too much, and it seemed she was content. Then I discovered she conspired against me, and I could not allow that to stand. I had fought too hard to make Valcotta strong to allow her to tear it apart. She gave me no choice. Just as you now have given me no choice. It's over, Zarrah."

"No," Zarrah answered, staring out over the sea of shocked and angry faces of the Imperial Army, each one of them having heard every word of the conversation, just as the stadium builders had intended. "It has only just begun."

The Usurper whirled, confusion rising on her face as shouts filled the air, voices demanding justice. "How . . ."

"I believe this is checkmate, Petra," a velvet voice murmured, seeming to come from nowhere and everywhere at once. "Peace's champion has won the day."

On the far side of the stadium, an armored soldier appeared from the shadows of the opposing pavilion. He pulled off his helmet, revealing blond hair, the sight of his face nearly bringing Zarrah to her knees.

"You're dead!" The Usurper shrieked. "Welran killed you after your filthy army handed you over!" And then, seeming to remember herself, she added, "Seize him!"

"No need to shout, Petra," Keris answered. "These are the whispering courts of Meritt, perfectly designed so that the game masters' voices can be heard by every player and every spectator, even if they speak no louder than a confession. A genius construction, though I understand you outlawed handball some years ago for being an *unworthy pursuit*. A good friend of mine never forgave you for it."

Keris started down the steps, and the Usurper shouted, "Seize him! This is the king of Maridrina! He is our enemy, come to destroy us!"

The soldiers ignored her, parting to make a path for Keris.

"You were clever sending Welran to make a deal with the men of my army in Nerastis. They were sick with guilt over what occurred in Vencia and desired not only for someone to take the blame but also to forestall it happening again," Keris said, nodding at the soldiers he passed. "But what you failed to consider was what their wives, sisters, mothers, and daughters would have to say on the matter. There is a mistaken belief that the marriage knives Maridrinian women wear are kept dull because they are weak and incapable of wielding them. That is a fallacy. The women

of Maridrina are the bastion that protects the heart of the kingdom, and while they may not be the first weapon you meet, they
will be the last, for their knives sharpen to the keenest edge. You
attacked the heart, and I'm afraid to say that as a result, there was
not enough left of Welran for me to return him to you."

The Usurper swayed, catching the side of the table for balance.
"Seize him! Don't you hear what he has done? He murdered Welran!"

Zarrah held her breath, but not one of the soldiers moved
against Keris as he walked slowly down the center of the stadium.
"My aunt Coralyn, who was the cleverest woman to ever live,
taught me that the secret to victory was not having the sharpest
blade or the strongest arm or even the keenest mind, but rather to
know one's opponent. Anyone who knows Zarrah Anaphora understands that she'd have fallen on her own weapon before pitting
Valcottan against Valcottan, yet you came here looking for exactly
that fight. Likely because you knew it was one you could win,
whereas a war of truths was one you were destined to lose."

He had reached the midpoint of the stadium now, light of the
setting sun glinting off the steel on his armor, and Zarrah could
still barely bring herself to believe that he was alive. That he was
here.

That they'd won.

"Hubris is the downfall of all, Petra," Keris continued, "as it has
been yours. So certain were you of victory that you split your
army in two, bringing half here to watch you take Zarrah's *surrender*, sending the other half to capture the rebel army. The latter, I'm
pleased to inform you, swiftly capitulated when they discovered
themselves caught between the rebels and the combined forces of
Maridrina and Ithicana. As to the other half of your army . . ." He
paused, looking around. "I ask, will you swear allegiance to the

rightful heir to the Valcottan Empire, Zarrah Anaphora, or will you continue to fight for the Usurper?"

He turned back to the pavilion in which Zarrah stood, and her breath caught as their eyes locked. She should have known that not even death had the power to stop him.

"This is madness!" The Usurper came around to the rear of the table as though to keep it between her and Keris. "Seize him! That is an order. Any who fail to listen will be given a traitor's death. Will be fed to the dogs!"

It was not one by one, but rather a tide as the soldiers of the Imperial Army dropped to one knee, pressing hands to their hearts. Then, to Zarrah's shock, Keris knelt. "On the blood of my family, as the king of Maridrina, I swear my life and sword to Zarrah Anaphora. May peace be had between Maridrina and Valcotta now and forevermore."

"No," the Usurper whispered, then screamed, "No!"

"It took me a long time to see what you really are," Zarrah said quietly. "But now my eyes are clear. As are theirs."

The Usurper went still; then she said, "If you are not mine, then you will be no one's."

It took a heartbeat too long for Zarrah to understand, Keris's screamed warning filling her ears right as the Usurper's knife pressed against her throat.

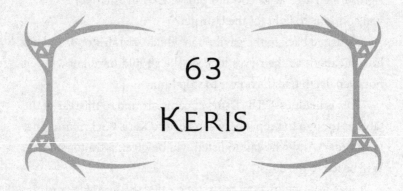

63

KERIS

EVEN FROM THIRTY YARDS AWAY, KERIS SAW THE SHIFT. FELT IT IN his chest like a surge of pressure that made his heart stutter and adrenaline surge through his veins.

The moment Petra turned on Zarrah.

He was on his feet and running, shouting a warning. Screaming Zarrah's name while the soldiers around him all leapt upright in alarm.

They were all too late.

In a flash of speed that came with a lifetime of training, Petra was behind Zarrah, a knife to her neck. "Come any closer and I'll slit her throat."

"You kill her, you'll die badly," Keris answered, though he drew up at the base of the pavilion steps, his heart throbbing. Zarrah struggled in her grasp, then fell still as blood trickled in rivulets down her skin. Her eyes met Keris's. *She'll do it.*

"You think that's any threat, you arrogant fool?" Petra hissed. "I would rather die than watch Valcotta be ruled by Maridrina's puppet empress."

"You know she isn't my puppet and never has been," he answered, lifting a hand to stop the Valcottan soldiers moving closer, for their desire to protect Zarrah was more likely to get her killed. "What you can't stand is that she's no longer yours to play with as you will, but rather her own woman."

"I gave her everything!" Petra stomped her foot hard. "She's nothing without me!"

She stomped her foot again.

Keris thought it a fit of temper; then Zarrah's eyes widened, and both women dropped from sight.

"Zarrah!" Keris sprinted up the steps, nearly losing his footing as he raced around the stone table, eyes latching on the square opening right as the hatch door was pushed back into place. He threw himself at the stone slab, hauling on the metal handle bolted to it.

But the hatch wouldn't budge. Was either stuck or latched from the far side.

"Pry it open!" he shouted at the Valcottan soldiers who'd followed him up, several of them taking his place to pull on the handle. It was to no avail.

Raking a hand back through his sweaty hair, Keris fought his panic. "Where does it lead?"

The soldiers exchanged looks, everyone shaking their heads; then Saam and Jor appeared, Arjun with them. "Where does the escape tunnel lead?" Keris shouted at Saam. "We need to find them before she hurts Zarrah!"

"I don't know." Light from the flickering lamp illuminated Saam's pale face. "When the games were active, it was a close secret known only to the game masters in case there was a riot. I never had a chance to explore the stadium myself. It's only because the tunnel from the other pavilion caved in that we knew where to find it."

"I shouldn't have left her alone," Arjun said, pressing his hands to the sides of his head in panic. "I shouldn't have let her risk it."

"If you hadn't, we wouldn't have known she was here," Keris snapped. "Does anyone know where the tunnel leads?"

A Valcottan captain stepped forward. "A dozen of the imperial guard rode northeast when we began the march to the stadium. No information was supplied as to where they were going, but they were all members of her personal guard. Someone among them must have known where the exit to the tunnel was and been waiting below."

"Fuck!" Keris slammed his hand down on the hatch door.

"You in charge?" Jor demanded of the captain, who nodded. "Send riders to the town. Those living there might have answers. Have the rest of your soldiers start a search heading northeast."

The Valcottan captain opened his mouth as though to argue but then thought better of it, turning around to shout orders.

Keris stood but didn't move from the pavilion. This was his fault. Zarrah had it in hand, and he'd had to provoke Petra. Had to twist the knife. Had to have the final *fucking* word.

Zarrah was fighting for her life because of it.

"Shit." He doubled over, his stomach roiling because he didn't know what to do. The Valcottan army was well trained, the thousands of soldiers pouring out of the stadium all going to search. "I need to find her. I . . ."

"You need to move your pretty arse out of my way is what you need to do."

He lifted his head to see Jor waving a hand at him. "Down the steps. We'll wait until that lot is clear before getting underway. We can't be certain all of them are loyal to Zarrah, and I'm not keen on being attacked from behind."

Confusion permeated Keris's panic, Arjun and Saam exchanging equally bewildered glances. "What are you talking about?"

"We're going to pursue them through the tunnels. Cover your ears, right?"

The old Ithicanian pulled two small bottles from his inner coat pocket, then disappeared around the stone table. A few seconds passed, then he scuttled back around and down the steps, hands pressed to the sides of his head. "Cover your ears and close your eyes!"

Keris clapped his hands over his ears and shut his eyes.

Through his eyelids, he saw a flash of light. The shock wave of the explosion made him stagger. Snapping his eyes open, Keris found plumes of smoke and dust coming from the pavilion and Jor already halfway up the steps. He went back around the stone table and nodded with clear satisfaction. "Let's go." And without waiting for Keris to respond, he disappeared from sight.

Keris took the steps two at a time, rounding the table to stare into the smoking hole, the stone slab that had been the door now in shattered ruins below. Jor's face appeared, a torch in his hand. "Hurry!"

Keris leapt down into the hole.

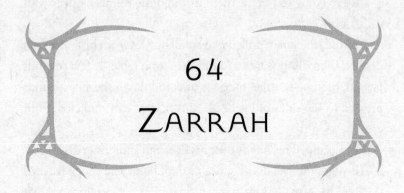

64

ZARRAH

HER THROAT STUNG, THE BACK OF HER SKULL ACHING WHERE THE Usurper had struck her, and Zarrah blinked as everything came back into focus.

She was being dragged by a large man in the uniform of an imperial soldier, and when Zarrah lifted her head, she recognized him as a long-standing member of the Usurper's bodyguard. These men were as indoctrinated as she'd ever been. Would be loyal to the bitter end.

Which was probably why the Usurper hadn't bothered to gag her.

"She's awake," the soldier rumbled, his voice echoing in the narrow tunnel.

"Good." The Usurper glanced over her shoulder, dark eyes meeting Zarrah's. "She does not deserve the mercy of death. I want her alive so that she can witness the horror of what she's done. Want her to witness Valcotta's fall from grace, to hear everyone curse the woman who brought them to ruin for the sake of her lust for a man."

"You'll be waiting for a very long time," Zarrah croaked, though in truth, with Petra discredited and Zarrah locked away, it would be a race to the throne among the Valcottan nobility.

Her unease must have shown on her face, because the Usurper gave her a cruel smile. "Yes, Zarrah. Civil war. Whether your lover involves himself or not will matter little. Valcottans will turn against Valcottans, and thousands will die. All their blood will be on your hands."

The accusation didn't have time to sink in as a roar of noise shattered Zarrah's ears, the walls of the tunnel shaking.

"Run!" someone shouted, and Zarrah was dragged back to her feet. "It's a cave-in!"

"It's the Ithicanians!" the Usurper shrieked at them. "They've blown the hatch. Go!"

Keris was coming.

Zarrah threw her weight backward, fighting against the soldier holding her. "Keris!" she screamed. "Keris, I'm here!"

Then the Usurper was on her.

Fingers caught hold of her hair, slamming her against the wall of the tunnel. Zarrah fell to her knees, only to be kicked in the kidneys.

She screamed in pain, trying to roll, to regain her feet, but she couldn't do it with her wrists bound.

A foot struck her in the ribs with a crunch of breaking bone, flipping her over. The Usurper knelt on her chest and slapped her, nails raking across Zarrah's cheek. "You think he'll still want you if you're ugly?" she screamed. "Do you think he'll march his army for you if your face is in tatters? You'll need me then because no one else will want you!"

Zarrah screamed as the monster clawed at her face; then one of the soldiers was pulling her off. "Empress, they're in the tunnel. We need to flee!"

For a heartbeat, Zarrah thought the Usurper would think

shredding her face worth the delay, but then she snarled, "Carry her! We need to reach the boat!"

Everything was agony, her head spinning, but she heard Keris's voice echoing through the tunnels. "Zarrah!"

Spitting blood, she grinned wildly at the Usurper. "It's a Veliant who is hunting you, *Auntie*. I doubt you can run fast enough."

For the first time in her life, Zarrah saw fear in Petra Anaphora's eyes.

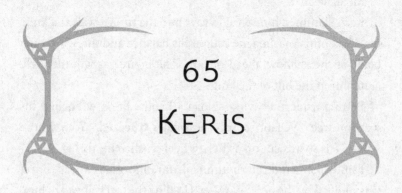

65
KERIS

"KERIS!"

His name filtered up the tunnel as his feet struck the ground. Pushing past Jor, he took a few steps, the smoke and dust making it hard to breathe. But it did nothing to muffle her screams of agony.

Something in him snapped.

Wrenching the torch from Jor's hands, Keris broke into a run, his companions' cries of warning barely registering in his ears.

The tunnel had been made by the hands of men, the ceiling high but the walls narrow. Too narrow to fight with a sword, so Keris pulled a knife. Caution screamed at him to slow his pace, warned him that ambush could be waiting around each bend. But the echo of Zarrah's screams of agony drowned it out.

He was going to cut Petra's goddamned heart out.

The tunnel reached a set of stone stairs, and he descended in leaps, his torch casting man-shaped shadows on the walls. His breath came in ragged gasps, a stitch forming in his side even as the scent of mildew and moisture filled his nose.

Metal flashed.

Keris slammed himself sideways into the tunnel wall as a knife flew past him. Snarling, he caught his balance and threw his own blade at the shadow ahead of him. The figure gasped, then fell, clutching at the hilt of the knife.

Batting aside the dying soldier's hands, Keris wrenched his weapon free. "Veliant scum," the soldier wheezed. "Your whore will—" His words cut off as Keris's heel crushed his throat.

Faintly, he heard the rhythmic drum of footfalls ahead, but it was muffled by the noise of water. Holding the torch ahead of him, Keris slowed his pace as he stepped out into a cavern.

It was massive, and unlike the tunnel, a product of nature. Overhead, stalactites dangled above an underground river, too wide and fierce to cross without risking one's life. A footpath wove down between the stalagmites protruding from the cave's floor, leading to a wooden bridge that stretched above the raging water. Figures carrying torches moved across it, and Keris's eyes immediately went to Zarrah's shape slung over the shoulder of one of them. She lifted her head, the torchlight revealing that the side of her face was a mask of blood.

And all he saw was red.

Shoving his bloody knife between his teeth, Keris drew his sword as he raced down the path. Two of the figures broke away from the rest, taking up positions blocking the bridge. Then, to his horror, one pressed his torch to the wooden planks.

No!

The word echoed through the cavern, and Keris realized that he'd howled it a heartbeat before his sword clashed with one of the soldiers' blades. He spun away, then threw his torch at the man setting the bridge ablaze. Screams ricocheted off the walls as the burning brand smashed the soldier in the face, and he rolled sideways into the river, disappearing beneath the rapids.

But it was too late. The bridge was already aflame, and the other soldier still blocked his path.

"Keris, wait!" Saam shouted, but as the soldier's eyes flicked upstream to where his companions had appeared, Keris struck.

He'd resisted it all his life, this skill. Refused lessons from his father's weapons masters and dragged his heels when Otis had made him practice, but against his will, it had sunk into his soul. Had been kept in check until now only because he hadn't wanted blood on his hands. Hadn't wanted to kill.

But Keris wanted this man dead.

Firelight flickered off their weapons as they exchanged blows, the collision of swords violent and quick.

Keris let instinct guide him, sensing each attack before it happened and meeting it with rising ferocity, for this man stood between him and Zarrah. This man had watched Petra brutalize her and done nothing.

He would die for it.

Keris feinted, and as the soldier moved to parry, Keris reversed his slice, taking the man's sword hand off at the wrist. Blood sprayed as he staggered, clutching the stump, but his pain was short-lived, for a heartbeat later, Keris's blade was through his throat.

Too late, for the ancient timber of the bridge was engulfed.

"Keris!"

Her distant scream sent a shudder through him, and pulling his hood up, Keris leapt onto the bridge.

Heat seared through his boots with each step, embers burning the leather of his trousers, but Keris ignored the pain and ran. Beneath him, the timbers groaned, and gathering his strength, Keris jumped right as it collapsed beneath him.

66

ZARRAH

SHE STRUGGLED AND KICKED, DRIVING THE TOES OF HER BOOTS into the soldier's body and slamming her bound wrists against his back. Threw her weight from side to side, every hiss of pain or stumble fueling her efforts despite the agony it inflicted upon her broken ribs.

"You betray Valcotta by remaining loyal to her," she growled as the soldier caught hold of one of her legs to stop her kicking. "She's a liar. A murderer. A monster."

"She is empress."

"She is a usurper!" Wasted words, Zarrah knew, for these men had not heard the confession in the stadium. Even if they had, she doubted their fanatical loyalty would be swayed.

But even the slightest doubt might buy her time, for as they reached the mouth of the cave, Zarrah knew she was running short of it.

The river poured out of the cave in a great spraying arc, plunging over a hundred feet to join the great river below. And if they reached the boat waiting for them before Keris and his companions caught up, the Usurper would escape.

And a monster like Petra Anaphora could not be allowed to run free.

"Hurry!" the Usurper hissed, leading the way down the narrow path cut into the side of the cliff face. "They won't be able to hold the bridge forever, and even if it burns, he'll find a way across the river eventually. We need to be gone before he does."

Zarrah's heart skipped. What if Keris tried to swim across, not knowing about the falls? She left off her struggles and lifted her head, seeing the waterfall had turned orange and red in the sunset.

"The boat is waiting," one of the soldiers said, and Zarrah cursed. For while the Usurper had not remembered the acoustics of the stadium, she had most certainly remembered the escape route the game masters took during the riots. She was prepared.

The pathway switched back, leading down, and Zarrah fought the urge to scream as she lost sight of the falls. "Keris!"

What if he fell and she didn't see?

What if he already had, his body broken and caught in the endless flow at the base of the waterfall?

Panic rose in her chest, making it hard to breathe, but Zarrah dragged in an agonized breath. *If he's fallen, then you must stop her. Whatever it takes, you must stop her.*

Zarrah slammed her weight sideways.

The soldier gasped as he swayed toward the deadly drop, letting go of her bound wrists to fling his arm out for balance.

She took advantage.

Lifting her torso, she twisted sideways. As his arm clamped around her body to try to lock her into place, Zarrah bit down on his ear.

The man screamed, shoving her away from him, only to lose his footing. He fell sideways off the cliff, his screams fading until they cut off abruptly.

Zarrah landed on her back on the pathway, the impact knocking the wind from her chest, the pain of her broken ribs making the world spin. *Get up,* she ordered herself. *Fight.*

She eased onto her hands and knees, lifting her face.

Only to find the tip of a blade pressed between her eyes.

The Usurper stood before her with a sword in hand, her last remaining bodyguard standing behind her on the narrow path. "He's not coming, dear one," she said. "So I think it safe to say that your usefulness is at its end."

A shadow moved above, soundless as a cat.

"You keep saying that he's not coming, Auntie," Zarrah said with a wild grin as Keris jumped from the switchback above, landing behind the soldier. "Every time, you are wrong."

Keris drew his sword. "Let her go, Petra."

The Usurper stumbled away from Keris as her bodyguard attacked. She tripped over Zarrah and fell against the rock wall. Zarrah reached for her with bound wrists, catching hold of her leg to keep her from running.

The Usurper fell, her sword sliding up the path. She crawled forward, but Zarrah held on. If she escaped into the cavern, there might be other ways out. She might get away. She might come back, ever remaining Zarrah's nightmare.

Zarrah could not let her go.

She clambered up the older woman's body, bound wrists not stopping her fingers from closing around her throat.

Zarrah squeezed.

The Usurper's eyes widened, and she clawed at Zarrah's hands, skin purpling. "This is for my mother," Zarrah said. "For Yrina. For Valcotta."

She heard Keris grunt behind her, then the scream of the soldier as he was tossed off the edge of the cliff.

"But most of all," Zarrah whispered, "it's for me."

The Usurper went still, staring into Zarrah's eyes. She twitched and jerked; then, with a last burst of strength, the Usurper threw her weight sideways.

Zarrah gasped, trying to counter the motion. But it was too late.

They were falling.

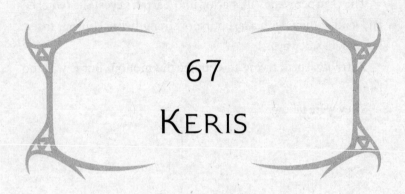

67

KERIS

"ZARRAH!" HE SHOUTED AS SHE CRAWLED AFTER PETRA, TRYING
to knock the soldier in his path out of the way to reach them.
There was nowhere for Petra to go, for his companions would
catch her on their way down. "Zarrah, let her go!"

It was as if she didn't hear him, her bloodied face a mask of
desperate determination as she reached for Petra's throat.

The soldier slashed at him and Keris parried, knocking the man
off-balance. A punch to the jaw sent him stumbling off the edge,
revealing Zarrah atop Petra, strangling her.

Then Petra rolled.

No.

Memories flashed before his eyes. Of himself diving and reaching, Otis's clothes brushing his fingers as he fell to his death. Of
Serin just out of reach, his plunge setting a nightmare into motion.

Not her.

Keris dove forward, the bare skin of her arm slipping through
his grasp as she dropped from sight.

68

ZARRAH

His fingers brushed over her arm, trying and failing to stop her plunge, and Zarrah screamed as she fell.

Only to stop short as Keris caught hold of the rope between her wrists, her shoulders nearly wrenching from their sockets, for the Usurper had hold of her as well.

"Kick her off!" he shouted. "I can't hold you both!"

Zarrah sucked in a panicked breath because with each heartbeat, Keris slid another inch over the edge; there was nothing for him to grasp for leverage.

"Zarrah, please!"

Her eyes shot downward to where the Usurper dangled from her belt. Below, the deadly plunge, the rocks on the riverbank already splattered red from the fallen guards.

"Dear one, please! Please don't let me fall!"

Their eyes met, and Zarrah's stomach flipped.

"I'm sorry. I'm sorry for everything," the Usurper pleaded. "I will make it up to you, I promise. I'll go into exile, never give you trouble again. Just don't let me fall."

They jerked downward, Keris cursing. "Goddammit, Zarrah! Don't listen to her!"

"I love you, Zarrah," her aunt pleaded. "More than anyone in the world. I gave you everything I had. Helped you become strong." Her lip quivered. "I was afraid of losing you, that's all. Afraid of being alone. Please!"

"Keris!" voices called from above. Familiar voices. Saam. Jor. Her father. "We're coming!"

"I was wrong to try to make you like me," her aunt sobbed. "You've always been better than me. Please don't change that."

"Zarrah, we're all going to fall!"

She looked up into Keris's face. His left hand was braced on the edge, tendons standing out white against his blood-smeared skin, but he was slipping. "Don't listen to her," he said between his teeth. "Don't let her take you down."

"Zarrah, please!" her aunt wailed. "Don't allow my death to stain your legacy."

It wasn't lost on her that her aunt was trying to save her own neck, but the words struck a chord. If Zarrah let her fall, it would weigh upon her conscience. Be forever how the world remembered her. Whereas if she showed her aunt mercy . . . "Climb up," she gasped out. "My wrists are tied; I can't. But you can."

"Zarrah, no!" Keris's arm was shaking, but the others were coming. He just needed to hold on a few seconds more.

Her aunt gave her a tight nod, then started to climb. Her fingers dug into Zarrah's body, legs wrapping around her waist so that they were face-to-face. "You are a good girl, dear one," she whispered, breath hot and sour on Zarrah's face. "Serving until the bitter end."

The Usurper let go with one hand, and Zarrah saw the flash of steel slashing toward Keris's face.

No.

Zarrah smashed her forehead against the Usurper's nose, hearing it crunch even as blood sprayed her in the face. The monster gasped and recoiled, losing her grip.

Then she was gone.

Zarrah looked down, watching as the creature who'd touched every part of her life, good and bad, fell. Petra Anaphora didn't once scream. Only stared up at Zarrah until her body smashed against the rocks below.

Thud.

She was dead. Zarrah stared at the broken body of the woman she'd once worshipped, barely able to comprehend that Petra Anaphora was gone.

"I've got you."

Zarrah looked up as Keris began to lift her, so she saw the moment his injured shoulder gave out. She dropped as he slammed down against the cliff edge, and then they were falling. Zarrah screamed, her nails clawing at the rock face, only for her body to stop with a jerk.

The ropes binding her wrists had snagged on a crag, leaving her dangling, knees banging against the cliff. "Keris!" she howled, terror and horror making her heart tear from her chest as she forced herself to look down, knowing it would be to see him shattered on the rocks below.

Only to see his blue eyes looking up at her.

He dangled from one hand on a crag below her, knuckles tight with strain. As she watched, he tried to reach with his other hand, but his injured shoulder refused to lift his arm. "Hold on," he gasped. "They're coming."

Above, Zarrah heard her father call her name. Knew that they didn't have a rope and wouldn't be able to get one in time, because

Keris's fingers were slipping, and with the way the cliff curved in beneath him, there were no toeholds to be had.

He was going to fall.

A shriek of defiance tore from her lips because she'd already signed his death warrant once tonight, and she refused to do it again. They would live together or die together.

Her toes scrabbled for holds on the rock, and ignoring the incredible pain in her torso, Zarrah heaved herself upward.

"Zarrah, no!" Keris shouted.

Even her father screamed, "Don't move! Saam's running to get rope from the boat below!"

She ignored them as her face drew even with her bound wrists. Her arms shuddered as she linked her fingers together over the crag, then caught hold of the knot with her teeth. The copper taste of blood filled her mouth as she ripped at the rope, ears deaf to the shouts telling her to stop.

I will not let him fall, she told herself. *I refuse to let him fall.*

Then the knot pulled loose. Her weight came down hard on her linked hands as the rope fell past her legs, and Zarrah sucked in a deep breath. *You can do this.*

"Zarrah, no!"

She lowered one foot, finding another toehold. Then she began climbing down the cliff.

Every part of her was shaking, fear like poison in her guts, but adrenaline gave her strength as Zarrah edged her way down, the deadly drop a blur of river and rock below. "Hold on," she shouted. "Please, Keris. Don't let go!"

Her progress was agonizingly slow, with each handhold her heart skipping with fear that she'd hear him slip. Hear his scream as he fell. Hear the thud of his body hitting the rocks.

"Zarrah, stop!" he pleaded. "Climb up, please!"

She didn't answer, focusing on finding handholds, her weight suspended on fingertips and toes. Her battered ribs protested every move, sending bolts of agony through her that made her see stars.

And then she was above him.

There was no way to go lower with the way the cliff curved inward, and Zarrah scanned the surface of the rock, trying to find a way closer. Tears were pouring down her face, because she could see his strength was failing, only sheer will keeping him dangling from his fingertips. "Hold on," she pleaded. "They're coming with a rope. Just hold on a little longer."

"I can't," he gasped. "You have to let me go, Zarrah. It's over for me, but you need to live. Promise me that you'll live."

"Do you think I haven't tried to let you go?" she shouted at him. "Over and over, I've tried, but I might as well let go of my heart. I cannot live without you, Keris. I will not!"

But he was slipping.

"I love you," he said, eyes locked on hers. "Close your eyes. Don't watch."

"No," she screamed, seeing his strength fail.

Right as the rope dropped past her.

Zarrah let go of the cliff, catching hold of the rope even as she reached with her free hand, the world a spiraling twist of darkening sky and rock and water as his fingernails scraped over the rock, grip lost.

Falling.

Then her hand closed on his wrist.

They swung sideways on the rope, legs tangling in the length, her palm tearing as the rope dragged across it, only to jerk to a stop as her ankles got a grip. "Hold on," she shouted at him, their bodies pressed together as their friends heaved, pulling them back up to safety.

Sobs tore from Zarrah's lips as her father dragged her onto the path, Saam and Jor doing the same to Keris. Ignoring the agony that was her body, she clambered on hands and knees, pulling him into her arms.

He was bruised and bloodied, hair tangled around his face, but the sight of him made her heart beat with renewed strength. "You came for me." A tear rolled down her cheek, stinging the scratches. "I knew you would. Even when they said you were dead, my heart wouldn't let go."

Keris lifted a hand, cupping it around the side of her face that wasn't shredded, his eyes locked on hers. "Every life I have, I will gladly spend on you."

He lowered his lips to hers, and she sobbed between kisses, wrapping her arms around his neck. Refusing to let him go as the others knelt next to him.

"Are you all right?" her father demanded.

Jor leveled a finger at Keris, shouting, "You're just like your sister, you mad fool!"

"We're fine," Keris answered, holding her tight against his chest. "Petra is . . ." He jerked his chin toward the edge.

"Very dead," Saam announced. "Although perhaps I should check again." He started down the path.

All she should have felt was relief, but Zarrah felt sick, her heart in as much pain as her body. Keris pressed his lips to her forehead. "Breathe."

Zarrah drew in a gulp of air, then slowly allowed the brief pang of grief to fade away.

Her father cleared his throat. "We'll capture those still claiming loyalty to Petra, but after what the Imperial Army heard, I think they'll be few in number." He met her gaze. "It's over."

She gave a tight nod, words beyond her, and with a small smile her father tugged on Jor's sleeve and led him after Saam. Leaving them alone.

"You are the empress now, Valcotta," Keris said softly. "The Empire is yours to raise up high."

"Just as Maridrina is yours," she answered, wishing this felt more like victory.

He didn't answer, and Zarrah understood why. They'd fought for this. Bled for it. Yet the greatest cost felt yet to come, as the roles they had secured would ensure they were ever kept apart. For a few moments, she didn't want to be empress. She only wanted to be his.

Finding Keris's lips, Zarrah kissed him again, losing herself in the heat of his mouth. Burying her fingers in his hair and relishing the feel of his hands on her body. For a few heartbeats, the world fell away, and there was only the two of them. No kingdoms or empires, no crowns or armies. Only touch and breath and an endless love.

But fate, as always, saw fit to remind them that it was a star-crossed love, and the horns of war once again began to blow.

69

ZARRAH

"DO WE KNOW WHAT IS HAPPENING?" SHE ASKED AS THEY reached the bottom of the path, the river running deep and swift through the ravine. In her periphery, Zarrah could see the Usurper's corpse on the rocks, splattered and ruined, but she refused to look directly at it.

"We aren't sure," her father answered. "No one knows where we are to bring a report. We need to rejoin the main army and march on Pyrinat, claiming it in your name."

More fighting. For while many in the Imperial Army knew the truth about the Usurper, Pyrinat would be held by those who still saw Petra as the empress and Zarrah as the enemy.

Zarrah took a steadying breath, feeling Keris's arm tighten around her waist, though he was mindful of her ribs. He'd had to half carry her down, for as her adrenaline had faded, the full extent of her injuries had made themselves known, pain stealing her strength.

"Aren and Sarhina have command of the army," he said softly. "They will not move on the capital without your blessing."

"Incoming," Jor growled, pulling the machete strapped at his waist. "Imperial Army uniforms."

Keris drew his sword, but as he moved to stand between her and the group of soldiers racing down the riverbank toward them, Zarrah said, "Give me a weapon."

She wouldn't be of much use in a fight, but neither would she hide. Saam handed her a knife, and Zarrah moved to stand at Keris's side.

Yet as the soldiers drew near enough to recognize her, they slowed, sheathing their weapons. "My lady," their captain said, inclining his head. "We have been searching for you. Feared the worst." His eyes flicked to the Usurper's corpse. "But I see you are victorious."

"I will not claim victory until Valcotta is united and at peace," she said. "Can you give me a report?"

"The Maridrinian and Ithicanian armies have united with the rebels," he answered. "The Imperial Army has surrendered, although many are part of the search for you."

Nodding, Zarrah stepped away from the group, going to stand at the water's edge and looking up at the waterfall that poured into it. One of a thousand tributaries that fed the mighty flow of the Pyr.

"What do you want to do?" Keris asked, coming to stand next to her.

"I don't want to march on my capital city as the enemy," she said softly. "I don't want my people to see me as a threat."

He rocked on his heels, and she looked up at him, seeing the exhaustion. Pushed to his limit and beyond, in so many ways, but still standing strong. "We can send emissaries," he finally answered. "They can share the truth with the people, ask them to surrender peacefully to you."

Zarrah exhaled, allowing her eyes to go back to the water even as she took hold of his hand. "If I do that, it will be the enemy's voice telling the story, and they won't believe it. It needs to come from the lips of those they trust. For them to surrender Pyrinat to me is an act of faith, and it requires an act of faith from me in return."

"What is it that you have in mind?"

Keeping her grip on his hand, Zarrah turned back to the waiting soldiers. "Bring word to Aren to release the Imperial Army," she said to Jor. Then she turned to the Valcottan soldiers. "I wish for the Imperial Army to gather and return to Pyrinat."

Her father hissed between his teeth. "This is madness. There is every likelihood they will turn against you, and we'll be faced with an army that won't be easily defeated."

"If that is the case, then we will leave." Her grip on Keris tightened, and though her nails were likely digging into his palm, she couldn't relax her hand. "I . . . I won't rule people who don't want me. Nor will I use fear to force them to pretend to."

"Zarrah, they only need time to watch how you rule," her father argued. "Expecting them to love you today is unreasonable, but with time—"

"I understand that after all your years of fighting for this, my words are hard to hear, Father. But I will not be her."

"Zarrah, you must—"

"Arjun," Keris interrupted. "Zarrah has heard your counsel, and I know she respects it. But do not think that gives you the right to tell her what she must do."

"Of course you'd support this madness," her father snapped. "If she walks away from Valcotta, you can have her to yourself. Make her queen of Maridrina, as all know you desire to do."

Keris silently met her father's gaze, and a shiver ran over Zarrah's skin as she realized that at some point in this long journey, he'd become a king. Not by law, but in spirit, and he was a force to be reckoned with.

"Zarrah is an empress," he answered. "Not a queen."

Her father looked away, the tension thick as she waited for him to decide. Finally, he said, "If those are your orders, Imperial Majesty, it will be done."

She shifted her attention to Jor, who scowled at her.

"I'm too old for this." Then he shrugged. "But fine, I'll bring Aren the message."

"We can't leave you two alone," her father said. "And Zarrah is not fit for travel."

Keris lifted a hand and pointed downriver to where the vessel the Usurper had intended to use was tied to the bank. "You know how to steer something like that?" he asked Saam, who lifted one shoulder.

"Can't be that hard."

"We'll give you a head start, then set out down the Pyr," Keris said. "Have a force meet us downstream before we reach the city."

Zarrah saw the argument rising in her father's eyes, so she said, "You all have your orders." The muscles in her legs were trembling enough that it was only a matter of time until they gave out on her, and she wanted everyone gone before they did. "Go."

Jor and her father departed, heading up the path they'd come from to find their armies, the group of soldiers ascending the cliffs by another route to gather up their fellows. Zarrah's legs lasted until they were out of sight; then her knees buckled.

Keris wordlessly caught her, lifting her into his arms while Saam went to the boat, drawing it close enough to shore that Keris could set her inside.

"You need my help?" Saam asked softly.

Keris shook his head. "I'll take care of her. Can you . . ."

"I'll watch your backs until dawn."

"Thank you."

The boat rocked as Keris climbed in, then helped her into the small cabin at the center. Grimacing in pain, Zarrah settled on the cot while he lit a lamp, used the light to dig through the supplies, and returned to her with a clear bottle of spirits and clean rags. "I need to clean the cuts on your face," he said quietly, sitting on the cot. "It was her who scratched you?"

Zarrah gave a tight nod. "She . . . she wanted to make me ugly."

"Well, we can add that to her long list of failures," he answered. "Nothing could make you ugly."

She bit her lip, then winced as he cleaned the long scratches down her cheek, his brow furrowed in concentration. "They aren't that deep," he said. "But Lara will have some sort of potion to help when we rejoin them."

His hands moved to the buckles of her leather corselette and unfastened them. Beneath, the dark silk of her blouse was soaked with sweat, peeling away from her skin as he carefully removed it, each motion sending lances of pain through her torso. Every inch of her was darkening with bruises, yet she gave no protest as he ran his fingers along her ribs, her heart's need for his touch far outweighing the pain. "I think only one is broken."

He cleaned the cuts on her knuckles, then helped her out of her trousers to bandage a cut along one of her thighs that likely needed stitches but would have to do without. Retrieving a blanket, he wrapped it around her and then handed her the rest of the bottle of spirits. She took a long swallow, grimacing at the taste as it burned its way down her throat. Then she reached out a hand and knocked her fist against his armored chest. "It's strange to see you wearing this."

He gave her a wry smile. "Don't get used to it. As soon as I have some certainty that no one is trying to stab me in the chest, I'm tossing the whole stinking lot into the river."

"Good." Her lip quivered when she tried to smile. "It does not suit you."

Which was only half the truth, for he wore it well. He looked the part of the blood-soaked commander who'd led an army to victory, but that was not how she wanted to see him. The man she loved carried a book, not a sword. Had fingers stained with ink, not blood. Used words to accomplish his ends, not violence. This was part of him, she knew, but she hoped, prayed, it was one their victory would allow him to set aside.

As if hearing her thoughts, he began unbuckling the armor, dropping pieces of it onto the deck with loud thumps, clothing following suit. The lamplight illuminated the muscles of his body, and she trailed her eyes over every hard line and curve before he slipped under the blanket with her.

"Don't think about taking liberties," he murmured as she rested her head on his chest, their bodies fitting together as though some higher power had designed them as a pair. "I feel as though a herd of horses has galloped over me not once, but twice. I couldn't manage it."

Her mouth curved in a smile. "Liar."

Keris didn't answer, only reached out a hand to turn down the lamp, allowing them to look out the rear of the cabin at the dark river. And the glitter of stars in the sky above.

There were so many things to say. So many uncertainties ahead of them that they needed to plan for, but Zarrah found she couldn't put voice to any of them. She didn't want to talk about the future, because it was not a future with them together, for they couldn't abandon their kingdoms and expect peace to continue.

And she would not be his queen.

Keris's fingers trailed up and down her spine, making her toes curl, an ache forming low in her belly despite her body being in no condition to do anything about it. Her jaw trembled as frustration built in her heart, the future terrifying her, the present not satisfying her, which left only the past to content her. "Tell me our story," she whispered. "From the beginning."

His fingers stilled on her spine, and for a heartbeat, she regretted speaking. Then he resumed the motion, saying, "I don't know all of it. Some of it is hidden inside your head."

"I'll tell those parts."

"All right," he answered quietly. "I suppose it begins on Southwatch. I believed I was traveling through the bridge to attend university in Harendell, but unbeknownst to me, I was part of my father's plans to invade Ithicana."

Zarrah watched the stars as he spoke, telling her the story of their love, giving her a thousand little details that she hadn't known, even as she did the same, their accounts painting a picture so vivid, it was as though they were experiencing it all again. Every heartbreak and sorrow. Every victory and pleasure. Everything revealed, so that it was no longer his memories and hers, but a singular one that they shared. One that, every time they looked up at the sky, they'd see written in the stars.

It was only as dawn lit the sky, the boat rocking as Saam set it loose into the current and stepped in at the stern, that she said, "I'm afraid of what is to come."

"No matter what happens, no matter what is decided, I will be with you," he answered, and a single tear rolled down Zarrah's cheek, because whether he was deceiving her or himself, it mattered little.

Their story was drawing to a close.

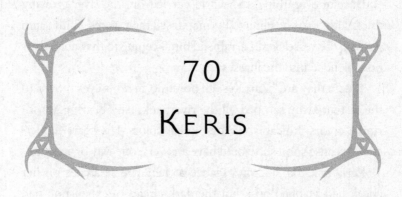

70

KERIS

THE LAST THING KERIS WANTED TO DO WAS PUT HIS SWEATY clothes and blood-splattered armor back on, but not only was there nothing else for him to wear, there was every chance he'd need the trappings of violence in the moments to come. Part of him wondered if there'd ever come a day when he could take them off.

He helped Zarrah dress, the grimace of pain on her face making him wish there were a way to bring Petra back to life so that she could be killed again, this time by *him*. But he kept those thoughts to himself, focusing on helping her comb tangles from her hair and clean away the blood that had seeped from her wounds during the night.

His voice was hoarse from talking for hours on end, but Keris wouldn't have given up last night for all the gold in the world, for it was perhaps the most precious night of his life. He briefly considered the idea of putting it to paper one day before he rejected the notion. Too much of them belonged to others. The whole of it needed to live with them and die with them, to be theirs alone.

Despite everything, the world carried on, the river growing thick with boats heading to Pyrinat to sell their wares. With Saam guiding the vessel, and Zarrah and him keeping to the cabin, their boat blended into the masses.

"There they are," Zarrah said, pointing, and his eyes moved to the distant army camped on the riverbank, flags bearing Maridrinian colors. Ithicanian colors. Rebel colors. His heart accelerated, because soon she would have answers, one way or another.

Keris risked a sideways glance at her. The scratches on her cheek had scabbed over, but the dark circles of exhaustion had deepened beneath her eyes. Beautiful and fierce, and he wanted to scream at everyone in Pyrinat that they were lucky to have her. That no one alive would rule them as well as she would. That they'd be fools to turn her away.

But he couldn't. This was not his moment—it was hers, and Valcotta's—and though it would kill him to remain silent, Keris vowed to do so.

The boat rode up on the bank of the river, several rebel soldiers holding it steady while they climbed out. Relief filled Keris at the sight of Daria's familiar face, though the rebel's expression was grim as she approached them. "The Imperial Army entered the city about an hour ago," she said. "Aren and Lara went with them under a white banner of truce, though they've yet to send word of the city's sentiment."

Keris tensed, disliking the notion of either of them taking such a risk, but before he could say anything, the army stirred, a commotion rising in the distance. Moments later, an exhausted-looking Jor approached, a folded and sealed letter in his hand. He said nothing, only handed the letter to Zarrah.

Please, Keris silently prayed. *Please be the answer she wants.*

Cracking the seal, Zarrah opened the letter.

71
ZARRAH

HER HANDS TREMBLED AS SHE TOOK THE LETTER FROM JOR, cracking the green wax holding the imprint of Aren's signet ring. She started to unfold it, but then paused, afraid to read.

Everyone had fought and bled for this moment. Many had died for this moment. Yet Zarrah found herself suddenly unsure what outcome she truly wanted, for both came with sacrifice. Both came with hurt.

Be brave, she silently whispered, then looked down at the page containing Aren's familiar scrawl, ever informal in his prose.

> *Zarrah,*
> *Your right to the throne has been recognized, and you*
> *are invited to enter the city and claim it in your name.*
> > *Aren*

Her fingers quivered, and because words were impossible, she handed the page to Keris. He swiftly read the lines, then met her gaze. "Congratulations."

Realizing that she'd been holding her breath, she exhaled and then sucked in another one, none of the air seeming to reach her lungs. Vaguely, she was aware that word of the city's decision was spreading through the army, men and women cheering, but it felt like the two of them stood alone.

Was this what she wanted?

For Valcotta, could she give him up?

Emotion churned in her chest, different futures playing out in her mind, and she didn't know the answer.

Then Keris said, "Do what you need to do to live with yourself, Zarrah."

She needed him, and it was past time she stopped believing otherwise. Past time she stopped believing that she needed to stand alone to be strong. But Valcotta desperately needed *her*. Zarrah's voice cracked as she said, "I'm sorry."

The corner of his mouth turned up, and he bent his head, lips near her ear. "This is who you are, Valcotta, and I love you for it."

Zarrah shuddered, fighting tears, but Keris straightened. "We need horses."

THEY RODE INTO PYRINAT side by side, Valcottans lining the streets and cheering. It felt like she'd stepped into a dream, only the pain of her injuries grounding her in reality. As they approached the gates of the palace, Zarrah lifted her face to the sky to look at the banners flying overhead. Valcotta, Ithicana, and Maridrina, united in peace for the first time in history.

Familiar faces greeted them in the courtyard. Aren and Lara stood together, the swell of the queen of Ithicana's belly covered with armor, Keris's sister clearly having been in the thick of it. A beautiful dark-haired woman stood at her elbow, blue eyes suggesting that this was Keris's regent and half sister, Sarhina. With them were the members of the Valcottan High Council, and Zarrah's heart clenched as they all dropped to one knee, hands pressed to their hearts. As did all the rebel forces gathered behind them, a sea of her people giving her respect.

Easing off her horse, Zarrah approached her kneeling people, then dropped to her own knees, hand pressed to her heart. "Without your courage and honor, we would not be here victorious!" she shouted. "Not only do you have my word that I will spend the rest of my life in service to Valcotta, you have my respect."

Zarrah stayed on her knees, so overwhelmed by the moment that she couldn't stand until her father approached, drawing her to her feet. Everyone else rose as well.

"In his final hours," her father shouted, "Emperor Ephraim Anaphora declared his daughter, Aryana Anaphora, as heir to the Valcottan throne. She, in turn, named her daughter, Zarrah Anaphora, her heir." His hand trembled, then steadied. "The Usurper murdered Aryana before she had the chance to regain the throne and bring peace to Valcotta, but Zarrah has honored her legacy by bringing legitimacy to the throne and ending the war. I ask you all now to bend the knee to the rightful empress of Valcotta."

For a moment, no one moved; then, nearly as one, the members of the High Council kneeled, pressing their hands to their hearts once more as the crowd did the same, shouting their declarations of allegiance.

"It is done," her father declared, and taking the crown that had been brought forth, he set it on her head. It was cold and heavy on her brow, yet somehow, she felt lighter for having it there.

"All hail Her Imperial Majesty, Empress Zarrah! Long may she reign!" her father roared, and all those around them echoed the words.

And not just them.

Like a wave, her name rose from outside the palace and into the streets, crossing the city.

All hail Her Imperial Majesty.

Only Keris, Lara, and Aren were not on their knees, but they stood with their hands pressed to their hearts as the sound slowly faded.

"Care to have your first act as empress be the signing of the peace you fought so hard to achieve?" Aren asked.

"Yes." She smiled. "Yes, I would."

A table was brought forth, an old scribe laying out a thick piece of parchment. Dipping the pen, the man moved to begin drafting a formal agreement of peace, but Keris reached forward and took the pen. "Allow me."

Zarrah felt her heart constrict as she watched a commitment to peace between the three nations flow onto the paper in his elegant script, and then he turned to her, holding out the pen. "Majesty, would you do the honors?"

His fingers brushed hers as she took the pen, hand trembling as she bent to sign her name. The scribe placed a glob of lavender wax next to it and stamped it with Valcotta's seal. She handed it to Aren, who swiftly scribbled his name, pressing his signet ring into the green wax Jor supplied.

"Keris," he said, holding out the pen, "it's your honor to complete this alliance."

Keris stared at the pen for a long moment, then stepped backward, shaking his head. "I'm afraid that I cannot."

A gasp rolled through the onlookers, and Zarrah's stomach dropped. "Why not?"

"Because," he said, "it should be signed by Maridrina's queen." Clearing his throat, he said loudly, "My last act as king was to change the laws of succession so that the eldest Maridrinian child, regardless of gender, would sit on the throne. Now, allow me to formally announce that I am abdicating the throne of Maridrina. Rule of the kingdom will pass to the next eldest child of Silas Veliant, Princess Sarhina."

"For which I'm never forgiving you," the woman in question muttered, but Zarrah barely heard.

"I don't understand," she croaked out. "Why have you done this?"

It was as though the whole world fell away as he approached, taking her hands. "A ruler must put their kingdom first," he said quietly. "That is the cost of the title, to ever and always put the nation and its people before all else, before even those he loves." His voice caught, and he swallowed before adding, "I find that an impossible task, for nothing in this world or the next comes before you in my heart."

"Keris . . ." Tears flowed down her face, cutting stinging paths over her ravaged face.

"Maridrina and Ithicana are bound by marriage," he said, dropping to his knees before her. "And soon to be bound by common blood with an heir. I . . . I would offer you the same union between Maridrina and Valcotta. If you'll have me."

This is a dream, she thought. *It has to be.*

Yet as she stared down into the azure eyes that possessed her soul, Zarrah knew that it was real. That against every odd, they would be together in a way that honored their nations, and themselves.

"I will have you." She dropped to her knees, kissing his lips. "From now until the end of days, I will have you."

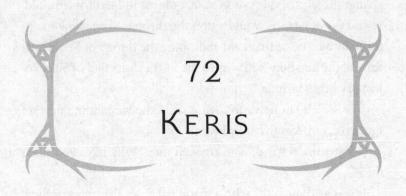

72
KERIS

"WELL, WHAT DO YOU THINK?" KERIS LEANED BACK, ADMIRING the white stone construction, the masons working on the final decorative touches.

"It's smaller than Ithicana's bridge," Dax answered, and Keris turned to glare at him, only to discover his friend was grinning. "It's a fine bridge, Your Highness. I look forward to walking back and forth over it many times."

It *was* a fine bridge.

Not just in its construction—Keris had approved every detail—but in the meaning of it, for it crossed the Anriot, connecting both sides of Nerastis. No more would Maridrinians and Valcottans skulk across the rubble of bridges torn down with violence, braving alligators and worse for illicit encounters with one another. Now they would walk freely, trade freely, and in time, he knew that Nerastis had the potential to become the greatest city on the continent, for it united the two most powerful nations.

"I need to get back to the palace," Dax said. "Her Grace holds to a schedule, and we are to be on a ship back to Vencia in an

hour. If I make Sarhina late, I'll be subjected to her verbal flagella-
tion."

"That's a big word, Dax," Keris murmured. "You're spending
too much time with politicians." For all his distaste of snakes and
his fear of Sarhina, his friend had taken well to the role of ambas-
sador, traveling back and forth between Vencia and Eranahl, as the
weather of the Tempest Seas permitted. Not that peace was in
question, with Lara's place in Ithicana more secure by the day and
Sarhina ruling Maridrina as its much-beloved queen.

"Likely so," Dax agreed. "But the pay is good, and I've come to
have a certain fondness for snake meat."

"There are worse things." Keris considered the date, then said,
"Ithicana might have its heir by the time you return again."

"I pray so," Dax answered. "Will give Aren's harridan grandmother something to do other than hassle the rest of us, though I
expect she and Lara may come to blows during delivery." He then
clapped him on the arm. "I should really go. Take care of yourself,
Keris."

"Likewise," Keris answered, watching as Dax crossed over the
bridge to the Maridrinian side, disappearing into the mass of construction along the waterfront.

Saam straightened from where he leaned against a pillar, the
rest of Keris's Valcottan bodyguard hovering behind him. "Ready,
Your Highness?"

Keris gave one last look at the bridge, the sight bringing an unexpected flood of emotion into his heart, and then he nodded.

"Good," Saam said. "Because it looks like the empress has arrived." Lifting a hand, he gestured to the Valcottan palace, where
Zarrah's personal banner slowly rose up the flagpole, the sight
causing Keris's heart to quicken.

She was here.

Keris forced himself to hold a measured stride as he walked through the streets, construction loud and raucous on all sides, his guard watchful for any threats, for there were still many who would not allow old grievances to die. People who clung to old ways and even older hatreds, and would not hesitate to put a knife in his back, prince consort to the empress or no.

He'd married Zarrah soon after her coronation, both of them still bearing bruises and wounds from their fight with Petra, and there had been something fitting about that. Theirs was a star-crossed love, but they'd fought long and hard to change the alignment of those stars, and their scars were markers of that victory.

Zarrah was Valcotta's empress. The Imperial Army's general. The rebellion's heart. And now she was his wife.

Keris relished the feel of calling her so, and sick of propriety, he took two quick steps and jumped onto a barrel. Reaching up, he hauled himself onto the roof of the building.

"Your Highness!" Saam shouted. Then, when he was ignored, "Keris! Come back!"

He left Saam's voice to chase him on the wind as he cut over the rooftops of the city, traveling routes he'd investigated many times before and arriving at the palace long before he would have if he'd taken the streets. Leaping the gap between a roof and the palace wall, he nodded at the wide-eyed guard watching him, then descended the steps two at a time to the courtyard below.

Zarrah, surrounded by an escort commanded by Daria, was handing off the reins of her horse to a groom. He drank in the sight of her. Her face still bore the marks from Petra's claws, and likely always would, yet rather than diminishing her loveliness, they gave her a fierce beauty. She wore no armor, and the silk of her trousers and blouse clung to every curve, the leanness of the starvation she'd endured in prison vanquished.

He watched the corner of her mouth curve up as she recognized the sound of his steps, though she didn't turn. Allowed him to watch her right up to the moment he stood before her, bowing low. "Imperial Majesty."

Her dark eyes caught his, pulling him into their depths as she murmured, "Husband. I was under the impression that you weren't supposed to be exerting that shoulder."

Husband. Hearing her say it sent a flood of desire rushing through his veins, and he lifted her into his arms. "Tell anyone asking for her time that she will be busy for the next few hours," he called over his shoulder at Daria.

Daria smirked and shouted, "A few hours? You're a man after my own heart, Your Highness."

But Keris was already walking, carrying his wife, his empress, into the palace. Bemused servants bowed low as they passed, and Zarrah said, "Your shoulder, Keris."

"Is fine." He climbed the stairs, heading down the hall to the royal chamber, the guards outside the door swinging them open at their approach. "No interruptions."

As soon as the door shut, her legs were around him, her lips on his.

"I missed you," she said between kisses, her fingers in his hair. "I'm sorry I took so long."

There had been demands for her in Pyrinat as she established her control, her rule, just as there had been demands for him here, negotiating terms with Sarhina. But Keris didn't want to think about any of that. "You're here now."

Laying her on the bed, he started on the buttons of her blouse, but there was no patience left in his soul, so Keris pulled. Tiny silver buttons rained across the bed, Zarrah laughing even as she made him promise to buy her a new wardrobe.

Though that was the last of their words.

Clothes fell to the floor, nothing left between them as he claimed her. As she claimed him. Over and over until they were both spent, darkness falling as the sun set outside their bedroom window while they lay tangled in each other's arms.

"Things went well with Sarhina?" she murmured. "Because I heard a rumor that you two fight like alley cats, and that she claims you have forsaken your Maridrinian heritage with your Valcottan favoritism."

"She's not wrong. But we came to a mutually beneficial agreement."

Zarrah gave him a lazy smile. "In our favor?"

"Of course." Rolling onto one elbow, he eyed the chests in the corner, which contained his books that had been salvaged from the ruins. When she'd arrived a week ago, Sarhina had both Sara and books in tow. While he'd spent hours with his little sister, he'd yet to check the chests. Rising to his feet, he went over and opened one, digging through the contents while Zarrah examined correspondence that had been left for him.

"This is a spy report from Harendell," she said, holding up a page. "You should read it, given your part in the problem."

A book in hand, he came back over to the bed and took the page from her. He skimmed the contents, his eyebrows furrowing at the mention of the troubles Lestara was causing the Harendellians in her exile and then rising in surprise at the spy's speculation at the end in regard to the king's bastard, James. "I expected a good many things from you, Ahnna Kertell," he murmured. "But definitely not *this*."

Casting aside the report, Keris climbed back into bed, pulling his wife into his arms.

"There is so much to do," she murmured. "So many things demanding our attention."

"Do you want to go do them?" he asked, feeling a prick of pain in his heart that there was always something pulling them apart, despite knowing that they'd always find their way back together again.

"No. I don't." Zarrah kissed him deeply, then rolled onto her elbow to retrieve the book he'd abandoned on the side table. "I want you to read to me instead."

Want a second look at a critical scene
from Lara's point of view?
Read on for an exciting bonus chapter . . .

LARA

LARA SILENTLY WATCHED AS AREN LEFT THE ROOM, THE REST OF their people on his heels. Part of her wanted to go with him, to eke out a few last minutes alone with him before they threw themselves headfirst into another fight.

But a larger part was unwilling to leave Keris alone. Her brother radiated a strange tension that made her uncertain whether he was on the verge of lashing out or breaking down entirely, and she was sympathetic to that sensation. Knew what it was like to cling to fragile filaments of hope, full well knowing that at any moment they might snap and send you plummeting. Knew what it was like to have selfish hopes burrowed deep in your heart that you refused to admit to anyone, even to yourself. Lara toyed with the buckle of her sword belt, then said, "Even if you free her, Zarrah may not be grateful. Aren certainly wasn't. His anger at seeing me came close to hindering our escape more than once."

"I don't expect gratitude. I . . ." Keris ran a hand through his hair, seeming to recognize that his words were a lie. "I . . . I just don't want her to be punished for making the mistake of choosing me."

His words struck her harder than they should, grief pooling in her stomach and binding her chest, making each breath feel difficult. It had been that way with him from the moment he'd stepped out of the harbor and into Eranahl, her emotions running high and unpredictable, which hadn't been what she'd expected. Most of their lives they'd spent apart but being back in her brother's presence had somehow brought to life every sentiment her childhood self had felt for him, the labyrinthine ties of blood and shared experience, good and bad, binding them together. Like with her sisters, but different because the way they'd been raised had made them all as much adversaries as they'd been siblings, causing each other endless harm as they reached for the goal their father had dangled before them. Whereas he'd been her older brother, always lifting her up and standing in the way of anyone who might pull her down.

Right up to the point he hadn't.

To be stabbed in the back by someone you believed would always have your back was the worst sort of betrayal, and for all she'd prattled at Aren not to trust Keris, some part of her had, with the absolute faith of a child, believed that she could. The shattering of that faith hadn't been a blow so much as it had been slow-acting poison that had eaten at her soul, the damage it had done not clear to her until the poisoner had stood before her.

Lara had been so angry at him that it felt like she was burning from the inside out, the desire to hurt him as much as he'd hurt her so overwhelming that she'd seen red until he told her what Zarrah had said to him at Southwatch. Words that forced her to see just how similar she and Keris were. Steel exteriors hiding hearts that feared losing the ones they loved. Fear that drove them to protect those they held dear without hesitation and often without consideration of consequences. Though they'd been raised apart, they'd been raised under the regime of the same man.

Where all weakness was punished, including displays of sentiment, which meant the only way to show love was strength. To endure the cruel words and vicious blows so those they cared about wouldn't have to. It was a flawed and broken way to live, but the emotion beneath was pure.

I just don't want her to be punished for making the mistake of choosing me, his words repeated in her head, making her heart ache, because God help her, Lara knew that terror better than anyone alive. "It wasn't a mistake."

Surprise filled his eyes, and it stung her heart that he believed she thought so little of him.

"You are an irritating, egotistical prick. But the only flaw in Zarrah's choice in you was that all the world was against it. They never gave you a chance."

He understood. She could see it in his eyes, the knowledge that this wasn't really about Zarrah but about them. That it was about the father who'd torn them apart, twisted and changed them so that it should be impossible for them to be family again. That it was about her desperately needing a chance to prove that wrong. "Lara," he said, "I—"

The draft coming from under the door abruptly struck her, carrying with it a stink that turned her mouth sour and sent her stomach roiling. "What's that godawful smell?" she asked, instantly regretting opening her mouth.

"It's—"

Because with words, so came the vomit.

"—dinner."

"Oh, God." She wiped at her mouth with the back of her hand, horrified that she'd spoiled the moment. "I'm so sorry. Normally the seasickness eases after this long on the water, but I can't seem to shake it this time."

Keris had a strange look on his face, but instead of mocking her, he murmured, "Congratulations."

She gaped at him. "What?"

"Congratulations on your pregnancy. I've lost count of my nieces and nephews, but this one will be special."

Pregnancy? Shock radiated through her. "No . . . no, I'm not . . ."

"You most definitely are," he said. "I grew up in the harem, sister. You're not the first pregnant woman I've seen vomit over the smell of cooking."

She couldn't be. Her last cycle had been on the journey from Nerastis to Ithicana, memorable because she'd been stuck on a tiny boat with Aren and Jor, but not since. She hadn't thought much about it because she'd been ill, then weak during her recovery, and because they'd been cautious every time.

"How is this possible?" She turned to the window, fear pooling in her stomach as the fallout of this revelation filled her head. Fallout she hadn't planned for because she'd done everything she could to avoid this.

"I'm not really the ideal messenger for this information, but when a man and a woman—"

"I know how babies are made, Keris!" she shouted at him, annoyed that he was teasing her when she was on the verge of bursting into tears, realizing that it had been after the battle for Gamire Island when she must have become pregnant. In that desperate union of blood, sweat, and tears.

Keris shrugged, giving her a smirk that didn't reach his eyes. "Just checking. There was the possibility that all your training was dedicated to learning how to poke holes into a man and not learning what happens when a man pokes you in—"

"If you say it, I'll stab you in the face."

He was quiet for a long moment, then said, "You don't want a child?"

The question stole the breath from her chest because it wasn't one she'd believed she would need to answer so soon. One she wasn't certain she *could* answer, because her feelings on the matter were so complex.

"No. Yes." Lara pressed her hands to her face, then dropped them, feeling a frantic need to move. To fight or flee. "We were taking precautions."

"I've been told the only certain method is abstinence, though I'm not one to judge."

As if she didn't fucking know that. "The Ithicanians are going to think I got pregnant to protect myself. To earn their favor."

"Is that such a bad thing?"

"Yes!" Lara paced the room, trying to release the tension simmering in her veins. "To use a child as a shield to protect myself is selfish and disgusting. They already hate me. No need to make it worse."

"And you think *not* having a child is going to change the way they feel?"

Yes, was the answer that rose to her lips, though she could not quite articulate why.

"You're the queen," he said. "Which means the vast majority of your subjects don't see you as a person. What you think, how you feel, how you *suffer*? They don't give a shit. All they care about is how the choices you make affect their lives. Putting yourself through hell will change *nothing* for Lara the queen and destroy everything for Lara the woman."

His words made sense—were what Lara might have offered as advice to anyone other than herself—but her heart recoiled from them. She wanted to suffer, needed to hurt, because it seemed fair given the hurt she'd caused. Why should she have a child when her invasion plans had allowed her father to kill or orphan the children of so many Ithicanians? She didn't deserve to have what they had all lost.

"You deserve to be happy, Lara," Keris said softly. "If this is what you want, please don't allow the joy of it to be destroyed by individuals who don't care about you."

Did she deserve to be happy? Part of her dreamed of feeling that way, of finally being free from the crushing guilt, but the rest of her screamed that she needed to spend the rest of her goddamned life atoning.

"It's not your problem," she said, and because she wanted time to figure out how she wanted to handle this, she added, "Though I'd ask you to keep this development to yourself. Aren needs to be focused on finding a way to get you out once you're in, not on my . . . condition."

A flicker of anger flared in her brother's eyes. "Except it's not just you anymore, is it?"

Her own anger flared because this was exactly how Ithicana would see it. How everyone would see it. Her hiding behind an heir to protect herself. But she didn't need fucking protection, and she certainly didn't want it. "Pregnant or not, I'm the one who will figure out a way to extricate you and Zarrah."

He huffed out a breath. "I'm not going to say a damn thing to anyone, but perhaps remind yourself of the outcome of the last time you kept secrets from Aren."

His words were an unexpected blow. "You're an asshole."

Wanting no more of this conversation, Lara strode from the room. Every breath she took was shaky because Keris's jab had struck harder than any of his words about happiness, because they struck at the fatal flaw in her logic. Her hypocrisy. For if what she wanted more than anything was to atone, why did she keep defaulting to the same behaviors that had caused the harm in the first place?

Because it is your weakness, her conscience whispered. *You guard your heart even at the cost of others. You claim you neither need nor want protection, but half of your actions are taken to protect yourself.*

Hypocrite.

Her eyes burned, her heart coming to terms with the realization that Keris was right. *Putting yourself through hell will change nothing for Lara the queen and destroy everything for Lara the woman.* Suffering would solve nothing for anyone. But forcing herself to be brave enough to change? To allow herself the dream of happiness? Maybe that would.

Her eyes immediately found Aren's tall shadow, backlit by the setting sun, and Lara went to him before her nerves could fail her. "I need to talk to you."

Her voice was tight, colder than she'd intended, given that *cold* was the exact opposite of how she was feeling.

His hands stilled on the rope he was holding. "What's wrong? What did Keris say this time? I swear to God, if he—"

"It's not Keris. But I need to talk to you alone."

"All right."

He followed her to the fore of the deck, but once there, Lara found her tongue frozen in her mouth, unable to put to voice the countless thoughts and emotions pouring through her head.

"What's wrong?"

He'd picked up on her tension, his agitation visibly growing, which wasn't what she wanted from this. *Say something,* she screamed at herself, but God help her, she was so terrified. More afraid than she'd been in all her life.

"Lara?"

"I threw up on Keris," she blurted out. "On his boots."

A laugh burst from Aren's lips, but then he stiffened. "Please tell me he wasn't an ass about that. It's not your fault you get seasick. Honestly, why does he have to say every goddamned thing that springs into his head? I'm going to throw him overboard, and then I'm—"

"He wasn't an ass," she interrupted, marshaling her courage. "And I'm not seasick. I'm pregnant."

Aren went still.

After what felt like an eternity, he asked, "You're . . . Are you sure? We were careful . . ."

"Not on Gamire, we weren't."

"Gamire . . . I . . ." He shook his head, and her heart shattered as she watched guilt fill his eyes. She knew him well enough to know what he was doing: blaming himself because no matter how much he might want this child now, he didn't think she felt the same way. For her to become pregnant in a moment that he already suffered so much guilt over made it all the worse.

"No!" Lara flung her arms around his neck. "Please stop what you're thinking. Banish it from your head."

"Lara . . ."

His strong arms closed around her, banishing the chill in the air and easing the nerves that kept trying to paralyze her tongue. She pressed her cheek to his chest, listening to the rapid beat of his heart. God help her, but she loved him. Loved him in a way that defied reason, and yet still she kept up some of her walls. Why? Why did she guard herself against the one person who loved her without condition? Who had proven time and again that he'd stand by her. Her husband, whom she trusted more than anyone in the world.

"I'm afraid," she whispered. "Not of being pregnant or giving birth. I'm afraid of being weak."

He inhaled, and because she knew what he'd say, Lara pressed one finger to his lips. "I need to speak."

When he nodded, she lowered her hand. "For me, to be happy

is a weakness, because it's something that can be taken away. I know that because it's happened to me before. But if I never allow myself to feel happy, then I have nothing to lose. No way for my enemies to strike at my heart. Better to suffer, better for people to remember my failings, because I can handle those blows. I don't know if I can handle people attacking my happiness, because I'm already terrified that I don't deserve it."

Aren's arms tightened around her body, the pain her words were causing him written across his face, but he didn't interrupt.

"It's easier to suffer," she whispered. "Easier to be sad. But it isn't only me that I'm hurting, it's you."

"Don't make this about me, Lara. I'm fine."

"You're not." Tears dripped down her face. "And how can it not be about you when you are my heart? The person I love so much that the thought of losing you makes it hard to breathe. This is not the first time I've hurt you for the sake of protecting myself, and I need to stop. For the sake of you, but also the sake of myself, because if I carry on down this path, what sort of woman will I become?" She drew in a ragged breath, then said, "I want to be happy, Aren, but I don't know how because it means being brave in a way in which I've always been more coward than not."

Aren gave a slow nod, and because he knew her better than anyone, he didn't give Lara platitudes. Didn't argue with her views of herself. Instead he helped her in the direction she wanted to go as he said, "Tell me one thing that you want."

Her fear screamed *no no no,* but Lara knew that if she wanted to change, she could no longer listen to that fear. "For you to hold my hand in front of our people."

He moved his arm, catching hold of one of hers and sliding his hand down until their fingers were interlaced. "Another."

Lara's bottom lip quivered, and she bit down on it as she dug into the hidden places of her heart. "To rebuild my Midwatch house, which *you* burned down."

"Agreed. I'm not interested in sleeping in the barracks during War Tides. Another."

Already, she felt greedy. Like she was taking too much, but Lara said, "I want to control Ithicana's intelligence network. I want to be our spymaster."

The corner of his mouth turned up. "*That* would make you happy? Reading spy reports all day?"

She fought against the smile rising to her own lips but lost the battle. "Yes. And I want to create schools on all the large islands, so children won't just learn to fight and survive, they'll learn reading and art and music. And I want an official military title so that when it comes time to defend Ithicana again, my voice will matter. As will my sword."

Aren nodded. "Anything else, Commander?"

Her eyes moved from his face to where Jor stood talking to Keris. He had been a father to Aren, she knew that. But he'd also been one to her in many ways. "I want you to go tell Jor that he's going to be looking after another Kertell."

ACKNOWLEDGMENTS

Some stories require the sacrifice of a piece of your soul to see them to completion, each word written in blood, sweat, and tears. The romance between Keris and Zarrah is such a story, but given the journey I put them through, perhaps it's only fair that I suffered alongside them as we fought to change the stars.

So many thanks to my family for their love and support—I'd go into Devil's Island for any of you, but let's hope it never comes to that! Though if it does, at least we know where one another stands on certain dietary choices . . .

Thank you to my incredible agent, Tamar Rydzinski, for all the work you do for this series. To Audible Originals, especially my editor, Jessica Almon Galland, I am so grateful to have the opportunity to work with you and I look forward to creating more novels together! Huge thanks to the U.K. team at Michael Joseph for your passion and enthusiasm for my work, and for helping me reach a global audience!

Amy, my incredible assistant, it's because of you that my head didn't explode writing this one—you are the best! Melissa, as always, your insights were beyond helpful, and Aren, in particular, appreciates you keeping my Keris's sass in check. Elise, you are my bestie for life. NOFFA, you ladies are so critical in maintaining my sanity—thank you!

Last but not least, all the love to my readers. It is your support that has allowed me to keep living in this tempestuous world of romance and adventure, and I am blessed to have you.

DANIELLE L. JENSEN is the *New York Times* bestselling author of *A Fate Inked in Blood*, as well as the *USA Today* bestselling author of the Bridge Kingdom, Dark Shores, and Malediction series. Her novels are published internationally in nineteen languages. She lives in Calgary, Alberta, with her family and guinea pigs.

danielleljensen.com
TikTok: @daniellelynnjensen
Facebook: facebook.com/authordanielleljensen
Instagram: @danielleljensen

DISCOVER MORE FROM
DEL REY &
RANDOM HOUSE
WORLDS!

READ EXCERPTS
from hot new titles.

STAY UP-TO-DATE
on your favorite authors.

FIND OUT about exclusive
giveaways and sweepstakes.

CONNECT WITH US ONLINE!
⊡ ⨍ ✕ @DelReyBooks

DelReyBooks.com
RandomHouseWorlds.com